PORTIA MASSAGED JAY'S neck and back. She needed to know if she had a chance, so she came right out with it. "Jay, do you wanna get serious with me?"

He took a second to respond. "I don't know. Maybe."

That wasn't what she'd wanted to hear. "Maybe" only led to false hope. Portia played cool and kept on massaging. "Now give me a real answer."

He rolled over so that they faced each other. "You want me to tell you what you *wanna* hear, or you want the truth?"

"The truth."

He licked his lips and folded his arms behind his head. "A'ight. Portia, you're a pretty girl, and I'm feeling you. I look forward to seeing you and all that. But you out there way too much. You hollering you about to slow down and all that, but how do I know that's not temporary? I gotta stay focused on achieve mode, so I don't have time to be wondering where you at or who you wit'. I can't even reach you half the time I call. You not home, *and* you got your cell phone turned off." He shook his head. "You too dangerous, Ma. You got the looks, the personality, and some pretty good conversation. But I can't wife somebody I can't trust."

You could've knocked Portia over with a feather. All she coul~~d~~ got up and played ing to fo

CAROLINE McGILL

A Dollar Outta Fifteen Cent

An Urban Love Story of Sex, Money, and Murder

POCKET BOOKS

New York   London   Toronto   Sydney   New Delhi

Pocket Books
A Division of Simon & Schuster, Inc.
1230 Avenue of the Americas
New York, NY 10020

This book is a work of fiction. Any references to historical events, real people, or real places are used fictitiously. Other names, characters, places, and events are products of the author's imagination, and any resemblance to actual events or places or persons, living or dead, is entirely coincidental.

First Pocket Books paperback edition July 2013

POCKET and colophon are registered trademarks of Simon & Schuster, Inc.

For information about special discounts for bulk purchases, please contact Simon & Schuster Special Sales at 1-866-506-1949 or business@simonandschuster.com.

The Simon & Schuster Speakers Bureau can bring authors to your live event. For more information or to book an event, contact the Simon & Schuster Speakers Bureau at 1-866-248-3049 or visit our website at www.simonspeakers.com.

Designed by Leydiana Rodríguez-Ovalles

Manufactured in the United States of America

10 9 8 7 6 5 4 3 2 1

ISBN 978-1-4767-3417-0
ISBN 978-1-4767-3418-7 (ebook)

This book is dedicated in loving memory

to my godfather, Dale "Uncle Dake" McGill.

You're forever my guardian angel.

This one is for you.

RIP.

*R*INNG! PORTIA HAD just laid down an hour ago, and was knocked out as if Mike Tyson had sucker-punched her, when the phone rang. She groaned and rolled over to peek at the clock radio on her nightstand. Its red numbers read 4:57 a.m. *Rinng!* Damn, who the hell was calling her at five in the morning?

It dawned on Portia that it had to be about money. She quickly cleared the sleep frog from her throat so she wouldn't sound crusty and picked up the receiver. "Hello?" It came out sounding sweet and velvety.

"Why yo' ass ain't sleep yet? What, some nigga over there? I'm comin' through in like fifteen, so get rid of that cocksucka."

Portia recognized the voice immediately but played him. "Who's this?"

"Yo, you on some bullshit. You got too many niggas. Bye, man." He sounded real pissed.

"Jay, wait! I'm just playing with you, dag. I *was* sleeping, boo. And ain't no nigga up in here. I told you I don't get down like that. Now, what's crackin', daddy?"

"I'm on my way to your crib now. Get up." Jay's tone was serious and demanding, as usual. "Take a shower and put on something sexy."

"Nigga, you know you ain't gotta tell me to wash my ass. I'm the cleanest chick you fuck with. But make it thirty minutes, Jay."

"Nah, man, that's too long," Jay exclaimed, as if he'd temporarily morphed from a thug to a child on Christmas Eve.

"Oh, boo-boo," Portia cooed, like he was a little baby. "Just go to the store and get the rubbers. I'ma make it up to you."

"Yeah, you better."

"Jay, buy the Magnums. You know how big Rocky is." Portia meant to boost his ego, but she spoke the gospel truth. Jay was packing. She casually threw in her pitch. "So, am I gettin' blessed?"

Jay sucked his teeth impatiently. "Come on, don't play me like some broke-assed chump. You know how I get down. I ain't that lame you was fuckin' wit' earlier. *Thirty minutes,* man. One." Jay hung up before she could say another word.

Portia stretched and gave herself a pep talk. "Get up and get that money, girl." Jay was a big tipper, so she smiled and slid out of her queen-size bed.

It wasn't just about the funds. Portia couldn't front; she really dug him. Unlike the others, Jay wasn't just some trick. There was something extraordinary about him. But Portia didn't want to cross that line. Their arrangement was fine the way it was. Still, Jay was the one guy she'd consider loving outside of the life. That is, if he would have her.

Portia glanced out the window of her third-floor apartment at the lamplit streets of Bedford-Stuyvesant. Bed-Stuy, aka "Do or Die," was the Brooklyn community where she'd been born and bred. As dawn peeked through the clouds, a sanitation truck made its rounds on the next block, and the B44 bus stopped at the corner of Nostrand Avenue for commuters. Their body language said it was cold as hell out there.

Portia was glad she worked at night. She admired morning people's drive, but that could never be her out there, freezing and waiting on no bus five o'clock in the morning in January. Sometimes she was just coming home at this hour, but never on no damn bus. Or train. She was far too high-maintenance for that. She'd either take a taxi or get whoever was spending some money that night to drop her off.

Portia was discreet with where she lived because she was no drama queen. She didn't like her business on Broadway, so outside of work, she kept a low profile. She fought to keep the two spheres of her life separate; the things she did for a living were taboo to her friends. They were all morning people with careers.

Portia didn't have to do what she did. She'd had a strict upbringing from decent, church-going parents with Southern roots. She'd seen her father dib and dab in a couple of things over the years, though he always schooled her about morals and respect and made sure she knew right from wrong. But Portia was a natural-born hustler. She had it in her blood.

She'd obtained her street savvy and prudence coming up in the learning institution of the 'hood, so she could take care of herself and wasn't afraid to go anywhere. She'd traveled along the coast paper-chasing, leaving a trail of satisfied men with lighter pockets in her wake. To Portia, pussy was gold and should be treated as such; men were just big wallets. She chose the life, although she could get down intellectually also, because she had an education. Portia was flexible and never ruled out any options.

Her friends knew she was an exotic dancer but were ignorant about the "privates" she did to keep her bank account fat and stay laced. Portia was a glamour girl, and it cost to dress in designer European threads. Make no mistake, girlfriend was fly as hell. When she wore Gucci, she did Gucci from shades to shoes. All official. She'd never be caught dead in any of that bootlegged knockoff shit. That's how Portia's whole crew rolled. They rocked top-of-the-line shit, like Marc Jacobs, Armani, Vera Wang, and Prada. The only difference was that they had day jobs, while Portia was queen of the night. Her girls didn't knock her, but they urged her to reach her full potential.

Ironically, Portia got turned out while trying to hustle up some extra cash in college. She completed school, but after she got accustomed to the fast money and excitement, she couldn't escape the nightlife. Her logic was simple: *Why work a day job for hundreds of dollars a week when I can make thousands?*

Five-five, hourglass-figured, and beautifully brown, Portia had a way with men. The kill to her was getting in their pockets. Her silver-tongued charm could disarm the cheapest "I don't have to pay for pussy" men and make them peel off. She was so classy that, by the time they gave up the money, they were convinced it was for an excellent cause. Portia had the gift of gab, a brain, and a nice package. Even more dangerous was the fact that she knew it and used it as her weapon.

Portia brushed her teeth and jumped in the shower. The hot water's force dug into her tired muscles like magic fingers. It felt almost like an orgasm. Minutes later, she patted herself dry and got out, and an arctic gust of wind hit her. Shit! She'd forgotten to close the window after a stinky number two almost made her evacuate the premises earlier. She ran and shut it and simplified her beauty ritual because she knew Jay was prompt. Oil of Olay, Dove deodorant, and Johnson & Johnson baby oil gel. Then peach-scented Calgon body spray. Portia skipped the FDS because Jay complained that her "cootchie spray" made his tongue feel numb. She smelled good enough for him to eat, pun intended.

Portia hung up her towel and walked down the hall to her exclusive Italian black-and-white-lacquer-furniture-filled bedroom. She backed it up naked in her dresser mirror. Personally, she thought her ass could use a little more weight on it, but men seemed extremely satisfied. Her 36D's, tiny waist, and full hips compensated for any shortcomings of the highly acclaimed ghetto bootie. Portia jiggled one of her butt cheeks at a time. That move drove men crazy at the clubs. She glimpsed at the clock. The time said eleven minutes till Jay.

She was really going to freak him this morning. Portia turned on the stereo and sauntered across her superior eggshell-white carpet to the closet for something sheer and sexy. She selected a pink Victoria's Secret teddy and a pair of pink strap-up, clear-bottomed stilettos from the collection that her homegirl Simone had christened "sexy stripper booty push-uppers."

Portia tied her shoes and decided to rock a wig, since her hair was damp. She picked out a cute doobie style that was similar to the way she wore her real hair. Portia put on the wig and adjusted it, sprayed on some oil sheen, and ran a comb through it. She painted her lips with brown-sugar MAC lip gloss that complemented her milk-chocolate complexion, and she was ready for Jay with two minutes to spare. Her full, shiny lips were perfectly shaped and enticing. Portia knew how to fuck with a man's head. She would intentionally OD on lip gloss because she knew the kind of thoughts that went through their brains when they saw a pair of lips like that. *Damn, I know she can suck a good dick.* Just then, the intercom's buzz startled her.

Portia ran over and pressed the talk button and inquired sweetly, "Who is it?"

"Buzz me in, man." Jay sounded impatient.

Portia obeyed and popped two mint Tic Tacs. She left the pack on display in case Jay felt doubtful about his dragons too. But he always smelled good from head to toe. At the thought of it, she yearned for his thug passion. Portia quickly lit two scented candles and switched the CD, and as she sashayed to greet her black stallion, Jaheim's album came on. She flung open the door and seductively smiled at her prey with her hand on her hip. "Hey, daddy!"

As usual, Jay's expression was hard, and he was cucumber-cool, but his eyes lit up when he saw her. "Why you in the hallway like that? Close the door before somebody see you."

Portia locked the door, and when she turned around, she caught him sizing her up. They embraced, and Jay squeezed her behind. His warm breath on her neck made Portia tingle. She reached up and removed the black hat he was wearing, then rubbed his head and stroked his jaw affectionately. "I missed you, baby. Where you been?"

"You smell so good, Ma." After being around a bunch of hardheads and dope fiends all night while he took care of his business, he found Portia a treat. Jay squeezed her tighter. "Let's go in the room. Come on."

Hypnotized by his Burberry cologne, Portia followed him and adored his lean, broad-shouldered frame. Standing six feet two with slightly bowed legs, Jay was the deepest and prettiest possible shade of pecan brown. He had dark eyebrows, sexy lips, and black spinning waves in his hair deep enough to make you seasick. He kept his hairline and goatee shaped up all the time. The brother was truly a work of art, designed by God in a younger Brian McKnight kinda fashion, but with extra thug.

Jay had on a black Iceberg hoodie and matching jeans, which didn't sag too low and sloppy on his narrow waist and hung nice and loose over his black Timbs. Portia loved the way he dressed. She hated when guys wore their pant legs too tight. And she hated when dudes wore their pants hanging all the way off their asses like they had a load of shit in them.

They went inside Portia's bedroom, and her hormones jumped double Dutch when Jay sat on the bed and stared at her. His expression was serious, and then he smiled and revealed a great set of white teeth. Jay hardly ever smiled, but when he did, it was like the sunrise. Portia didn't know which Jay tickled her fancy more: the nonchalant boss or this little boy with the melting smile. He was so handsome.

Suddenly, he was serious again, but this gaze was intense. The heat was building between them.

Portia stood in front of him and palmed his face in her hands. "You are such a fuckin' dime, baby."

"Man, go 'head with all that sucker shit. Save it for them lames you fuck with." Jay knew Portia was full of shit, but he was attracted to her hustling acumen. Most of the chicks he knew depended on a day job and didn't know how to get money any other way. He knew Portia was the type of chick who kept some scratch and didn't wait on no man to bring it home. He knew she made a living playing niggas for dough, but he was attracted to the unrelenting "bout it, bout it" shit. She went about hers a different way, but she was grindin' just like him, and he had come to respect that. For that reason alone, Jay spread love. The more he helped her out, the fewer dangerous things she had to do for money. He dug her and was going to look out anyway, so she could save the G for them lames in the clubs.

Portia laughed. "It ain't no sucker shit, Pa. You *are* gorgeous." His humble demeanor and scent were intoxicating. Portia looked into his eyes and wound her hips to the beat of the music. Jay ran his hands along her thighs.

Portia turned around and did her infamous jiggle, and then she bent over and gave Jay a 3-D view of the goods. Peeping between her legs, she saw that his eyes were hooded with lust.

Jay watched thoughtfully as Portia slowly peeled off her pink lingerie. Sexily, she pushed him back on the bed and stood over his face in one motion. She gyrated her hips down to barely six inches from his face. Unable to stand it anymore, Jay pulled her thighs toward him, and she sighed in bliss when his tongue probed her feminine flower. He appeared to be enjoying himself too. Portia couldn't help but ask him, "What my pussy taste like, baby?"

"Like candy." Jay's voice was barely audible, and he took his time until Portia floated on ecstasy's magic carpet. He ate that pussy so good, it was hard to tell that he was still a novice to the art of oral love.

Moaning, Portia bent down to kiss him. His breath was sweet. Now it was his turn. She dismounted Jay's face, trembling, and knelt at his feet as if he were a statue of Buddha. Portia unlaced and removed his Timbs; she was satisfied with his clean white socks and lack of foot odor. She couldn't stand a funky nigga. Portia mentally noted another gold star for Jay and unfastened his belt.

Rocky was already standing at attention. She slid down Jay's pants and gray Ralph Lauren boxers, and nine inches of ebony manhood sprang in her face. Portia gasped and fetched the box of Magnums from his back pocket. She tore open one of the gold packages and timed Jay's usual protest. *Five, four, three, two . . .*

"Wait, don't put that on yet," Jay said as if on cue.

Portia had been messing with Jay for eight months, and he was so predictable. He hated getting head with a condom. It wasn't that Portia didn't trust him; it was Jay who'd insisted that they be tested for HIV after their first rendezvous. He said he was feeling her and wanted to fuck with her but needed assurance. She was kind of offended at first, but his caution turned her on.

She had always been responsible and practiced safe sex, but she was still afraid, because she hadn't been tested previously. Portia had agreed, then spent the week beforehand mentally reneging and recommitting.

But Portia kept up with the news, so she knew that all across the world, young black women were dying from AIDS faster than any other demographic. Afraid of becoming a statistic, she went ahead and did it. In the last eight months she and Jay got tested twice, and each yielded a negative result, thank God! It was to her benefit, because knowing she was disease-free erased Jay's qualms about going down. He used to say he didn't eat pussy. It took him six months to do it the first time.

Ironically, they continued to use condoms, since AIDS wasn't the only issue. Portia was twenty-five, with no children, and Jay was twenty-eight, with a four-year-old son and baby-mama drama, so they were both content in the kiddie department. As far as giving him blow jobs, she didn't mind the actual act, but the thought of cum in her mouth made Portia sick. Though she expressed this to him every time, she made sure Jay left her house feeling pleased.

Jay knew the routine. "I promise I won't bust in your mouth, Ma. Just do it for a little while."

She took an escape route. "Jay, I care about you, and I really wanna please you how you deserve. It's not you, it's me. Let me get past this mental-block thing first. Okay, baby?" She massaged his balls and kissed the tip. When he moaned, she rolled the condom on and slid Rocky down her throat. Portia tongue-teased the head in small, circular motions.

Soft moans escaped Jay's throat and proved he loved

it. He placed his hand on the back of her head, and Portia faked a heavy ghetto accent. "Dang, nigga! Don't make my wig come off!"

"Why you got this shit on, anyway? I like your real hair better."

"So get it done, then, 'cause my head is tore up."

"You ain't said nothin' but a word. Hold me to it."

She silenced him by deep-throating and sucking the way he loved. Portia sensed he was ready, so she lay down and spread her legs. "I want Rocky now, Poppy."

Jay slid in and fulfilled her wishes with his big, stiff dick. He was pleased by how wet she was. "Ssss. Damn, Ma. Sss, ooh, this pussy so good." He pounded her with slow, deep strokes, up and down and side to side.

Portia squeezed the muscles she'd learned to master and transformed her magical hole into a vacuum. She tightened up as he pulled out, and let loose as he slid in. Jay got up inside her to the point where the pressure was a little pain and a whole lot of pleasure. Portia relaxed and let him do the work, and their bodies melted together like warm butter. He was an amazing lover.

That uncontrollable preorgasmic twitch forced her to blurt out her true thoughts. "It feels so good, baby. It's all the way in my stomach! It's so big, Jay. Unhh! Ooohh, I'm cumming!" She pulled him closer and deeper inside. Jay's thrusts continued for about six more seconds before he joined her.

He groaned, probably in an effort to withhold a scream. Portia figured his macho ego wouldn't let him go out sounding like a bitch. He lay inside of her, and she playfully squeezed his softening manhood. Jay protested but made no effort to withdraw. She held him close and massaged his back. Her pussy was an asylum; he was snoring in under a minute. Portia was lazy with sexual satisfaction also. She rolled Jay off of her and floated to the bathroom to freshen up. The CD changed again, and the sounds of Maxwell filled the room.

When Portia came out of the john, Jay looked like an innocent child sleeping. She grabbed a tissue and removed his condom and tossed it in the trash. Afterward, she used a hot, soapy washcloth to clean his penis and balls.

Jay awakened and peered at her through dreamy eyes. "Come lie down, Ma," he insisted, and patted the bed.

Portia slid in bed, and he held her tightly from behind. The clock read 7:23 a.m. Together, they drifted into the peaceful calm of a slumber that only two satisfied lovers could share.

RINNG! PORTIA OPENED one sleepy eye. It was 11:24 a.m. She still smelled Jay's Burberry on her sheets, but he was gone. Typical Jay. Gone to do whatever he did to afford her so often. Jay spent more money on Portia than a mortgage cost every month. He had to be ballin', because it didn't appear to hurt him.

Rinng! She knew Jay didn't have a nine-to-five, and she was attracted to the fact that he was grindin', just like her. That shit really turned her on. She didn't know what he was into, because he wasn't the type to tell his business, and she wasn't the type to pry. But no matter what a person's hustle was, Portia respected the grind.

Rinng! And she loved the thug in Jay. He disguised it well with polite overtures and gentlemanly gestures, but his gangsta was clearly recognizable. She'd never been attracted to squares, since she was so wild and adventurous.

Jay's aroma comforted Portia as if he were still there, and she tried to hold on to it. Boy, she could really love him. *Rinng!* That was probably Laila or Simone calling about a lunch date, which she was tempted to cancel. She decided to let the answering machine pick up. After the fourth ring, her greeting began: "Hi. I'm unavailable. Leave your name, number, and a brief message, and I'll holla back ASAP. Thank you." *Beep!*

There was laughter. "I hate your corny-assed, wannabe-sexy greeting." It was Simone, loud and jolly, as usual. "Portia, don't be try'na act like your ass ain't home. Pick up the damn phone." She switched to a mock-preacher voice with a deep Southern drawl. "Portia La-eeen . . . You can't run! You can't hide! Out all night sinnin' and gyratin' yo' hips. But y'all don't hear me-ee . . . Raise up, Portia! I said raise up and get on the scene! Hey, hey, hey, take me off the machine." Now Simone was imitating James Brown. She started singing, "Please, please, please. Ple-ea-ease, pick up the phone."

Portia picked up the horn, just to shut her dumb-ass homegirl's mouth. "Shut up, shut up! I'm woke. Just hush, Mone!" Her voice was crusty with sleep.

"Damn, girl, you sound like a frog. It's eleven-thirty. We supposed to do lunch at twelve. You know how slow you are. Girl, get up and get ready. Me and Laila are already a pair, and I gotta be back to work by two. And don't try to back out either." She didn't even pause for breath.

"Simone, I just laid down a couple of hours ago. I'm too tired to—"

Simone cut her off. "We'll pick you up at twelve. Bye!"

Portia groaned. Boy, were those bitches annoying. She checked the nightstand drawer and saw that Jay had left her money in the usual place. Four, five . . . oh, shit, six, seven C-notes. Jay had left an extra two hundred dollars, probably for the hairdo he'd promised. That dude was all right with her! Portia was starting to have strong feelings for him, though she didn't want to cross the line between business and pleasure. What a paradox, because business with Jay was always pleasure. Portia dozed off, and the phone rang again.

This time it was Laila. She spoke softly, as usual. "Portia, get out that bed. We on our way over there. Get your behind up, girl!" Laila hung up, and Portia reluctantly dragged herself out of bed.

In the mirror, she saw that she was a sight. Her wig was cocked to the side, and she looked tore up from the floor up. She snatched it off and hurried to get ready before her girls got there. Portia slayed her morning-breath dragon with Colgate Total and jumped in the shower. She didn't want to hear her homegirls' mouths. Having been best friends since the seventh grade, they knew one another to a tee. There were four of them in the original clique.

Back in '89, Simone Benson and Portia Lane had become friends instantly when they met in junior high school; Simone was as zany and outgoing as Portia. Laila Atkins had taken a liking to them and started hanging around. Though soft-spoken, Laila was succinct and spoke her mind. She was real calm and laid-back, but her close friends knew that she had a flip side if pushed.

Fatima Sinclair was the mother hen of the clique. Always verbose and full of advice, Fatima was the one they used to keep secrets from so that she wouldn't lecture them. For example, she was the last one to know about their first sexual experiences—Tima was an anti-teenage-sex advocate until the eleventh grade. The rest of them had started by the tenth.

Portia wondered what was up with Fatima. She hadn't heard from her in three weeks and made a mental note to track her down. She hoped girlfriend was all right. Portia was an only child and held her homegirls close to her heart. They were true blue, not the kind who would stab you in the back and fuck your man. Portia rinsed off the soap and paid her cootchie area special attention with Summer's Eve feminine wash. Her mother had taught her to be particular about feminine hygiene when she was a small child, and it stuck.

Drifting down memory lane, Portia remembered the time before her father passed, when the shower was broke and he took his time fixing it, like he did most things in the house. In the morning before school, her mother supervised while Portia washed from a basin. She used to say, "Get over that basin and scrub your twat real good." Portia smiled at the recollection and turned off the water. Her parents were originally from North Carolina, and they'd kept their Southern accents.

Sadly, her father, Dwight "Daddy D" Lane, was killed in an attempted bank robbery, just after he made a deposit into his business account in '96. Portia's family used to own a store. Ironically, Daddy D had recently, under the close scrutiny of his wife, Patricia, ceased his illegalities, like selling weed out of the store. He'd cleaned up his act and started walking a straight line business-wise, trying to keep his books and banking records up to par. He'd abandoned his old method of "They can't tax it if they don't see it, so I'll keep it in the house in the stash" only to be killed in a damn bank. Worse, he got caught up in some shit he had nothing to do with.

Portia missed her pops like crazy. His death had drawn her closer to her mother than a sister; she made a mental note to go visit soon. Portia poured some carrot-oil cream in her palm, rubbed it through her hair, and combed it into a ponytail. She looked decent but didn't feel glamorous enough to be up in no restaurant. She knew Laila and Mone wouldn't be trying to hear anything about her backing out, but later, she was definitely going to the beauty salon.

She wasn't in the mood for panties, so she slid on a pair of tight Chloé jeans and got her beige Gucci loafers from the closet. Working at the club in five- and six-inch stilettos made a sister appreciate a pair of comfortable kicks now and then.

Portia snatched the sex sheets from her bed and tossed them in the hamper, and before she could fasten her bra, the intercom sounded. She tripped over a Gucci shoe box on the way to the door and put on a beige Chloé turtleneck sweater. She flung the door open and grinned at her ace booms. "Bet y'all thought I wasn't ready. Aha!"

They greeted one another with traditional sisterly hugs and diva kisses to each cheek. "And I can't believe it. It's gonna snow," Simone said sarcastically. "What the fuck is up, girl?"

Laila smiled. "Hey, baby girl. What's good?"

Portia replied, "Same shit, different day. What y'all got in them bags? It sure smell good."

"We didn't think your ass would be ready, so we copped some takeout from Kum Kau so we can sit in and chitchat."

"Shrimp?"

Simone said, "But of course, girlfriend."

On their way to the kitchen, they passed the bedroom. Detective Simone peeped the unmade bed and blurted out, "No wonder this heifer been 'sleep all day. Ain't no sheets on the bed, so this bitch was *fuckin' all night.*" She'd hit the nail right on the head.

"Don't be thinkin' you know me, bitch." Damn, Simone knew her. Portia playfully punched her on the arm. They had been using the word "bitch" freely since seventh grade, when Fatima had worn a button to school:

> **B**eautiful
> **I**ntelligent
> **T**empting
> **C**harming
> **H**eadstrong

It pleased Portia to see her comrades looking well. They were immaculately dressed, as usual, and appeared stress-free.

Tall and slim as a model, Simone had no worries about getting a man. With cappuccino-colored skin, almond-shaped gray eyes, and shoulder-length auburn hair, Mone towered above them at five-ten. She was dressed in a purple Escada pantsuit, with high-heeled gray Gucci boots and a striking gray and purple silk scarf, and she carried a gray Hermès handbag. She was an attractive sister, but her beauty was in her personality and modesty.

Simone was humble because she'd known hard times. She never knew her father, and she grew up in Marcy Projects with a negligent, forever-boyfriend-switching, alcoholic mother. She also was molested by one of her mother's boyfriends at a young age. Simone used to have a lot of anger pent up in her on the low, and she used to fight all the time in school.

Fortunately, Simone realized she had a purpose, so she beat the odds and made something of herself. Now she was single and focused on achieve mode on Madison Avenue, the advertising mecca of New York City. Simone's dark past wouldn't allow her to trust anybody, so girlfriend always played it safe and carried a gun.

The complete opposite of Simone, Laila was a petite sister of five-one, with coffee-bean-colored skin as smooth as satin, snow-white teeth, and ebony Cleopatra-like slanted eyes. Her glossy jet-black hair usually flowed down her back, but today it was pinned up in a roll. She had on an earth-colored hooded Moschino sweater with a pair of Moschino jeans rolled to the calf and brown pony-skin stiletto boots, and she carried a brown zucchino-print Fendi tote. She looked real chic with her hood pulled on and wearing tinted tortoiseshell Fendi glasses.

Though petite, Laila had an extra helping of bootie. The boys in junior high school used to say she had the biggest butt out of their crew. But she was never the type to flaunt it. In fact, she was the only sister Portia knew who tried to demote her ass. Laila was meek and had an air of wisdom that most people felt a connection to upon introduction. Laila was always the rock of the crew. She had been through a lot at a young age too, but her story was different.

Both of her parents were dead by the time she was thirteen, so her grandmother stepped up to the plate and raised her. Laila's granny passed away two weeks before their high school graduation. With no mother or father figure, Laila continued her education, and now she had a burgeoning career as an RN and was married with two little girls. She never complained about anything. Her motto was "We just gotta deal with it."

Portia complimented them. "Y'all look cute. Thanks for being considerate. A bitch barely had three hours of sleep the last three days. What's poppin'?"

Simone said, "I know you got some sunshine. Roll up, so we can get an appetite."

Laila feigned disgust. "Y'all are such weed heads, it's sickening."

Portia stuck her tongue out at her. "It takes one to know one." She went to get her stash. Since she copped an ounce at a time, she kept her weed in a medicine bottle in her underwear drawer. The bottle concept was her father's theory, which he'd concocted to keep his herb from drying out. Plus, he believed it was his medicine and should be treated as such. Portia grabbed a vanilla Dutch Master from the box of fifty on the dresser. Dutches burned slow and made smoking an el an extended ritual.

Portia returned with the goods. "Laila, smell this shit. I got it from this Jamaican cat named Wicked who deejays at the club sometimes."

"Hell, yeah, that's some sweet sticky icky," Laila agreed.

Simone sniffed the bottle and nodded her approval, and then she crumbled a couple of buds onto the table. "You taking too long, P. I'm ready to smoke, shit." She used her thumbnail to saw open the cigar and dumped the tobacco into the trash can. Then she sprinkled the chronic inside and twisted it up in seconds. "Give me some fire," she insisted. Laila passed her an orange Bic from her purse, and Simone sparked up. "I'm still the quickest blunt roller-upper in the whole wide world. Y'all wish y'all was nicer than me."

Laila and Portia were used to her blunt-rolling boasts, so they laughed and rolled their eyes. Simone inhaled deeply a few times, then grinned and passed it to Portia.

Portia nodded in Laila's direction and slid her an ashtray. She checked her mental notepad. "Have y'all heard from Fatima lately? We ain't touched bases in over three weeks."

Laila passed her the peace pipe. "I called her last week. Girlfriend got her head in the clouds over that young cat she messin' with. He's in one of the hip-hop groups she does A and R for. She was rushing me off of the phone just because he was leaving the house. Bitch was like 'Where you goin'? I'm lockin' my door if you leave. Yo' ass gon' be homeless. Don't fuck with me tonight!' Then I heard the door slam, and she was like 'Laila, I gotta go.' She followed his punk ass outside, and he came back. I know because I called her back like thirty minutes later, and she was like 'Laila, we 'bout to go to the mall. I'll call you later.' Tima must've bribed him or some shit. Up there behaving like some fuckin' sugar mama. He's only like nineteen. She should be ashamed of herself."

Simone looked at Portia. "Yo, that dick must be slammin'! Fatima got herself a fuckin' boy toy."

They all laughed. It was no secret that Fatima liked to trick on her men. Her parents were well off and spoiled her, so Tima kept money and flaunted it in her men's faces in an effort to keep them loyal. None of her friends understood why she felt she had to be so generous, because she was real pretty.

Portia commented, "That's cool. I'm not hatin'. I just don't want her getting used. You know how some mothafuckas are. They'll chew you up and spit you out if you let 'em. Tima's heart is too good for that. If you gotta buy a nigga, you don't need that mothafucka. Laila, stop OD'ing and pass the blunt."

They decided to each contact Fatima to make sure she was on the right track. The topic switched, and the blunt grew shorter as the conversation went on. Portia's homegirls filled her in on all she had missed from their lives in the past week.

Laila reminded them of her kids' birthday party coming up. Her girls were one year and one week apart, so most people mistook them for twins. Every year she gave them a double birthday party. Laila and her husband, Khalil, had bought their first home a year ago, and she said since their finances had stabilized, they were going on a cruise to Barbados for Valentine's Day next month. She was also contemplating taking a leave from the hospital to help Khalil with the clothing store they'd opened recently.

Simone was having an affair with her manager. They'd had sex at the office after he asked her to stay late for a meeting. She said that the sexual attraction was reciprocal and unbearable, so it had been only a matter of time. That was unlike her, so Portia figured he must really be something. Mone said he was doing her special favors, like giving her paid time off and three-hour lunch breaks. Portia told her to enjoy the fruits while they lasted, but be careful about mixing business with pleasure. The two combined was like a time bomb, and Portia warned her to keep her emotions intact.

Evident from their red dreamy eyes, they were all high, and it was time to grub. Simone passed out take-out trays, and they feasted on shrimp and broccoli over white rice and Snapple. Time must've been on crack— before they knew it, the microwave clock read 1:48.

Simone jumped up. "Oh, shit, I gotta get back to work."

"Girl, please. You're fuckin' the boss. You can be a few minutes late," teased Portia.

"P, I'ma chill for a minute," said Laila. "If that's okay."

"Since when you gotta ask?"

Simone came back from the bathroom, where she had gone to touch up her lipstick and apparently drop some Visine in her eyes. "Ladies, I must love you and leave you. I'll call you chicks later. I'm ghost." She yelled from the hallway, "I'll lock the door. Don't get up. Bye, Portia! Bye, Laila!" With that, she was gone.

Laila rose and began straightening up the kitchen. Portia gave her a hand, and then they went in the living room. When she noticed the new stereo, Laila said,

"Girl, that is bad. Turn it on and let me see what you got. When you got this?"

"Oh, I bought it from this cat at the club. He can get any kind of electronics or household shit you could imagine. That's the same cat who sold me my laptop and my new blender and juicer. Just let me know if you need something." Portia hit the power button. "I'ma play our song, Lay."

She put on Maxwell's "This Woman's Work," which they had fallen in love with when they heard it during the sex scene in the movie *Love and Basketball*. She turned the volume up to six, and Laila took off her boots. Weed and good music went great together when you had an appreciative soul. They loved hip-hop too, but they had old souls and loved songs filled with feeling and emotion. The friends grooved in peace.

"Portia, how much power that amp got?"

"A thousand watts."

"I know that's right."

Portia sensed something was wrong with her friend, who looked troubled, so she was frank. "Cut the bullshit, Laila. What's the matter with you?"

Laila's shoulders slumped, and she sighed. "Khalil's fuckin' around on me. I need actual proof, but I'm convinced. He's changing lately. He been staying out late the past few weekends, and I let that slide, but he came home late as hell last night, smelling like a fuckin' liquor barrel. On a Tuesday. I played it cool when I questioned him, but he still tried to turn it around, talking 'bout I'm accusing him of shit. He slept on the couch, and we didn't even speak this morning. This shit been goin' on for three weeks now. I feel like I'm losing him, P."

"Damn. Don't let this shit get you down, Lay. Khalil knows you're the best thing that ever happened to his ass. He owes you everything, 'cause you made him the man he is!" Portia tried to calm down a little. Though hearing the news had ticked her off, she wasn't shocked. After what she'd seen some married men do at the club, she didn't trust a man as far as she could see him. "Besides, two can play that game. Don't stress Khalil. Just disappear on his ass sometimes to show him how it feels. He's too comfortable with the fact that he got a good wife sitting home taking care of the kids. That nigga needs a reality check to make him appreciate you, and we shall start his damn reawakening today. Get a babysitter for the girls this weekend, 'cause we goin' out. And don't tell him shit."

Portia had Laila pumped up. "A'ight, Porsh, I'ma give him a taste of his own medicine. I love Khalil, but I will not let that mothafucka break me down. I'm too strong for that shit," she assured herself.

"I know that's right," Portia cosigned.

"**S**LOW DOWN RIGHT here," Portia told the cabbie.

The taxi driver pulled over to the curb in front of the Twilight Tower, where a blue neon sign blinked on and off atop the building.

"You are a dancer. I should've known," the cabbie said in a Middle Eastern accent, and smiled. "You do private shows?"

He was cute in an *Arabian Nights* kind of way, so she flirted with him. "Maybe for you." Portia passed him a card. "How much?" She was referring to the fare.

"Nothing, it's on me. How much?" He was referring to other things.

Oh, what the hell. She propositioned him. "Five hundred."

"I'll give you two hundred," he said.

She laughed. "What's your name, sweetie?"

"Mohammad." He stared at her, intense.

He was very handsome. But not fine enough to screw for no deuce. "Well, Mohammad, call me when you get your money straight. You have my card. Thanks for the ride." She flashed him a smile and reached for the door.

"Wait, wait! You are so fucking beautiful. I will give

you three hundred. That is all I can give. I am dead serious. Please."

His accent was cute. He was about twenty-eight, with tan skin, dark eyes and hair, and dazzling white teeth. Portia could tell he was a clean person from the way he kept his cab. It was comfortable and didn't have that funky-ass smell a lot of cabs had. He easily could have been an Arabian prince. Portia pictured herself belly dancing for him, draped in a chiffon genie getup. "Three-fifty," she negotiated. Fuck it.

He nodded. "Okay, three-fifty is fine."

"When do you want to hook up, sweetie?"

He said, "Right now. Go with me for a little while, and I will bring you back to work. It is only eight o'clock. I can have you back by nine-thirty because I also have work to do. We can go to my place."

Portia thought about it. If she got this jump-start, she wouldn't have to work as hard tonight. It was a Wednesday night, and there was no guarantee that the club was jumping. She rarely worked Monday through Wednesday; she was going in to compensate for the loss from Saturday night, when she, Laila, and Simone partied at Mars 2112. It had been a long time since Portia had hung out just for enjoyment, and they'd had a ball. She didn't regret it, but her weekend stash was missing a hefty chunk.

In order to stay ahead of the game and stack, Portia had to meet a quota each week. That was her life story. Always trying to make a dollar outta fifteen cent. Portia had set a deadline to end her dancing career the following year, but if she hustled hard enough, she could accomplish her goal quicker. She'd started dancing as a stepping-stone in life and had never intended to make it a career. Time had gone by real fast, and she knew she was getting too old for this shit. Plus, it took up all of her time.

Portia decided she'd feel more comfortable in her apartment. "Let's go to my place. And don't try nothin' crazy, 'cause I will cut you too short to shit." She hit him with the "I'm dead serious" expression, and he assured her he'd behave.

Portia silently prayed as he made a U-turn. *Please, God, watch over me and keep me safe. I know this ain't right, but I just need the money. Please protect me, God, and don't let Mohammad turn out to be a maniac.* She was usually a good judge of character, so upon hearing no little voice in the back of her head, she relaxed and hummed softly to the music.

IT TOOK ONLY forty-five minutes to give Mr. Cabbie a striptease and incontestable pleasure twice. Lucky for Portia, he was a two-minute brother, so most of the time was spent on foreplay. Thank God nothing had gone wrong. She had taken care of business, showered again, and he'd taken her back to work.

At the entrance of the underworld, she greeted Biggs and Tree, the twin gorilla-like bouncers. "What's good, fellas? Any money up in here?"

Biggs rushed to help her with her bag. He greeted her by her stage name. "Mystique, what you doing here on a Wednesday? It must be gon' snow! You lookin' good tonight. Smell good too. You know something? You the classiest chick up in here tonight, so I know you gonna make all the money." Biggs babbled all the way to the dressing room. His compliments went in one of Portia's ears and came out of the other.

He opened the door without knocking, but none of the girls seemed alarmed. A few just threw bored glances in their direction. Portia noticed how some of their expressions changed when they saw her up in the house. She didn't see one welcoming smile. Only ice grills. But she was there to make money, not friends.

Portia thanked Biggs for carrying her bag and set an empty chair in front of a mirror. She saw Snow, a white dancer who was convinced that she was a sistah, coming offstage. Portia was a little relieved to see a familiar, friendly face.

Snow noticed her, smiled, and headed her way. "Hey, Mystique! What the fuck you doin' in here tonight? I *never* seen you in this mothafucka on no Wednesday." Snow was loud, with a slight Latino accent, from growing up in a Puerto Rican neighborhood. "How you been, girl? Where were you on Saturday? You missed a *lot of money*. Mad niggas was asking about you, yo. You know how *you* be getting that money, girl!"

Portia peeped the eye rolling and smirks between two chicks standing a foot away and eavesdropping on their conversation. She lied to give them a reason to hate, since they already were. "I flew to Jamaica for a few days, Snow. I needed a vacation. You know I do the Caribbean every few months." She winked at Snow, who got it and smiled. The skinny player-haters were sick. They strutted away.

Snow laughed and waved her hand. "Girl, fuck them ho's. Surprisingly, there *is* some dough up in here tonight. The VIP room is *jumping*." She patted her money, which was stacked and tucked neatly in her thigh garter and secured by a rubber band. "You better hurry up and get dressed and go out there, Mystique. Let me change. I got a VIP." She sauntered off to her station.

Portia undressed and oiled her body again, then lightly dusted her breasts and butt with shimmering powder. For her first number, she selected a short, glittered, sheer purple dress with side splits, over a purple-and-silver-tasseled G-string bikini. She suffocated herself with smell-goods and slid on her silver thigh-high stiletto boots, and then she locked her street clothes in her huge rolling suitcase with her dance stuff. She wore the key on a gold anklet because some of the girls had sticky fingers.

Out of the corner of her eye, Portia saw Hollywood, a young girl from out of town who worked weekends too. She'd just had a baby two weeks earlier, so Portia was surprised to see her back in the club. The buzz around the dressing room was that the guy who picked her up from work every night was her pimp, and she was a runaway from Wisconsin who'd gotten pregnant by a trick. Whatever her story was, Portia felt kind of sorry for her; she kept to herself, but she looked so lost all the time. Portia looked closer and saw that Hollywood had a black eye and was applying makeup in an attempt to cover it up. That nigga must really be her pimp. The bastard probably had whipped her ass and made her come back to work. Portia's tender heart almost made her ask the girl if she was okay, but she decided to mind her own business. She had problems of her own. Besides, in New

York City, there was plenty of domestic violence assistance available.

According to the stage schedule on the wall, there was one chick ahead of her, named Queen, with a two-song set. Portia peeked out the curtain and saw that Queen was on her last song. It was almost time to hit the stage, and she was glad, because time was money.

The deejay said, "Gentlemen, give it up for her highness, Queen!" There were whistles and some clapping, so girlfriend must've worked it.

Portia heard her intro. "Gentlemen, we gonna slow the music down a little bit, but y'all speed up that tipping. These ladies are working hard to please y'all. Act like you know. Fellas, we have a special, sweet treat for you. When you see her, you'll know what I mean. She's sexy and full of surprises. Coming to the stage is the lovely Mystique."

The sounds of R. Kelly's "Feelin' on Yo Booty" began to fill the club, and Portia seductively paraded onstage real slow. She made eye contact, and she moved with class, unlike some of the grungy dancers of the new breed who bombarded the clubs. Some of them started humping the floor as soon as they got onstage. Several men came forward from the bar and joined the others at the front and side of the stage. Portia worked the pole gracefully and seduced them, and they tipped. And tipped.

By the end of her set, she wore only thigh-high boots and a tasseled G-string; both her silver garters were filled with bills; and money littered the stage. As Portia gathered her pile of earnings, she got six requests for VIPs. Men whistled, clapped, and barked like wild dogs as she headed for the dressing room.

Portia was counting the proceeds when Candy, the bartender, came to the dressing room and said, "This guy just paid me twenty bucks to come tell you he wants a VIP, and he said he doesn't have all night, so if he can be first, he'll pay you double per song. What should I tell him?"

Portia said, "Tell him to give me five minutes, 'cause I'm changing. Good lookin' out, Candy." Candy nodded and left.

Portia freshened up and changed her outfit. After she checked her hair and lipstick, she secured her money in a sequined garter on her thigh and hit the floor. Candy eye-signaled to a guy in a nice Coogi sweater and jeans. His back was turned, but there was something familiar about his physique. At least seven men fought for her attention before she got to him. One of them hollered out, "Damn, girl, you fine! What they call you, Titties? 'Cause you sho' got some pretty ones!" A few guys grabbed at her hand. "VIP? VIP?"

"I'll be back in a minute," she repeated over and over.

When Portia reached him, he smelled real good. She smiled and spoke softly in his ear. "Hi, handsome. You ready for your private dance?"

When he turned around, her smile faded and her jaw dropped. Lord, it was Khalil, Laila's husband! Portia flipped. "Khalil, what the fuck are you doin' here? You know I work here. What's wrong with you?" The drink in his hand smelled like Hennessy.

Khalil smiled. "Damn, Portia—I mean Mystique. That ain't the reaction I was hoping for. I didn't know you worked here weeknights, but it *is* nice to see you." His manner was easy, as if he saw her like this every day.

She toned it down. "You caught me off guard. It's not every day my best friend's husband catches me dancing onstage half naked. This shit is embarrassing. What are you doing here?"

He stared at her funny. "Right now I'm trying to get a VIP with this pretty chick I saw earlier. Don't be embarrassed, Portia. You're perfect, and you make dancing an art."

"Thank you, but it's not about that. I don't feel right doing this. I'll find you somebody else to VIP—"

He cut her off. "I don't want nobody else. I'ma pay you two times the regular rate. That's forty dollars a song. Just to talk, Portia. That's all."

"Khalil, we can talk somewhere else. This is inappropriate. You're practically my brother-in-law, so let's not go there. And quit calling me Portia. In here, I'm Mystique."

"Mystique. That's the perfect name for you. Well, *Mystique,* you wastin' time. Make this money, girl. I ain't gon' do nothin' to you. Why you actin' like that? If I'ma drop some paper on somebody in here, it's gon' be you. You the baddest anyway." His voice got low. "Come on, I promise. Just to talk. Be professional, Mystique. You're at work."

Portia sighed. "Okay, Khalil. Let's go." He smiled and followed her inside the dimly lit VIP room.

Big Bruce, the VIP room security, nodded at them

and told Khalil, "Ten bucks a song for the booth. You pay the lady separate, whatever she asks for. Follow the rules." He nodded at the list of rules on the wall. "And don't gimme no problems back here, man."

Khalil passed him a twenty. "A'ight, man."

Big Bruce pointed to an empty booth at the back. "Get your money up front," he told Portia, clearly tired of arguing with customers who didn't want to pay after a lap dance or VIP. Bruce didn't have to tell Portia that, though. It was always business before pleasure with her. She wasn't born yesterday.

The booth was dark except for a flashing black light. Portia knew she shouldn't be back there with her best friend's husband. She had never been so nervous. She took a deep breath and commanded herself to relax. Khalil sat down, and she stood in front of him like a lost, afraid child. Boy, she needed a drink.

Portia blurted out, "I'll give you twenty dollars back. Let's just leave, Khalil. I'm sorry, I can't do this."

He laughed. "Calm down, man. It's a'ight." He stood up and massaged her shoulders to help her relax. "You want a drink?"

She nodded, and he disappeared. In what seemed like less than a minute, he returned with two drinks. "Is Hennessy okay? Or should I have gotten you a chick drink, like a daiquiri or something?"

"This is fine." She sipped it. "Damn, Khalil! What happened to the chaser? This is straight!"

"My bad. You want me to . . ." Khalil didn't bother finishing, because she guzzled it down fast. "You better slow down, girl."

Portia just wanted to avoid the horrible taste and

numb herself a little. "I'm good. You paid for two songs. Do you wanna talk?" She stood up and felt kind of woozy.

He shook his head.

"You want me to dance?"

He nodded. "We got one song left." Khalil pulled out a bankroll and peeled off three fifties and pressed them in her hand. "Dance," he insisted.

Portia took another deep breath and began. She tried to imagine Khalil as another person. She closed her eyes, and with the help of the Henny, it kind of worked. She turned around, and he lifted her dress and massaged her ass.

"Can I touch you?" He asked that a little too late.

She just shrugged, because she was unsure about anything at this point.

"I paid for more time when I went to the bar. Take this dress off and give me a lap dance."

He hadn't touched his new drink, so she asked for it. Khalil gave it up, sensing that she needed it more than he did. She wolfed that one down too, ignoring the little angel stripper on her shoulder that said, "Slow down." Portia slowly slid her dress straps down and rubbed her breasts while Khalil stared at her like he was in a trance. When she took off the dress, he breathed deep, as if fighting to maintain his cool. He pulled her toward him, to sit on his lap. By now she was tipsy as hell from the Hennessy rush and needed to get off her feet for a minute.

Portia sat on his lap, leaned forward, and placed her hands on the floor and wrapped her legs around his chair, which gave him a full view of her ass. She squeezed her muscles and made her butt cheeks jump one at a time. Khalil rubbed in circular motions and squeezed simultaneously, and then he tried to slide her thong strap aside, but Portia shifted quickly. She rose from the floor and swung around to sit on his lap face-to-face, then continued lap dancing and avoiding eye contact.

Khalil held her waist and slid down on the chair. Now her breasts jiggled right in his face; he cupped them in his hands and gently squeezed her nipples. They were too close for comfort, so Portia leaned back and rested her palms on the floor. Khalil rubbed her thighs. His touch was gentle, as if she were breakable. She usually enjoyed the power she had over men, but under these circumstances, she was afraid of it.

Khalil rubbed her stomach, and his fingers rested on her navel ring briefly before treading over the bulging turquoise thong that housed her womanhood. She was usually proud of her ample lips down there, but at this instant she wished they weren't so fat. Khalil felt Portia tense up, so he continued his trail to her inner thighs, where his hands rested for a second before going back to the bulge and squeezing it, as if he couldn't help himself. "Damn, you got a fat pussy. It look like a fist."

Portia sat up, and he leaned down and took her left nipple in his mouth and sucked on it like a hungry baby. Shame flooded over her because it felt so good. She tried to push him away, but the Hennessy had taken its toll. He starting working on the right one, and he was the type of man who sucked a titty good enough to make a chick cream. Portia stifled a moan and pushed him away. She jumped up from his lap. He stood up too, then she sat down. Khalil knelt in front of her and rubbed and kissed her thighs. Gently, he spread her legs apart and kissed between them.

Portia intercepted. "Khalil, please stop."

He was hardheaded, and her resistance was getting weaker. Without a word, he slid her panties down and off of one foot, then he put his face in the place. Khalil sucked on Portia's clit and tongued her pussy until she trembled. She clenched her teeth to keep from crying out when she exploded, and he wouldn't come up until she climaxed again.

Suddenly, Khalil rose and turned to leave. He stopped short and dug in his pocket and quickly peeled off some bills and dropped them, and then he left without a word. Portia could count money in the dark, and she knew its sound. She'd counted ten bills, and they'd better not be singles.

She sat there in shame for a minute, feeling lower than a dirty dog. She wasn't shit. She never should've done a VIP with Khalil, because she'd jeopardized her friendship with Laila, as well as their marriage. She felt like cousin Faith, that traitor bitch who fucked Teri's husband in the movie *Soul Food*.

How many songs had Khalil paid for? They were back there for over thirty minutes, and Big Bruce hadn't come to collect once. "Girl, you fuckin' up big-time," she told herself while she got dressed. She'd broken her rule of never drinking at work, and she'd gone way too far with Khalil. She wasn't usually so careless; she turned up her nose in disgust at girls who got drunk on the job because they were wild and sloppy and caused men to stereotype the rest of them. Portia looked in the hall mirror to make sure she was straight, then headed to the dressing room to clean up.

Big Bruce gave her an approving nod when she passed him. "You been back there long enough. Your moneybag should tell the story. Shit, if I had it like that, I'd take you back there and keep you all night! Girl, you one sexy mothafucka!" He laughed at his own wit.

Portia went back on the floor dressed in a hot-pink number to solicit her other VIPs. On VIP number three, she became annoyed when the fat greaseball burned her on the hip with his cigarette, even after she'd insisted he put it out before the lap dance. He'd sworn he'd be careful, but lardass got overexcited, just as she'd predicted. The extra twenty he threw her didn't take away the sting, and she needed a break.

Portia changed her outfit again to black leather, then hit the bar. She was grateful that Khalil had left. Burdened by the guilt of betraying her best friend, she threw back four double shots of Hennessy. When she finally stood up to leave the bar, the room swayed, and the faces in the club moved from side to side. She was drunk as hell.

Candy was concerned. "Mystique, you need to call it a night and go home. You had *way* too much to drink. Go get dressed, and I'll call you a cab."

Portia just nodded and stumbled to the dressing room to get her things. She stuffed her money into her purse and grabbed her bag, and she bounced. This would be the first time she'd left before changing back to street clothes, but she was so drunk she needed to get home ASAP.

"I'll make sure you get home safe, baby," some guy yelled, and scored some laughter.

She sat at the front entrance on a stool with her bag at her feet and waited on her taxi. Biggs and Tree expressed concern about her safety, because they knew it was unlike her to drink at work. After she assured them that she was fine, she went outside. Just as she reached the curb, a horn blared at her from behind her cab. The blue Ford Expedition's driver jumped out and came toward her. It was Khalil. She hurried to her taxi, but he was right at her side. Portia ignored him and opened the cab door.

"Let me give you a ride. We need to talk. What you doin' out here dressed like that? Close your coat."

"Khalil, I'm fine. I prefer to take a cab. Go home," Portia slurred.

The cabdriver asked her, "Is everything okay, miss?"

Khalil said, "Yeah, man. Everything is good. Go 'head, I got her. Come on, P. You fucked up. I just wanna make sure you get home safe. How much did you drink?"

The cabdriver looked real impatient. "Do you need a cab or not, miss?"

"Tell him to go. I'ma take you home." Khalil took her bag to his truck.

Portia told the taxi driver to leave and followed Khalil. When he opened the passenger door, she fell into the seat. She heard the back door open and close when he put her bag in the back, then he climbed in the driver's seat and took off.

Not a word was exchanged on the nine-minute drive to her apartment, and Portia fell asleep before they got there. When Khalil shook her awake, he was outside the truck holding her bag. Portia couldn't walk straight, so she leaned on him for support. He zipped up her coat and tied something around her waist to make her look halfway decent before they entered her building. It was late, but you never knew who might be stirring about, because the city never slept.

They got on the elevator, and Khalil said, "I wanna make sure you get to your door safe." His face was serious.

"I'm all right," Portia asserted.

"No, you not."

She fumbled in her purse for her keys and opened both locks, and they went inside. Portia kicked off her shoes and ran to the bathroom just in time. After she peed, she splashed some cold water on her face. When she came out, Khalil was sitting on the couch.

"You all right?"

She nodded and went to her room because she felt faint and nauseated. She needed to lie down. Minutes later, he came to her bedroom door and called her name. When she didn't answer, he sat on the foot of the bed and touched her arm.

"Yo, Portia. I'm sorry. I was just attracted to you tonight. I didn't mean to . . . I love Laila to death, and I know y'all like sisters, so I hope I didn't make a big mistake. Well, I know I did, but fuck it, I don't regret it. I know you liked it too, 'cause . . . Never mind." He got up. "I'ma leave so you can get undressed and get some sleep. You need anything?"

Portia shook her head, and a wave of nausea hit her. She was going to be sick. She jumped up but was unable to make it to the bathroom, so she fell down on her knees in front of the trash can by her computer desk and threw up. She vomited with such force that the spray ricocheted all over her face and dress. After what seemed like an eternity, her stomach stopped turning, and she trembled in a cold sweat.

Khalil had gone to the bathroom to get a wash-cloth, and he wiped her face. She snatched it from him and cleaned her mouth. Damn, she wished he would quit asking if she was okay. Portia looked down at her clothing and saw she was a mess, so she walked to the bathroom on shaky legs to rinse her mouth and clean up. She'd peed on herself while throwing up, so she took off her fouled thong and dropped it into the sink with some detergent to soak. She quickly showered and half-towel-dried, and then she went and fell in bed butt-naked.

She looked up and saw Khalil standing over her like a concerned father. Shit, she'd forgotten he was there. She pulled the covers over herself and mumbled, "Go home, Khalil. I just need some sleep, 'cause I feel real woozy."

"You sure? Do you need anything? You should eat something to settle your stomach."

Portia had voyaged to dreamland at the speed of light, so she didn't hear his last words.

N A DEEP sleep, Portia dreamed a pleasant feeling was rising in her groin. She was in a daze but realized she wasn't alone. In the dream, her assailant's head was between her legs, and he was finger-rolling her nipples, but she couldn't see his face. Portia was paralyzed with pleasure and fear as he manipulated her joy button with his tongue until she got that itchy feeling right at climax. Just before, the mysterious figure rose and penetrated her, gliding into her wet tunnel with ease.

Wait, she wasn't dreaming! She wanted to stop him, and her mind screamed *NO!* Her mouth just didn't have its back, so she surrendered without protest. Dark Man held her wrists and slid in and out. Portia gasped, and on the seventh or eighth stroke, she climaxed.

Dark Man shuddered and slumped, breathing heavily in her ear. He rolled over and disappeared, and Portia sat up and tried to grasp what had happened. She felt a sticky wetness between her thighs. She panicked and prayed it wasn't what she feared. Her prayer was rejected. The sticky substance was semen. He hadn't worn a condom; she hadn't even checked to make sure he had one on. Portia dashed down the hall to clean herself, and she bumped dead into Khalil at the bathroom door. They avoided eye contact.

Portia had a word with God in the bathroom as she washed down there several times. *Please forgive me for being so foul. I am so sorry, Lord. Please don't let me have no disease or get pregnant or nothing. Please forgive me for stabbing my best friend in the back. And God, please don't let this thing blow up in my face. Don't let him have AIDS, or herpes, or anything, God. And please don't let me be pregnant. And God, please help me cope with this evil I've done.* Portia felt so bad, she had tears running down her cheeks.

She washed her face with cool water and took a deep breath. She hoped Khalil was gone, but then again she wanted to kill him for taking advantage of her when she was out of it. No, she should kill herself for lying there in a drunken stupor and just letting him fuck her. That was something only a stupid bitch would do, not her. She didn't get down like that.

Khalil was dressed and ready to make his exit. Portia grabbed her robe from her bedroom door to cover her nakedness and shame. He kept his head down and stuttered, "Yo, um, Portia, I'm sorry. You looked so sexy sleeping that I couldn't help myself. Damn, I'm sounding like some pervert, and shit. I didn't mean to bother you. Umm, I umm . . . I know I should've pulled out before—"

She cut him off. "I looked sexy sleeping? What the fuck you talkin' 'bout, Khalil?" She paused and took a deep breath. "You should have used a rubber, at least. What were you thinking? Lord, what was *I* thinking? This is so fucked up. You know, we ain't shit. Why did you cum in me, Khalil?"

Portia had sense enough to know that even if he had pulled out, she would still be at risk of pregnancy or disease. She was more afraid of disease, because she didn't know how many strippers he was eating out in VIP. Did he always get down like that? She just wished she could rewind and erase the whole night, because it felt like a bad movie script.

"It's my fault, Portia. I should've left when you fell asleep. I went to the door like three times, but I kept thinkin' 'bout you under the covers with no clothes on. Temptation got the best of me. I should've been a man and left."

Portia rolled her eyes at him. "That's the reason you stayed, 'cause you're a man, and you think wit' your dick! I, on the other hand, should have been a *woman* and stopped you. But I ain't even know that was you! Oh, God. You're my best friend's husband. What decent woman would let her best friend's husband fuck her?"

Khalil shook his head and shifted the blame back on himself. "Nah, you was 'sleep, and I shouldn't have messed with you. I should've just took my ass home."

Portia faced up to her responsibility. "I was out of it, but I *still* could've protested or something!" She sighed. "Khalil, there's no point in discussing what we could've, should've, or would've done. It's over, so let's just forget about it. Laila can never, *ever* find out about this, 'cause it would hurt her to her heart. She does not deserve this. You better not run your fucking mouth, Khalil. Let's just sweep it under the rug and pray there are no repercussions, like pregnancy or disease, God forbid. Oh, man, we played our fuckin' selves." She shook her head in disbelief.

Khalil raised an eyebrow. "*Disease?* Is you a'ight, Portia?"

She looked at him like *nigga, please.* "You should've been concerned *before* we had sex. I haven't had un-protected sex in years, and I took two AIDS tests last year. I'm pretty sure that *I'm* fine. Well, I *was* sure. How often are you out cheating? Do *you* use con-doms? Are you fuckin' around on Laila with a lot of women? Khalil, tell me something before I freak out, please."

"Calm down, girl. I'm not fuckin' around on Laila. I only cheated on her twice since we've been married, and both times I used a condom. I wouldn't jeopar-dize my wife's health. Or mine. I can't take something home to my family. I got two little girls. I don't get down like that, Portia. Trust me."

"I just wish you'd used a condom. God, Khalil, we played ourselves. What if I'm pregnant? I know I was fucked up, but this wasn't the way I wanted to sober up." She was real scared now. What the fuck had she done? This was around the time Portia ovulated every month, so she was in her fertile stage.

Sensing her panic, Khalil tried to soothe her. "Don't worry, you ain't pregnant. But we'll deal with *whatever* happens, okay? Be cool. You hungry?"

Portia nodded. Her stomach was on E from the Hennessy-induced vomiting episode.

"I'll go to IHOP. Call the order in so it can be ready."

She fished for the number in the Yellow Pages, then called and ordered steak and eggs for Khalil, and grits and eggs with toast for herself. Portia told him the food would be ready in about twenty minutes.

To get an appetite and ease her mind, Portia got out her pill bottle stash and twisted up some sunshine. She lit up and passed it to Khalil, who refused the first time, then accepted her second offer. He said, "No wonder every time Laila come from your house, she so high."

"Don't front like she only smoke when she come over here."

"You right. I smell it sometimes when I come home. Probably be having my daughters high off contact."

They both laughed.

"She don't smoke around them, Khalil, you know that. She's a good mother," Portia assured him.

He nodded. "I better go get this food."

He left, and she was glad they could have a half-decent conversation after their betrayal. She didn't want them acting suspicious, even though they were both guilty as sin.

Khalil retuned in under twenty minutes, and he looked in her eyes like she was on exhibit. "You *mad high*."

Portia said, "*Duh*."

In the kitchen, she took a half-gallon of Tropicana out of the fridge and got two glasses, and they shared small talk while they ate. Soon the microwave's clock read 5:47 a.m. Khalil must've read her mind, because he decided it was time to leave. He said it was his turn to take the girls to day care that morning.

"Khalil, Laila's gonna kill you for coming in at this hour."

He played tough. "No, she won't. I'll think of something to tell her."

"She ain't as dumb as you think." Portia walked him to the door, and he hugged her and kissed her on the cheek like a sister, the way it was supposed to be.

"Good night, Khalil. Take care of yourself."

He looked at her for a second. "Ditto. Thanks, P. Get some rest."

"**G**O WITH THE peach, Patty-cake. And work that peach hat too. That's a real nice wedding color," Portia told her mother.

Patricia lowered her brow. She hated when Portia called her Patty-cake. "Girl, you don't wear pants to a wedding. Appropriate wedding attire for a *lady* is a dress that hangs below the knees."

Portia giggled. "Ma, it's not gon' be in a church. It's not traditional. They're getting married in a banquet hall."

"A wedding is a wedding. And it's a nice hall. I think I'll wear the pink."

Pat was as sweet as pie, with her soft-spoken demeanor. Portia was glad she'd caught her today, when she was off and they could spend the whole day together. It had been a while, because Patricia worked second shift and Portia was a night owl and usually asleep when her mother was stirring about in the morning.

Pat looked great at fifty years young. She had cocoa skin and light brown eyes, with full lips, dazzling white teeth, and shoulder-length silky black hair. Because of her girlish smile and small waist, most people thought she and Portia were sisters. Patricia Lane was a proud woman whose modesty enhanced her beauty. She was a widow with only one child, and they were exceptionally close.

She reappeared from the huge closet in her bedroom and stared at Portia as if taking inventory. "You're losing too much weight, girl. You need to stop running so much. Child, it's time for a change in your life. You said this dancing mess was just a stepping-stone. It looks to me like you done got comfortable. Baby, that's not a career. You're smarter than that. You can have a better life. You got a college degree. You got to get up off your butt and work. That fast money will get you in trouble. A lot comes along with it, baby. Those are risks that you don't have to take. For God's sake, Portia, you could be raped or killed by some lunatic and left 'side a road, God forbid."

She paused and sighed. "You my only child, but you're a woman now. You're twenty-five years old, and it's time for you to become successful and establish yourself in the world. Enough of this bullcrap. You blessed with your health and strength, and you can become so much more. Don't run yourself down young. You don't have to be stripping and doing what you're doing to earn a living. And don't think I don't know what you're doing. Don't waste your God-given talents, baby. Quit lookin' at life through a fool's eyes."

"Ma, I'm not stupid. You right. I don't know what happened." Portia shrugged.

"Whatever happened don't matter no more. It's time to turn it around, Portia. I raised you to be an intelligent, respectable lady. The things you do in life will follow you. One day you may want to settle down and have a family. Let your husband and children be able to be proud of their wife and mama. You may think you're getting over in life, 'cause you takin' the fast road and bypassing success's struggle, but sooner or later what's done in the dark will come to the light."

Unable to meet Pat's gaze for fear she might burst into tears, Portia looked down at the mauve carpet. It was time to move on to the next level. That shit was getting old. Or was she just burdened by guilt from the night she and Khalil had played themselves? Three weeks had passed, but she was still tripping. She hated herself for being for sale that night. If she hadn't been trying so hard to make a dollar outta fifteen cent, she wouldn't have agreed to VIP with Khalil. Lately, she felt like she'd lost touch with herself. She used to love to write, though now she didn't feel inspired by anything but money. Portia had been born with a poet's soul, but the last few years of paper chasing had limited her creativity. "I know, Ma." The concern in Pat's eyes triggered a self-pity trip, and she broke down.

Pat handed her a tissue. "Don't cry, do something about it. You're still young and have plenty of time. If you don't waste it."

Portia nodded and blew her nose. They spent the rest of the day catching up and watching movies on Pat's favorite channel, STARZ in Black. By the time Portia went home, she'd been strengthened by the kind of understanding and guidance that only a mama could offer. She felt lighter than she had in weeks.

When she got home and checked her answering machine, there was a message from Laila. They hadn't talked much the last few weeks, since Laila was working so much overtime. Portia was glad, because she felt too guilty to face her. Khalil had called twice since that night, but Portia had avoided him. She'd even opted to send gifts and money to the girls' birthday party, missing it for the first time. She'd called Pebbles and Macy during the party and told them that she couldn't make it, and they said they loved the presents she'd sent.

Portia returned Laila's call to make sure everything was okay. Nobody answered, so she left a short message, and then her call waiting beeped. It was Fatima on the other line, and Portia greeted her with gusto. "Hey, stranger! What up, babygirl?"

Fatima laughed. "The mothafuckin' rent! I'm downstairs, P. Diddy. Buzz me in."

A minute later she was at the door, and they embraced like long-lost sisters. Portia was delighted to see her. She looked healthy as ever. Almond-complexioned, voluptuous-figured Fatima was decked out in camel-colored leather from her cowgirl hat down to her skirt and stiletto boots. That color brought out the honey-colored flecks in her eyes and new strawberry-blond highlights in her curly hair. She was working that outfit, and Portia let her know.

Fatima accepted the compliment with grace and followed her into the living room, where Portia immediately began to query. "What's his name? I don't hear from yo' ass no more, so tell me what the fuck is goin' on."

Fatima laughed and revealed cute dimples and gold-framed bottom teeth. "Portia, don't play dumb. I know y'all mothafuckas been talkin' shit about me. But I've been real busy working with these new acts. There's a lot of marketing shit to be done, and it's time-consuming. My days been real long, girl."

She continued, "And his name is Troy, aka Felony. No pun intended, 'cause he ain't even twenty yet. That young boy got some of the sweetest tongue and dick I ever had in my entire life. I need to thank his *mama!* Hell, that's all he *can* do for me is suck and fuck me. He ain't got shit but a big dick. He stays with me a few nights out the week, but I see him when I *wanna* see him. You know how I get in my moods."

"Fatima, you so nasty!"

They both laughed. Portia wasn't worried about Fatima. She liked to be in control of her relationships, and she loved herself some younger men. Portia wasn't about to lecture, because Tima would do as she pleased anyhow.

"Girl, I can't stay long. I just had to stop and holla for a minute to puff some trees and play catch-up. How *you* doin'? What's up in *your* life? Still shakin' that ass for cash?"

"Hell, yeah! Nah, seriously, Tima. I'm about to square up. It's time to move up a level. I ain't try'na make that no career. What I'ma tell my kids? Mommy is a stripper? I'm tired of this shit. I gotta make some serious changes, girl."

"Portia, you can do anything you want to. Do you. The sky is the limit, boo. You got plenty of life left in you. And a lot of strength. You just got to use it."

Portia's eyes watered up again. It had to be PMS making her so damn emotional. She escaped to the bathroom, and Fatima had the blunt fired up when she came out. She was glad, because she needed the tranquillity.

Fatima passed her the el. "Porsh, you all right?"

She nodded and inhaled. They passed the peace pipe back and forth, and the weed must have been like a truth tonic, because Portia almost confessed details to Fatima about her rendezvous at the club with Khalil. She chose to shut the fuck up because she couldn't let Tima know she was trifling and had broken the code. She was especially ashamed of having enjoyed it. What kind of weak traitor bitch was she? Tima's laugh drew her back to reality, and she faked a smile.

About twenty minutes later, Fatima had to bounce. She reminded Portia to give her a copy of her résumé the following day. "I'm telling you, I can get you on at the label. Make sure you call me tomorrow, P. That can be another stepping-stone for you. Until we start up our *own* company."

Portia grinned. "I know that's right." They hit high five and bade each other farewell, and then she heard Tima's heels clickety-clack to the elevator.

Portia decided to lie down for a little while and listen to some music. She drifted into a light sleep, until a knock at the door startled her. She checked her breath and appearance and went to investigate. She tiptoed and peeked through the peephole. It was Khalil. How the hell did he get into the building? Portia walked away from the door, and he knocked again.

She sighed and opened the door. "What's up, Khalil? Did you lose somethin' here?"

"Damn, don't bite a nigga head off. I just came to check on you. Ain't no need to act so stink."

She softened up a fraction. "I'm fine, Khalil. And you?"

"I'm good. Can I come in for a minute?"

Part of her wanted to slam the door in his face, but she figured they were adults, and they had to put this thing behind them in order for things to get back to normal. Khalil was her best friend's husband, so they'd be forced to interact eventually. She let him in, and they sat in the living room and shared small talk about the kids, the news, and the neighborhood. Neither of them mentioned that night. He told her the store was finally out of the red and seeing a profit.

Portia noticed how excited he got when he talked about the store, so she was happy for him. She remembered what Laila had said, and she grinned. "Laila told me she was thinking 'bout taking a leave from work to come help you with the store."

The light in his eyes died, and he didn't respond for a few seconds. Portia sensed she said the wrong thing.

Khalil sighed. "It's like this, P. I love my wife, and I'd kill for her. But the fact is, we're not attached at the hip, and there's no need to be in each other face twenty-four/seven. The store, that's *my* thing. I mean, everything I got is hers too, but sometimes a man just needs his own thing. I hope I'm not coming off like some selfish, ego-tripping asshole, but I'm just being honest."

He looked sincere, and Portia felt him. But she knew Laila would be hurt if she heard how he really felt. "I guess Laila doesn't know how you feel, huh?"

He shook his head. "I can't tell her that."

Portia figured this was the reason Laila had com-

plained that Khalil was so distant with her. He was trying to change her mind, but he didn't know how to
express himself without hurting her feelings. Instead,
he had done like most men and run away from the
problem.

She transformed into a marriage counselor. "Khalil,
communication is the key to a lasting relationship. If
it's bothering you, then you have to face it, 'cause your
reaction to the situation is only causing more problems. Simply discussing it with her can avoid some
permanent damage you may regret. Laila may not love
what you have to say, but she'd rather you be honest
with her. She's very understanding, and she *is* strong.
Talk to your wife, Khalil. She loves you."

He looked like he was listening. "Thanks, Portia. I'll
let her know."

"Be easy," she warned him.

The phone rang, and before she answered it, Khalil
got up and kissed her on the forehead. "Good night,
Porsh. Take care of yourself," he said, and left her
apartment.

Portia picked up on the fourth ring. "Hello?"

"What took you so long?"

It was Jay! She smiled like she was taking a picture.
Cheese! "Hi, baby!"

"What's good, Ma? I'm back, and I'm comin'
through in a few, so be on the lookout. One hun'ed."
He hung up.

Portia put the phone back on the hook. Her black
knight had returned, and she was as happy as a faggot
with a bag of dicks. Fuck the money, she genuinely
cared about Jay. She melted inside when she heard his

voice. Jay could really be her soul mate, because he'd understood and accepted her for who she was even before he knew what she really had to offer. She knew she was slipping, but she decided to follow her heart and tell him how she felt.

Portia took a shower and rehearsed what she would say. She didn't want to come off sounding half as vulnerable as she was feeling. Midshower, she changed her mind. She would just let the cards play out and see what he wanted first, because tonight he would be exposed to the real Portia. She wouldn't be all dolled up and wearing no damn stilettos. She was cozily clad in a baby-doll T-shirt and a pair of Jay's plaid boxers, with pink bunny slippers on her feet and two ponytails in her hair.

The phone rang; it was Laila returning her call. She sounded tired. "I'm just shoutin' you back out. I just got in twenty minutes ago, girl. I worked till twelve, and I'm beat. Everybody's asleep in this joint. Khalil dozed off on the couch waiting for me. He looks so cute. He must be tired, 'cause he never goes to sleep this early. I'ma take a shower and crash. What's poppin', P? You a'ight?" She had barely stopped for a breath.

Portia laughed. "Yes, I'm fine. It's you who's wired up. Get some sleep. I'll talk to you tomorrow. Oh, Fatima came over here earlier. She said to give you her love. That's all, boo. Night-night."

"Okay. I'll call you tomorrow. Nighty-night." Laila hung up.

Portia had purposely left Khalil's visit out of the conversation. Not that Laila would be suspicious, but she would want to know what they'd talked about, and

Portia wasn't about to run her mouth. Besides, as soon as Khalil brought it up, Laila would call to get Portia's opinion on how to react. She would just tell Laila to give him his space. Portia flicked the idiot box to *Midnight Love* and sang along with slow-jams videos. She lit two mango-scented candles for aromatherapy, then relaxed on the couch.

Fifteen minutes later, Jay arrived. She popped a stick of gum and unlocked the door and was grinning and showing all thirty-two teeth when he entered. He looked extra-good in a navy blue Rocawear velour suit, and he reeked intoxicatingly of expensive cologne and masculinity.

She hugged him tightly. "I missed you so much, daddy. I hate it when you leave me."

Jay disagreed. "Since when? You don't be thinkin' about me, Portia. You think you fuckin' superwoman. Wildin' out and shakin' your ass all up in them clubs and shit. You think you real tough, right? Since when do *you* need a nigga?" Sarcasm dripped from his voice, and then he laughed. "Girl, you got some serious game. You should've been born a dude, with all that G."

She would have to fight to get past the image he had of her. She couldn't blame him, because he'd asked her to slow down before, and she hadn't even considered it then. She swallowed and looked in his eyes. "Jay, I'm serious. I really care about you, and I'm tired of being tough all the time. I just wanna be loved. I'm leaving this dancing shit alone because it's time to square up. And I'm *not* superwoman. But I want you to be my superman. I'm in love with you, Jay."

Jay looked at her strange and sat on the couch. She

joined him and studied him quietly. It was the first time she'd ever seen him without a haircut. She stroked his jaw.

"I gotta hit the barbershop in the morning. I only fuck with my man Tweeze. I just wolf out till I get back up top, 'cause them country barber niggas be molesting niggas' hairlines. I gave a nigga one chance, and he fucked my shit up. He had my shit starting all the way back here, Ma." He pointed to the middle of his head.

Portia laughed. "Well, I'm content. I love you wolfing out or bald as an eagle's ass. It don't matter, I'll take you however I can. But imperfection can be sexy, Jay." She snuggled up under him.

He laughed. "Yo, you acting real weird tonight, P. You high? You been smokin' weed?"

"I'm high off of you," she replied. "I'm not acting weird, I'm seriously expressing my true feelings."

Jay changed the subject. "So what you been up to? What's going on?"

Portia gave him a quick rundown, carefully leaving out details he didn't need to know. There was no need to tarnish his image of her any more than it already was. Now it was his turn. "So what's going on in Jay-ville? Let me into your world? I yearn to know more about you."

He was staring at her funny again. "After you tell me what happened."

Portia was confused. "What happened when?"

"What happened to you while I was gone that made you start talking 'bout squaring up all of a sudden? Usually, when somebody suddenly starts talking about changing, something happened to make 'em see the light. Did you have some kind of bad experience at the club or at one of your little *private parties*? I ain't no slow leak. What happened to you?"

Portia knew the guilty look on her face gave her away, so she bent the truth. "This fat mothafucka burned me with his cigarette while I was giving him a table dance. I'm just extra fed up with this bullshit. That made me feel kind of cheap, I guess. It's been building up, though. You get tired of niggas lookin' at you like a piece of meat. Plus, my mother been getting on me and tellin' me I should be doing more. And my friends. I already know that, though. I never intended to dance as a career. It was just like a stepping-stone to hustle up money for school. Now I'm just smartening up, 'cause it's time to move on. And Jay, you have the wrong idea. I don't do private parties like that. I told you that when we first met. I don't get personal with just anybody." She looked in his eyes for reinforcement of her last words, then continued, "I earned my bachelor's degree in accounting almost two years ago, so it's time to do something with it. I'm thinking long-term because I'm concerned about my future. Now it's your turn."

Jay appeared satisfied with her explanation, because he nodded. He looked thoughtful and remained quiet for a minute. "Well, me and a partner just started a trucking company. I got three trucks in VA, with drivers and some accounts set up already. A little more paperwork, and they'll be loaded down and rolling. Plus, I'm trying to get this production company off the ground. There's a lot of money in this music shit. I'm trying to stay legit from now on. I gotta be around because I got a lot of people depending on me. I dib and dab in a few things, but I'm looking at the future, man. The big picture."

He crossed his arms and scratched his chin. "In the streets, a nigga havin' a good run right now, I can't front. Everybody on the team eatin'. I ain't fucked up right now, but I know all good things come to an end. You just gotta stack and know when it's time to get out. Timing is everything. You gotta stick and move, but you gotta have a *plan*, Portia. Money ain't shit without a good plan. That's the path to long-term stability. A plan."

She was impressed by his prudence and wished him success in all of his endeavors, though she knew his last words were aimed directly at her. She had a little bit of money saved up, but she didn't exactly have a good plan. She just knew she wanted out of the life.

They talked for hours about things they'd never discussed before, and it was three a.m. before they knew it. Jay must've been getting sleepy, because he yawned. Portia lay across the bed while he took a shower. When he was done, she would give him a massage and put him to sleep like a baby. She marveled at how deep they got that night. It was beyond sex. They connected on a higher level, and now they shared a kinship. Jay had the power to make her bare her soul.

Portia kept on hearing his words: *You gotta have a plan . . . That's the path to long-term stability.* Damn, he probably thought she was some chicken-head with no plans, and his opinion mattered. She really had to get her shit together; she was definitely no pigeon. She had dreams and goals, just like he did.

He emerged from the bathroom, wearing nothing but a few drops of glistening water and a navy blue towel tied around his waist. He looked like fine dark chocolate dipped in midnight, with stardust sprinkles. "Get me some boxers," he demanded in that sexy thuggish way he couldn't help.

Portia was ahead of him. She pointed to a brand-new plaid pair at the foot of the bed. He'd left a three-pack of Fruit of the Looms there one night, so he'd have fresh ones when he crashed. Jay sat at the foot of the bed to put them on. He shyly turned around and slipped them up under his towel. Portia thought that was so cute. Jay stretched out on the bed on his stomach, and she lay on top of his back.

"Yo, get off my ass, man. I don't play that gay shit."

She laughed. "I'm just smelling you. I love your scent. It turns me on."

"Ma, you crazy."

Portia sat upright and massaged his neck and back. He was tense, so she dug deeper in circular motions until he relaxed. She needed to know if she had a chance, so she came right out with it. "Jay, do you wanna get serious with me?"

He took a second to respond. "I don't know. Maybe."

That wasn't what she'd wanted to hear. The word "maybe" only led to false hope. Portia played cool and kept on massaging. "Now give me a real answer."

He rolled over so that they faced each other, and he got serious. "You want me to tell you what you *wanna* hear, or you want the truth?"

"The truth."

He licked his lips and folded his arms behind his head. "A'ight. Portia, you're a pretty girl, and I'm feeling you. I look forward to seeing you and all that. But you out there way too much, and I can't wife somebody I can't trust. You're too fast for me. You hollering you about to slow down and all that, but how do I know that's not temporary? Portia, I can't let you fuck me up. A nigga ain't got time for heartbreak and shit. I'm too old for them type of games. I gotta stay focused on achieve mode, so I don't have time to be wondering about where you at or who you wit'. Shit like that *already* crosses my mind, 'cause I can't even reach you half the time I call. You not home, *and* you got your cell phone turned off."

He shook his head. "You too dangerous, Ma. You got the looks, the personality, and some pretty good conversation too. Portia, you got a banging body and skin soft as satin, but I can't fuck wit' you. I hope I don't sound fucked up, but that's what's up."

You could've knocked Portia over with a feather. All she could come up with was "Word?" She got up and played it off, so he wouldn't see the tears starting to form in her eyes. "You thirsty?"

"Yeah, get me some cold water."

In the kitchen, she set her tears free from willpower prison. She shouldn't have been shocked by his reaction. Who was she kidding? He'd met her in a fucking strip club. But it still hurt. No matter what he said, she knew he cared about her. They would get past this trust thing, because she really was about to change. She couldn't give up that easy; they had something. She felt it too much. Portia got herself together and poured two glasses of spring water from the fridge. She went back in the room and handed Jay one.

"Is it safe to drink this?"

She smiled. "Don't be silly. Jay, I respect your honesty, but I can't give up that easy. There's something between us, and I know you feel it too. You gon' change your mind about me, because this is right. Therefore, accepting a 'no' from you isn't even an option. I'ma take you away from that other chick. Permanently. That's my word."

He looked real amused. "Look at you, you *serious*. Tough girl, huh? You staking claims? Sit your little ass down."

Portia probed on. "Do y'all live together?"

"Y'all who, Portia?"

"You and whatever her name is. I don't know." The "black woman attitude" was coming out.

"So you don't need to know. Don't worry about it."

Now she wanted to know more. "Be straight up with me. What's going on?"

"What's with all the questions? If I asked you who you fuckin', would you be honest? *Do* I ask you? No, 'cause I don't wanna know all that. Now, this discussion is *over*."

"I'm not finished. I still wanna talk about it," she demanded.

He got up and pulled back the covers. "You heard what I said. That's a wrap. Lay down, and let's go to sleep." He patted the bed beside him.

She took off her clothes and slid in bed naked. In minutes, Jay was snoring softly, holding her.

When Portia awoke at nine the next morning, Jay was still sleeping. It felt good waking up beside him, and he looked adorable. She went to the bathroom to brush and freshen up, and she drank some water to wet her whistle.

She went and got back under the cover and massaged Rocky. He stiffened under her caress, and she pulled him out and licked his tip. He stood at attention like a proud soldier, and Portia kissed his shaft and slid him in her mouth. She knew Jay was awake, but he played possum. She continued her oral conquest and heard him stifle a moan, which excited her more. She sucked gently up and down and feather-kissed and licked.

Jay abandoned the possum role and ran his fingers through her hair, brushing it back so he could see her face. She looked sexy as hell. When Portia deep-throated and squeezed the back of her throat, he moaned uncontrollably. After that, Rocky vibrated in her mouth, so she pulled her head back and hand-pumped him to bliss. He shuddered, and then babies shot out all over her hand. Curtains.

She went to the bathroom to clean up and gargle and came back in a flash. "Good morning, sunshine."

Jay flashed her a lazy, appreciative smile. "Nice wake-up call. Is my toothbrush still in there?"

"Of course. And I left a green washcloth and towel in there for you."

When Portia heard the bathroom door close, she sat on the bed and thought about what she'd just done. She'd done Jay without a condom for the first time. That was a big step, and she hoped it wouldn't backfire on her ass. It wasn't as bad as she'd thought it would be, so she must have strong feelings for him.

Portia decided to cook some breakfast. She was hungry, and he probably was too.

She made pancakes, scrambled eggs with cheese, and turkey bacon for two, and then she poured two glasses of Tropicana OJ and fixed Jay a man-sized plate. She was eating when he found her in the kitchen.

"I didn't know you could cook. I don't even smell nothin' burning."

"You *crazy*? I can cook my ass off. Sit down and eat, boo. You might need to put your plate in the microwave for a few seconds. And that's turkey bacon." She knew he didn't eat pork either.

Portia wasn't lying. She had learned how to cook from her mother, her father, and her grandmother. Each of them had a different style, so she'd combined what she'd learned from all of them to create her own. Jay reheated his food, and she headed for the shower, leaving him to enjoy his meal alone.

When she came out, Jay was on the living room sofa, watching TV. He wore only boxers and white cotton crew socks, and he looked deep in thought. She sat astride his lap, wearing only a burgundy bath towel. "A penny for your thoughts," she whispered in his ear.

"Nah, they cost more than that."

"I'll give you whatever you want."

"Whatever?"

Portia looked in his eyes. "Anything."

He slid his hands under her towel, and seconds later, she rode him on the couch. And then once again in the bedroom.

Shortly after, they lay sleeping in each other's arms, and Portia didn't wake up until the phone rang. It was a telemarketer trying to get her to switch her long-distance carrier to MCI. She wasn't interested, so she hung up. Jay had to be real tired, because he barely budged. He hardly ever got enough sleep, so she didn't disturb him.

Three hours later, she was in the living room, up-dating her résumé on her laptop, when he appeared, dressed and ready to make an exit. She grinned at him. "Did you get enough rest?"

"More than I'm used to. I usually keep one eye open. It's a little too comfortable in your crib. Why you ain't wake me up?"

"Evidently, you needed the rest."

"I got a lot to do today, and I'm running behind schedule. I turned my phone off last night, and I got forty-three new messages. Mothafuckas act like they can't do shit without me. I gotta run, Ma. Don't get up, I'll lock the door." He kissed her on the forehead. "I'll call you later."

"Be careful, baby. Have a good day."

"I will." He winked at her and shut the door.

After he left, Portia got back to her résumé. She was pleased with her current love interest, and now she needed to work on the other areas of her life.

When she went to her bedroom later to print the ré-sumé, there was money on the nightstand. She counted five hundred dollars! Portia didn't know how to take that. Last night was on her. Did the money mean that he wanted to leave things as they were? Was a relation-ship completely out of the question? Or was he just looking out for her? She decided to let the cards play out by themselves. Jay wasn't going to drive her nuts. If it was meant to be between them, then it would be. But she was sure hoping for the best.

She needed to get out of the house and get some fresh air. She called Fatima, who answered on the third ring. "Fatima speaking, may I help you?"

"Girl, this Portia. What's goin' on?"

"Hey, Ma-Ma! What's crack-a-lackin'? I'm down here at the studio with our latest act. We're trying to get this single done. It's by an R and B chick named Raven. Her vocals are almost finished. My lil' squeeze has sixteen bars in the song, and he has to lay down his verse, and then there's editing and mixing and shit to be done. We'll be in session for a few more hours. You should come on down here, girl. We up in here jammin'."

"Well, I ain't doin' shit anyway. Give me some directions. I finished that résumé, so I'll bring it with me." Portia jotted down the address and called a cab.

Fifteen minutes later, she looked up at the high-rise building in the city and then back down at the yellow Post-it she'd scribbled the address on. Yup, that was it. She headed on inside.

When the elevator reached the twenty-sixth floor, she got off and looked up at the cathedral ceiling and beautiful brass chandeliers. Her red pony-skin Dior stilettos sank into the plush green carpet. This was definitely no low-budget basement studio.

Fatima had told the security guard she was expecting Portia, so he buzzed her in. When the black door opened, Fatima was standing in front of a wall-sized aquarium. It was filled with exotic tropical fish swimming around beautiful rocks and greenery. At the bottom was a life-size deep-sea diver carrying a flashlight aimed at a treasure chest filled with gemstones and golden treasure. With the exception of the purple neon aquarium light, the hallway was dark. The effect was awesome.

"Beautiful, right?" Fatima asked.

Portia nodded. They stood there for a minute, admiring the fish, then Fatima pushed a button and a doorway parted in the aquarium. They went inside and stepped into a blue-lit lounge with a bar in the middle of the floor. There were yellow and purple couches with oversize leopard-print velvet throw pillows strewn about, and the sound of bass shook the whole room. It was a real cool atmosphere.

Portia stopped Tima on the way to the sound room. "Girl, I have to use the bathroom."

"When you come out, I'll be in there." Fatima pointed to a steel door.

"I'll be right out." Portia rushed for the toilet. When she opened the bathroom door, there was a guy peeing at a urinal. She said, "My bad. I thought this was the ladies' room."

He smiled and said, "Don't mind me, love. It's unisex. Those stalls have doors." He pointed left, zipped up his pants, and left the john.

Portia hurried to relieve her bladder. She peed so much lately. She hoped her kidneys were okay. She had taken her mother's advice and scheduled a routine physical. Her appointment was in two weeks. Portia washed her hands and had barely made it out the door before a guy grabbed her around the waist and whispered in her ear, "Wanna roll with me, sexy?" He opened his palm and revealed several small colorful pills.

"I'm not into E, boo. Roll on." Portia kept it moving. She just smoked a little weed. Ecstasy was not her thing.

"Don't go, baby. Let me squeeze that juicy ass," he crooned at her backside as she went down the hall. She threw up a middle finger without even looking back, and the guy laughed. "Yeah, fuck me, baby! That's what I want you to do, shorty!"

Fatima motioned Portia over and introduced her to the crew as her God sister, and everyone greeted her warmly. When Portia met Felony, Fatima's young squeeze, she immediately understood her friend's infatuation, because that young boy was fine as hell. He was about six feet tall and caramel-colored, with dark eyebrows and zigzagged cornrows. To judge from his complexion and cheekbones, he looked like he could be of Native American descent. He was perfect, but to his benefit, he had a thuggish air that eliminated him from pretty-boy status.

He was in the booth laying down his bars, and he had a pretty tight flow. The song was hot. It was about a girl messing with a guy who was already involved with someone, and she was threatening to sabotage his relationship. Felony was playing the role of the guy. He rapped about her not being able to break up his family, and her being weekend booty, never to be wifey. When he was done, they played back the entire song. Portia dug the concept and thought it was a potential hit.

Hours later, the crew finally was satisfied with the mix, and it was time to go. Fatima suggested that they go get some grub, and Portia was down. They decided on buffalo wings from Pluck U. The weather was nice, so they walked the seven blocks down Sixth Avenue to Greenwich Village.

"Did you like the song?" Fatima asked.

"Hell, yeah, girl. It can be a big hit, 'cause the concept is hot. It's real scandalous. Who wrote it?"

"A newcomer named Shante Taylor. She's only twenty. I smell a hit too. Portia, the label is recruiting some fresh new writers. I remember you used to write all the time in school. You ever thought of songwriting?"

Portia gave her the *yeah, right* face and laughed. "Girl, I think I lost my inspiration."

"Find a new love," Fatima offered. "If some new dick don't inspire you, then nothing will." They laughed, and then she got serious again. "On the real, though, Porsh, you used to write some deep shit. You need to dig down in your soul and find that part of yourself again. Let the world know how gifted you are. It ain't never too late to shine, babygirl. I'm in a position where I can help you. I worked hard, and I moved up, so I finally got a little power. I can help you get a job and maybe get some of your writing out there. It's all up to you. What do *you* want to do? Sky's the limit. Oh yeah, give me that résumé."

"Word, let's start with a job first. I haven't started looking anywhere yet. I just made my decision, so I'm still green. I need to get it together big-time, girl."

"Don't worry about a job. There's an opening coming up in our fiscal division. It's a good spot and pays well above your average starting position. I know you're qualified, so I'll put in a good word for you. The head of that department, Charlene, she's a sister. And she's a friend of mine. We do lunch sometimes. I just need to know that you're serious, Portia. If you are, you know I'll stick my neck out for you. All the way, 'cause you my girl. If you take the job, it can be good experience for you. Until we start our own company. Sistahs got to get busy. The future is right on our heels."

Portia agreed. "Word. But I feel like I'm living in the past. I'm a ghost of who I used to be. Tima, I'm dead serious about this job. I'd be a fool to blow this. When is this position gonna be open?"

"In four to six weeks. The guy who has it now went with a better offer. He's relocating to L.A. Several people are waiting to fill his spot, but Charlene owes me a favor. And by the time I finish telling her how much you were born to do this, she'll hire you. Bet your bottom dollar."

"Give me a job description, Tima. What would be required?"

"I don't want to put my foot in my mouth, but nothing too strenuous. Just some accounting, probably A/P and ledger posting. Done on a computer, of course. Maybe some trends and projections. Nothing you haven't seen before, I'm sure. This is baby stuff to you, Porsh. You graduated with a 4.0."

"I know, but it's been a minute since I've done this stuff. I hope I didn't get stupid, girl. I better dig out those books and play catch-up, huh?"

"Do what you got to do, but I know you can do this," Fatima assured.

They ordered buffalo and honey barbecue wings, curly fries, and root beer. Portia unzipped her purse, but Fatima stopped her and slid the cashier a twenty. "My treat, Portia. You need to save all the money you can."

She looked so concerned, Portia had to laugh. "Stop looking at me like I'm a damn orphan. Thanks, girl, but I ain't broke. I've been saving a little bit. I have ten G's in my bank account. I knew this day was coming sooner or later. I'm not set for life, but I can make it till this job is open."

Fatima looked impressed. "In that case, you should be treating me, shit!" They laughed and proceeded to get their eat on.

SOONER OR LATER, *what's done in the dark will come to the light.*

Pat's words echoed in Portia's head over and over. The shit had hit the fan and come back in her face with a force more powerful than a head-on collision. Portia felt like shit. And she knew she wasn't shit either.

For three days she'd isolated herself from the world like a hermit. She was a mess. She hadn't eaten a single thing or taken a bath, and she wasn't taking any calls. The last few weeks were really a blur now.

Things had been going great between Portia and Jay. They were seeing each other three or four times a week. They hadn't discussed commitment again, but they were definitely getting closer. Portia just about had that new job sewn up. She'd done lunch with Fatima and Charlene, and she and Charlene really clicked; their opinions on a lot of things were almost identical. Before they parted, Charlene promised to treat Portia's résumé with special priority. Portia felt so confident that she hadn't even searched for employment elsewhere.

Shit was all good until three days ago, when a phone call sent Portia's world crashing down around her. That terrible memory she'd repressed had resurfaced and given her a black eye. Now she was in a heavy fog of denial.

Jay and Portia had slept late Tuesday morning. The night before, she'd turned off the ringer on the phone and turned down the answering machine, so they wouldn't be disturbed. After they got up and Jay went to take a shower, she checked her messages. There were two new ones. The first was from her mother to confirm Portia's attendance at the first sermon preached by Aunt Gracie, Pat's sister, in New Jersey. Gracie was recently ordained as a minister, and Portia had promised Pat that she wouldn't miss it. She jotted a reminder on the date in her planner.

The second message almost led to a nervous breakdown. It was her gynecologist. "Good morning, Miss Lane. This is Dr. Jacobs. I'm calling in regard to your visit last Friday. Your blood work has come back this morning, and it appears you have a reason to celebrate. Congratulations, Miss Lane. You're almost eight weeks pregnant! Feel free to contact me with questions. If not, I expect to see you soon for prenatal care. Please call to schedule an appointment. Thank you. Have a blessed day." The doctor sounded chipper, as if she'd given Portia great news.

Portia just stood there, dumbfounded. There had to be a mistake. Maybe they'd mixed up her blood work with somebody else's. This couldn't be. She quickly rewound the last few weeks. My God, she hadn't seen a period last month. Her heart sank, and a lump rose in her throat. She heard Jay coming out of the bathroom, so she got it together.

Jay could tell something was up from the look on

her face. After he put on his boxers, he asked her, "What's wrong, Ma? You all right?"

Portia lied. "I have to go down south with my mother. My grandmother is real sick."

"I'm sorry to hear that. I hope she gets well soon."

"Thank you."

"You just found out?"

"Yeah, my mother left a message this morning, so I called her. She's freaking out and worrying to death." Tears welled up in Portia's eyes from the guilt of lying about something so terrible. She hoped God would forgive her. Her maternal grandmother had been dead for seven years. Nana was probably turning over in her grave, hearing Portia misuse her memory like that.

Jay placed his hands on her shoulders. "Don't cry. She'll be okay. You gotta have faith, P. Stop crying."

Portia broke into an uncontrollable sobbing fit, and Jay held her and rubbed her back until she regrouped. They stood there embracing in silence for a few seconds. It really hurt because she couldn't keep it real with him. She would take this secret to her grave.

"When you leavin'?" he asked.

"This afternoon. We're flying."

"It's eleven-thirty. You better get ready. Hurry up and take your shower, and go be with your mother."

When she finished in the bathroom, Jay was watching the noon news on the sofa. He came down the hall and watched her get dressed with a real concerned gaze. "You good, Ma?"

She nodded. "I'm straight."

"You want me to take you to your mother's house?"

"No, because I have to pack, and I'll hold you up. I can take a cab, or she'll pick me up."

"Can you drive, Ma?"

Portia was honest. "I can't parallel-park that good, but I do have a license. Why?"

"You need a car, man. I worry about you, 'cause you think you're invincible, and you be in the streets too much. We gotta get you a ride, Ma."

"If I practice parking for a little while, I'll get it. I catch on fast."

"A'ight. I gotta go, Ma. You need anything before I leave?"

"Just a hug and a kiss."

Jay pulled a brick from his right pants pocket and peeled off. "This should take care of your traveling expenses and leave some spending money in your pocket." He pressed the money in her hand. "Don't hesitate to call me if you need anything else. A'ight?"

She nodded and wrapped her arms around his neck, and he kissed her on the lips. Not sloppy but tender and passionate. It was then that she knew for sure she loved him. Portia was close to tears again, but she didn't let them fall this time. Jay cupped her chin in his hand and raised her face. "It'll be all right, Ma."

"I ain't even leave yet, and I miss you already. Keep in touch, Jay. You have my cell number. It should work down there. I'll call you."

He planted a gentle kiss on her forehead. "Have a safe trip, Ma. Be safe."

"You be careful too. Thanks, baby." She walked Jay to the door, and when the lock was safely in place, she sank to the floor and cried on the carpet like a baby.

Three days later, she was still wearing the same clothes she had on when Jay left, and she'd cried so much that her eyes were swollen shut. She'd wept herself into brief troubled naps, and each time she awoke, she did it again. Portia was nauseated and weak to the point where she felt she would die, and she almost wished she would. She didn't deserve to live, because she was worse than gutter shit.

Portia figured that if she didn't eat anything, then she'd miscarry, and the problem would take care of itself. Shame swept over her for having such evil thoughts. What kind of heartless bitch had she become? She wanted to lose the baby because she knew that she could never have the child under these circumstances. What would she do, relocate to South America and raise the baby without telling anyone? She weighed other options. She could lie and say it was Jay's. No, she couldn't live with that lie; plus, they used condoms. What if it came out looking just like Khalil? Then Laila would know, because both of her girls looked just like him. He had very strong genes. Maybe she would have it and give the baby up for adoption. No, she couldn't do that.

The truth was, she didn't want anyone to know about the pregnancy. The selfish, low-down bitch in her had already decided the poor baby's fate. If Portia couldn't miscarry, she'd be forced to abort. Damn, having an abortion was something she'd vowed she'd never do, no matter what the circumstances were. But she hadn't planned on ever being in a predicament like this. She was carrying her best friend's husband's child. That was some sick television shit. Her life had become a fucking *Jerry Springer* episode. In desperation, she called Dr. Jacobs and insisted that there must be some kind of mix-up. Dr. Jacobs said she doubted it very seriously but to come on in for another pregnancy test that afternoon.

After Portia showered, she tied a Chanel scarf over her messy hair and threw on her darkest shades, a pair of charcoal Versaces, and she hurried across town with high hopes. Almost thirty minutes later, she was blindly thumbing through *Elle* magazine when the nurse called her. "Portia Lane? The doctor's ready for you now." Portia followed her, and the nurse placed her file in the metal slot on the door and left the examination room.

Five minutes later, Dr. Jacobs came in, bright and cheery, as usual. She was an attractive dark-skinned black woman in her late forties. She was tall and slim, with small, neat dreadlocks that grayed at the temples and hung to her waist. "Well, hello, Miss Lane. So you think I made a mistake, huh?"

"There has to be a mistake, because I can't be pregnant."

"Have you not been sexually active in the last two months? That's the only way pregnancy is impossible. And some will dispute that."

"I had sex, but I can't be pregnant."

"Oh, I see. This time we'll try a urine test instead of a blood test, for immediate results. How's that? I'll need a urine sample, Miss Lane. You know what to do with these." She passed Portia a lidded cup and two sterile wipes.

In the stall, Portia prayed for negative results. It was hard for her to pee, because she'd drunk barely anything the last three days. She managed to squeeze out a little, and she noticed it was dark yellow from the lack of water intake. She took the cup back to the doctor.

Dr. Jacobs handed Portia a gown and instructed her to change, and she took the urine off to wherever. When she returned for the examination, Dr. Jacobs put on fresh latex gloves. "Please lie down and place your feet in the stirrups, Miss Lane. You just had a pap smear last week, so we'll skip that." She placed two fingers against Portia's cervix and pressed down on her pelvis. "Are you feeling any pain?"

Portia admitted it did hurt a little. When Dr. Jacobs had finished the exam, she trashed her gloves and scribbled something on the chart. "Miss Lane, I'll be back with your results. You can get dressed." She left the room.

"God, please let her come back and say it's negative. Please don't let me be pregnant," Portia said aloud.

Her prayers were in vain, because Doc came back and confirmed the nightmare. "Are you one hundred percent sure?" Portia asked, still in denial.

Sister doctor was direct. "If you're not pregnant, I'll eat my hat. I was sure three days ago, but *you* needed persuading. You're obviously not happy about this. I know that you have no children, but you're no teenager, Miss Lane. I don't have to tell you about your other options, because you know them as well as I do. No matter *what* you decide, it's imperative that you realize you are definitely pregnant. You're dehydrated, Portia. Have you not been drinking anything?"

Portia shook her head.

The doctor continued, "Well, whether you decide

to have this child or not, that's not the healthy way to go about it. And you know better. I can look at you and tell this has you baffled, because you don't look yourself at all today. I've known you for years, Portia. Get it together, honey. A baby isn't the worst thing in the world. And you also have a choice. This is the new millennium, dear. It's your decision to make, and yours alone. I don't know your situation, but I'll advise you, just don't wait too long, because if you're going to have this child, you'll need prenatal care. And if you decide to abort, I don't recommend a second-trimester abortion, if you can help it. Though legal in some states, those procedures can be much more complicated. Go home and think about it, but don't sit on it too long. Try and talk to someone. You'll find that getting it off of your chest will help you to cope. Do you have any questions?"

The lump in Portia's throat made it impossible to speak, so she just shook her head. She finally managed to say, "Thank you."

"Feel free to contact me at any given time. You have my personal number."

Portia had one question. "Um, do you do that procedure here?"

"No, but I can recommend several good clinics that do. I do follow-up exams here. I'm going to give you a prescription for some prenatal vitamins. If you do decide to have the baby, these will be crucial for healthy development. Take them either way. They won't hurt you. They're just vitamins."

"Thanks, but I'll weigh my options for now." Portia felt like she was going to be sick, so she took the prescription and stuffed it into her jacket pocket. She made it to the bathroom just before spilling her guts into the toilet. Her empty stomach yielded only dry heaves and bitter yellow bile. There was nothing to spit up, but her stomach just kept on turning. That was worse than any hangover.

On her way home, she stopped at the corner store for some saltine crackers to settle her queasy stomach. She placed them on the counter and peeped Hector, the store owner, looking at her all funny. She said to him, as usual, "Hey, poppy. What's crackin'?"

He gave her a concerned look and said in his thick Hispanic accent, "You no look so good today, mami, what's wrong? You looka so sad. Every other time I see you, you happy, smiling. Today you so sad. Is everything okay?"

Portia smiled. "I'm good, papi."

Hector said, "You face smiling, but you eyes no smiling. Cheer up, baby, it's okay." When she reached for her change, he patted her hand.

As soon as Portia got in the lobby of her building, she ran into Simone coming off the elevator. Damn, she'd spotted Portia, so it was too late to duck. Shit! This just wasn't the time.

Simone hollered over, "Girl, I just left your house. Damn, I'm glad I ran into you." She walked up and looked Portia up and down. "You okay? Where you been, lookin' like that?"

The elevator came back down to the lobby, and they got on. Thank God it was empty, because Portia knew Simone would continue running her big mouth. She peered into Portia's eyes through her shades, and then she snatched the glasses off before Portia could stop her. She looked like a mother checking a teenager's eyes for signs of narcotic use. Simone stood over six feet in the heels she wore, so she tilted Portia's chin up to get a better look. "Oh my God! Look how swollen your eyes are. Your face look all sunk in. What happened to you, Portia? What's goin' on?"

Portia tried to sound nonchalant. "Nothing. I'm just on a hangover."

The elevator doors opened on her floor. They didn't speak again until Simone followed her into the kitchen. Portia barely had enough energy to open up a can of vegetable soup. She popped a few crackers while her soup heated, and Simone's gray cat eyes peered at her every move. Portia avoided eye contact and took a jug of spring water out of the refrigerator. She was so thirsty, her tongue felt like sandpaper. She drank four cups of water back to back.

Simone poured the hot soup into a bowl and placed it on the table. "Sit down and eat, child, 'cause you look like death." She passed Portia a spoon and sat opposite her at the table.

"That's how I feel." Portia finished the meal and the gallon of water in silence. The soup and crackers tasted like paste, but she forced them down because she had to put something in her stomach. She would never do that to herself again. When she was halfway done, she put her head down on the table.

"Go lie down for a little while," Simone suggested.

Portia took her advice and went in the bedroom and stretched out on the bed.

About two hours later, she woke up to the smell of

weed. Portia got up and went in the living room. Simone was chilling on the couch with her shoes kicked off, watching that stock market news channel, Bloomberg.

"I didn't mean to go to sleep on you, girl. I was out of it. You a'ight, Mone?"

"Please. You know I make myself at home. Besides, you looked real peaky, so you needed some rest. Feel better?"

"I'm good now. Let me wash my face and shit. I'll be right back."

When Portia joined her on the couch, Simone said, "This is one hell of a coincidence, P. I don't believe this shit. Guess what?" She lit up the clip in the ashtray and passed it to Portia.

"What?" Portia took two pulls, then shook her head and gave it back. The weed stank to her. She couldn't get high right then. She didn't even want to smell it.

Simone took a few more pulls and put it out. "If you can't smoke, I know it's true. You wasn't gonna tell me, Portia? I know your ass is pregnant. And girl, me too." She grinned.

Portia denied it. "You crazy, I'm not pregnant. What in the world you is talkin' 'bout? But congratulations, girl! That's wonderful! How far gone are you?"

Simone gave her a *you're full of shit* look. "Bitch, please. Don't play with me. What's the big secret? We're friends. Right?"

"Of course, silly. We're like family."

"Then why are you lying? I looked in your jacket pocket to see if you had a lighter, and I found *this*." She held up the prescription. Detective Simone continued,

"And don't try to lie, 'cause I have the same damn vitamins. How far gone are you?"

Fuck it, she was caught. "About two months."

"I'm almost three now. I'm having some doubts, P. I need some advice, because I'm running out of time. That's why I came over here. You the first person I told, but I didn't plan on your ass being knocked up too. This is a real coincidence."

"Coincidence? Shit, more like a curse, on my behalf. I can't have this baby. That's out of the question, Mone. I've already made my decision. Now, what are *you* having doubts about? *You* can do this."

Simone sighed. "I got pregnant by mistake. We were just fuckin' around, Portia. This wasn't supposed to happen. He's married, for God's sake. I didn't know at first, but when I found out, I kept on fuckin' him. I'm so fuckin' stupid. Look at me. Knocked up by my boss, who happens to be a married man with three kids. I don't know what to do, girl."

What kind of advice could Portia offer at this point? She was in a worse predicament than Simone, because she was knocked up by her best friend's husband, who was also married with kids. She wished that she could tell Simone what happened, just to get it off of her chest. But she couldn't.

"Simone, you're doing good in life. You're independent, and you have a career. If you want to have this baby, do it. It's not like you can't afford it. Look how many women are doing it by themselves. Life don't always go how we plan it. But you know I got your back, whatever you decide. Have you told Kyle yet?"

Simone shook her head. "I stopped messing with

him when I found out. He keeps on pressing me at the office and calling my house, trying to find out why I don't wanna fuck with him no more. He has no idea, girl. But what if I tell him and he try to play me like some hoe, like it's not his? I'm scared, Portia, because if he plays me like that, I just might kill him. I'm serious. Not that I need him, but I don't wanna have a baby whose father isn't a part of his or her life. That's not my style. Not if I can help it. But I ain't no home wrecker either. I ain't try'na break up his happy home, because I know his kids need their father. But mine gon' need one too. Portia, you know I never knew my father. I don't want my baby to grow up like that."

Portia felt her. "You need to weigh your options. What kind of man is he? How good does he treat you? It doesn't really matter what happens between you two. It's your baby."

Simone sighed. "He's *too* good to me. That's why it's been so hard to leave him alone. He spoiled me, girl. Money, presents, perks on the job. He bought me this and these." She touched her diamond-flooded tennis bracelet and pointed to the huge princess cuts in her earlobes. "And this ain't the half. You should see my place. You ain't been over in a long time. Girl, I got so much new shit. Furniture, new carpet, a big screen, and the works. *And* we went on vacation to Bermuda. Oh my God, we had so much fun. He's the perfect man. But he's married. He treats me like a lady, but that doesn't mean he'll be delighted that his mistress is pregnant. That defeats the whole purpose." She sighed again. "He ain't never gon' be mine, 'cause he already has a family. What kind of damn fool am I?"

They just sat there for a few minutes, until Simone broke the silence. "Portia, I'm sorry for being so selfish. Here I am, wallowing in self-pity, and you're going through something too. Tell me why you seem so confident that *your* decision is right. You ain't no spring chicken either, Miss Thing. How come you said having your baby is out of the question? Jay's the father, right?"

"Yeah," Portia lied.

"And you really like him, and he's a good guy, right?"

Portia nodded.

"So have the baby, Porsh. At least Jay's not married. Y'all been spending a lot of time together lately. He must care about you. Does he know?"

Portia shook her head. "I just found out, and I'm not telling him either. There's no point. I didn't really want *nobody* to know, so please don't tell Laila and Fatima. You know neither one of them is pro-choice, and I don't need them running a guilt trip on me, because I feel bad enough. I've already made my decision, Simone. That's my final word, so please don't keep on. It wasn't an easy decision to make, so don't think I'm some cold, heartless bitch."

Simone just looked at her, and then she blurted out, "Let's go together. This week."

"You sure?"

She nodded.

Portia felt bad. "Mone, don't do this because I am. I have my reasons. Trust me. Please don't do what I do."

"Let's call and make the appointments. They'll tell us what we gotta do."

Portia got the Yellow Pages, and they selected a

clinic in Queens called Options, because they figured they wouldn't run into anyone they knew over there. Portia called to get some information, then she filled Simone in.

"The woman said they take walk-ins. It costs two-fifty. That's forty for the examination and two-ten for the procedure. She said they're open every day except Sunday."

"Let's go soon, P. The sooner, the better."

Portia agreed. Lord, why couldn't Jay really be the father? No way she'd get rid of it then. She felt so bad, she hadn't even called him since she was supposed to have left town. She had to call him today, because she didn't want to make him suspicious, which he probably already was. She didn't deserve him anyway, after this.

Simone hung out for a while. She said she had a taste for some of Portia's chicken and rice, so Portia made some.

After they grubbed and consoled each other, Simone had to break out. "Girl, I don't mean to eat and run, but I have some paperwork to finish. I guess I'll go back to work tomorrow. Then I'm taking a personal leave for a few days. I'll call you tomorrow, Porsh. Love you."

After she locked the door, Portia was sort of glad Simone had left, because she needed some "me" time in order to think. She had to talk Simone out of getting an abortion, but how could she, without being a hypocrite? She couldn't tell Simone that she'd keep her baby if it weren't Khalil's. She was too ashamed, and she didn't want her friends to hate her. Simone would probably be just as mad as Laila, and so would Fatima. They'd have every right to be, because she was the most trifling friend ever. She cared about Laila too much to ever hurt her with news like that. Portia would go to her grave with the terrible secret.

It was time to call Jay, so she had to take her mind off of it. She used her cell phone, because he had caller ID, and she wasn't supposed to be at home. She dialed his phone number, and he picked up. "Yo."

"Hey, baby."

"What up, Ma? You a'ight?"

"I'm good. You doin' okay?"

"No doubt. How's your grandma?"

"Not so good. They might have to do surgery. I'm scared, boo. They said she might not make it. I don't know, baby."

"Just have faith, Ma. I hope she gets better. What you doin' down there? What took you so long to call me? I know they got phones down in them woods."

"I'm sorry. I couldn't get no reception on my cell, and I didn't have a calling card. I'm in town now, so I got a signal. I miss you so much, baby. I can't wait to come home. Hopefully, it won't be long. You just better behave yourself while I'm gone. Don't act up. I got people watching you, so you better beware."

Jay laughed. "You just make sure *you* don't act up. Don't make me have to come down there and pound on one of them country niggas. Ma, right now I'm in the middle of taking care of something. Call me later."

"If not, I'll call you tomorrow. Be safe, baby. I love you."

"A'ight." He hung up.

Portia wished she hadn't said those last three words, because he sure as hell hadn't said them back. She was feeling very vulnerable, but it wasn't Jay's fault, so she couldn't look to him for comfort. Not about that situation. She did love him, because everything with him felt right. He'd never done a single thing that turned her off, and that was unbelievable. He was perfect. She was the trifling one with all the skeletons. A bone should fly out her mouth and ricochet off the wall and hit her between the eyes. Portia regretted having to lie about something so fucked up. At this point, her life could've been a soap opera script.

She knew what she had to do. She put it on a back burner and dug out some of her college books to brush up on accounting. Portia read for the remainder of the evening, and then she drifted into a troubled sleep.

That night she dreamed she was drowning and being sucked underwater into a whirling black hole. Every time she managed to get her head above water, the force overpowered her. She lost the battle in the end.

HOEVER SAID WOMEN couldn't keep a damn secret had hit the nail right on the head. Simone couldn't keep her fucking mouth closed. Her lips were looser than Wendy Williams's were. Portia wished she had never found out. She was suspicious the night before, when Mone called, sounding hesitant about going to the clinic. Portia had told her not to go with her, so she should've just left it at that. But Simone ran her damn mouth. And Laila came over at nine o'clock in the morning.

Laila must've lucked up and caught an open door downstairs, so Portia didn't have time to prepare. She just heard a "police" knock on the door and ran to the peephole.

Laila said, "I know you in there. I'm *not* leaving."

Portia opened the door and brightly faked it. "Hey, girl. What you doin' over this way?"

Laila just stood there looking at her, like, *Well? Don't you have something to tell me?*

She knew. That damned Simone. Portia shrugged. "What?"

Laila followed her to the bedroom. "I knew you were gon' try to front. That's fucked up, Portia. I thought we were bigger than that. How could you keep something this important from me?"

"I wasn't keeping it from you. I just ain't told you yet. Don't take it personal. My decision is already made, and I'm going in the morning."

"Don't do it, Portia. This is a blessing from God. I know you think you're unprepared, but you can do this, girl. You can have this baby. God does everything for a reason. If He put it there, it's meant to be." She got right up in Portia's face. "A baby is a *blessing from God*. God don't make no mistakes. If you kill this baby, you'll distort your destiny. Think about it."

Portia took a slow, deep breath. "I have thought about it, so please hush. This shit is painful enough already. Trust me. You don't understand everything, Lay."

"What's so terrible about a precious little baby? You're right, I *don't* understand. You gots to help me with this one, sis. How does Jay feel about this, huh? The fact that you wanna *kill* his child." She raised an eyebrow at Portia in suspicion. "You haven't told him, have you? I wished *I* had his number, 'cause I'd call him and tell him what a big mistake you're about to make."

"Mind your own business."

Laila stopped and sighed. "My bad, P. I'm outta line. I don't wanna make you feel worse. I just want you to realize that you're capable of being a loving mother. This baby might be just what you need, Portia. My kids are my inspiration. They give me that extra drive I need. Everything I do, it's all for them."

Portia was curt. "I have my reasons. I don't wanna discuss this no more. I have some things to do this morning, Laila."

"I'm not leaving until I get through to you. Simone called me last night and confessed about y'all little clinic plans. I think I got through to her. At first she was talking about she'll change her mind if you change yours. Then she asked me to convince you not to go. As if I wasn't gonna try anyway. I know how you screen your calls with that damned answering machine, so I figured you wouldn't answer the phone. That's why I called in late this morning and came over here. You can say what you may. I'm sorry, but you'll thank me for this when you hold that bundle of joy in your arms. We'll get through this. Portia, you know I'll help you out in any way I can." She opened her Coach briefcase and took out some papers. "Before you make a snap judgment, take a look at these. Look at these poor babies that didn't even have a chance because somebody else decided their fate."

Laila was armed with anti-abortion literature! She had pamphlets, magazines, and some stuff she'd printed off the Internet. Her mission was clear. She held up a picture of a tiny undeveloped fetus. It was lifeless and missing an arm. Across the top of the picture read "This is abortion. This is murder. Think twice."

On the verge of tears, Portia turned away. That was too much. Laila was playing hardball. After seeing those pictures, who could be that heartless? A lone tear ran down her cheek, and she wiped it away. After tomorrow, Laila would think she was repulsive. What could Portia say to convince her that she didn't have a choice? She couldn't tell her that she was pregnant by Laila's husband. That wasn't even an option, so she played tough. "Are those pictures supposed to make me change my mind? I appreciate your concern, but this is *my* life and *my* decision that *I* made by *my*self, and I don't have to answer to nobody but God about it. This is between Him and me."

Laila's rebuttal was "I know it's your life, but that baby has a life too. Don't be so fuckin' selfish. That ain't even like you. You acting like you still in high school or something. You're a twenty-five-year-old woman, so take responsibility for your actions. You got pregnant, so have the baby. You owe it to that child to give its life the benefit of the doubt. It's not all about *you* now, bitch. There's a *baby* inside of you."

Portia was petulant. "I'll answer to God about it, not to you. Don't judge me, Laila. Please, okay? I have my reasons. I can't talk about this anymore. Enough is enough! I'm getting a headache. Stop making such a big thing out of this. It ain't no great debate. I told you my mind is made up. It's a wrap." Portia couldn't tell her friend that she felt like killing herself more than the baby.

"Girl, you makin' me wanna grab you and shake some sense into your ass. Is there anything I can do to change your mind? Am I just blowing out hot air, Portia? Am I speaking Chinese? What the fuck is wrong with you, P? Tell me you're not this foul. Tell me you have a heart. *Please?*"

"Oh well. I guess you don't know me as well as you thought you did."

"That's foul, Portia." Laila looked at her like *You fuckin' bitch!*

Portia looked down at the carpet. She did have a heart. This shit was tearing her apart. Laila had no idea how foul she and her taboo secret really were. Portia felt tired and burdened by betrayal's guilt. She'd stabbed Laila in the back, and here she was, close to tears from trying so hard to stop her so-called best friend from making a mistake. Portia had already made the worst mistake in her life, and she would never forgive herself for it. She had to get rid of Laila. She meant well, but Portia just couldn't be around her right now. This scene was just too appalling. She felt horrible. She didn't deserve a friend like Laila. She'd committed an atrocious, inexcusable act, and there Laila stood like a saint, wasting her good intentions on a traitor. Portia wondered if she should just lie and say she'd changed her mind so Laila would relax and go home. Or start an argument and tell her to get the hell out. Or should she just say she'd reconsider, to buy some time?

Portia went with option C. "I'll think about it, okay, Laila? That's the best I can do right now. I *will* think about it."

Laila smiled. "I'll accept that. Make the right decision, Portia. I know you will."

Portia smiled too, but her heart wasn't in it. "I'll try."

Laila rubbed her hands together. "At least I have a little peace of mind now. I gotta go, P."

Portia walked her to the door, and Laila grabbed her hand and squeezed it. It was the same thing Portia had done at her mother's funeral, when she walked with Laila up to the casket to view the body. Then Laila said the same words Portia had told her: "I'm right here. Don't worry, girl, we'll get through this."

Portia hugged her and cried. You always hurt the ones you love. She wished that were just a song.

PORTIA WAS UP reading at about two a.m. when some-body knocked. Shit, she hoped it wasn't Jay. She tiptoed to the door in the dark and looked through the peephole. It was Khalil. Of all the people in the world, why him? She didn't want to see him.

He knocked again louder, and she walked away from the door. Then the phone rang and startled her. Portia let the machine pick up. It was that asshole, call-ing from his cell phone in the hall.

"Portia, I just wanna holla' at you. I know you home. You probably lookin' at me through the peephole right now. Yo, open the door for a minute. Just for a min-ute. If you don't, in five seconds, I'ma wake up all your neighbors."

Whatever. She wasn't letting him in. Then that fool started knocking real hard and screaming her name in the hallway. Didn't he know what time it was? Por-tia's landlord lived right upstairs, and he would have a fit. She tried to ignore him, but Khalil got louder. "Yo, Portia! Open the door. Open the door!" *Boom, boom, boom!* "Open the door! Portia, open the *fuckin'* door!"

That mothafucka done lost his damn mind! Portia stormed back in the living room and yanked the door open. "Nigga, is you crazy? Stop banging on my damn door, making all that noise! Do you know what time it is? What the hell do you want, Khalil? Go home to your wife."

He pushed his way in, and she smelled liquor on him. "You should've just let me in. I know you heard me knocking."

"I have company," Portia lied. "You have to leave."

"No, you don't. You lyin'." He touched her stomach.

She pushed his hand away. "Stop."

"Why? Stop why, Portia?"

"Because I said so. Go home, Khalil."

He closed the door and locked it. "Not until you talk to me. What's going on?"

"Nothing."

"That's bullshit. Stop lyin'. Is it mine?"

"Is what yours?"

"Stop playing fuckin' games, Portia."

"What the fuck do you think?"

"Why didn't you tell me?"

"For what?"

"What do you mean for what? Don't I have a right to know? It is mine, right?"

"What the fuck you think?"

"So don't I have the right to know? I had to hear this from Laila. She was yapping about her two friends expecting babies. Talking 'bout she finally gonna be an auntie. I didn't know she was talking about you until she said she had to keep a close eye on you before you did something crazy. What's *something crazy*, Portia? What she talking about?"

Portia didn't like his tone. "Who you think you is, coming up in here questioning me? Don't ask me shit." Married couples must really share everything, because Laila sure felt free to share Portia's damn business with her husband.

"Portia, can we talk like two adults, please?"

She sighed impatiently. "Okay."

He sat on the couch and grabbed her hand. "Sit down."

She stood over him and shook her head. He placed his hand on her stomach. Portia wished he wouldn't do that. She sat on the other end of the couch. "Well, what's up?"

Khalil looked serious. "What you wanna do?"

"You mean what am I gonna do? I'm getting an abor— I'm going in the morning." It was so painful that she couldn't say the word.

"You sure that's what you wanna do?"

"No. But considering the circumstances, it's best. This was a mistake."

"It's not a mistake, it's a baby, Portia. A life."

"Yeah, well? I know you didn't come over here to run a guilt trip on me. You're just as guilty as I am."

"I face up to my responsibilities. I'm a man."

"If you weren't, I wouldn't be pregnant."

"Won't you have it?"

"Are you crazy?"

"I'm against abortion. That's against my faith. That's murder, and it'll haunt you for the rest of your life."

"You the father. It'll haunt you too."

"I know, so don't do it. I'll take care of it, Portia. I promise. Have the baby."

"It's not that simple, Khalil. *Hello?* You married to my best friend. I can't have a baby by you."

"Yes, you can. You're pregnant, right?"

"Not for long."

He put his head down, and they didn't speak for a minute. When he finally spoke, his voice was full of pain. "I know we didn't mean for this to happen, but it happened, so let's deal with the consequences. Laila wouldn't want you to kill the baby. She'd be upset at first, but then she'd understand, 'cause she's strong. She'd get over it, 'cause she would want me to take care of my kids."

Lord, he was talking crazy. Portia cut him off. "Hold up. It's not like you just made a baby on the side with some strange woman. This is *much* more complicated than that. Laila's my *best friend*. Don't fool yourself, Khalil. This would destroy your marriage *and* me and Laila's friendship. She's like a sister to me, and I don't want to fuck that up any more than I have. Our friendship is tattered, and you want me to destroy it. I don't wanna lose my best friend. We were friends way before you met her, and she *cannot* find out about this. Do I make myself clear? You don't wanna lose your family, do you?"

He shook his head. "I'm sorry. I know this shit is probably hard enough without me coming over here putting more pressure on you. But ever since I found out, that's all I could think about. I'm not okay with this."

He was going to make her cry. "Think of Laila, Khalil."

"So let's not tell her. Say somebody else is the father.

I'll be like a ghost parent. I promise I'll do my part. She ain't gotta know. Please don't kill my baby, Portia. We can work it out."

He was dead serious. Portia was torn inside. This man was begging her not to abort his seed, which had been conceived in illicit lust with his wife's best friend. Portia toyed with the thought. "What if it looks like you. You have strong genes. Both Macy and Pebbles look just like you. Laila would know. The truth would come out sooner or later. Besides, I couldn't live a lie like that. That's too devious."

"So what? By the time it come out, the baby will be done grown up. I'd rather live a lie than live with a baby's blood on my hands."

That was one hell of an ultimatum. What a low blow. "Damn, Khalil. That's fucked up."

He was being harsh, and she didn't need it the night before. She rolled her eyes and took a deep breath, because she didn't want to cry in front of him. "How do you think I feel, smiling all up in Laila's face, and I'm pregnant by her husband? How you think that make me feel? That's my best friend! Don't you see how fucked up that is?" Her voice cracked, and she broke down and cried the way her daddy's whippings used to make her. Trembling lips, runny nose, and the whole nine.

Khalil softened up. "Damn, I'm sorry. Don't cry, Portia."

She couldn't stop. All of this was too much on top of what she faced in the morning. She bent over and shed torrents of tears. She was tired of playing so tough. And she was scared God was going to punish her and let something go wrong during the procedure. What if she hemorrhaged and died? If it happened, she deserved it.

Khalil moved closer to comfort her and rub her back. "Shh, it's okay. Shhh! It's gon' be all right. Don't cry."

Portia leaned on his shoulder and wept for what seemed like an eternity. Neither of them spoke for almost an hour. Not even when he went and got the box of Kleenex off of her dresser and came back.

Khalil broke the silence first. "You okay?"

She blew her nose again and nodded.

"What's the verdict?"

Heavyhearted, she shook her head.

"Is that your final word?"

She nodded.

"How much the butcher shop charging now?"

"What?"

"That slaughterhouse you goin' to in the morning."

Bastard. "Two-fifty."

He peeled off three C-notes and threw them on the coffee table. They landed right by the Bible. "Take a cab."

Khalil bounced just like that. He was obviously pissed. Now Portia felt like she was crossing him. No, it was Laila she'd betrayed. She really needed God to give her strength. She knew when it was time to pray. She didn't go to church every Sunday, but she spoke to God on a daily basis through quick prayers and a *Lord, forgive me* here and there. Right now she needed something more. She picked up the Bible and flipped to the 121st Psalm. It was the verse that her father had taught her to read in a crisis.

I will lift up mine eyes unto the hills from whence cometh my help. My help cometh from the Lord, which made heaven and earth. He will not suffer thy foot to be moved . . . After Portia finished reading the Bible verse, she prayed aloud. "God, I know I've done wrong, and what I'm going to do in the morning is immoral and a sin. Please forgive me, God. I stand before you humble. I'm a sinner with foul intent in my heart. I know I can't fool you, because you know my every move. I'm sorry for being so cruel. I don't want to do this, God, but these circumstances place the odds against me. I know I should deal with the consequences of my act, but I don't want to hurt Laila. I know it's not up to me to end a life that you blessed me to bring forth. God, I know it's wrong to pray a selfish prayer, but I need you in my corner on this. I apologize for taking this blessing you bestowed upon me for granted. I don't mean to defy you, but the setting just ain't right this time. Please forgive me. I know that you're merciful, God, but I accept any way you choose to punish me. Please forgive me, God. I'm so sorry."

Portia's tears formed wet spots on the Bible pages. No part of her wanted to go through with it, but she was constrained because this thing was larger than just Portia.

PORTIA WAS AWAKE before eight a.m., but she couldn't get out of the bed. She was wishing she had someone impartial to accompany her. Somebody she could borrow a little strength from to help her through the ordeal. Her legs felt like weights, and she was paralyzed with fear of what lay ahead.

She was thirsty, but she wasn't supposed to drink anything after midnight. As soon as Portia finally got up and switched her ringer back on, the phone rang, and Laila's cell number popped up on the caller ID. Portia knew she was calling to chastise, but she answered so that Laila wouldn't rush over and start up again. "Hi, Laila."

"Hey, Ma-ma! How're you feeling this morning?"

"I'm good. What you doin'?"

"I just dropped the girls off at day care, and I'm on my way to work. What's up for the day?" Laila didn't want to come right out and ask.

Portia didn't want to hear her fuss, so she lied. "Don't worry, I haven't made up my mind yet. I'm still thinking about it. I'll let you know, so don't be at work worrying today. Okay?"

"Okay, girl. Have you been eating right?"

"Um-hmm," she lied again.

"Good. Take care of yourself, Portia. Call me if you need anything. I'd better get off this phone. A cop car is behind me. Let me go before I get a ticket. Love you."

"Ditto. Talk to you later." Portia noticed she had two new messages on her answering machine. The first one was from Simone: "Hey, boo! Just checking in to make sure you're okay. Laila called me. I'm glad you're reconsidering." She paused. "I'm scared too, Portia. Oh yeah, let me apologize for running my mouth. I guess I knew that she would talk us out of it, and I'm glad she did. You said we could do this, P. Right? Girl, I'm home today. Later, let's do lunch or something. Holla back."

Not now, Simone. Not now. The next voice on the machine was Patricia's. "Portia, this is your mother. Pick up the phone. Portia? Where you stirring around at this morning? Tired of being a night owl? Don't forget about church on Sunday. You gave me your word, so try to make it, baby, okay? Call me. Oh, I hope you have something nice to wear. Nothing too short, showing all your behind. Let me know if I have to find you something. Don't wait till the last minute. I'll talk to you later."

Pat's voice was comforting. Portia called her back, but voice mail picked up. She tried her mother's cell phone and got her on the third ring.

"Hey, lady. What you doin'?" Portia asked.

"Hey, baby. I'm just running around tending to some business."

"Anything major?"

"No. Just paying some bills. Then I'll probably head on to the nail salon to get a fill-in before I go to work."

"I might need you to take me somewhere this morning."

"Like where?"

"I have to go to the doctor."

"What time is your appointment?"

"They take walk-ins, but I wanna go in early."

"What direction are you going in? Oh, downtown. Okay, I'll drop you off and go get my nails done. Then I could swoop you back up."

"I gotta go to Queens, Ma. On Woodhaven Boulevard."

"Queens? Did you change doctors?"

"No, Mommy."

"Did you let your insurance lapse, Portia? Health insurance is a priority. You know better than to—"

Portia cut her off. "No, Ma. I have insurance. Just give me a ride, okay?"

The levels on Pat's "concern-o-meter" rose. She knew her child. Something was wrong, "Why are you sounding all funny? What's the matter with you?"

Portia couldn't answer because a lump was rising in her throat.

Patricia raised her voice. "Portia? What's wrong?"

"Nothing. I just need you to come with me."

"Are you crying?"

Yes. "No."

Pat knew her daughter was lying. "I'm on my way." She hung up.

Portia was relieved Pat was coming. She didn't know if her mother would approve, but she was the one person who wouldn't judge Portia for this, because she loved her unconditionally.

In under ten minutes, Pat was on the intercom. "Portia, it's Mommy. Let me upstairs."

Portia buzzed her in without trying to fix herself up, because even if she altered her disheveled state, she'd still be suspect after that phone conversation.

A minute later, Portia opened the door and embraced her mom. "Hey, Patty-cake!"

Though Mama knew something was up, she was cool. She'd always tried not to be a panicky parent. "Hey, baby. I thought you were ready to go. Look at your hair." Pat attempted to smooth Portia's hair, and then she began her inspection of the apartment. She nodded her approval. "The house looks good. You've done some things since I was last here. You inherited my good taste." She smiled.

"Thank you, Mommy. Let me just run a comb through my hair and slip on my sneakers, then we can roll out."

"Take your time." Patricia sat on the papasan chair by the bed.

Portia could feel her mother's eyes glued to her as she moved about. Pat was attempting to read her. Not wanting to make her play guessing games, Portia said, "Ma, we'll talk about it in the car on the way."

"Okay, that's fine."

Portia grabbed her purse and jacket, and she was ready. The final glimpse around her apartment reminded her that when she returned home, she'd no longer be with child. She wished she could feel relieved, but it was a sad and eerie thought.

She rode shotgun in Pat's Lincoln Town Car, and

they headed toward the Van Wyck Expressway. Portia changed the radio station to Hot 97 and leaned her seat back and crossed her arms behind her head. She studied the partly cloudy sky and thought of how to break the news to her mother. She decided not to beat around the bush because that wasn't their style. "I'm going to an abortion clinic." She stared straight ahead but peeped Pat's shock in her peripheral vision. After a few seconds, it passed.

Pat spoke calmly. "How far gone are you?"

"Two months."

"Have you thought this through?"

"Thoroughly. It's for the best."

Pat sighed. "I guess you know what's best, huh?"

Portia just nodded and turned toward the window.

Pat kept on. "Who's the father? Does he know?"

Patricia treated Laila like a daughter, so of course Portia lied. "The guy I told you about. Jay. I ain't even tell him."

"Do you think he'd approve?"

"Approve of what? Me being pregnant or me getting rid of it?"

"You tell me."

She paused. "I don't know, Ma. I just don't know."

"How long have you known?"

"About a week."

"That's a hard decision to make, Portia. Are you sure, baby?"

"Yes, Ma." She tried to say it firmly, but it came out sounding doubtful.

Patricia was quiet for a minute. A cabdriver veered

around the corner and cut her off. She hit the brakes and honked at him. "Lord Jesus! Just signal next time. I'll let you go, don't kill somebody."

Portia stuck her middle finger up at him. Her mother must've been the only person left in New York City who didn't get road rage. New Yorkers drove like fools. "That asshole! Excuse me, Ma. You all right?"

"Yeah, I got it." She placed her hand on Portia's knee. "Portia, I'm going to choose my next words wisely, because I imagine this has been hard enough for you already. I figure the reason you asked me to go with you instead of one of your friends is because you need my support. In that case, I'll try and be more of a friend today than a mother. So all lectures set aside. You're a grown woman capable of making your own decisions, for whatever reasons. I respect that, and I support you on whatever decision you've made. I'm here to hold your hand, baby. I know this isn't easy."

"Thanks, Ma."

They drove the rest of the way, each immersed in her own thoughts.

"IS THAT IT?" Pat pointed at a white building across the street.

"Yeah," said Portia. It was hard to believe that the innocent-looking premises could be what Khalil referred to as a slaughterhouse.

Pat parked across the street. "There's a meter. I wonder how long we'll be . . ." She didn't finish her sentence, but she turned off the car and took some quarters from the ashtray.

Portia took a deep breath. Her hand was on the handle, but she couldn't open the door. *Come on, Portia. Get out the car and get it over with,* she told herself. Her body complied, and Pat was at her side. Hand in hand, they crossed the street and entered the building.

Ironically, the atmosphere in the clinic was bright, but the floors must've turned to quicksand, because each step Portia took seemed to get heavier. She felt like she had on lead-filled combat boots.

The receptionist at the front desk, a plump Caucasian redhead, was on the phone. When she hung up, she smiled at them. "Hi, I'm Julie. What can we do for you today?"

I'll have an abortion, with a side of fries and a Coke, Portia thought. What kind of stupid question was that?

Sensing her loss for words, Pat spoke for her. "We'd like to discuss your services."

"Sign in, and take a seat. Someone will be with you shortly, and they can answer any questions you have."

Portia thanked her and signed the roster. The waiting room was pretty crowded. There were women of all ages and ethnic origins. She tried to guess who was going under the knife. She gave up and zoned back to her own dreadful reality.

A young Asian couple came through swinging doors on the left. They were oblivious to the crowded waiting room; the girl was crying hysterically, while the guy hugged her and whispered in her ear. She didn't look a day over sixteen. Portia felt her pain, and from the way some of the women looked at each other, so did they. The silent communication between the adversity-faced women went on for a brief moment before they averted eye contact and hurried back inside their shells to their own troubles.

Pat kept a close eye on Portia. "Are you okay?"

"I think so."

A tall, blond, middle-aged woman came out and called Portia's name. She introduced herself as Jill Andrews, and the Lane women rose and followed her. They reached an office with a desk and three chairs.

When they were seated, Jill smiled and asked, "Which of you is Portia?"

"I am. This is my mom."

"Well, hello. I can certainly see the resemblance. I would have guessed you were sisters, though." She turned to Pat. "You look great."

"Thank you." Pat smiled.

Jill looked at Portia and got down to business. "So, Miss Portia Lane, I assure you that everything discussed here will be kept confidential, regardless of what you decide today. Now, I need to get some information from you. How far along are you?"

"Two months."

"Okay. We're required to do a sonogram before any procedure, since pregnancy can be misdiagnosed. This way, all parties are a hundred percent clear on everything."

Jill proceeded to find out Portia's family medical history, and then she asked if Portia had any children, previous pregnancies, or abortions. Jill said that, by law, she was required to inform her of other options, but Portia didn't want to hear them. She only wanted to know if it would be painful. Jill said she'd be under anesthesia and wouldn't feel a thing. In her opinion, it probably hurt worse to get a tooth pulled.

Then the counseling session was over, and they got down to business. Portia kept crying, but she wasn't turning back. Jill handed her some forms to fill out and give to a girl named Karen in billing.

Karen in billing was a light-brown-skinned sister of about thirty. She was a shade darker than Simone, but their resemblance was uncanny. She even had the same gray eyes. She smiled and took the paperwork. "I just need to call in and confirm your insurance. I'll just be a minute." She called in and got a yes, then typed some information into her keyboard. "Miss Lane, go down the hall and through the green door to your left. They'll take care of you back there." She smiled.

According to the sonogram, Portia was in the first trimester. After that, she was directed to another room, and it was time. Her mother wasn't allowed in the back with her. When she changed into a hospital gown and slippers, Portia gave her belongings to Pat, who assured her that she'd be fine. Portia didn't tell her, but she was having trouble breathing. The air was getting thicker and thicker, and she didn't want her mama to leave her. She held Patricia's hand tight.

Pat looked real concerned. "Portia, are you sure about this, honey? We can leave right now. All you have to do is put your clothes back on. You know you don't have to do this."

Here came those damn tears again. "Yes, I do, Ma. I have to." Had Pat been aware of her terrible secret, she probably would have understood. "I'm all right, Ma. I'm fine."

Portia gathered herself, and Pat looked at her like she wished she could make things easier. Portia felt guilty for dragging her into this, but she needed her. She felt a little stronger.

"I'll be all right, Ma. Just pray for me." She followed the nurse through the doors, praying silently the whole time.

In a super-sanitized-smelling white room, Portia was instructed to lie down on the examination table while Mary, the nurse, prepared a shot of anesthesia and made small talk to deter her from the needle. Mary asked, "So, what kind of music are you into? Do you like Jay-Z? I think he's fabulous. And his lips are so sexy."

Portia agreed that Jigga was the man, and Mary rubbed her hip with an alcohol pad and rattled on. "His last CD was so hot. He's my favorite rapper."

Portia was tickled that this country-music-video-hoe-looking white nurse was a hip-hop fan. Hip-hop was definitely universal. Mary gave her the needle and kept talking. She said her boyfriend managed a female rap duo from Staten Island, and she asked Portia who her favorite female rappers were.

Through a fog, Portia noticed a gray-haired woman enter the room. She must've been the doctor. "I like Eve, that new chick Remy Ma, oh, Rah Digga, Lil' Kim, Foxy . . ." The dope kicked in and knocked her out.

She dreamed she heard a voice in the sky. "Hello? Hello? Wake up, sweetie."

Who was disturbing the best rest she'd had all week? Portia opened an eye, and a chubby redheaded white woman in a white uniform looked in her face and swayed from side to side.

"How many fingers do I have up?" the lady asked.

Portia managed to mumble, "Four."

"You're in recovery, dear. Sit up and enjoy your high, honey," the lady said. She cackled at her own humor and disappeared.

While Portia tried to recollect, she looked around the room. There were about thirteen other hospital beds with women who appeared to be coming out of a trance; a few of them were crying. Her head was swimming, and she felt real sleepy. She fought it as best as she could.

A few minutes later, the woman came back and told her to try and get up. She said hot tea and Tylenol were available if she felt cramps. Portia was still on her trip, so she only half heard. The lady helped her sit up. "Come on, honey, you gotta come out of this. Work with me here, doll."

Portia peeped the lady's strong Jewish accent. She was starting to get through. Portia sat up and realized there was something between her legs. She reached down. The nurse noticed and said, "It's a sanitary napkin for the bleeding."

Portia feebly got up. She was ready to shake this, because she didn't like feeling out of control. Plus, the crying and screaming of the woman on the bed next to her was becoming annoying. With the nurse's help, she made it to the chairs on the other side of the room, where some girls were sitting. Portia accepted the offer of Tylenol, crackers, and hot tea. She felt light cramping in her stomach but nothing major. Though it was over, she didn't feel better.

An auburn-haired Puerto Rican girl sitting next to her nudged her. "You'll be okay, mami. Don't worry, you'll heal like that." She snapped her fingers. "This is my fifth one, and I'm already ready to go to the club tonight. Shiit, fuck that!" She laughed.

Her sympathetic words immediately turned Portia against her ass. Fuck the recovery shit. She was ready to go home.

J AY HUNG UP his cell phone, not bothering to leave a message this time. He was tired of talking to her voice mail, and he was on the verge of saying "fuck Portia," because he wasn't the type of nigga to press no bitch. He made a right on DeKalb Avenue by the Roosevelt Projects and honked at his little mans Nino and them on the corner. In his rearview mirror, he saw fat Kareem flagging him down. Not in the mood for the usual complaining, Jay turned the music up and hit the gas. If it was that important, Kareem could page Wise.

At the stoplight on the next corner, three scantily clad young girls walking across the street vied for Jay's attention. The skinniest one got bold and approached his truck. "Yo, excuse me. Yoo-hoo," she said. When she caught his eye, she gave him a knowing look and said, "Pull over, boo."

Jay just looked at her and said, "Nah, shorty, I ain't that easy." Then the light changed and he hit the gas. She looked too young, but even if that had been Tyra Banks out there, he probably wouldn't have hollered at her right then because he was preoccupied. Jay was tight because he wished he hadn't bought Portia the damn car. It seemed like girlfriend had done a 360 on him since she bounced.

Portia had been gone for three weeks and had hardly called. Now Jay was feeling like he was the bitch, like she had the upper hand. She was probably fucking some bamma down south. Good thing he hadn't told her about the car yet, because at this rate, she was going to fuck around and be assed out. He could always give it to one of his sisters, Kira or Laurie. He'd bought them the cars they drove now.

He wondered if Portia was really down south. Was her grandmother really sick? He was beginning to doubt her whole story. He'd known from the time and place he'd met Portia that she had mad game. But she was trying to play the wrong one now. Jay was tired of focusing on her. He was too serious about getting money to let a bitch distract him from his goals. He pulled his Excursion into the car wash on Atlantic and made some phone calls while his truck and twenty-threes got a bath.

When he was on the phone, Portia beeped in on the other line with some "Hey, boo" bullshit. He was gruff with her and told her to call him back because he was taking care of business. She must've been crazy. He wasn't waiting on her fucking call like no bitch. Deep down inside, he was relieved to hear her voice, but he'd never let her know she had him open. Jay had more important things to do then sweat Portia.

Money over bitches. MOB. That was the code he and his mans lived by. The ones with the most cake, anyway. As a matter of fact, he had to break out of town later to pick up some money from VA. Shit was gravy down there at the beach, and his whole team was eating real good. As usual, he'd catch a flight and get a rental down there.

On the way to the airport, Portia called him back and said she'd just gotten back from down south. He played nonchalant and told her he was on his way out and would catch her on the comeback. Had he been honest, he'd have told her he wanted to leave a first-class ticket at the airport for her to meet him in Virginia, because he didn't want to spend another night without her. He missed her touch, her scent, her smile, and that juicy snapper. Despite himself, Jay's penis became erect at the thought. It dawned on him that he hadn't had any since Portia left.

He didn't count the head from Tiffany the night before last as sex. She couldn't turn him on the way she used to, and he didn't even want to pipe her after the oral. She'd gotten upset and started talking slick because he didn't want to fuck her. She'd said he was turning sweet on her and probably fucked around with niggas now. He told her he just didn't want her drunken-assed pussy no more. Lately, every time he saw her, she was fucked up. And what a turnoff that was.

Tiffany had swung on him, so he smacked her and yoked her up. She was a real drama queen and loved shit like that. Jay was so disgusted and through with her that he tossed her a C-note and told her to lose his fucking number. Now he placed her in the same category with Stacy, his son's mother. That stupid bitch was done off.

Jay's mind drifted back to Portia. He wanted her so bad right now, and he was used to getting what he wanted. But he was a man, and his pride forced him to play silly high school games. Lately, he'd gotten tired of playing games. He needed a real woman in his life, and it seemed like Portia had it all. She had class, beauty, brains, a great personality, and street savvy. She smoked a little weed, but she was no alcoholic or nicotine fiend like Tiffany. Portia was all that, and regardless of where they'd met, she was his work in progress. She had wifey potential. He felt it. She just needed guidance.

He reminisced about the night they'd met. Jay and his peoples had gone to the Dragon's Lair for drinks and entertainment. Unlike his friends, Jay wasn't really turned on by strippers, so he usually avoided the stage and played the bar. He was the type to refuse lap dances from the girls but still tip them a five or a ten, just to show love and not hurt their feelings. It wasn't personal. He was just kind of old-fashioned in a sense.

Then he saw Portia. There was nothing mediocre about her. She stood out like a sore thumb. Jay did a double take and beckoned her to the bar. Unlike the red-bone chicks he usually found himself attracted to, babygirl was chocolate and literally thicker than a Snicker. Her beauty was natural, and her face wasn't packed with all that foundation he hated to see sisters OD on. His ex Stacy used to spend an hour putting on all that face and eye bullshit, and she held him up every time they went somewhere.

This girl didn't need makeup; she had flawless skin. She introduced herself as Mystique, but he told her a stage name was unacceptable. She was feeling the kid, so Portia revealed her real identity. She had a radiance about her that drew him like a bee to honey. Jay never got a vibe that strong from any woman before, let alone a stripper. Her aura read that she didn't belong there, that it wasn't her calling. To his surprise, he found he wanted to rescue her from the smoky sin hole and place her on a pedestal. A diamond in the rough, Portia had been intriguing from day one.

When it was her turn to go onstage, he felt a twinge of jealousy: He didn't want his friends and the other men watching her. Not only was she sexy, she was real acrobatic on the pole, and she could do a full split. She made a lot of tips up there, and mad brothers requested VIPs when she was done. Jay had her locked down from the time she came out of the dressing room, so he hadn't realized how popular she was. He guessed she had that effect on everybody.

Jay couldn't help feeling possessive after that. He was so smitten with Portia, he spent about a thousand dollars in lap dances and VIPs that night, just to keep her from dancing for anyone else.

Jay never tricked on strippers, so his mans Casino and Wise were shocked to see him go in the VIP room. They really broke his balls about it later. But they were happy that Jay finally had loosened up. He and Portia wound up going to IHOP for an early breakfast after the club and spending the night together.

Now she had him fucked up, and she didn't know it. And she wouldn't know it, because Jay kept it gangsta. She knew he dug her, but that's as far as it would go. Even though she claimed she'd changed her lifestyle and wanted a commitment, he had to be positive he could trust her. He was feeling Portia, but a woman would never be his Achilles' heel. Jay was a thug, and he didn't wear his heart on his sleeve. He never would.

PORTIA HAD SPENT the last three weeks going through postpartum blues and recuperating at her mother's house. She'd finished the prescribed pills that were supposed to stop the bleeding, and her two-week follow-up exam had gone well. During her hiatus, she'd prayed for forgiveness and attended church with Pat to witness Aunt Gracie's first sermon.

The topic had been "Faith Versus Adversity," and her aunt had done well. Portia was touched and felt like the words were directed right at her. When she went to the altar for prayer, she couldn't hold back her tears. Patricia was moved too, but she later joked, "Everybody that ain't been to church in a long time feels like the preacher is talking to them."

Portia had called Jay and acted like she'd just returned from down south. She wanted to see him, but he said he was going out of town for a few days. He sounded kind of snappy. She hoped she hadn't fucked around and messed up the good thing they'd started. She regretted having to disappear like that. Portia just wanted to get back to normal life, whatever that was.

She was grateful to Pat for the solace of her old room, but she went home and awaited her prince. She missed Jay like crazy, and she didn't like that cold-shoulder vibe he gave her.

Portia touched base with Laila, Simone, and Fatima to let them know she was okay. They all fussed at her, but they were more concerned about her health than the fact that she'd disappeared without calling. They knew it was done already, and they all seemed to forgive her. Thank God, Simone was going on with her pregnancy. Portia wanted to be the baby's godmother.

Two days later, Jay came back up top, and that midnight Portia was in his arms, praying he didn't notice anything different about her down there. He obviously didn't, because he made love to her so sweet that tears ran down her cheeks.

The next day, Portia saw that Jay hadn't been kidding about buying her a car, because he surprised her with a champagne-colored chromed-out Lincoln Continental. She was a '99, with cream Coach leathers and a sunroof, and she was sitting on eighteen-inch rims. It was Portia's first car, and she was so happy, it might as well have been a Bentley.

Jay blushed when Portia showered him with hugs and kisses, and he spent the afternoon teaching her how to parallel-park. After chauffeuring him around on his errands for driving practice, Portia spent the evening thanking him in every position she could think of. Everything was a go. Jay was her ebony prince, and there was no turning back.

Within a week, Portia learned to master her whip and was all over the city with her girls, who seemed really pleased. Simone joked that Portia "must've sucked a mean one to get such a nice ride," and Laila and Tima told her not to "dumb out and blow it, because Jay's a keeper."

Patricia was kind of suspicious of Jay's intentions. She told Portia to make sure the registration papers were legit, and to be careful, because "men don't just buy cars and expect nothin' in return."

Patty-cake made it a point to come by and be nosy one morning, so Portia introduced her to Jay. He was so polite that Pat warmed to him immediately, and they wound up conversing for over an hour. Like Pat, Jay was up on his politics and current events. Portia loved that about him. She couldn't stand a man who didn't keep up with what was going on in the world.

Over the next weeks, Jay proved himself to be an asset. He did more than his part. He made sure Portia had enough bread to cover her bills and her student loan payment, and he kept money in her pocket. On average, he was spending at least four nights a week at her house, and he savored the home-cooked meals she prepared for him. Things were going so well, Portia doubted there was anyone else for her in this lifetime.

Jay completed her. He filled that empty space she had disregarded for so long. Being in love was beautiful. Exotic dancing didn't even cross Portia's mind anymore; she was sure that he wouldn't see her fucked up. They talked about business a lot, and they were impressed with each other's intelligence. Jay was serious about his goals, and Portia had business and accounting knowledge. They complemented each other and had the makings of a powerful couple.

On a Tuesday morning, when Portia came out of the bathroom, Jay was dressed and getting ready to go.

He slapped her on the butt when she walked past him and said, "Ma, your friend Fatima said to call her right back. She said it's real important. She called while you were in the shower. Be good, P. I'm out."

"A'ight, be safe, boo." She blew him a kiss. After Jay left to handle his business, Portia locked the door and dialed Fatima's office.

Fatima was expecting the call, and she answered on the first ring.

"What's crackin', Tima?"

Fatima was excited. "You got the job! Charlene wants to see you for an interview first thing in the morning, but I already know you got it."

"Are you sure, Tima? What time?"

"Ten o'clock, in her office. The building on West Fifty-seventh, suite 304."

"Good-lookin'."

"No doubt. I have to make some calls. Holla at me later, P." Fatima hung up.

Portia marveled at her new opportunity. And it was all thanks to a hookup from her homie. What would she wear in the morning? She had to go get her hair done, and a manicure too. Portia was determined to get that job. She was in love, but she was no fool. She knew she couldn't live off love alone, and Jay wasn't obligated to sponsor her. Besides, she'd be a better catch for him if she brought something to the table.

How would Jay react to her news? She hoped he wasn't the type who needed his woman's universe to revolve around him. She'd had a jealous boyfriend in the past, and he always got all quiet when she told him about her accomplishments, as if thinking, *Once she gets something going for herself, she won't need me anymore.* Like a woman couldn't be capable of doing both—taking care of home and having a career. A man should want his woman to succeed. Portia hoped Jay wouldn't disappoint her by acting uninterested. She decided she wouldn't tell him until she was positive she'd gotten the job.

Portia prayed God's punishment for the abortion wouldn't be her not getting the job. She knew she had to pay for the sin somehow. Portia had tried to put it behind her, but she was haunted by it and having two recurring nightmares. In each dream she had a beautiful baby girl, and then the baby either died in the dream or she lived, and Portia woke up to realize that there was really no baby because she'd killed her before she even had a chance. No matter the conclusion, she wound up teary-eyed. When Jay was at her house, she was careful not to let him find out. Luckily, he was always asleep when it happened.

Portia decided to put it in the hands of the Lord. If it was meant to be, she would get the job. She wasn't about to fret. Portia headed for the hair salon, hoping to beat the afternoon rush.

"**Y**OU A'IGHT, LIL' MAN?" Jay smiled at Jayquan, his four-year-old son, whom he'd just picked up from day care. His mini-me nodded.

His mother wouldn't let him wear the outfits Jay matched so carefully when he shopped for his son. The boy was wearing Rocawear jeans and a Polo shirt; he had a bunch of Rocawear shirts that Stacy could've put on him. She did stuff like that just to irk Jay. He'd complained about it before, so now she deliberately did it on the days when he picked Lil' Jay up. It wasn't that he was sweating baby clothes; it was just the principle of the matter. She got stupid the second he did one little thing that she didn't like.

He copped Lil' Jay a Happy Meal from Mickey D's and headed toward his Clinton Hill brownstone. When he passed Putnam and Franklin, he honked at the cats on the corner. When his main man, Cas, and company recognized Jay's truck, their icy grills melted into smiles. They motioned for him to pull over and get in the game.

Jay was tempted to stop, but he had his son with him, and something could jump off. Sometimes niggas were sore losers, and shit could get ugly at a dice game. Consistent with the head cracks, Jay was known for dead-busting niggas in dice. But some niggas hate a winner. He'd had to back down a couple of fools in his time. Sometimes they weren't satisfied even if you gave them a walk.

That was why Jay kept his Desert Eagle and .45 within reach. He referred to them as his girlfriend and his mistress, respectively. His man Twan had been killed in a dice game stickup in Brownsville last summer, and his little man Munchie was paralyzed from getting shot up at another dice game in the Stuy. Jay slept on no one, because sleep was the cousin of death. Especially in NYC, because the Big Apple was full of worms.

Jay was very careful, but he loved to gamble. He bet on ball games, pool, dogfights, boxing matches, cards, you name it. He set aside a certain amount of money just to fuck up every week. That was why it was nothing for him to give Portia so much dough. Sometimes he threw away more than that. When he won, he won big. And luck was usually his lady.

Jay pulled up in front of his house and took Jayquan upstairs. His cell phone rang for the millionth time, and the caller ID read Moe's number. He must've been finished.

"Yo," Jay answered.

"Your laundry is ready. What time are you picking it up?" Moe spoke in code all the time; he didn't trust talking business over the phone.

"In thirty minutes," Jay replied. He hung up and left Moe wondering how he could make the three-hour trip upstate that fast. Little did Moe know, Jay already had Wise up there to collect and then restock him with product. Wise was Jay and Casino's lieutenant, and he had proved himself to be true blue. He was compensated well for it too. Jay made the call for him to hit Moe with another big eighth.

Moe was all right with Jay. He'd been an "L7" college boy when he came to Jay two years ago and expressed interest in getting money. Jay saw something in the little nigga, and on the strength of Maurice being Stacy's cousin, he had put him on. Moe had come straight ever since.

Jay was proud of Moe because he was about to graduate. He couldn't fault Moe for taking advantage of all the money those rich white kids at his college spent. And he liked the fact that Maurice was extra-careful over the phone. Moe hadn't seemed to let hustling go to his head. He was just trying to get some paper, and Jay respected that. He was going to give Moe a legitimate salary one day, if he stayed humble and stuck with him.

Jay had cut off a lot of niggas lately for being on that bullshit and feeling themselves just because they were getting a little money. They were wannabes, drunk off of themselves over pebbles. They didn't understand long money, and a petty nigga couldn't be trusted.

Jay kept a close circle and hit only two or three good dudes with major work. He wasn't trying to be a kingpin, but it was "ball or fall" in New York. Jay was on top of his game, and he had other things going for himself. His main man Casino's mother was a real estate broker, and she had advised them early on to make some wise investments, to clean up their dirty money. They took heed, so now both of them owned property. So far, Jay owned a house in Clinton Hill, a house in Bed-Stuy, and a six-family building in Park Slope, all paid for and free and clear of mortgages. Because of this, he had a steady passive income from collecting rent on eight apartments. Jay's next goal was to get up in the entertainment industry. He knew he belonged up there with the big boys.

As far as hustling, he broke down only a couple of kilos at a time, to serve a few good men some weight. Two chicks on their payroll, Reecy and Tina, usually made the deliveries upstate and down south. So Jay didn't really get his hands dirty until it was time to cop. Manuel, his Colombian connect, would deal with only him and Casino, who got money together but ran separate cocaine and heroin operations. They were equal partners, but Jay dealt with the "girl" and Cas supplied the "boy." Other than cop, all they did was pick up money. Their subordinates handled all the footwork.

Jay peeped in on his seed, who was in the living room sitting in front of the plasma big-screen, watching *Dr. Dolittle 2* on DVD. Jay joined him on the recliner at the end of the tan L-shaped Italian-leather sofa. His little man could work the remote better than he could. Lil' Jay had picked up fast ever since he was a little baby, when he'd started walking at seven months old.

"Don't you have some homework, Jayquan?"

"Just a little bit. I can do it later, Daddy. I always watch TV first."

"No, you can do it now. Then you can look at TV."

Jayquan scowled, but he went to get his book bag, and Jay went over the homework with him to make sure it was correct and legible. Only after that did he award the boy playtime. He tried his best to be a good father; there was no way he'd let Jayquan grow up like he did, angry at his pops for not being there for him.

Jay looked around at the immaculate bachelor pad. You could tell that no women lived there: He had chosen masculine decor. Over in the corner by the window stood a bonsai tree he'd had imported from China. The late-afternoon sun shone through the window and bounced its shadow off the freshly waxed parquet floor.

Jay looked around proudly at the collection of expensive genuine African art displayed about the living room. His aunt Yaz was a sculptor, and she used to take him and his sister Laurie to art galleries and museums all the time when they were kids, so Jay knew authentic art. His favorite piece was a nine-foot statue of a proud, topless African woman carrying a basket on her head. She was sculpted from mahogany wood and had exaggerated facial features and perfect ample breasts. Everyone who saw her loved her.

That made Jay think of Portia. She'd never been to his crib. He never brought chicks here. He'd usually get a room or take them across town to another hideout he had, because he didn't want them trying to stay. His baby mother, Stacy, had turned him completely off of having a relationship. Until he started fucking with Portia.

Lately, he'd been staying at her house a lot. It was comfortable over there, and he'd paid the bills the last couple of months, so he felt okay staying. Plus, she acted like she wanted him there. Jay wondered if he was moving too fast, but he was thinking of moving her into an apartment in his Bed-Stuy building that would be vacant next month. The tenant had bought a house and was waiting on the closing. The apartment was in Stuyvesant Heights, so she wouldn't have to move far. And he would foot the moving expenses. In the long run, it would be cheaper than paying rent to her landlord. She had a nice crib, but this one was in a better section of the neighborhood. Plus, the bathroom and living room were bigger, and she'd have an extra bedroom. There was no way she could refuse that offer. Unless she was still fucking around and didn't want him watching her.

He hadn't told her about his idea yet, because he had to be certain he could trust her. He'd told her he owned only one house. Portia didn't nag him about coming over. He liked that about her. She hardly ever nagged him about anything. Of course, she didn't have to, because he was on his job, but for some chicks that wasn't enough. He was really feeling shorty; he provided for her out of the goodness of his heart. He just wanted to make sure homegirl wasn't playing him like some trick.

He could tell she was dealing with something she hadn't opened up to him about yet. He hadn't let on, but he knew she woke up in the middle of the night sometimes, from bad dreams or something. He'd be holding her, and her body would go rigid for a minute, and a time or two he could've sworn she was crying. He played possum every time, because he figured she'd discuss whatever it was with him when she was ready. Jay couldn't help wondering what was eating at her. He wished he could fix it, whatever it was. Or at least make it better. Portia was so mysterious sometimes, and Jay was both attracted to that and fearful of it. He hoped he knew her as well as he thought he did, because he'd invested a lot more in her than he had any other woman in years.

All she had to do was stay out of the clubs, and by any means necessary, he would make sure she was straight. Portia didn't know it yet, but Jay was seriously considering making her his wifey. He dug her mentality. If she got it together, she could really be something. She was educated, and she needed to use that, and he could use her for a lot of things too. She was the kind of chick he needed in his corner right now; never mind that his peoples knew how he met her. He didn't give two fucks about what niggas thought anymore.

He didn't discuss their relationship with his mans, but they knew Jay and could tell he was sweet on her. Portia was so bad, they could understand why. On the low, Jay knew each of them would've tried to get a piece of that fine chocolate if he didn't care so much about her.

"Daddy!" Jayquan snapped Jay out of Portia-ville. He had a guilty look on his face. He'd probably broken something.

Jay asked him with patience, "What happened, lil' man?"

"Promise not to get mad at me first."

"What did you do, man? All right, I promise I might not be mad at you."

"You cheated, Daddy. You said you *might not*. Say you won't!" Jayquan was no slow leak. He didn't fall for trickery when it came to bargaining his way out of trouble.

Jay laughed and picked him up and spun him around high in the air. Jayquan usually loved to play helicopter with his tall daddy because he could touch the ceiling, but he protested this time, kicking and squirming, and Jay realized his pants were wet one second before he hollered, "Put me down, Daddy! I pee-peed on myself 'cause I couldn't hold it. Don't be mad!"

He sounded so cute that Jay couldn't get mad if he tried, even though Jayquan had been potty-trained since he'd turned two. He knew better, but he always waited too long to go to the bathroom. Jay carried his little pissy pride and joy upstairs at arm's length to clean him up and change his soiled clothes.

" **I** GOT A JOB! I got me a jizob," Portia sang while she walked down the block to the parking lot on Fifty-ninth Street in Manhattan. Charlene had just briefed her on the job description on the elevator ride down, because she was running late for an appointment. She warned Portia to get ready for work in a fast-paced environment.

The interview had gone great, though nothing like she'd expected. Dressed to a tee in a slim-fitted cream-colored Versace pantsuit, Portia had arrived fifteen minutes early to check out the record company headquarters' vibe. Black Reign Records was an independent label, and they appeared to be handling their business. The atmosphere was a professional but relaxed hustle and bustle, and the race ratio was about twelve to two.

On her way down the hall to Charlene's office, Portia peeked in doors and checked out the attractive, well-dressed brothers and sisters. She received smiles from a few sisters, some appreciative stares and nods from the brothers, and an Asian girl waved at her. Portia wanted to be among them. She was excited by the possibility of coming to work every morning in such a cool environment. She'd become a morning person for this in a heartbeat. She crossed her fingers and sat with Charlene and answered a few questions based on her slightly embellished résumé. The interview was a breeze, and it ended with Charlene telling her when she could start.

In two weeks, she would be employed. And not at some regular boring job. She'd be working in the industry. On the drive back to Brooklyn, Portia was thrilled that the FDR Drive wasn't crowded. She headed for the Brooklyn Bridge and thought about how Jay would react to her news. She'd left the house at eight this morning, while he was still asleep. That was the first time she'd ever left a man alone in her apartment, but she trusted Jay. He'd come in late the night before, so she hadn't gotten a chance to tell him about the interview. She'd gone to bed earlier than usual, determined not to have bags under her eyes when she woke up.

Thinking of Jay made Portia feel warm and tingly down there. She was in the mood for some celebration sex. She turned the radio up; 98.7 Kiss was jamming all the oldies. Portia sung along with Marvin Gaye. "'When I get that feeling, I need sexual healing. Sexual hea-ea-ling is good for me, makes me feel so fine, helps to relieve my mind.'" She decided to locate Jay on his cell phone—she wanted to tell him about her job right now. She knew he was out of the house, because it was half past twelve. She speed-dialed him, and he picked up. "What up, Kit Kat?"

"Hey, baby. Where you at? Are you busy?"

"Not really. I'm on the avenue. I'm 'bout to go get something to eat in a minute."

"You gambling, Jay?"

He laughed and lied. "Nah."

She lied too. "Okay, I just called to say hi. I'll see you later, boo." Portia hung up and busted a U-turn. Today she was going to do something she never did. She was about to roll up on Jay on the avenue and scoop him up. She knew the gambling spots he frequented, so she'd surprise him. She pulled up and parked on the corner of Grand Avenue, by an ensemble of Timberland-throwback-and-white-T-shirt-wearing, do-rag-and-fitted-cap-having young brothers with ghetto swaggers and complexions that varied from extra-light toast to black coffee.

A dice game was in full swing, and Portia spotted Jay in the crowd. He looked real crispy in a gray Akademics velour sweat suit, and like always, his white tee, do rag, and Jordans were brand-spanking-new. Jay was standing next to his main man, Casino, who looked good as hell too, wearing a royal blue, red, and white Philly Sixers jersey with a matching fitted cap over a royal-blue do rag.

Portia knew about half of the guys out there. Craig, who was Fatima's first; Robbo, whom Laila used to talk to; Bokeem; Puerto; and abusive-assed Wayne-o, whom she herself used to fuck with back in high school. He was older and had tried to control her every move by slapping her around. He smirked and nodded at her, and she remembered the black eye he gave her in ninth grade that almost made her parents send her down south to go to school. She halfheartedly waved at the bastard, and then she smiled at Jay's back and hoped he didn't see her creeping up on him.

Wayne-o ice-grilled Jay as Portia approached him.

She had the nerve to try to style on him when she knew he'd tamed her. He used to wear that out, and now this bitch was trying to act brand-new. That nigga Jay thought he had something. That bitch Portia was looking good, though.

Jay didn't see Portia roll up, but the look on Cas's face told him they had company. He turned around, and he fought back a smile when he saw who it was. Portia was decked out in cream, looking real classy and sexy. Her hair was blowing in the wind, and she was smiling like she was happy about something. She looked beautiful. Portia always had a sunny disposition, and she said "What's up?" to everybody on the corner, and Jay saw niggas looking at her like she was a piece of candy when they spoke back. Even Cas was smiling at her.

Jay quickly pulled her to the side. "What you doin' out here?"

"I came to get you. I have something for you." She ran a freshly manicured nail down his chest and eyed him seductively.

Jay looked interested. Fuck those niggas and a dice game. He would catch them later, because his lady looked and smelled real good. Just then, Jay decided it was time to take Portia to his place. "You hungry, Ma? You ate lunch yet?"

She shook her head. "Let's eat later. Can we go home for a little while?"

Jay shrugged. "It's a go. Let's roll."

He had parked his truck earlier and ridden with Cas in the Range, so he'd ride with her. He told Cas he'd holler in a little while, and he gave his peoples pounds.

Jay noticed how hard that clown Wayne-o from Quincy was clocking his shorty. That cocksucker better watch it. Portia didn't give that nigga any eye contact, though. She knew better than to disrespect him like that.

Jay drove them off in Portia's car, bumping H-Town's "Knockin' Da Boots." Was she dropping hints? He smiled to himself about her choice of music. She was always listening to old jams.

Portia was so eager to share her news that she blurted it out as soon as they turned the corner. "Guess what? Today I got a job!" She let go the breath she'd been holding when he smiled.

"Word? That's good, Ma! Go 'head and do you. Where? When you start?"

Portia gave him a rundown on everything about the hookup from Fatima, the interview, and the company, and Jay seemed genuinely impressed. He said she would benefit from the experience and could use it to help him too. Portia beamed. Jay was a dream come true. It was official. She was head over heels, and she would reward him for his support when they got home.

Jay pulled up on a nice quiet block in Clinton Hill. Portia figured he had to make a stop on the way. He got out and told her to come on, so she followed him up the stairs and didn't ask any questions, because she knew men hated that.

Upon entrance, she didn't have to inquire as to their whereabouts; there was a huge painting of what had to be his son on the living room wall. The little boy was the spitting image of his father. "Oh my God, that is beautiful! He is *so* cute! He looks exactly like you."

Jay laughed and excused himself to the bathroom,

and Portia took it all in. She walked down the hall and examined every nook visible. She was definitely impressed. Jay was a man of cleanliness and expensive taste. Her baby's house was bad as hell, and there was no sign of a woman yet. She would check the bathroom cabinets later.

Jay took his time, knowing that Portia was snooping around. Women were nosy like that. He wanted her to look for herself anyway, since he wasn't into the tour-giving thing. He figured she was checking around to see if some chick stayed there. He went upstairs and caught her coming out of his master bedroom. Portia tried to look nonchalant, but she realized how guilty she looked, and she laughed. Jay's eyes were drawn to her wide hips. She sure looked good in that suit.

"Baby, your house is beautiful. I love the art, the furniture, I love everything. You have exceptional taste."

"Yeah? And you look exceptionally tasty in that cream, Ma." He pushed her back into the bedroom. Portia fixed her eyes on him and slowly removed her clothing until she wore only tangerine satin underwear. Jay wanted to taste her female essence intensely, so he slid off that thong barrier and positioned her spread-eagled on his king-size bed. When he first met Portia, he didn't even eat pussy, but she was real clean, and he enjoyed doing it to her.

"Take off your shirt," she whispered. Jay snatched off his shirt and stepped to his business, and he didn't come up for air until she squirmed. Yearning to offer reciprocity, she planted a trail of kisses from his lips down to the wonderful, thick nine-inch extension of him she had so come to love. There were no holds barred in their lovemaking; even condoms were forgotten. Their bond was strengthened. She had come into his world. Portia had passed the test.

LATER THAT NIGHT, Portia was snuggled in the big bed, clad in Jay's T-shirt, thumbing through the satellite channels on the bedroom wide-screen. Jay had to go take care of something, so he'd told her to make herself at home. Her inspection of both bathrooms had yielded only expensive fixtures and Jacuzzis with gold faucets and no evidence of a female. Portia was satisfied and so comfortable that she didn't want to leave. You could fit her apartment into his house five times. She pictured little Jay and a miniature Portia running around the house and was shocked at her sudden urge to bear Jay's child. A warning bell went off in Portia's conscience. Seconds later, the image returned, and she succumbed to her imagination.

ACROSS TOWN, JAY was done handling his business, so he stopped by Portia's crib to pack her an overnight bag. He grabbed a set of red satin underwear, some feminine products, and a change of clothes. He headed out the door but stopped short because he'd forgotten the shoes she'd told him to bring.

When Jay came out of the bedroom, some chick had her head stuck in the door and yelling, "KNOCK, KNOCK! HELLO!" She stopped when Jay emerged from the back. After she gave him a suspicious once-over, her expression softened. "Hi! Is Porsh here?"

"Nah."

"Well, I'm Fatima," she introduced herself. "You must be Jay. Nice to finally meet you."

"Likewise." He'd heard of her. "Portia's over at my house. I just came to get some stuff for her."

"I stopped by to congratulate P on getting hired at the label. I am *so* proud of her. This is a real good move she's making."

Jay agreed. "No doubt. She's too intelligent to be shaking her ass for a living."

Fatima nodded. "You're right. But she did that 'cause she *chose* to, not 'cause she *had* to. Don't think you messing with no dummy. Porsh always got the highest grades out our *whole* crew. She's a math wiz. Shoot, she helped me struggle through algebra, trigonometry, *and* calculus. It's like that stuff came natural to her. You know, she has a BA in accounting. I'm not just saying this 'cause she's my friend, but you got yourself a good catch, Jay. Make sure you do right by my girl."

Jay was humble, as usual. "I'll do my best." He chatted with Fatima for some time about Portia's well-being, and her friend seemed genuinely happy with her transition. Fatima suggested they give Portia a party to celebrate her squaring up. Jay told her he had a friend with a sports bar he could rent for little or nothing, and he insisted on paying for the catering and a fully stocked bar. Fatima said she'd be responsible for the cake, and she and her girlfriends would handle all the planning and the guest list, including whomever he wanted to invite.

They exchanged numbers and agreed to keep Portia in the dark. On the elevator ride down, Jay offered

Fatima a ride to her destination, but she said she had a friend waiting in a cab outside. They parted with a great first impression of each other.

When Fatima got back to the cab, Felony was looking all swelled up and impatient. He started bitching, but she ignored him because she didn't give a damn how he felt. He wasn't paying for nothing, so if he thought she took too long, he should've started walking. He was starting to get on her nerves with his damn whining all the time. Later, she would sit on his face, then send him home to his mama for a few days. Shit, maybe permanently.

She wondered if Jay was going to invite some of his cute friends to the party. She would make it a point to be alone that night. Maybe it was time to pull a switch of companions. All of her friends had men who could do something for them. This young nigga didn't have shit but a dream, and he wasn't serious about that. He bullshitted when she booked him studio time and made excuses left and right, so he didn't even have a demo recorded. Her generosity had spoiled him, and quite frankly, she was getting bored. That nigga was about to be black history.

She continued to ignore Felony and took out her cell phone to call Laila and pregnant Simone to pull their coats about the surprise party for Portia. Fatima remembered she didn't want him hanging on her coattails that night, so she decided to wait until she had some privacy later.

Felony sensed Fatima's shortage of patience and put his pouting to rest. He knew how far to go. At first he had her on lock, but lately, Fatima played him indifferent and acted like she didn't care if he left or not. He wasn't going to lose his meal ticket that easy. Honey kept him jigged out in all the latest hot shit, and she was that bridge he needed to get on in the industry. If all else failed, then fuck it, he would marry her for security. Tonight he would have to work on her, give her a few more reasons to keep him around. Hell, he knew how to work her big ass. He would lay his pimp game down once more and tighten that thang up. In the end, he'd have her meowing like a cat.

JAY HEADED HOME in high spirits. His girl got a job, and he was pleased to throw her a celebration the coming weekend because he was proud of his lady. He got a good vibe off of her friend Fatima. She was the kind of girl Portia needed to hang with, not strippers. Fatima had something on her mind. Jay knew his man Wise would be on her, because he was a breast man, and he loved real thick girls.

Portia heard the key turn in the lock and broke into a grin. Her black knight had returned. Jay came in and playfully threw her in a headlock. "What you been searchin' through my house for?" He knew she had been nosy.

She giggled. "Stop, Jay. You know I had to make sure ain't no bitch livin' here."

"I don't bring bitches here. Consider yourself lucky."

"Don't you mean special, boo? I hope I'm special to you."

"No question, Ma. You wifey." He looked sincere.

JAY WAS PISSED the fuck off. Two days before the party, and now this bullshit. He felt like an asshole. Earlier, he'd wanted to call Fatima to make sure she had everything under control and a big enough budget, but he'd misplaced her number. So when Portia drove to the supermarket and left her cell phone home by mistake, he checked it for Fatima's number and saw that Portia had a new voice mail. The last incoming call had an 804 area code. He wondered who was calling her from Virginia. Jay couldn't help but be curious because he had a lot of peoples down there, so he listened to the message.

It was some country dude. Dude said, "What it is, sexy? This Big Q. You need to come on down here for a couple of days. Why you be acting like you don't want no mo' money? I ain't heard from you. You retired? I got something for you that you ain't even got to work for. You can lay flat on your back if you want, and make 'bout two or three G's a night for the weekend. I need you so bad, I don't even want no cut. I'm just putting you on, 'cause a lot of these mo'fuckas been requesting you. We missing you, Mystique baby! Quit playing wit' it, wasting all them goods you got. That nigga you obviously done fell for ain't gon' be good to you as the game is. The game been good to you, so now you gotta be good to the game. Let's get this money. Call me ASAP, fo' I give some other young lady this golden opportunity. You number one, and I got two and three already. Give me a commitment. I know you still got the number. Just in case, it's 804–582–9942. Holla at Big Q, baby!"

Rage and jealousy filled Jay, and he bit his lip. He was mad enough to choke that bitch out for playing him. He knew he'd better bounce before Portia made him catch a charge. As a cover-up for her to run out of town and whore, she was going to act like a relative was sick again or some shit. That's probably where she was before, at some fucking private party servicing a million dudes. Who the fuck was that nigga, her pimp or something? Jay wasn't into this drama shit.

He was kicking out all this money for a celebration for some liar. Portia was insulting his intelligence by acting all innocent and shit. Now he had proof that he couldn't trust her. He never should've gotten serious with her ass. Jay called Wise to come get him immediately, because he couldn't even look at that bitch right now. He broke out before Portia returned, because as tight as he was, he might kill her ass.

PORTIA CAME HOME and wondered where Jay had gone. She had his truck, and her car was parked in the same place. *He should've waited until I got back to help unload all these damn bags,* she thought. She did it alone, making several trips up and down the stairs and sweating in the heat.

When she was done, she cranked up the AC and put

away the groceries, and then she started dinner. She remembered she'd left her cell phone home earlier, so Portia checked her voice mail after she put her chicken in the oven. There was a message from Laila and one from a promoter named Quentin, whom she knew from Norfolk. It had been a while since she'd gone down there. She made pretty good money locally, so she hadn't felt the need to travel for a while.

When she used to go out of town to hustle, Q would set up parties for her and other dancers. He provided security for their safety, plus made sure the ballers showed up, so that the girls got paid every time. In exchange, they would throw him a small percentage of their earnings. Some of the girls opted to pay Q with sexual favors. Portia always hit him off with dough; she made good money when Q set something up. They maintained a mutual respect because Q had a "treat 'em like they wanna be treated" philosophy, and he knew Portia wasn't like those who preferred to service him.

She called him back to politely decline his offer and tell him she'd thrown her guns down. He was disappointed, but he congratulated her when she told him where she was working. Q said he'd always seen something in her and was glad she knew she had other options in life and hadn't gotten swallowed up in the belly of the beast. Before they hung up, he promised to check on her sometimes. Q was of good-hearted nature, and they understood each other.

There was no way Portia would backslide and jeopardize her relationship anyhow, even if she didn't have a job. Jay was such a good provider, there was no need to. Her phone rang before she could put it down. It was Laila calling her back. Portia answered, "Hey, Lay. What up, girl?"

"You're a hard person to catch up with. You never answer your phone. I forgot you be at *Jay house* all the time now. You ready for next week?"

Portia said, "It's now or never. I start Monday."

"It'll be here before you know it. Keep your schedule free Saturday night. We gon' do something. We should take a cruise around the city. It's summertime now, and we're taking the beautiful weather that God's blessing us with for granted. You down?"

"No doubt. That'd be nice. I'll call Fatima and Mone to see if they rollin' too. You think Simone can stand a boat ride, being pregnant?"

Laila laughed. "I hope so. Have you seen her lately? She looks so cute! She's carrying big for six months. She's way out there, girl. It looks like a boy to me, 'cause her stomach is sitting up high. She said she don't wanna know what it is till it comes. With all this technology we have today. Can you imagine? *I* want to know, so I can start shopping for the baby."

"Me too. I feel so bad, 'cause I ain't seen her in weeks. I put my girls on a back burner since I got with Jay. I'm sorry, Laila. We definitely doin' something this weekend, even if it gotta be mommy-to-be friendly. Oh, how my babies doing?"

"They're fine, girl. Khalil took them to buy another computer. We need two so the girls can use one for learning and we can use one for business. They've been asking about their auntie Portia too, 'cause they ain't seen you in a while."

"I know. I miss them too. Tomorrow is Friday,

right? Matter of fact, they can stay with me tomorrow night. Okay?"

"Like I'm gon' stop you. Come and get 'em, girl. Or I can get Khalil to drop them off. Whichever is more convenient for you. Just let me know."

"Okay, just drop them off around six. I'll talk to you later."

"A'ight, one." Laila hung up, and immediately dialed Bigmouth to warn her once more not to blow the surprise.

"Hello?" Simone sounded sleepy when she answered.

"Hey, Miss Mommy, you okay?" Laila didn't mean to wake her, but she didn't want Mone to run her mouth when Portia called.

"I'm good. Kyle and I just came from the doctor. He left, and I fell asleep for a minute. What up?"

"What did the doctor say? Is everything a'ight?"

"Yeah, she just said back off of the salt. My fingers and ankles swelled up a little bit, but I'm fine. What up?"

"Portia thinks we goin' on a city cruise Saturday. She's probably gonna call you to see if you're okay with it. Just play dumb. Don't say nothin' about the party."

"Duh! I ain't gon' spoil the surprise, don't worry. Fatima called earlier. Y'all gettin' on my damn nerves. I know how to keep my mouth shut. She said all we gotta do is pick up the cake on Saturday. Everything else is done. Jay peoples we rented the club from wanted to put a cap on drinks at first, but I guess Jay really blessed him, 'cause now there's an open bar all night. And I can't even really get my drink on. Ain't that some shit."

"I drank a little champagne at my wedding. You know I was pregnant with Macy when I got married. I didn't get sick. Just make sure you eat right first."

"Girl, speaking of eating, the doctor said I gained eighteen pounds so far. I'm only supposed to gain twenty-five my whole pregnancy. At this rate I'ma be a damn blimp. I gotta stop eating so much junk. I eat healthy, but I do eat a lot of junk. I been craving some crazy shit lately."

"Just stay away from the salt. That's real serious, Mone. Take care of yourself."

"I will. Let me get a nap before Kyle's worrisome ass comes back. I'm 'bout to send him back to his fuckin' wife. I'm having second thoughts about this whole situation."

"Simone, you don't know *what* you want. Be glad he didn't ditch you when you got knocked up. A lot of men would have. He's just aggravating you 'cause you're pregnant and moody. Don't you run him away."

"He claims he didn't break up with his wife for me, that they were having problems before me. He said they haven't been happy for years, they were just waiting for their kids to grow up. And I sure didn't ask him to leave her. Oh, well. He does treat me good, though. That nigga rubs my feet and all. Plus, he already set up an account for the baby. I told him just don't come over here so much. He said he gon' put me and the baby in a house, in my name. We'll see. Girl, I'm tired. Bye, Laila, I'll talk to you tomorrow. Love you."

"Love you too, Ma-ma. Take care." Laila figured it wasn't necessary to call Fatima, because she already knew the deal. She would touch base with her tomorrow to find out what time they would be decorating for the party.

THAT NIGHT, JAY decided he wasn't going home. He was still very angry and didn't want to see Portia. Wise looked over at him, slumped down in the passenger seat. He had been quiet the entire ride. Wise turned onto Conduit Boulevard en route to Eden, a new strip joint in Queens that they hadn't checked out yet. Although Cas was Wise's usual strip club partner, he was out of town. Jay didn't look like he was in the mood; still, Wise figured he could use a few drinks to take his mind off of whatever had him so tight. He wasn't going to ask any questions, but he was pretty sure Jay's temperament had something to do with his main squeeze, Portia. His man Jay was real private about shit like that. Any other night, he'd be home by now. Wise knew Jay loved her, and he hoped that chick wasn't playing his man, because Jay did meet her in a titty bar. Not to throw salt, but niggas had to stay on point—these bitches would take you if you let 'em. Portia seemed cool, but she could be taking Jay for a ride. It was a woman's nature to be deceptive.

Jay was Wise's man fifty grand. It was Jay and Casino who put him on, when he came home from up north three years ago. Now he stood on his own two feet and had his own shit. To show his gratitude, he held them down. They weren't sonning him, because the money was good. Wise was no dummy. He had his own work too, but he hung around Jay and Cas because he learned a lot from them.

They taught him how to have something. They

didn't bullshit and just talk about the shit they wanted to do. Them niggas made power moves, and they weren't your average street-hustling dudes. Because of them, Wise got his moms and little brother out of the projects and into a home last year. And they taught him how to flip houses and shit. Eventually, they were getting out of the game and fucking strictly with real estate. Plus with the music shit Jay kept on talking about. Wise usually stayed in the paint, but he was nice on the mike, and he wouldn't mind seeing his name up in lights. He knew it could happen, because Jay always did what he said. Wise turned in the parking lot of Eden, and Jay finally spoke. "A couple of drinks, and we out. I don't feel like fuckin' with no bitches tonight."

Wise felt quite the opposite and hoped the drinks would change Jay's mind. They paid the cover and headed for the bar. The deejay was playing some heavy-metal shit, and a stiff white girl danced onstage like she was doing aerobics. This wasn't their usual domain, but they were there already, so they might as well chill for a minute. Wise ordered their first round of Hennessy double shots and proceeded to get in the groove. Out of about twenty girls, only two or three were black. And they were all skinny. He didn't see one thick girl so far. Wise preferred big-butt sistahs.

Being in a gentlemen's club made Jay think of Portia even more. He just couldn't get her off of his mind. Though his image of her was somewhat shattered, he'd rather be in her company instead of these skinny white broads. Not that he had any racial qualms. He just wasn't into snow. Jay hated to admit how much that voice mail had hurt. How could she be his girl and still be getting calls like that?

Wise said, "Drink up, man. What you sipping for? Yo, look at that bitch titties. You think they real?" Wise was referring to a suntanned brunette coming their way.

"Ask her." Jay didn't care if they were real or not. He knew Portia's were real. Damn, everything reminded him of her. He finished off his drink and ordered another round, and Wise called the brunette over.

She smiled. "How's it going? I hope you gentlemen are enjoying yourselves. I'm Victoria." She asked Wise, "What's your name?" She loved black men and appreciated both of these Adonises, but she could tell this one was feeling her more; his friend appeared distant. She knew who to work on. This one looked sort of like that rapper Memphis Bleek, with cornrows, and his friend was a young hard-core replica of Brian McKnight. She'd love to get acquainted with these two.

"Tell me your secret, Victoria. Then I'll tell you my name. Is all that you holdin' real?" Wise eyeballed her breasts. The Henny had him feeling frisky.

She winked at him. "I can show you my secret better than I can tell you. Wanna see?"

"Yeah, let me see what you working with. When you go onstage, shorty? Make me come up out these pockets."

"I'm up after the next girl. Stay tuned, 'cause you're in for a thrill." She flicked her tongue ring at him.

Damn, shorty had on red lipstick. Wise was really thinking naughty now. "A'ight, I'ma check out your stage show. Freak off enough up there, and you might be the one to get this money tonight, girl." He flashed her a bankroll from his right pocket.

"You look like the type who knows how to pick a winner. I'll let you decide."

When she sauntered off, Wise was shocked to see that she had a plump little booty. He had to comment. "Yo, shorty got a lil' onion for a white girl. Let me find out."

Jay had to agree. Though she was real slim, she did have a nice little bump in her dress. Jay drank on, but Wise chilled on number three, because he had to drive. Wise knew he had to stay on point. He could see that Jay was getting hammered.

Jay nudged him when Victoria came onstage. She had changed into a red outfit. They recognized the song she danced to from MTV, but they didn't know the name of it. Wise had undoubtedly seen sisters dance better, but she was something sexy. Her melons jiggled when she moved, so they had to be real. Wise stayed back in the cut and checked her out. She grabbed this guy by his tie and flicked her tongue ring at him. Suddenly, the song changed to a slower, sexier beat, and a tall, slim blonde with big boobs and a deep suntan joined her onstage.

The girls were imaginative, and they used hot candle wax and honey, and they had props like whips and chains. The men at the front of the stage went wild, delighted with the freak show. The strippers sucked on each other's nipples, but they didn't go down on each other. Wise was willing to bet they had before, since they seemed so familiar with each other. They danced and caressed each other provocatively, and then for the grand finale, the blonde poured champagne on her breasts and Victoria's and used a lighter to set them on fire briefly. Then the girls kissed and rubbed breasts to put out the flames.

"These bitches is crazy," Wise mumbled. He was turned on. He wanted to take that party to a telly room and freak with them. A new girl came onstage, but she couldn't hold a candle to either of her predecessors. Wise waited on Victoria to get cleaned up and return to the floor. If Jay wanted the Barbie doll look-alike, he would treat him to a private dance.

Victoria resurfaced, and Jay motioned her over. "Where's your friend?" As soon as he asked, Malibu Barbie came out, and Victoria summoned her. Wise put a bug in Jay's ear. "Let's take these bitches in the VIP room and see what they working with, son."

The liquor had taken its toll, so Jay thought, *What the hell.* "Yo, Barbie! What's your name?"

She answered, "My name *is* Barbie. How's it goin'? Wanna be Hot Chocolate Ken tonight?" She gave Jay an approving once-over that proved she was into black guys.

She was so tall, they were eye to eye. Her eyes were green, and it was uncanny how much she looked like a life-size Barbie doll. Her waist was tiny enough to fit in a handcuff, and her suntan was so perfect, it looked paid for. It had to be done under an artificial light at one of those salons. Jay wondered if she could do a full split. The Henny made the "Portia issue" less impor- tant, and Jay was on his way to seeing how anatomically correct Barbie was under that little neon-green dress. He gave Wise the go, and they slid to the VIP room.

Once inside, they settled into adjoining booths. Despite the doorman's warning about throwing them out of the club and fining the girls fifty bucks apiece if he caught them exchanging sexual favors, Wise still made a lewd suggestion. "Yo, let me feel them red lips and that tongue ring, Victoria." He patted his zipper.

Victoria feigned shock. "Do I look like the kinda girl who does that?"

Wise kept it gangsta. "Hell yeah, shorty!"

They all laughed. Barbie draped her leg over Jay's and seductively murmured, "I get off at two. What are you in the mood for? I'm down for whatever, 'cause you're really fuckin' hot."

Jay was with it. He could see Victoria giving him the eye too, while she rubbed Wise over the pants. These bitches wanted to freak. It had been a while since he did some shit like this. Maybe it was time to act up a little. It was almost two, and he was horny, so he told Barbie to get dressed fast because he was ready to roll. Wise was ready too. They knew they could hit those freaks for free, but if the bitches acted right, they might get tipped.

WHEN THEY REACHED the hotel room, Jay reneged. He'd sobered up some during the ride, and homegirl was looking more like Trailer Trash Barbie. Her shoes were cheap, and he noticed she had bad skin underneath too much makeup. Jay doubted he'd be able to get it up if he tried, because his unattraction to white girls had resurfaced. Maybe if she were a classy-looking broad, he would have felt differently, but he and Wise had clearly bagged some scallywags. Now Jay wanted out.

Just as they'd figured, the broads weren't thinking about money. They wanted some E, so Wise made a call and had his son Mark deliver some ecstasy and powder to the room. The girls tripped on E and got skied up off the snow, and then they fulfilled Wise's request of eating each other out. Next, Barbie and Victoria wanted to give them head. Jay declined, and they tried everything to get him to participate, but he went outside and waited in the truck. He was ready to go. Wise told Barbie he had enough dick to spare, and he hooked her up too.

Jay sat outside and wondered what Portia was doing. Wise should've been finished by now. Jay wasn't trying to cock block, but he didn't want to leave, because he didn't trust those drug-head bitches. He didn't want the nigga to get pickpocketed or some shit. Jay knocked on the door and told Wise to hurry up.

Fifteen minutes later, Wise came out dressed and ready to go. Jay threw the broads a fifty for cab fare, because he and Wise weren't about to drive them home. He could tell by their accents that they lived in an Italian neighborhood like Bensonhurst or some shit, and he didn't want to wind up in beef with some white boys over no hoes. Victoria gave Wise her phone number, and Barbie gave Jay hers. Jay took it to avoid hurting her feelings.

Barbie said, "Hot Chocolate, she sure is lucky, that lady in your life. Not a lot of guys would've passed on this opportunity. I really hope I'll hear from you one day. Look, I don't want anything from you. We can just be fuck buddies. It'd be great. Please call me. You won't regret it."

When Wise pulled up in front of Jay's crib, he said, "Man, you ain't really miss shit. Them silicone titties don't feel real. I'll take a natural thick sistah over one of them skinny-ass mannequin bitches any day."

The two friends laughed and gave each other a pound, and Jay headed upstairs.

WHEN JAY GOT inside, Portia was asleep on the couch. She must've been waiting on him to come home. She was wearing a colorful candy-striped panty and tank top set, and she had her hair in two ponytails. She looked so cute and innocent, it was hard for Jay to stay mad at her. He watched her for a few seconds and decided to wait it out and see if she disappeared in the next few days. If she did, he would kick her to the curb. He didn't know if he could trust her anymore, but it was after four in the morning, and her thick brown thighs looked like succulent Thanksgiving turkey drumsticks compared to Barbie's and Victoria's. He was horny, and he needed Portia to put him to sleep. It was her duty to ease his frustrations. Jay crept upstairs to shower off the scent of Barbie's cheap perfume.

Portia had been up waiting on Jay all night, but she played possum when he came in. Once she heard the bathroom door close, she ran upstairs. She had to know where the hell her man was all damn day that he couldn't answer her phone calls. Jay was in the shower, and he'd stepped out of his pants and left them on the bedroom floor. Portia was tempted to check his pockets, but she didn't want to behave like some insecure wife. She could trust Jay. Seconds later, her inner insecure wife overruled.

In Jay's right pants pocket was a folded stack of money. The left contained his car keys, an open pack of Trident, and a box of condoms. Portia's heart fell in her ass. They were Magnums. The pain in her chest turned to fury. That mothafucka was cheating on her. She paced the floor and took a deep breath. This was the first time in their relationship that Jay had fucked around on her. Or was he fucking around the whole time?

Portia decided to play dumb and see what he had to say for himself. She dug out her "fake bitch" and walked in the bathroom and pulled the shower curtain back. "Hey, baby. Why you came in so late? Is everything all right?"

Jay jumped. Damn, Portia had scared the shit out of him. "What the fuck is you creepin' around for? I thought you were sleep, man. Hand me that black towel over there." He turned off the water, and then he thought about it and turned it back on. "Yo, get in."

That nigga had a lot of nerve. Portia obeyed him and undressed and climbed into the shower. That bastard looked real good with all that water running down his chest. He didn't say a word, but he lathered her with Dove body wash, spending extra time on her breasts and buttocks. He squeezed some feminine wash from Portia's bottle of Summer's Eve, but she felt funny about that and took her washcloth and finished the job herself.

Jay placed his hands on Portia's shoulders, and she

felt him pushing her down. At this point in their relationship, she knew what that meant. She knelt and fulfilled his wish so well that he grabbed her ponytails.

"Get up," he commanded. Portia rose to her feet, and Jay picked her up and backed her up against the shower wall and thrust himself deep inside her. He pounded her hard and steady. Portia wrapped her arms around his neck and attempted to relax her muscles and receive him with ease, but he was being rough this time, and it was kind of painful. She couldn't help crying out. Water cascaded down their bodies, and Jay climaxed. After he caught his breath, he put Portia down and washed his dick with soap again, and then he rinsed and exited the shower silently. He grabbed a towel and left Portia alone in the bathroom to clean the sticky mess he'd left between her legs.

Portia wondered what was up with that shower episode, but she wanted to address the condoms first. They'd agreed to be open with each other about everything. Jay was lying down in the bedroom, wearing a wifebeater and boxers. Portia walked in the room naked and slipped into one of his T-shirts. She was tired of fretting, so she came right out with it. "What's with the condoms, Jay?"

He had forgotten about those. What was she doing in his fucking pockets, anyway? "What condoms?"

"The ones in your left pants pocket."

He sat up. "I bought those for you, 'cause I don't know what the fuck you been doin'."

"Don't fuckin' play with me, Jay. We don't even use condoms."

Jay stood up and came toward her. "You fuckin' somebody else, Portia?"

Typical male. He was trying to flip the script and find her guilty of something, but Portia wasn't going for it. "Hell no! Are *you*?"

"I should be. Somebody worthy."

"What the fuck is that supposed to mean, Jay?" He was going too far. She didn't know where he was coming from with this shit.

"Take it how you wanna take it, Portia."

"I don't know where that came from, but I'm gonna act like I didn't hear you."

"So act like it. That's all the fuck you do *is* act. I don't know who the fuck you is no more. But I know I can't mothafuckin' trust you."

"Jay, you must be really guilty of something, coming off on me like this. Yeah, you guilty. The bitch you fuckin' with must have you brainwashed."

"Hell yeah. You! You *had* me brainwashed, but not no mothafuckin' more." He angrily grabbed Portia by the shoulders and spoke through clenched teeth. "You still fuckin' dancing and selling yo' ass? As much as I do for you? You just can't help being a fuckin' hoe, huh?" Jay was unwilling to share pussy. He grabbed Portia by the neck and pointed his finger in her face. "I'ma make you take another AIDS test before I fuck you again."

She felt dirty and humiliated. "Get off of me, Jay! Please! You hurtin' my neck! Please! Jay, I swear I don't know what you talking 'bout. What's wrong with you? You gon' flip like this after I just sucked your dick in the shower? Why you ain't come with this bullshit first?"

"I should've left you in the fuckin' club." He mushed her in her face, and she fell on the bed.

Portia jumped up. "You knew I was dancing when you met me, but I quit. Look at me, Jay. I *swear*. Why you trippin' on old shit all of a sudden, try'na make me feel dirty? I wanna be with you forever, baby. I would *never* cheat on you, Jay. I love you! Whatever you thinking, it's not true."

"It ain't no lie. I heard for myself. You don't fuckin' love me. I heard the message that bamma pimp nigga left you. That's your pimp, Portia? I gave you too much mothafuckin' credit. I didn't think you was dumb enough to let some nigga pimp you."

Now she understood his irate behavior. Q's message! "Oh my God, Jay, you misunderstood. I ain't heard from him in a long time. Word to God, it wasn't like that!"

"I don't believe a word you say. I ain't shit but a trick to you, but you won't play me no more, bitch! I'm not fuckin' wit' you no more. You cut off."

"Please don't say that, Jay. You don't mean that. I would never play you like no trick. Are you crazy? I love you! Calm down and listen to me. Ain't nothin' in this world that would make me jeopardize what we have." She grabbed his arm. "I'm not lying, I swear."

This wasn't the time for reconciliation. Jay was pissed and seriously regretting the fact that he was sponsoring a party for her lying ass this weekend. "Don't fuckin' touch me! I *thought* I had something, but everything that glitters ain't gold. You pretty, but you ain't shit. You can't turn no fuckin' hoe into no housewife. You stupid, fuckin' gullible, dumb *bitch!*"

He shoved Portia across the room, and she fell on the floor and cried. Jay stormed out and slammed the bedroom door.

T WAS FIVE o'clock Friday evening, and Portia was in a fog. Jay had left a couple of hours ago, and the only communication between them had been the looks of contempt he threw her when she tried to explain and reconcile. She was clearly on his shit list, and she felt desperate and exasperated, and she didn't know what to do. All Portia knew was that she wasn't leaving. Not even if he threw her out kicking and screaming. No way was she giving up that easy. Not when she was completely innocent. It was a total misunderstanding, and she had to make it right. She loved Jay way too much to let him go over that bullshit. And she knew he loved her too, or he wouldn't have reacted like that. She hadn't lied to him about anything since she told him she went down south, and she would never lie to him again under any circumstances.

Laila called Portia to say she was on her way to drop off Macy and Pebbles. Amid the chaos in her relationship, Portia had forgotten all about her commitment to keep them overnight. She told Laila to come on over because she hadn't seen the kids in a while, and she thought perhaps some children's laughter would lift her spirits. She'd take them out somewhere, maybe a movie if they wanted. She was already dressed in a cute outfit, because she'd tried to look attractive for Jay, even though he'd just ignored her.

Portia looked out the window and saw a white Escalade on dubs pull up. Laila had told her that Khalil had traded the Expedition for something newer, and it was nice as hell. Laila parked and got her daughters out of the truck, and the three of them walked up the stairs. Her darling daughters looked like twins, as usual, dressed alike in Baby Phat sweat suits. Their long, thick, curly hair was cornrowed in zigzag designs, with pretty, colorful beads at the ends. They looked adorable.

Portia flung open the front door to greet them. "Hiyee! Ooh, y'all got so big. Come and give me a hug!" They both looked like their daddy had spit them out.

Macy, the more talkative and the older of the two, ran to Portia first. "Auntie Portia! We came to stay with you!" Pebbles followed, and they were all over her, hugging her and touching everything from her jewelry to her hair.

Portia loved every second of it. "Oh my goodness. Y'all giving me all this love. I can't take it." She picked them up one by one and kissed them and tickled them. They giggled uncontrollably, and Laila smiled because she knew her daughters loved Portia as much as she did. She placed their bags on the floor by the couch.

Portia led them into the den and turned on the Cartoon Network. *Scooby-Doo!* was on, and they were delighted. "I'm going in here to talk to Mommy for a minute. Then we're gonna go and have some fun. Okay?"

"Okay!" they said in unison.

Portia went back where Laila was. "Laila FaLana! What's goin' on, girl?" she yelled.

Laila laughed at her silly friend. That was what Portia used to call her in junior high school. "Same shit, different day. I got a little running around to do this evening. Thanks for keeping Macy and Pebbles, 'cause I could sure use a break." She looked around the house. "Girl, this is a nice-assed place. No wonder you don't want to take your ass home. Y'all up in here playing married. Jay got you cooking for him and shit. At this rate, it may not be long till he asks you. I can tell he's really into you. By the way, how is Jay? Maybe one of these days I'll get to meet him."

Portia didn't know Laila had met Jay three days ago, when he dropped off some money at Fatima's house for party stuff. Portia looked down. "He's fine. You'll meet him soon."

Laila sensed something was wrong. "What happened? You think he'll have a problem with you keeping the kids over here?"

"No, he loves kids. He's just kind of upset with me right now."

"About what?" Laila hoped Jay was just acting, to throw Portia off. Now wasn't the time for him to be upset with her, because the party was tomorrow.

Portia said, "Nothing. Just some damn phone call. Ghosts from my past." She waved her hand like it was no big deal. She didn't feel like talking about it because it was depressing. She couldn't spoil the kids' evening and have them worrying about her.

"Work it out, whatever it is. You know you love

him. If it's worth having, it's worth working for, mama. You okay?"

"I'm good. We're about to go to the movies. When was the last time they ate?"

"They ate a late lunch when they came home from school. That was about four."

"So we'll eat after the movie. Go do what you gotta do, girl. We gon' catch the next show. Did you bring jackets for them? It's probably cold in the movie theater."

"Yeah, everything is in their bags. Toothbrushes and all. I have a checklist."

"I believe you." Portia laughed.

Laila kissed her babies goodbye, and Portia walked her to the door. The girls weren't the least bit sad to see their mommy leave; they knew they were in loving hands.

"Oh yeah, don't forget about tomorrow. It's girls' day out. Fatima's down, and Belly is too. I'll call you later." Laila was in a hurry to get to her hair appointment. She didn't want to be running around looking crazy at the last minute tomorrow. She had enough on her plate. She had to meet Fatima at the sports bar, take care of her duties at home, and get ready for the party. Then she held the responsibility of detouring Portia from a so-called boat ride to the club. She hoped Jay's friend Wings would agree to let them decorate early tomorrow. Simone was pregnant, so all of the weight was on Laila and Tima. It was okay, though. They were all excited about the theme they'd chosen.

Portia loaded Macy and Pebbles into her car and secured their seat belts. After they agreed on a radio station, she and the little ladies headed for Sunrise Cineplex. Portia prayed Jay wouldn't have had the locks changed by the time she returned.

JAY LEFT HIS apartment building to get some grub. He'd just responded to a complaint from his tenant Mrs. Rivera about extra-slow drainage in her tub. All Jay had done was put on rubber gloves and stick his hand down the drain and pull out a wad of hair wrapped around a plastic ring she said belonged to her grandson, and then he poured Liquid-Plumr down the drain. It was so simple she could've done it herself, but women always overreacted. She'd called him an hour ago, breaking like it was some big emergency, and she said if he couldn't come, she'd call a plumber and deduct the bill from her rent. Jay was a responsible and easygoing landlord, but sometimes his tenants got on his nerves.

He decided to get some fish from a Halal restaurant on Fulton. The Muslim brothers who owned the joint were cool, and he liked to support black businesses. Fatima had called him a little while ago and asked if they could decorate early the following day, so he called and got an okay from Wings for three o'clock and called her back. "Fatima? Go meet him over there at three. He'll be expecting y'all, so be on time. You need anything else?"

"No, we just gotta pick up the cake. We already bought everything else. What time is the deejay coming?" Fatima asked.

"He'll be there to set up around seven. I already took care of him, the bar, and the caterer. Just be around when they come to set up. If you need anything else, just call me, 'cause I'm not coming."

Had she heard him correctly? "Why not, Jay?"

He sighed. "I'm not try'na be funny, but I don't want no credit or recognition for this. If she asks, just say y'all did everything. I'm not trippin', Fatima. Just leave it at that."

"Jay, I don't mean to be nosy, but what's going on? Did something happen between you and Portia?" Fatima's last words caused Laila to raise an eyebrow.

"Nah."

"So you'll be there, right?"

"Nah. Your friend can't be trusted."

"Hold up a second, Jay. Elaborate, please, because I know Portia loves you, and I know you care about her too. What did she do that you suddenly can't trust her?"

"Let me ask you something. Off the record." Jay needed a little closure.

"Sure," Fatima said.

"Is Portia still dancing?"

"Hell, no! She quit for good. Jay, I know Porsh, and she has an honest soul. She wouldn't lie about something like that. And I'm not saying that just because she's my friend. When she quit, she quit. Trust me. That girl loves you." Fatima crossed her fingers, and Laila followed, just like they used to do when they were younger.

"A'ight, later." Jay hung up. He didn't know why he'd asked her in the first place. Like Portia's homegirl would actually tell the truth about what she did. Portia was so damned slick, Fatima might not know anyway.

Jay thought about their early-morning episode. He felt kind of bad about the way he'd grudge-fucked her all hard and spiteful in the shower. And he'd choked her and pushed her. He wasn't an abusive guy, but he snapped a little. Truth was, the thought of another man touching and sexing her drove him mad. He hadn't meant to physically hurt her and make her cry, but if Portia was going to be his wifey, he had to be able to trust her completely. He didn't even fuck around anymore, so how could she? He wasn't the female in the relationship, and he wasn't about to act like no bitch and sit home being faithful while she was somewhere whoring around. He would cut her off completely first. He had to stay focused on his business, so he couldn't have a slut for a girlfriend. He was too old for that kind of shit. He'd known she was a thoroughbred when he met her, but his lady had to be respectable also. If he hadn't tamed Portia's wild ass by now, he would set her free.

Now she was at his house. His original plan had been to move her into an apartment, but they'd moved too fast. She still had her apartment, so if he cut her off, she would be okay because she had a job. But Jay couldn't front: Portia had him spoiled. He was used to sleeping with her every night. It was nice to be able to roll over and hit something first thing in the morning, but it wasn't just the sex. She was good for a lot of things, and they had become good friends. Jay discussed things with Portia he'd never considered opening up to a girlfriend about. They had a whole lot in common, and even their differences seemed compatible. He loved her, but he had to stay away from her for a few days. It was time to go out of town to collect. If she disappeared while he was gone, he would know she was lying.

His cell phone rang. He looked at the caller ID. It was his baby mama calling. "What up, Stacy? Is my son okay?"

"Jayquan is fine. I need more money, Jay. You slackin'."

"Here you go. How am I slacking? I take care of my son. I know he got everything he need, 'cause I buy it for him. Food, clothes, sneakers, boots, socks, under-wear, toys, his computer, games, school supplies, *and* I take him to the barbershop. You don't gotta buy shit. Plus, I throw you a buck-fifty a week for your pockets. What are you talking about?"

"Like I said, I need more money. I have bills. You got the easy part. I'm the one struggling with your son, and I need money."

"After we broke up, I offered to set you up in a crib, and you acted stupid. Remember? Your car is paid for, and I paid your insurance up for a year. You chose to have whatever bills you crying about. You wanted to play high post, and now you calling me talkin' 'bout you need bill money. You got a job. You make money. And where's that nigga Tony at? He ain't helping you with shit?"

"Don't worry about Tony. You need to worry about Jayquan, because if you don't start coughing up, you won't be seeing him anymore. You got bitches living with you and shit. And driving your fuckin' truck. If you can take care of that bitch, you can help take care of your son!"

Jay knew she had an angle. She must've seen Portia somewhere with his truck. He stayed calm. "Why you worried about who drives my truck? What is this phone call *really* about, Stacy? Didn't I tell you don't call me with this stupid shit no more? Threaten me about not seeing my son one more time. If you can't take care of him, he can live with me. I told you that a million times. I'm not fuckin' you anymore, and I'm not obligated to pay your bills. I take care of my son. That's it."

"You black mothafucka! How dare you just fuckin' brush me off when I call you about your son. Who the fuck do you think you are? That black bitch must got your head swollen. Don't fuck with me, Jay, 'cause I'll have the last laugh. You know!"

"Stacy, you should know by now that all that rah-rah shit don't faze me. That's not the way to get something outta me. That's why you're being sanctioned now. Because you run your mouth too fuckin' much. Grow up, Stacy. It's not all about you. Call me when you're ready to have an adult conversation. Kiss my son for me." *Click.*

Stacy stared at the receiver and wished she could jump through the phone. He'd hung up on her again. She hated when Jay pulled that nonchalant shit. She hated to admit it, but he was right. She did know that Jay hated that ghetto shit, and it wasn't the way to get something out of him. She was pissed because she'd ridden down his block and seen some dark-skinned bitch parking his truck. Then the bitch hopped out with some shopping bags and sashayed upstairs like she was the shit.

Stacy was tempted to go after her, but she didn't want Jay to think she still gave a fuck about him. She didn't want that black piece of shit anymore. But that didn't mean she wanted some other bitch to have him. She would further investigate this new bitch in Jay's life. It wouldn't be hard, because she had eyes everywhere. As a matter of fact, her homegirl Maisha lived up the block from Jay and probably knew something. Stacy would give her a call later. Jay's bitch thought she had it going on, but Stacy was going to burst her bubble. If Jay couldn't make her happy, damn if she was going to let him treat that black bitch like a queen.

SATURDAY MORNING, PORTIA gave Macy and Pebbles their baths and got them dressed early. They were settling down for a breakfast of Lucky Charms and orange juice when Laila called at eleven and said Khalil was on his way to pick up the kids, so Portia would have time to get ready for girls' night out.

Portia had enjoyed keeping Pebbles and Macy. They'd gone to the movies, the arcade, and then to Captain D's for seafood. The girls had been exhausted when they got in after eleven o'clock. Pebbles was afraid of the dark, so Portia left a lamp on in one of the guest rooms, and they slept like logs. Portia tossed and turned all night because Jay didn't come home or answer her calls.

The girls finished their cereal and were watching cartoons in the den when the doorbell rang. Portia peeked out the peephole. It was Khalil, all right. She let him in, feeling slightly awkward because she hadn't seen him since the night before she went to the clinic and got the abortion.

"Hey, Khalil. How you doing?" She didn't want to act all stiff in front of the kids.

"I'm good, Portia. How 'bout you? You been taking care of yourself?" He looked at her with genuine concern.

She relaxed a little. "Yeah, I'm fine."

Neither of them spoke for a few seconds. Khalil looked at her stomach, so Portia crossed her arms. He tried to cover up what he was thinking. "You lost some weight. You on a diet?"

"Not really. Just watching what I eat. Trying to stay healthy, you know."

"No doubt. We only get one body a lifetime."

Portia nodded. "Well, let me go get the girls' stuff. I'll be right back. Have a seat." She motioned to the couch.

When Portia came back downstairs, Khalil stood up, and she handed him their overnight bags. He said, "Oh yeah, Laila told me about your new job. Congratulations, girl! Do the damn thing."

Portia grinned. "Thanks, Khalil. The kids and I had a lot of fun last night."

As if on cue, Pebbles ran into the living room. "Daddy!" She ran over and hugged Khalil. He picked her up and tossed her in the air. Pebbles loved to play rough. Macy overheard the commotion and greeted Khalil with the same enthusiasm. The love between father and daughters was apparent.

Khalil said to them, "Thank Auntie Portia for keeping y'all." They ran over and hugged Portia. Macy said, "We had so much fun. When you gonna come and get us again?" Pebbles said, "Yeah, when we coming back?"

Portia grinned and hugged them. "Soon. I promise. Give me some kisses. I love you two so much! Be good, girls, okay?"

"We will. Love you. Bye!" They headed down the stairs behind their daddy.

Khalil turned around and said, "Take care, Portia."

Portia nodded and smiled. When she stepped back inside, the house's emptiness engulfed her, and the desolation was unbearable. She dialed Jay's cell number again, to no avail. He still wasn't taking her calls. Her hopes fell once more. Where was he? He could've called to let her know he was alive. Portia hated feeling so powerless.

She settled onto the couch and planned her schedule for the day. She had to go to the beauty parlor and the nail salon, and then she was taking a hot bath in the Jacuzzi and getting ready for the evening. She was glad she and her girls had plans, because she really needed to get out of the house. Sitting around brooding wasn't helping the situation. She just had to reinforce Jay's trust in their relationship. This time would be a bigger challenge than the first time.

Later on that day, Portia left the nail salon and strolled downtown Brooklyn. She passed the Ink Spot, where she got her navel piercing and tattoos done. When she reached the corner of Fulton and Duffield, she did an about-face. Portia knew she was going out on a limb, but love drove her to act on impulse. She headed to the rear of Fulton Jewelry and down the stairs, where Big José ran his business. His girlfriend and partner, Marisol, was there too. Portia was glad because Marisol had José's name tattooed on her leg, her chest, and God knew where else. She greeted the couple, and they looked happy to see her.

"Long time no see, mommy," Marisol said in her

heavy Puerto Rican accent. "What can we do for you today?"

Marisol looked slimmer since Portia had seen her last, so she complimented her. "Mari, you lost some weight. You look good, girl."

Marisol beamed. "Thank you, mami. Everybody notice but him." She nodded at José. "He doesn't notice nothing. I come here to work naked with tube socks, and he still no say nothing." She laughed at her own joke, and Portia joined her.

"You know how men are, Mari. But you can't help but love them mothafuckas. I came to get a tattoo. I want my man's name on my bootie, but I want it spiced up. Maybe with a little Cupid or something. What do you think?"

"Mami, come with me. I go to show you something perfect!" Marisol headed for a booth in the back, and Portia followed.

An hour later, she was lounging at home in a thong, with gauze taped over her latest body art. She couldn't wait to show Jay how much she really loved him. He would think she was nuts, but it proved that she belonged to him only. Either that or he would think she was obsessed with him. And she sort of was, but fuck it.

Laila pulled up around nine and hopped out of the Escalade. She looked terrific in a tawny-colored, low-cut Christian Dior one-piece, bad-assed tan Dior open-toes, and a matching Dior bag and belt. Her hair hung down her back in a long wrap, and she wore a pair of toast-colored Christian Dior shades on top of her head. Portia came out with cute spiral curls in her hair, looking scrumptious in a sky-blue Chanel flare-skirted sundress, blue-tinted signature Chanel glasses, with a sky-blue Chanel purse and matching ankle-strapped stilettos. They nodded approval at each other's outfits. That was how they always did it—"give niggas a heart attack" style. They were both showing a lot of skin and curves, and it was high-fashion time.

Laila said Simone and Fatima were meeting them at the pier because they'd caught a ride with her cousin Rizzo. She cracked up when Portia told her she'd tattooed Jay's name on her ass.

Portia drove her car, because if she got in touch with Jay, she was flat-leaving them before the boat sailed. Laila pulled off and put the plan into effect, and Portia tailed behind.

JAY AND CAS had caught a red-eye from Virginia and were en route to New York. They were scheduled to arrive at La Guardia at ten to midnight. Jay had taken Casino's advice. They were going to the party that he'd paid for.

ACROSS TOWN, STACY was getting ready for her usual Saturday-night outing at Club Cheetahs. She was still heated with Jay and working on her plan to keep him miserable for the rest of his life. Maisha had told her that Jay was serious about that bitch; she was always at his house even when he wasn't. Stacy suggested she and Maisha hang out that night. Up to one of her schemes as usual, Stacy needed a reason to be in Jay's neighborhood. Plus, she needed a spy, so she had to get buddy-buddy with Maisha again.

Stacy dialed Maisha's cell phone to remind her to

pick up beer from the store on the way over. Maisha's voice mail picked up, so she left a message: "Yo, Mai, this is Stacy. Don't forget to bring me two Heinekens. Don't worry, I'll reimburse you. And don't forget the straws. I'm getting dressed. Hurry up, Mai. One." Stacy wanted to get her buzz on before they went to the club. The night was young, and with Jayquan at her mother's house for the weekend, as usual, she was ready for action.

Maisha heard the phone beep, but she didn't answer it because she was talking to Wings on her other line. They'd been kicking it off and on for a few years, since she was sixteen. Wing had a wife, but Maisha was sort of his mistress. Wings had casually mentioned that his man was throwing a party for his girlfriend that night at his sports bar. He said he wanted to get up with her later, so she should come through when she was finished with whatever she had planned.

Maisha made a note to end her evening early, no matter what Stacy said. Her boo Wings was her priority. Their relationship was one of understanding. She knew Wings's home situation, and she played her position as mistress well. She was always ready and willing to meet his demands.

It wasn't all for nothing, because Wings was crazy generous and treated Maisha like a queen. As long as she went to school, he looked out for her and provided everything she wished for. He gave her everything except time; she wished he could spend more time with her. Still, she treasured what time they did share, and she didn't nag him because it wasn't her place. That was for his wife. Maisha was his comfort zone and wished to remain so. She would dead their affair only at his request, and even then she couldn't let it go that easy. She felt like she'd put in enough time with Wings to stake a claim.

Aggravated, Stacy dialed Maisha's number once more. She was dressed and ready to roll, and Mai was running late. If she didn't hurry, they'd wind up paying the cover at the club, and Stacy wasn't trying to hear that.

Maisha answered this time. "Hello?"

Stacy tried to stay calm. "It's after ten o'clock! *Hello?* Where you at? We get in free before eleven. After that, it cost a dub. Where the fuck are you at, Mai?"

"Girl, please. I'm not about to break my damn neck trying to save no twenty dollars. Save that for them birds. I'll be there in a little while. I'm 'bout to go to the store. Chill, Stacy."

Maisha hated getting to clubs all early, trying to get in free like some chicken-head. Stacy was out of her mind if she thought Maisha was going out like that. She preferred to make her grand entrance after midnight, hair swinging and hips sashaying. Maisha remembered her commitment with Wings later on. Stacy's ass was lucky this time. They could leave early so they could go ahead and get the night over with. Maisha wasn't that into clubbing anyway.

Quite the opposite, Stacy was a straight-up club head, and she was pissed at Maisha's nonchalant brush-off. Stacy didn't pay to get into clubs. Or buy drinks. She left that up to the ballers and high rollers. "Can you *please* hurry up, Maisha? Matter of fact, where you at? I'll just pick you up, and we can roll out."

"All right, fuck it. I ain't gon' front, I'm still at home. But don't worry, I'm already dressed. I'm doing my hair, so come on. Call me when you get downstairs."

"A'ight. I'm on my way." Stacy grabbed her keys and her purse.

LAILA PULLED UP in front of a sports bar and got out. She walked over and leaned in Portia's car window. "Park and let's go in here and get a drink first, P. It'll probably be a lot cheaper than drinks on the cruise."

"Laila, you're not usually that cheap. I'll pay for your drinks, damn. Come on, before we miss the boat. Tima and Mone gon' kill us if they sail without us. It's probably mad crowded in this sports bar. Look at all these cars. It'll probably take us an hour just to get served. Laila, let's go!"

Laila was adamant. "Come on, it won't take that long." She dialed Fatima's celly and gave her the cue. "What's up, Tima? We're on our way. Word? Okay, just hold our spot." She hung up and said, "See, Portia. Tima said take our time. Half of the people ain't even boarded yet."

Portia shook her head, but she parked and followed her bossy little friend to the door. After security scanned them and checked their purses, they headed inside. Portia didn't see the doorman wink at Laila. He knew what time it was.

It was darker inside than Portia thought was normal, and she felt an uncomfortable vibe. "Laila!" she whispered. "It's too dark in here. And ain't even no music playing. I got a bad feeling. This shit is kind of spooky. Yo, let's get the fuck outta here, Lay!"

Laila boldly grabbed Portia's arm and moved toward the darkness. Portia didn't think now was the time for Laila to be so courageous, because she had a real bad case of the creeps. Maybe she was paranoid from the half-blunt she smoked on the way, but she began to think of horror movies, and her heartbeat sped up. She snatched her hand back from Laila's, and Laila laughed at her. Portia was scared for real now.

Suddenly, lights flashed on and people appeared. "*Surprise!*" they yelled. Portia jumped—they'd scared the hell out of her. But when she realized all those people were yelling at her, she was happy. Oh, shit, Simone and Fatima were right there. There were Patty-cake and Aunt Gracie, and her cousin Melanie was filming with a camcorder. There were her old friends Neicy and Kisha. Portia couldn't believe it. It wasn't her birthday, so what was the surprise for?

Laila finally told her. "This party is to celebrate your new lifestyle and job. Me, Mone, and Tima planned it, but Jay paid for *everything*."

Portia's eyes watered up. She group-hugged her girls and then went around greeting people. First she hugged her mother and her aunt, then all of her cousins, friends, and extended family. There were people she hadn't seen in years. Everyone was there except Jay. Portia kept high spirits and prayed he'd show up soon.

CASINO AND JAY had a quick flight. They'd both suffered from lack of sleep the last few days, so they dozed off. It seemed like only seconds passed before the pilot announced their arrival at La Guardia Airport.

Keeping a low profile, they quickly collected their bags and hailed a cab. In under an hour, money was stashed, burners were collected, and they were back on the avenue in Brooklyn, hollering at Wise and B.J. The partners were content because Wise made sure B.J. and them stayed on top of business, so all of the paper was straight.

It was a warm summer night, and the corner was packed. The corner was a ghetto forum where uncensored ideas and free expression flowed freely, and everyone from atheists and alcoholics to thieves and thugs was welcome to the open discussion. A heated debate could arise at any given time on the corner, with topics ranging from "Who's the nicest emcee, Jigga or Nas?" to "Are they ever going to capture bin Laden?" Tonight the debate at hand was religious—Christianity versus Islam. The men were civilized but very loud and opinionated. That's the way it was when birds of a feather flocked.

Nate came through and tried to get a dice game started up. Jay was tempted, but Cas reminded him about the party for his wiz. When niggas heard that, they all wanted to roll; they knew there was sure to be plenty pussy. Plus, Jay said the bar was free all night. The homies ran into some of their peoples from Brownsville on the way, so five cars deep, the men were bound for Jay's wifey's party.

CLUB CHEETAHS HAD been packed, and the heat inside was Maisha's excuse to vacate the joint. She wasn't interested in any of the guys at the club who'd tried to holler. Stacy said she'd acted like a stuck-up bitch.

Maisha hadn't meant to, but she was preoccupied with thoughts of Wings from jump. She just didn't feel like meeting any new guys. She had something she'd worked on for a long time, and she didn't want to avert her attention. She was ready to go see Wings. Stacy complained about leaving so early but agreed that it was too hot in the club.

Maisha gave her directions to the sports bar. "It's gon' be mad ballers there. I'm telling you. Let's roll, Stace."

"A'ight. Let's do the damn thing." Stacy giggled. She was real tipsy, and she swerved when she pulled off.

"Stacy! You all right? You want me to drive?" Maisha hadn't drunk as much as Stacy had, and she wanted to get to Wings in one piece.

"Nah, Mai. I'm good. I got this." Stacy laughed and headed for the Manhattan Bridge.

MAYBE IT WAS twisted fate or perhaps plain old coincidence that would place Stacy at Portia's surprise party. However, when the two collided, there was drama for your ass.

Maisha found out who the evening's honoree was when she ran into Kisha, a girl she used to go to school with. They hugged each other, and Kisha said, "Hey, girl, how you been? I didn't know you knew Portia. It's a small world. I ain't seen you in eons, and look how we both wound up at her party! Jay is a sweetheart, throwing her a gala like this, right?"

Maisha put two and two together and realized that she'd fucked up by bringing Stacy with her. Stacy had just finished talking about how she couldn't stand Jay, and now she was at a party he was throwing for his girlfriend, whom Stacy hated before she'd even met.

Maisha knew Stacy had seen Portia before and would recognize her and probably spaz out. She decided to be direct. "Look, I'ma tell you now. I just found out that this party is for Jay's girlfriend. We can leave right now if you want. What you wanna do?"

Stacy was shocked but disguised it well. "You crazy? I ain't leaving. Fuck Jay and his bitch. I might just get wit' one of his mans tonight. Matter of fact, that's what I'ma do. I'ma fuck with one of his friends. Watch."

"Okay. Just don't do no crazy shit, 'cause I'ma tell you now, I ain't no fighter. You'll be on your own."

Maisha wasn't about to turn Wings off with no stupid shit. In fact, she should go and tell him now. "Stacy, I'll be right back. Let me go holla at my boo for a second."

"Go 'head. I'ma go use the bathroom," Stacy lied. She just had to see that bitch Portia. She went off to look for trouble.

Maisha located Wings. "Baby, I kind of messed up. Stacy is here with me."

Wings grabbed Maisha around the waist and pulled her to him. "So? We can drop her off later or put her in a cab."

He obviously didn't know who Stacy was. "Baby, Stacy is Jay's baby mother. And she's kind of bitter."

Wings's expression said he understood now. No wonder Maisha was looking all dumb in the face.

Maisha continued, "If I knew who was throwing the party, I wouldn't have brung her. I'm sorry, baby. I just wanted to let you know ahead of time, in case something jumped off. But I already warned Stacy not to act stupid."

Now Wings knew she hadn't intentionally brought drama to his establishment. He raised an eyebrow. "You think shorty gon' wild out?"

"I hope not. She better not."

"Well, this nigga Jay ain't even here yet, so I hope not too. I'm not try'na have no physical confrontation with his baby moms, but if she act up, she got to go. I'd hate to have my security throw her out. Damn, man. Go find her. Control your friend, man."

Just then, Wings spotted Jay coming through the door, followed by Casino, Wise, Nate, and B.J. Then two cool cats from Brownsville, Lloyd and Black, came in behind them. Wings caught Jay's attention, and Jay headed his way.

The men greeted each other with a pound. Wings was jovial. "This nigga roll up in the joint 'bout two in the morning. What's crackin', man?" Wings gave all of his peoples a pound and a man hug and told his bartender to hook them up. Then he came back to Jay. "Son, you *may* have an unwanted guest." Wings gave him the rundown on Stacy.

Jay looked unhappy about the news. "Fuck is she doing here? How'd she find out?"

STACY SPOTTED PORTIA in a group of girls coming from the bathroom. She walked past and bumped her real hard and kept going without saying "excuse me."

Whoever that bitch was, she was very rude, and Portia was offended, so she turned and called her. "Hello? Girlfriend?"

This freckle-faced, light-skinned chick looked back with her face all screwed up. Portia didn't know who she was—there wasn't a single picture of Stacy in Jay's house—but she sure looked unapologetic.

Portia reacted accordingly and checked her. "You invaded my space. The words are *'excuse me.'* Watch where you goin'." Then she blew it off and kept going because she was tipsy from too much champagne and felt lighthearted. She was unperturbed because it was her night, and she knew her girls were on point. They watched out for one another like that.

Stacy approached her and demanded, "Yo, what's your name?"

Portia fired back, "You up in *my* party, so you *obviously* know me." She didn't like the vibe she was getting from this hoe. She was trying to come off hard. Portia suspected that it had something to do with Jay. "What's *your* name? And why did you bump me? Do we have a problem?"

"Yes, there's a problem! I just don't like you. I'm Stacy, Jay's son's mother. I'm *sure* you've heard about me."

Portia didn't miss a beat. "Actually, Stacy, Jay doesn't talk about you at all. I never even heard your name."

"Well, you better remember my name, 'cause *I'm* the only important bitch in Jay's life. We got strong ties together, so you shouldn't bank on him too much. He's just using you. Like a little black maid."

Portia laughed in her face. "You're just jealous. But get used to it, Stacy. I'm Jay's queen. I know you heard. That's why you came here so mad."

This bitch's confidence was really starting to irk Stacy. "What, bitch? Your black ass ain't no fuckin' queen. You sound stupid. Bitch, you ain't nothin'!"

Portia was cool, calm, and collected. "I'm Jay's wife, *bitch*. You washed up, and you ain't got no class. No wonder Jay don't want your low-budget ass. Now it would behoove you to get out my mothafuckin' face."

Stacy's ghetto inner child prevailed, and she got real loud. "You black bitch! I don't want Jay, you can have his ass. He just use bitches like you to suck his dick—"

Portia cut her off right there. "Trash-assed, piss-colored hoe bitch, you must be crazy, disrespecting me at my party. I'll slap the shit outta you and have you escorted the fuck out of here! This is *my* night. *I'm* the queen up in here, and Jay paid for *all* of this. For his wife! Portia! Don't get shit twisted, bitch! You gon' respect me at my party."

"Who the fuck you think you is? You just as stupid as you is black. Bitch, I'll fuck you up in this mothafucka!" Stacy lunged forward but was stopped dead in her tracks by Portia's ice-grilled friends.

"Calm down! Fall back, sweetheart. It ain't gon' be none of that," Fatima said.

Big-bellied Simone stood right beside them, Cristal bottle in hand. If Stacy made a move, she'd bust her head to the white meat. Plus, Simone was strapped, and she wouldn't hesitate to go in her Prada bag if she had to. "About-face, bitch. Just let it go while you ahead," Simone threatened.

"Word. You better pipe down, rusty," added Laila. "Because you not gon' fuck up my sister night. And I don't recall your name being on the guest list, so you need to get up outta here."

Portia knew they wouldn't falter, because she'd do the same for them in a fraction of a heartbeat. They were so close that they reacted automatically to protect one another, without thinking, even. Portia kept her cool. "Let that bitch go. She ain't crazy. She's just the new president of my fan club. Stacy, Jay loves chocolate now. Kick rocks, hoe."

Stacy wanted to fight but realized the odds were against her, so she turned the violence down a little.

That scary bitch Maisha was avoiding eye contact, so it was clear she was neutral and wasn't going to help if those bitches jumped her. They couldn't shut Stacy's mouth, though. She went off. "Fuckin' tar baby, you wish you was chocolate. You ain't got shit up on me, hoe! Jay *always* gon' be in my life, 'cause I got his son. We'll see who the fuck be around the longest. I guarantee you, bitch! You will see!"

"The old me would've whipped your ass on GP, but I don't catfight with birds no more. I'm a lady, and I don't have time for this shit. Get out my face, bitch. You're dismissed." Portia waved her hand as if Stacy bored her. She was glad her mother and aunt had gone home before all this drama started.

Stacy stomped her foot in rage. "Bitch, that's my word! I'ma see you. That's word on my son and everything I love. I'ma see you!"

"Be careful what you wish for, you bum-assed bitch. 'Cause you really might fuckin' see me!" After that, Portia walked away. When she turned the corner, she bumped right into Jay. Her face lit up, and she hugged him immediately.

Jay asked, "What's goin' on, Ma?" Portia didn't look upset, but he knew there was commotion, because Wise pulled his coat.

Portia said, "Your ghetto-assed baby moth—"

Stacy turned the corner before she could finish. The women's reception of Jay was like night and day. Portia had greeted him with dreamy eyes and a warm smile, but Stacy's glare was subzero, and her eyes were like deadly daggers of ice aimed at his head. Spotlight was on him.

Stacy went off. "Mothafucka, you better keep your bitch in line! You mean to tell me you can't take care of my son, and you throwing bitches birthday parties and shit? And you ain't even doing what you 'posed to do for your son?"

Casino and Wise were trying hard as hell not to laugh. If Portia and Stacy locked up, they would help break it up, but they stood back, amused, for the time being. They had to see how Jay handled this shit. On the low, most of the guys there wished the girls would just go ahead and throw down, because somebody's titty was bound to pop out in a chick fight.

When it first jumped off, Wise was by the bathroom, trying to holler at Portia's easy-looking cousin Melanie. He was pleased when Portia and her girls were about to whip Stacy's ass, because Stacy was out of line. Portia's girls held her down, and Wise was impressed by how ladylike they handled it. He couldn't stand Stacy's stuck-up ghetto ass, and he would've loved to see her get her ass beat, but on the strength of her being his man's baby moms, he let Jay know they were about to scrap. Portia's whole crew was dimes, but the thick brown-skinned one could get it, boy. She had a nice set of knockers.

Jay said, "Shut up and stop acting stupid, Stacy. Don't fuckin' play with me! You know I take care of my son. Stop making a scene wit' all this drama shit."

"You done lost your mothafuckin' mind, nigga. This shit ain't over, you hear me? You gonna pay for this shit! You better let that bitch know who the fuck I am!"

Jay didn't even raise his voice. "Calm the fuck down. You outta line, Stacy! What you doing here, anyway?

You ain't even supposed to be here, so you upset yourself."

Stacy boosted up the drama, cursing louder and louder. Portia couldn't believe that bitch was yelling all up in her man's face. By now, the whole club was watching them. Portia told Jay, "Baby, any other bitch would be slapped by now for disrespecting you like this, but I know this your baby mama, so it's *your* call. Say the word, and I'll stomp a mudhole in this low-budget bitch *right now* for you. Let me handle this shit, Jay."

Ninety-eight percent of him wanted Portia to bust Stacy's ass, but Jay just shook his head. "Nah, Ma. I got it. I'll be right back. Stay inside, man." He knew Portia wanted to follow him outside and put it on Stacy. Jay wished she could, but he knew Stacy would use Jayquan to punish him for it.

Portia said, "Yeah baby, go 'head and eliminate this problem so we can enjoy our evening. This bitch is violating my space." She aimed the last words right at Stacy.

Stacy made a move, but Jay grabbed her before she could touch Portia. She violently swung on him, so he snatched her up and carried her toward the exit, kicking and cursing. Jay tried to handle it like a man because she was the mother of his son, but he wanted to choke the shit out of her stupid ass and throw her out of a fucking window. She always had to start some drama. Jay wasn't with that bullshit.

When he got Stacy outside and restrained, he tried the impossible task of reasoning with her. "Calm down, Stacia. What's the matter with you? We got a son together. We supposed to be bigger than this. What's with all this public shit?"

"Jay, you just a foul-assed nigga. I'ma have the last laugh. Watch. You messed up putting that bitch before me and Jayquan. I'ma fix your black ass."

Jay let her go. He was so tired of this shit. "You know, this is getting so old. You stay comin' at me with that bullshit. Stacy, I take care of my son, and that should be your only concern. We're not together anymore, and you shouldn't be worrying about my personal affairs. I do right by my boy, and that's all you should be stressing. Where'd all this extra shit come from? I'm curious. What you got up your sleeve?"

"Mothafucka, if Stacy ain't fuckin' happy, then ain't nobody gon' be happy!"

"What, you want some attention? I *see* you, Stacia. I fuckin' see you!"

"Eat outta my asshole, nigga!"

Jay shook his head in disgust. "You got a nasty mouth. You were never a lady, Stacia. That's why I don't fuck with you now, 'cause you ain't got no class."

"What, mothafucka? You think that bitch is better than me? You ain't got shit, Jay! Fuck both of y'all black mothafuckas. I'll whip that bitch ass! Matter of fact, I'ma beat her ass right now!" She started for the club door.

"Go up in Portia face again if you want to. You gon' make yourself look real stupid getting stomped out. She ain't with all that drama like you, but she ain't no punk. You better chill, Stacy. I'm telling you."

"Nigga, I'll kill that bitch and you too! I should get you smoked for this shit."

Jay clenched his teeth. That bitch was going too far. "You threatening me, Stacy? You better watch your mothafuckin' mouth!"

Stacy did know how far to go. She piped down and glared at Jay.

"Go home, man. As a matter of fact, come on. I'm taking you home, 'cause you're too upset to be driving." Not that he wanted to be around her dumb ass, but he was afraid she might kill herself in the state she was in. To Jay, an emotional woman behind the wheel was the equivalent of a drunk driver. Stacy had his son, and he already knew she wasn't a cautious driver. Not even when she wasn't upset about anything.

"I don't need you to take me no fuckin' where! I got a Benz, nigga! I can go wherever the fuck I wanna go!"

"I know you got a Benz. I bought it, remember? Knock it off and stop acting so hostile, Stacy. Let's act like adults for once."

Stacy stopped breaking and crossed her arms. "You wrong, Jay."

"How am I wrong?"

Jay was being patient and humble, as usual. Stacy hated that about him. She'd rather get under his skin and dig a reaction out of his ass. Now she felt defeated.

"Fuck you, Jay. Go back in there with your bitch and enjoy your little party. Rot in hell, nigga. Just stay out of me and Jayquan's lives. As a matter of fact, give me some money, because my son needs things." She held out her hand.

Jay just wanted to get rid of her, so he peeled off some C-notes and threw them at her. The money landed on the ground. Satisfied, Stacy picked it up and started talking shit again. "And wait until I catch one of your peoples out here. I'ma fuck his brains out on GP. You'll hear all about it, you bastard." She gave Jay an evil grin and walked to her car with her head held high.

After she said that, Jay doubted he'd have tried to save that stupid bitch if a speeding car turned the corner and hit her. He waited until she pulled off before going back inside.

Jay didn't know that Stacy wasn't going home just yet. After a few minutes, she doubled back to vandalize Portia's Lincoln. She used a knife to slash the tires, and she keyed the car with no mercy. Then she got a hammer from her trunk and tried to bust the windshield. She hit it twice, but it wouldn't give, so she swung at the front driver's-side window, which broke on the first impact. Extra satisfied, Stacy crept to her car and pulled off, giggling hysterically.

Inside, the party had shifted back into fifth gear. Though Portia mingled, she kept an eye on the door. She wanted to go out there, but Cas stopped her and told her that Stacy wasn't on her level and wasn't worth messing up her pretty outfit for.

Laila and Fatima, the hostesses of the party, directed Jay's people to the open bar and hot buffet. Everybody was getting their drink on, and the deejay was playing R&B and oldies.

Jay finally came back in, and Portia was relieved. He stopped to let his mans know everything was cool, and he must've asked about her, because Wise pointed her way. Jay came around to her side of the bar.

"Hi, handsome. Let me buy you a drink. Your girlfriend won't mind." Portia gave him the sexy eye.

He played along. "What she don't know won't hurt her."

"Crown? Straight?"

"Make it a double, Ma."

"I'm on it, boo." Portia summoned the bartender and ordered their drinks. "Let me get a double shot of Crown Royal and a Rémy Martin and Coke on the rocks with two cherries."

Jay laughed. "Cherries in cognac? If you wanted a girly drink, you should've ordered a daiquiri or a margarita."

"Shut up, Jay. I know what I'm doing. You all right?"

"Yeah. You?"

"I'm good. Now that you're here." She slipped her hand into his.

After they tossed their drinks back, Jay ordered three bottles of Cristal. Portia gathered their close friends and proposed a toast to love, friends, and the pursuit of success. She thanked Jay and kissed him, and then she thanked everyone else for coming and ordered the party back into full swing.

Everyone appeared to be having a good time. Jay was feeling good now too, with his lady by his side. He looked around at his mans, getting hammered and laying their mack down. They were starting to pair off with chicks. It looked like Wise was infatuated with Fatima, because he was all over her. Casino had Laila cornered by the bar, finessing her, and she was giggling and flirting right back. Usually stony-grilled Nate was smiling and appeared intrigued by Simone's gray eyes while they conversed in a booth. Wings's PYT, Maisha, was sitting on his lap, Lloyd and Black were pressing a set of identical twins, and B.J. had discovered Melanie, with her butt cheeks hanging out of her too-small white shorts.

Jay was pleased when they all started heading to the dance floor. The liqs and champagne had them feeling no pain, and there was no shame in none of their game. Jay stood back, amused. Next thing he knew, Portia had him out there too. He didn't have to do much, because shorty was throwing it on him, giving him plenty of eye contact. With her hair curled real wild and sexy, and in that blue Chanel getup, she looked sweeter than candy. Wait until he got her home later.

The deejay was rocking all the R&B oldies. He played jam after jam, like "Ooh and I Like It," "Before I Let Go," "Fools' Paradise," and "Mary Jane." Portia sang along and danced her ass off. She looked around for her girls; the party was jumping. She saw Laila throwing it on Casino, Fatima backing it up on Wise, and even Simone hooping with Nate. That was what you called a real party. Portia couldn't have been happier. To her far left, she saw that two of Jay's friends had Melanie in a sandwich in the corner, and she was freaking both of them. Portia hoped Mel's drunk ass wouldn't embarrass her that night by messing with half of Jay's crew.

The deejay switched to slow jams, and when "Feelin' on Yo Booty" played, Portia damn near gave Jay a lap dance. She was grinding on him, and he palmed her ass and loved it. She couldn't wait to show him her tattoo when they got home.

A little later, Fatima suggested they cut the cake because it was already five in the morning and time to call it a wrap. After they handed out cake slices, people fixed themselves plates and headed on home. All of the guys who came with Jay spread mad love and gave Portia money for the occasion before they left.

Everybody who went outside noticed the aftermath of Stacy's revenge on Portia's car, and people began to whisper. Nate peeped it and nudged Cas, who went back inside to quietly inform Jay that his stupid-assed baby mama had flipped the script again. Together, they went out and checked out the damage before Portia came out.

That shit had Stacy written all over it, no questions asked. Jay didn't want Portia to flip, so he hurried back inside to catch her before she and her circle came out. He caught her right at the door and blocked her path. He was direct. "Listen, Ma, don't get upset. Stacy fucked up your car, but don't worry about it, 'cause I'ma get you another one. Okay?"

Portia couldn't believe him. But Jay looked dead serious. "That bitch did what?"

"Please, Ma. Don't get upset and wild out, 'cause it's mad people outside waiting for you to react. Trust me. Don't let this faze you, Ma. I got you. I'ma make it up to you. That's my word. Go get the truck and pull around front. I'll be ready in a minute." He pressed his keys into her palm.

Tima, Mone, and Laila were pissed, but they agreed with Jay. Stacy was long gone, so getting upset right now wouldn't solve anything. They went outside, and Portia ignored the onlookers' stares and played it cool, but they vowed to get that bitch Stacy if Jay didn't make it right.

Laila's phone rang. It was her husband, and she told him she was on her way. She hung up and rolled her eyes, then said her goodbyes and took her ass home. Portia offered to drop Fatima and Simone off, but they declined. Fatima said she was riding with Wise, and Simone said Nate had offered to take her to breakfast. Portia told them to be careful and call to let her know they were okay. She figured the guys had to be good people, since they were friends of Jay's.

"**P**ORTIA, WE'VE GOT some major cutting to do this fiscal. We've got to minimize our losses, because I'm catching heat like hell from the big dogs. Some of this spending has to be nipped in the bud immediately. Print the expense reports so we can review them."

"Okay, just a second." Portia pulled up the reports, hoping she would finally get a chance to show off her skills. She declined to comment to Charlene now, but on her first day, she'd noticed that some of the company's costs were way too extravagant. She'd mentioned it to Charlene, who had brushed her off and said that the account balances were normal for that line of business. And now she was standing there, telling Portia that corporate felt the same way she did. Ain't that a bitch?

Portia knew accounting in depth and was disappointed to find that her job consisted of such minuscule duties. She hadn't been dumb enough to think she'd be company CFO, but she thought she'd be doing more than reviewing invoices and vouchers. Still, a paycheck was a paycheck, and she was confident that, with her ability, she'd move up fast.

Portia and Charlene spent the entire morning auditing the books and analyzing red areas, and by lunchtime she'd pointed out several of Charlene's errors. By five o'clock, Portia wondered who the hell Charlene had screwed in order to become head of her department. Portia hoped she was having an off day, but she kept her comments to herself; no matter how dense girlfriend was, she still had the power. Portia had been working there for seven weeks, and she wished to remain there under pleasant circumstances.

As soon as she got home from work, Portia kicked off her shoes and dialed Laila. She was eager to drill Laila about some news Jay had given her when she called him on her lunch break. She couldn't believe she had to hear it from him.

"L-Boogie, what's good? Where's Khalil? Can you talk?"

"He's gone. I got the girls, but they're taking a nap. Today I took half a day off from work to take them to the doctor. They got their shots, girl. And it was holler city! Neither one of 'em can stand the sight of a needle. They were breaking before the doctor even touched them, so I had to bribe them with all kinds of shit. My girls are troupers, though. They admitted it didn't even hurt that much, and they promised not to cry next time. We'll see." She and Portia laughed. "So what's crack-a-lackin', P? How's work coming along?"

"Work is fine, but that's not what I called to talk about, miss. As a matter of fact, I'm comin' over. I'm on my way, bitch. Bye." Portia wanted to see Laila's reaction when she asked her.

KIRA DROPPED HER homegirl Jenny off on St. Marks Avenue, and then she rode through Jay's block and saw his Excursion parked in front of his house. She decided to pop up on her big brother because it had been a hot minute since she'd seen him. Plus, she wanted to ask him to lease her an apartment in his building. She and her mother had been having it out a lot lately since she'd taken a semester off from school, and Kira needed some space.

She parked her Maxima behind Jay's truck, jogged up the stairs, and rang the bell. Instead of Jay, some hoe came to the door! Who the hell was she?

Portia was just about to leave for Laila's when the doorbell rang. There was some tall chick at the door. "May I help you?"

The girl stared her up and down like she had a problem. Girlfriend clearly didn't appreciate a woman answering Jay's door, so this had to be some drama. Portia got on point and hoped she wouldn't have to whip any ass in her new Jean Paul Gaultier outfit.

"This is my brother's house," Kira spat. "And you are?"

Portia relaxed because she remembered Jay had said he had two sisters. This was obviously the wild, smart-mouthed nineteen-year-old. Now her attitude didn't alarm Portia; she had to smile because the girl reminded her of herself at that age. She'd thought she was bad too. "I'm Portia, his girlfriend. Hi, Kira. Nice to finally meet you. Come on in. Jay's in the shower."

The girl knew her name, so apparently, her big brother did acknowledge her. Kira went inside the house. She was kind of sorry she'd come off on Portia like that, because she seemed nice. Even more shocking, she was dark-skinned. Jay usually messed with stuck-up, high-yellow hoes whom Kira disliked. Especially that bitch Stacy, her nephew Jayquan's mother. Kira returned Portia's greeting.

"Nice to meet you too. My bad. It's just that Jay never mentioned you, so you threw me off when you answered the door. That nigga don't tell the family nothin'." Wait until Kira told her older sister, Laurie, and Mommy that Jay had a girl. She wondered if Portia lived with him.

Kira realized that she and Portia resembled each other. They had about the same complexion, both wore their hair in long wraps with Chinese bangs, and they each had cute button noses. Portia looked more like Kira than her blood sister did. Kira was just taller, a little slimmer, and had a smaller chest. She peeped Portia's open-toed Guccis and gave it up. "Nice footwear."

"Thank you. Make yourself comfortable, Kira."

Just then, Jay came downstairs, dressed, but he had on slippers and white socks. Portia excused herself so he could talk with his sister privately.

Jay playfully mushed Kira upside the head. "Big-head, what you doin' over here? You must want something, 'cause that's the only time you come around."

Kira patted him on the belly to show that she noticed he was eating good. "I came to get some money, fat boy. What else? Nah, I'm kidding. I miss my brother, *dag*! I can't just come see you? Oh yeah, son! What the fuck is up with your baby mother? I went to get my nephew to take him to Tasha's little girl's birthday party Saturday, and that bitch wouldn't even let him go! Jayquan was like, 'I wanna go with my auntie Kira!' and Stacy said,

'No! We have stuff to do today.' My boo-boo started crying and shit. I wanted to bust that bitch in her face. For real, son. For real." Kira nodded.

Jay shrugged. "She's probably mad at me about something. You know how Stacy is. She's just stupid."

"Hell yeah, that stink bitch. You didn't tell me about your *new girlfriend*. Son, let me find out you're in love."

"There you go. Did I say all that? Don't insinuate shit, Kira."

"She got you open, bro, 'cause she done moved up in here."

Jay didn't deny it so Kira laughed and blurted out, "*Damn!* Girlfriend must have some good shit!"

"Yeah, whatever. Don't go home promoting my business."

"You should know me better than that. But on some real shit, I need my own crib, Jay. Word. Rent me an apartment in your building, son. I'll pay you. Please?"

"Pay me with what, your looks? Won't you take your ass back to school? That's where you need to be. You fuckin' up, Kira. And what about ball? I thought you said you wanted to go to the WNBA. Go back to school. Trust me."

"Look, fuck all that. Can you hook your sister up or what?"

"You're not responsible enough to have your own crib yet, Kira. You don't even have an income. Even if I don't charge you rent, how you gonna pay your bills? You think I'ma do everything? Well, you wrong. If you want some privacy, then stop being so grown and ask Mommy if you can move in the basement. That's an apartment right there. That's where I started out. It's hooked up down there, and that's enough space for you."

Kira kept it real. "Look, I might wanna have some company, and your mother is just too nosy."

"Is that what this is about? You wanna have *boys* laying up with you? Hell, no! I wish I would give you the opportunity to get pregnant. You need to take your ass back to school. Niggas ain't about shit."

Kira wasn't trying to hear that bullshit about no school. She was tired of everybody trying to play her like she was some little kid. She was legally grown and could make her own decisions. And she knew she belonged in the industry, so she was fucking with music. Jay had no idea how nice she was lyrically. Her homeboy Andre had booked her some studio time, and she'd hooked up with her music-producing nephew Dave, who was in school for audio engineering. It wouldn't be long before Kira blew on niggas. That was the reason she'd left school. She was trying to get on, but she knew Jay wouldn't understand. "Yeah, yeah, yeah. Whatever! Yo, let me get some pocket money, bro. I wanna cop them new Jordans. I'm broke as shit."

Jay peeled off three hundred dollars. "I knew that's why you came. I ain't no money tree. If you don't go back to school, I'm cutting you off. I'm dead-assed. You think I'm acting sheisty now. Don't go back. You'll see." He knew he had his baby sister spoiled, but he wasn't kidding this time. He was going to make sure she finished college. He hollered upstairs. "Yo, Portia! Bring me them white-on-white Uptowns out the closet. The new ones in the top box." He bought at least twenty pairs of Nike Air Force Ones a year. The smallest scuff made them old to Jay, and then he just used them for playing basketball or gave them away.

Portia brought down his sneakers, and he quickly laced them up and slipped them on. "I'm on my way out, Kira. Come on, I'll walk you to your car."

"A'ight. What's up with your fine-assed man Casino? You know I'm still in love with that nigga, right?"

Jay mushed her. "Don't get fucked up, Kira! Cas don't want your little young ass no way, so stop being so grown."

"That's what you think. I'ma marry that nigga, watch." Kira rolled her eyes at Jay and jumped in her car. She had Cas's cell number, and she'd called him a few times since she'd been back from Howard. He kept fronting and hit her with some "I take you for a little sister, I watched you grow up" bullshit, but Kira was a fighter. She was going to keep pressing him until he came around. It was that serious.

PORTIA WAS FLOATING on air, courtesy of Jay. She drove to Laila's in the comfort of her new money-green 600 with sunroof and beige butter-leather interior.

When she got there, Laila answered the door, grinning. "If Portia's at my door, it's gon' snow for sure," she teased. "You look snazzy in that new Benz, Miss Lane! I saw you pull up out the window. Work it, bitch!"

Portia walked in, smiling. Then she remembered why she'd come and tried to look stern, with her hand on her hip. "I'll be frank, because you know we don't beat around the bush. You talking to Cas, Laila?"

Girlfriend just burst into a fit of giggles. "Who told you that? Jay?"

"Yes. How do you plead?"

"Guilty like a mo'fucka, girl."

"Ooh, how could you not tell me? Jay just said Cas told him y'all talked on the phone. Y'all hung out yet?"

"Which time?"

"*Which time?* You sneaky bitch! Hold up, y'all met at my party almost two months ago. Let me get this straight, Lay. You having an affair with Casino?"

"Yes, and don't judge me. I'm very much attracted to Caseem, and he treats me like a lady."

"Caseem? That's his real name?"

"Yeah, but I prefer to call him Casino, 'cause I wanna get lucky." She winked at Portia. "Nah, seriously. I'm getting attention from him that I'm not getting from my own husband. Khalil and I barely speak if it's not about the girls. Lately, he don't even touch me no more. We used to do it at least five times a week. Now it's been almost a month. I know there's somebody else, P. I ain't slow. Girl, please. We're up to talking divorce." Laila nodded for reinforcement because Portia looked shocked. "It's getting that bad. And I can't honestly say I want to hold on. Khalil and I got married real young, and I haven't experienced anything else. He was my first and my only, Portia."

"You act like that's a bad thing. That's good, Lay." Portia thought about it and understood somewhat. Then she looked at Laila, kind of puzzled.

"Don't look at me like that. I haven't messed with Cas yet. We just went on three lunch dates. I wanna fuck him *so* bad. But he's a gentleman, and he doesn't pressure me. Plus, he knows my marriage situation." Laila paused and looked down for a few seconds. "Portia, I don't know if he's spitting game or what, but it seems like he's really feeling me." She sighed and rolled her eyes. "I just need this right now, P. Diddy. Even if it remains innocent. Cas makes me feel like a teenager again. I'm all giddy and shit. Marriage can be tiresome, girl. Hell, Khalil has somebody else! Maybe I just need to get this out of my system. I'ma gamble for the first time." She paused to ponder what she'd just said. "Yup, fuck it, P. I wanna fuck the shit outta Cas. He turns me on so much!"

Portia couldn't believe it. She'd never heard Laila talk about any other guy like that except Jay-Z, and that was just a fantasy. She was talking about some real shit this time. Portia sensed danger for her friend. She understood the dilemma, but she didn't want shit to backfire on Laila.

"Girl, just be careful. Not to burst your bubble, bitch, but Khalil will kill you if he finds out. Laila, don't throw your marriage away just for an affair. You have a beautiful family. You're a married woman with two children. Think this one through, boo. Remember, what's good *to* you may not always be what's good *for* you. But I do understand, believe me. Cas *is* a dime."

Laila smiled dreamily. She was acting like a teenager indeed. Portia had to laugh. "Tell you what, Lay. I'ma get some background on this cat. Cas is Jay's right-hand man, so I believe he's straight. But Jay's honest. He'll tell me what type of nigga Cas is. I just don't want you getting too wrapped up if he's only out to hit something."

"Quit being so overprotective. Shit, the way I'm feeling now, a one-night stand might not be so bad. I done made up my mind. He can definitely get it. We're both adults. Portia, just because I haven't been around as much as you have doesn't mean I'm some naive dummy. Besides, sex is healthy. It relieves stress, and I have a lot of that. I'll let you know what goes down. Just don't run your mouth, Porsh."

"Your secret is safe with me." Portia knew she was the last person on earth who should tell somebody what was morally right or wrong. She had so many skeletons in her closet, she'd probably do life in a fed joint if they found the bones. "Laila, did you cook?"

"Yeah, I made spaghetti, cheesy breadsticks, and a garden salad. You hungry?"

"Hell yeah, hook me up a little plate. Don't get outrageous, though. I'm not starving."

"Don't play. Girl, you at home, you know the rules. Help yourself, 'cause you ain't no guest. But wait." Laila reached under the coffee table and pulled out a freshly rolled blunt. "Get your appetite right first."

She lit an incense stick, and she and Portia got high and talked about their love lives. Then they started planning Simone's baby shower, because she was seven and a half months already. They set a date for three weeks later.

TO PORTIA'S SURPRISE, Jay was at home when she got there. Pac's *Makaveli* CD was thumping on the stereo, and Jay was on the couch, playing *The Getaway* on PlayStation II and talking on his cell phone. She greeted him with a kiss, and he raised an eyebrow at her.

Portia went upstairs to change into some sweats and a T-shirt, and she noticed three boxes of Jordans stacked at the foot of the bed. There was a pair for Jayquan, a pair in her size, and a pair for Jay. They were the latest ones, supposed to come out the following week. Jay had a sneaker connection. He always copped kicks before they were released on the street.

Jay came upstairs. "Why you getting home so late? Where you been?"

Portia unsnapped and slid off her bra. "I was at Laila's house. Do you want me to fix you something to eat?"

"Nah, when you took so long, I went and got some fish. It's like three big-assed pieces left. You want some?"

"Nope, I just ate. Thanks for the sneakers, boo. Those are hot." Portia slipped her T-shirt over her head and looked at him funny. "What *you* doin' home so early? I'm happy, but I'm shocked."

Jay smiled. "I should've stayed where I was, 'cause you wasn't here no way. I do have to go back out, though. How was work today, Ma?"

"Work was okay, boo. Jay, can you stay in the house tonight? Please?"

"I'm not gon' be gone long."

"I'm holding you to that. Oh, yeah. What's up with your man Cas?"

"He's a cool dude. Cas been my ace since we was lil' niggas like nine years old. What up with your homie? Ain't she married?"

"Yeah. Is Cas a womanizer?"

Jay laughed. "A womanizer, Portia? Where do you

get this stuff from? Stop watching so many talk shows. Cas is a good dude, man. He don't fake no moves, and most importantly, I respect and give him credit for one thing: He's a money-getting nigga. That's about all I can tell you. You better find some of his ex-chicks to fill you in on all that womanizing stuff." Jay paused. "He did speak very highly of Laila, though. He said he dug her style."

"She digs him too. That's what I'm afraid of. I hope he not just try'na skeet."

Jay laughed again. "Mind your business. They're both grown."

"You're right."

"Your girl Fatima must've put it on Wise, 'cause that nigga been staying at her crib almost every night. She got that nigga open. He said she cooks better than his mama!"

Portia laughed. "Yeah, Tima told me about Wise. She thinks he's real good for her. We did lunch yesterday, and she gave me the rundown."

"Oh yeah! And I found out Nate been messin' with your tall friend. What's her name? Simone?"

"What? You crazy? She's pregnant!"

"Yeah, and? I'm telling you. I know!"

"She would've told me."

"When is the last time you talked to her? Nate said they just started really kicking it like a week ago. He said after the party, she was fronting because of that belly, but he told her he didn't give a fuck about that shit. Now she starts calling him a couple of weeks ago. My man laid his gangsta down, and shorty couldn't help herself."

"I haven't talked to her in a couple of weeks. You might be right. Nate better be careful before Simone throw that pregnant pussy on his ass. You know what they say about pregnant pussy. Isn't that what y'all say?"

"I *am* right, Portia. And what the fuck I care about pregnant pussy? You ain't pregnant."

"True. Damn, let me find out my party was love connection for our friends. I hope your peoples got good intentions. I don't wanna have to put the hut-fut-choo on none of them cats."

"Sit your little ass down, Mighty Mouse. You always talkin' 'bout fighting somebody." Jay playfully yoked her up.

Portia slipped out of his vise and threw up her dukes like a tomboy. "Come on and throw your dick-beaters up, Jay. Let's do this. Brooklyn-style."

Jay laughed at his comical shorty and picked her up in the air. "I ain't gon' fight you, I'ma just body-slam yo' ass."

Portia felt ten feet off the ground. Jay lifted her over his head and spun her around like a propeller. She was afraid of heights and pleaded with him. "Jay, put me down! Please! Aahh! Please put me down, Jay!"

He dropped her on the bed, and she bounced like a rag doll. Jay fell down beside Portia, and they laughed like two third-graders. They were both dizzy, and the room was still spinning.

FATIMA CELEBRATED HER good fortune over a solo lunch in her office. She was feeling lucky this time because her new fine-assed, thugged-out man Wise was the best catch she'd ever had. He was an asset, not a liability, like all her former boyfriends. He paid his own way and provided for her too. When they'd gone out the night before, he'd actually gotten upset when she tried to pay for dinner. He told her not to play him like no chump, and he picked up the check. That was a first for Fatima, and it was refreshing. Her previous mates had expected her to pay for everything. She wasn't a bum magnet anymore. For the first time in her life, she had a good man.

She thought about her past relationships. Thieving, crackhead-assed Larry was first. When she got an apartment at nineteen, he moved in with her for two years, and he stole just about everything in her house that wasn't bolted to the floor. When she confronted him, he told all kinds of bullshit lies to cover his tracks, and then she was forced to run the same unbelievable bullshit by her parents when they came over and questioned why her TV or microwave was missing. They had every reason to be upset too, because they were paying her bills and putting her through school back then. Fatima's father got pissed about having to replace so much shit, and he demanded she get rid of Larry. Good dick had her blind for a while, so she refused. Plus, she felt like Larry needed her for strength. Eventually, she got fed up. Larry got abusive when she spoke up and said she knew it was him robbing her blind and she wanted him the fuck out. He refused to leave in peace, so it took a court order to get rid of him.

When she turned twenty-two, she met insecure, greedy-assed Mike. Two months into their relationship, he moved in and quit his job a week later. After that, their relationship went from sugar to shit. Mike had too much time on his hands and was jealous of everything she did, including hanging with her friends and going to school. Every single day she came home, he would accuse her of fucking around. He was even jealous of what she had. If she came in the house with shopping bags and didn't have anything for him, his selfish ass would destroy her stuff while ranting and raving about her spending unnecessary money on bullshit. As if he'd contributed one copper penny. Fatima started stashing things at her friends' houses, just to keep Mike from messing up her shit. After she found out he was cheating on her—which was after he gave her gonorrhea—she realized what a lunatic and loser his ass really was. She took her girlfriends' advice and put him out a month later.

After Fatima graduated, her parents surprised her with the huge two-bedroom condominium in Clinton Hill that she owned and occupied now. After that, she just played around with men and kept a friend or two. She had a good job and wealthy parents, so she didn't need a man's financial contributions for support. It was more of a physical and emotional thing. It was during those single years that Fatima learned how to deal with men. She used them for sex and didn't mind providing for them; that made her feel like she had the upper hand in the relationship. Fatima liked to call the shots.

So when she met immature, mooching-assed Felony, her most recent ex, she didn't have a problem taking him in and lacing him with hot getup. The clothing was good for his image because he was a struggling rapper trying to get on. The boy was so attractive, Fatima had pushed up on him. And then she stole him from his mama's house and moved him in. All she needed was sex and affection from him, but he was unable to love her on the level she required. He wound up being entirely too much work because she'd been too kind to the bastard. She spoiled him rotten, and he started taking her for granted. That's where he fucked up. The spell of his good looks wore off, and his constant whining started to irritate her, so she sent him back home to his mama.

Fatima had traded Felony in for Wise, because they became an item right after that. Wise was a little younger also, but he exposed her to the real meaning of being treated like a lady, and it felt damned good. She was going to stick with Wise. She was turned on by the way he handled things. The way a man should. Wise was always taking care of business, and he brought home the bacon to prove it. That's why Fatima let him call the shots.

STACY EXITED FAMILY court, grinning, and headed home. She had just turned Jay in for child support. Mrs. Terwilliger, the woman she'd met with, had said they were going after him and he'd have to pay back money from when Jayquan was born. Stacy couldn't have been more delighted. She didn't care if they'd cut off her public assistance benefits for Jayquan.

Deep in her heart, she knew Jay took care of their son, and he didn't even know she had been receiving welfare for almost five years, ever since Jayquan was born. She didn't care. Stacy was out for blood. She was doing everything in her power to break him so he would have less and less to provide for his bitch.

Stacy wanted revenge. After she'd sabotaged his whore's car at the party that night, that bastard Jay had the audacity to buy that bitch a newer and bigger Mercedes than hers. Stacy was sick. Her plan had backfired on her; the streets were talking about Portia's new money-green 600 with the tint. Instead of putting that bitch to walking, Stacy had put the hoe on a higher level than she was!

That was the final slap in the face. Jay was going to pay for sure. He'd be getting papers in a day or two: Stacy gave up every piece of information on him she possessed, from his social security number to the amount of real estate he owned. She even gave them his mama's name.

Jay hadn't said a word to her about destroying his bitch's car. That mothafucka played nonchalant again. But he sent a strong message by upgrading Portia's wheels. Stacy would have preferred Jay beat her ass or even press charges against her. His reaction took the cake. Her narrow one-track mind led her to believe that Jay's only motive for buying the Benz for Portia was to spite her. To Stacy, that meant war.

Not only was she giving Jay hell financially, she also had Jayquan stashed at her mother's house. The last five or six times Jay had come to get him, she'd made up excuses about Jayquan having more important things to do with her family. Stacy wasn't even releasing him to Jay's mother. War meant war. She felt not the least bit contrite about her actions. At this point, only in Jay's demise would her satisfaction lie.

ATIMA HURRIED TO light the last two scented candles in her living room before Wise came in. He had a key now and would be barging in at any second. She looked around at the effect she'd created. Only lava lamps and candles dimly lit the house. Dinner was ready, and so was dessert. Fatima was serving grilled teriyaki chicken breasts over a bed of rice pilaf, and corn. For dessert, she'd purchased a Mrs. Smith's Dutch-apple pie and a half-gallon of vanilla ice cream. There was no shame in Fatima's game. She enjoyed eating, and so did Wise. They ate good food and had good sex. Correction—they had great sex.

Fatima knew she had moved fast when she gave Wise a key to her condominium only two weeks into their relationship. They'd jumped in headfirst. It happened fast, but it felt right, and Fatima was known to follow her heart.

It was in her nature to treat her man well. It was the reciprocity she wasn't used to. She couldn't believe when Wise started offering her money for groceries and bills. And when she refused, he insisted. That did it. She was gone, and this time it seemed like it wasn't in vain. She'd picked herself a winner.

She heard Wise's key turn in the doorknob. He was right on time.

Wise's entrance was loud, as usual. "Yo, Ma! Where you at?"

"I'm back here, boo." Fatima grinned when he came in the kitchen. "Hey, baby. You hungry?"

"Nah, not yet. I got you something." Wise threw Fatima a Ziploc bag.

She caught it and squealed with delight when she saw what it was. "Umm, I can smell it through the bag. Where you get this shit from?"

"From my man. You gon' stop smoking all that seedy bullshit. That shit almost killed me last night. That's blueberry, Ma. Fo' hundred a ounce."

She laughed. "What you know about weed? I just started you smoking, and suddenly, you're an expert." She examined the contents of the bag and inhaled its pungent aroma. It had a bluish hue, and the fuzzy buds looked like tiny crystal trees. And there wasn't a seed in sight. Fatima knew weed, and this was definitely some killa. "Hell yeah, baby. This is some *shit*. You get *two* gold stars for this."

"Twist something," Wise urged. "Let's try that shit out."

"Lord, what I done did? I done turned you out. Look at you telling me to roll up. Two weeks ago, you were telling me ladies shouldn't smoke weed."

"If you can't beat 'em, join 'em. Fuck it." As an after-thought, Wise added, "But if it was crack you smoked, you would've lost me."

Fatima laughed but set him straight. "Nigga, the

only crack I fuck with is the crack of my ass when I wash it."

Wise shook his head and laughed. Tima's sense of humor was part of the reason he was so attracted to her. He hated a stuck-up prissy chick.

ACROSS TOWN, LAILA and Khalil were finishing a heated argument over absolutely nothing. That's what they fought about these days. Nothing. Laila glared at Khalil, who'd had the nerve to come in smelling like a liquor barrel and then try to get some. When she denied his sexual attempts, he went off and demanded some, talking about it was her job because she was his wife. Funny how he wanted to play husband all of a sudden because he was horny.

In an effort to shut him up so he wouldn't wake the kids with his loud bullshit, Laila relented and gave him some so he would go to sleep. Khalil smelled like an alcoholic, and she couldn't even get wet until she pretended it was Casino inside of her instead of her own husband. If Khalil only knew. But how did she know he didn't imagine he was inside some other pussy? She timed him. Not even fifty pumps, and he was out cold.

As Laila washed Khalil's sperm from between her thighs, she wondered what had become of her perfect family. She realized they were bonded by marriage, as well as two little lives that would be affected by every decision they made. Suddenly, desperation overcame her. She had to do something to save her marriage. They had built something together, and the foundation wasn't just sand. It was rock-solid. She and Khalil had started at the bottom and grown from having nothing to having something, and Laila was proud of that. Maybe they just needed some counseling.

Laila wasn't going to take all of the weight for their problems. Khalil had started this shit with his all-nighters and drinking. Lately, he wasn't the man she'd married. But she knew she had to hold on for the sake of their children. She didn't want them growing up feeling abandoned and insecure, like she had. No, she would try to resolve the differences. She decided to throw herself into her family life. If she gave it her all, hopefully, it would rub off on Khalil. They had to have a heart-to-heart first thing in the morning. Perturbed, Laila drifted into an uneasy sleep.

SIMONE SLAMMED THE door behind Kyle after he left her apartment. It was two in the morning, and all of a sudden he couldn't stay the night. Since when did he care so much about his loving wife at home? Something was fishy. Simone couldn't put a finger on it, but her gut told her something wasn't right. She'd had a bad feeling for the last couple of weeks because Kyle had been acting kind of suspicious. That bastard was probably cheating on both her and his wife.

Simone thought she might be paranoid until she found a number in his pocket. When she searched through his things, she knew she was behaving like a jealous wife, but she didn't care. And her search wasn't in vain. She found evidence. She ran to call the number on the matchbook she'd confiscated from Kyle's jacket pocket. It was from some establishment called the Risqué Café, and it had a number scribbled inside but no name. What the fuck was that, some strip joint? Trick-assed Kyle was probably sponsoring some stripper. Simone knew how he loved to trick. She didn't give a damn as long as she got hers.

That was bullshit. She was about to have his child. Not that she was in love, but she wasn't about to let Kyle be fucking around. Shit, it was bad enough that he had a wife. Simone was pregnant and didn't have time to be worrying about catching something. She was expecting a married man's child. Damn. Why had she started fucking him raw, anyway? She wished she could turn back time. Then she would've never gotten pregnant by him. She was having second thoughts like a mothafucka. For no reason other than wanting to hear her competition's voice, she picked up and dialed the number. It rang three times before an answering machine picked up. The voice was male but extremely feminine. It sounded like a gay man! "Hi, you've reached Vanity, and obviously, you've missed me! Leave me a message. Ciao!"

Simone hung up. Who the hell was that he-she? She had a queasy feeling in the pit of her stomach. She took a deep breath and prayed she hadn't discovered what she thought she had. What kind of bullshit was that? Simone's mind was racing. She'd expected a woman to answer the phone. She had to find out what kind of place the Risqué Café was. Was Vanity a drag queen or something? Could that son of a bitch Kyle be flaming?

FATIMA TOOK THE afternoon off from work and headed across town for a mammogram appointment.

After a breast exam during her last GYN visit, her doctor had discovered an unfamiliar lump in her right breast and recommended follow-up. When Fatima heard that, she almost went into cardiac arrest, because breast cancer ran in her family on her mother's side. Her grandmother and her great-aunt Dora had died from it. And three of her mother's sisters and her cousin Meagan had each undergone preventive surgery in which one or both of their breasts were removed.

Fatima whispered her billionth prayer since the doctor's findings and paid the cabdriver when he pulled up in front of Dolcire Diagnostics. Fatima noted that it was the same place where she'd had an MRI done a few years ago, after she'd been involved in a car accident. At the time she hadn't been really hurt but was trying to get a settlement from the insurance company. She got paid back then, and wished this visit were as worry-free.

Not only did she fear death, but she also couldn't bear the thought of having her breasts removed. She pictured herself frail and cancer-stricken, with sunken eyes. Fatima shuddered, remembering the image of her grandmother after cancer had eaten her alive. In six months, she had gone from 250 to 117 pounds. Her grandmother was merely skin and bones when they buried her. That could possibly be her fate as well. Fatima immediately rejected the thought. *God's got me,* she told herself.

She got off the elevator on the fourth floor and marched up to the front desk. "Hi, I'm Fatima Sinclair, and I have a two o'clock mammogram."

Amil, the pretty Hispanic receptionist, greeted her

with a smile. "Great, you're on time. Have a seat and fill out this paperwork. Bring it back to me when you finish. Then the technician will call you."

In under ten minutes, Fatima was getting a painful, titty-squeezing mammogram. She had no idea how much the damned thing would hurt. Why did women have to go through so much? Minutes seemed like an eternity before the agony was over. Fatima put her bra back on and checked her appearance in the mirror, and then she headed home.

She would get her results in four days, and she would hold her breath until then. She hadn't told her own mother about the lump, let alone her girlfriends. There was no need to alarm anyone until she was certain of a problem, God forbid.

PORTIA'S CELL PHONE rang while she was on the toilet. She wiped herself and washed her hands in just enough time to catch it before the call went to voice mail.

"Hey, cuz! What you up to, girl?" It was Melanie.

"Nothing, just got in the house. Whassup, Melly Mel?" What did she want? Portia knew she called only when she needed something.

"I'm chillin'. I was wondering, do you got a red shirt I can borrow? I bought these new jeans, and I didn't have enough to cop a matching shirt. I figured my fly big cousin would have one." She giggled.

"Look, Mel. I told you I'm not lending you nothin' else. You never returned the last shit I let you hold."

"Oh, my bad. I'll bring it when I come. See you in a few minutes." She hung up.

Portia was sick of Melanie asking to borrow her shit. She never had any money but was always giving up some pussy. That didn't make sense to Portia. Why be a broke hoe? Portia had heard a lot of rumors in the streets about her, including that she was messing around with girls now. Plus, Jay had told her some disturbing things Wise said about Mel drinking his babies. But what could she do? Mel was twenty-one now, so Portia couldn't beat her ass anymore, like she'd done six years ago when her homeboy Carl came and told her that his younger brothers and their friends were at his house, running a train on Mel. Portia had marched right over there to get her fast ass. Mel tried to be defiant and refused to leave, but Portia smacked her up and dragged her out of there. After she made Melanie take a shower and douche, she put her foot to her ass for sassing her and being so stupid.

Now her worrisome ass was coming over to bum a shirt. Portia should act like she wasn't home. But come to think of it, she did have a red shirt that she no longer wore. Melanie could consider it a gift; it wasn't like she was going to bring it back, anyway. Mel was hot in the ass and dumb, but she didn't have any older sisters or brothers, so Portia had to look out for her. Trollop or not, she was family.

Five minutes later, Melanie rang the bell. Portia let her in the house and saw that she hadn't brought the stuff. She knew she might as well write it off. As usual, Portia disapproved of Melanie's outfit: an extremely revealing purple halter top, some low-waist jeans, and a pair of purple Timbs. The child had no sense of season with that summer shirt on.

"Girl, what the hell you doin' dressed like that tonight? It's October, it's cold, and you got your back out. Bitch, this ain't California. Yo' ass gonna catch pneumonia."

"My jacket is in the car with Tim. I'm gettin' with him later. Let's go look in your closet, P. I need something sexy. Oh, and I need a dub, a'ight? I get paid tomorrow." Melanie headed upstairs.

Portia liked her nerve, all up and through her man's house. Mel was lucky Jay wasn't home. "Hold up, chicken. Slow your roll. I didn't even tell you to come over here."

Melanie didn't pay Portia any mind. They went upstairs to Portia's closet, and Mel asked the same questions over and over. "Ooh, where you bought that from? How much this cost? Can I have these?" Portia wound up giving her two pocketbooks, three shirts, two pairs of jeans, and two pairs of last-season Jimmy Choo open-toes. Mel had the nerve to ask for her brand-new red stiletto Gucci boots. Portia told Mel she didn't love her that much, and she tried once more to school her baby cousin. "Mel, you fuck wit' Wise?"

Mel giggled. "Yeah. I got that nigga open, P. He be *fiendin'* for my shit."

Portia was succinct because she didn't have the patience for Mel's ignorance. "So how come yo' ass always broke? Wise got dough. Why you never hit him up? I know for a fact that nigga will kick, 'cause he goes with my friend, and he's paying *all* her bills. *You* gettin' the short end of the stick. Or I should say the *dick*. Don't be no fool."

Mel got defensive. "I know Wise go with Fatima. She be calling his phone when he at my house. Her fat ass must not be satisfying him, or what he doin' wit' me? And I *got* a job. I don't need Wise money."

Portia figured Mel should keep her day job, because she wouldn't make any money in the nightlife. She was pretty, but she'd make a poor hustler, because she'd be too busy enjoying the attention. Mel was way too slow for the life. "Well, just stop giving so much and getting so little."

"I can't help it. I love sex, and I don't care what niggas say about me, 'cause they always come back knockin' on my fuckin' door."

Mel sounded real dumb. Portia didn't see her logic, so she continued getting on her. "You need to care. And you *better* stop letting niggas dig your shit out for free. As much as you throw pussy, you *should* be a fly bitch. *And* your ass should have a ride by now. Niggas in the streets is talking about you, and there's nothing *cute* about being known as a broke, free hoe. If you gon' hoe, do your shit right. You over here begging me for *my* shit and asking *me* for twenty dollars. Come on, Mel. Get it together, bitch. You're my cousin, so the shit you do makes me look bad too."

Now Mel was absorbing Portia's every word. "So teach me your style, P. I wanna be more like you. What's your secret?"

"First of all, start carrying yourself like a lady. Have some class. Men see your body, you don't have to promote it so much. Like now. You look like you cold, Mel. Like a cheap-ass hooker. Everybody see your hooters. They'll still show if you cover up a little. Tone it down. You gotta look like money to attract money. You can't look cheap and expect niggas to kick. You be lookin' easy all the time, Mel. If you wanna get in niggas' pockets, you have to change your image. Stop trying so hard. Relax. You're a pretty girl. Just chill, and don't appear so desperate for attention. Men love a challenge."

"Give me some stuff so I can dress different."

"No, I'm giving you some advice so you can buy your own stuff. I know that rent is kickin' your ass. If you gonna take company, just make niggas pay like they weigh. Stop letting them lay up *on* you and *in* you for free. It's simple. You have to recondition your mind so that you understand *you* got the gold and you can demand whatever ransom you want from men. That's up to you. You have to decide what you're worth. People pay for what they really want. You get it, Mel?"

"Yeah, I get it. No doubt, P."

They went back downstairs, and Portia went to the kitchen to get Mel a shopping bag. When she came out, Jay had just come home. Portia caught Mel acting like a bimbo, smiling all up in his face and giving him the *I wanna fuck you* eyes. Portia wasn't surprised, because that was typical Melanie behavior around a cute guy: She transformed into a whole new bitch. That damned girl was just whorish, and that's all there was to it. She couldn't even help it.

Portia greeted Jay and gave Melanie the bag. "Put your stuff in there. You better go before your ride leaves you, Mel."

After she bagged up her score, Melanie slowly and dramatically bent to tie her shoe. Portia knew she just wanted to stick her butt out in front of Jay, because her shoestrings weren't even untied. Jay ignored Mel's hot ass, so there was no need to scream on her. Portia didn't feel threatened by her, so she gave Miss Microwave a pass.

Mel stood up and adjusted her breasts. "Thank you, cousin." She used that dumb whiny voice she put on when she was trying to be cute. Portia hated that voice. "You know you're my big sister. I don't know what I'd do without you, girl!" Mel hugged Portia. "Make sure you call me, P. Good night, y'all!" She waved at Jay and theatrically sashayed out the door.

Jay looked at Portia, who burst into giggles. "Is she serious, Portia? What's with all that Lil' Kim Hollywood shit? Yo, your cousin is a little off, P. She is loco, for real."

Portia shrugged. "She can't help it, she's a fake bitch. She should've been born a blonde, right? Melanie's just a bimbo. I tried, Jay."

"Give it up, man. You can't help her, Ma. Not with the stuff I heard about her." Jay shook his head. "No disrespect, but your cousin nasty. She *should* be a porno star. You cooked, Ma? I'm starving."

"I'll fix you a plate. What you heard about Mel now?"

Jay told Portia about all the freaky stuff Wise told him he'd done to Mel lately. He had penetrated her with everything from a banana to a bottle, and apparently, she preferred a good old-fashioned "cum gargle" to Listerine. Portia sat his hot plate in front of him, and Jay said his grace. He continued the story while he ate.

"Wise said he be try'na hit her off, but she don't

never *want* no money. She's really a hoe that just love to freak, Portia. That nigga Wise is dumb. The mo'fucka said he was curious and outta shit to do to her, so he put on one of them thin latex gloves and stuck his whole fist in her pussy. He said she laughed and told him she could take a foot." Jay put down his fork and laughed for a few seconds before he finished chewing his food. "You know this nigga said he took his sock off and rolled a condom on his foot, and she actually laid down on the floor while he stuck it in. *And* she told him to measure how far in it went." Jay backed his chair from the table and stood up laughing. "Look, Ma. Wise told me he foot-fucked her like this." He made a serious face and lifted his leg up and down with his toes pointed, as if doing aerobics.

Portia cracked up. "Ugh! Jay, you lying." She was sick with Mel but couldn't help laughing because she could vividly imagine her dumb ass laying there looking stupid and getting foot-fucked by tape-measure-holding, one-sock-wearing Wise. And all for free. Portia wondered how they had the same blood, because Melanie was pitiful. She wished she had followed in Portia's footsteps more. "She is so fuckin' dumb."

"She ain't dumb. Let Wise tell it, she's a straight-A student, 'cause she give good brain."

Portia laughed. Being Jay's girlfriend and Fatima's homegirl had her caught in the middle. She knew Fatima cared about Wise and thought he was faithful, but Portia knew otherwise and had sworn to Jay that she'd keep her mouth shut. Plus, Mel was her baby cousin, and Portia didn't want Fatima to go upside her head about Wise, even if she was fucking him.

Really, they'd both met Wise the same night at Portia's party, so both had a fair chance to bag him. Fatima won, hands down. He respected her more and provided for her, but he couldn't seem to resist Mel's "open leg" policy. And from the shit Jay said Mel let Wise do to her, Portia could see why he kept going back. A gullible chick like Mel was a dream come true to Wise's kind. He was the type to take care of home but still fuck around with dumb chicken-heads he knew wouldn't make any demands. And that's exactly what Melanie was. Portia had to call a spade a spade.

AFTER WORK THURSDAY evening, Portia hung out with Charlene in the city at the new hot spot, Club Azure, for an album release party for Celestial. Celestial was a girl group of four whom the label had signed a year ago. The party was a nice jump-off, with industry heads, executives, and groupies all rubbing elbows. Charlene had promised they'd stay only an hour, but a few laughs and drinks had time on crack, and eleven o'clock crept up on Portia before she knew it.

All at once, she was feeling disoriented. Portia prayed it would pass, but it worsened. The faces in the club looked distorted. Dear God, somebody must've slipped something into her drink! Frantically, she tried to focus and find Charlene or any other familiar face from work. Portia stood up and stepped away from the bar, but she was so woozy, she stumbled and grabbed the nearest person's shoulder for support. It happened to be a guy she didn't know from a can of paint.

He spun around on defense, but his stone stare softened upon notice of a pretty girl. "You a'ight, shorty?"

Unable to speak, Portia just shook her head.

"Where your peoples at? You here by yourself or what?"

She shook her head again. Fear of the unknown settled in, and Portia began to panic.

Homeboy was no slow leak. He caught on. "What you took, shorty? Did somebody slip you some E or something? Hell yeah, that must be what happened. You can't be trustin' niggas to buy you no drink these days. You gotta stay on point, Ma."

Shorty was just giving him a blank stare, like what he said to her wasn't registering. He took her by the arm. "Let me help you find your peoples. You can't trust these niggas up in here."

Portia followed his lead, praying that he was her salvation and not the asshole who'd done this to her.

Some strange guy stopped them a few feet away. "Pardon me, man. Yo, she with me. Thanks, duke, but this me right here. I got her."

The saint leaned over and asked Portia, "Yo, you know this cat?"

She finally found her voice. "Hell no." That nigga was probably the one that did this to her.

Her saint looked at the dude. "Nah, man. We ain't doin' it like that. She don't know you. And she's with *me* now."

The asshole countered, "Damn, bro, from a player to a player, you know it ain't no fun if the homies can't have none. Shit, we can pass this thick bitch around. Look at them titties. Man, look how fucked up she is. Come on."

Her saint's expression hardened, and he stood firm.

"Fall back, homie. I *said* we ain't doin' it like that. This a lady, she ain't no scallywag. What's wrong with you, man?"

Homeboy got the message. "A'ight, super save-a-hoe. Go on and save her." He moved out of their path and mumbled, "Cock-blocking-assed mothafucka!"

Halfway across the club, Portia spotted Charlene with some people she didn't recognize. She tugged at her saint's shirtsleeve and pointed in their direction.

"You wit' Charlene?"

Grateful to him, she nodded, and they headed over.

Charlene noticed Portia and smiled. "Hey, Portia, I see you met Sacred. I'd like you to meet Danny and Kim from marketing." She looked closer at Portia. "Girl, are you okay?"

Saint Sacred spoke for her. "No, she's not okay. She needs to go home. Some nigga slipped her an E pill or something, and she's on a bad trip. Watch out for your peoples, Char."

He turned to Portia. "You good now, shorty. Next time be on point. Wish I could've met you under different circumstances, Ma. Maybe next lifetime, huh?" He winked at her and disappeared.

Portia was so thankful. She needed to get home to the comfort of Jay. Seeing Portia's condition, Charlene bade her coworkers farewell, and they bounced. She insisted that Portia leave the Benz parked and ride in her Lexus. Portia was knocked out on the passenger side before they pulled off.

When she came to, she didn't recognize her surroundings. She was in a strange apartment and didn't know how she'd gotten there. She focused in on Charlene, who was rubbing her back in circular motions, but she was too out of it to really notice.

Seeing that Portia was awake, Charlene smiled. "Welcome back, girlfriend. How was your trip? Drink this orange juice. You'll be okay. Somebody spiked your drink, girl. And you're not supposed to mix ecstasy and alcohol."

Portia sipped the juice, and Charlene kept rubbing her back. Gradually, her sisterly backrub seemed to turn to seduction. She ran her hands up and down Portia's thighs, and when Charlene cupped her breasts, Portia was positive that girlfriend was feeling her up.

She jumped up. "Hold up, Charlene! What the hell you doin'? I'm not gay, I don't get down like that. I'm leaving. Now! Where my keys and my pocketbook?"

Charlene grabbed her arm. "Calm down, Portia. You don't have to do anything you're uncomfortable with. I'm not gay either. I just swing sometimes, and I assumed you did too, being Fatima's friend and all. My bad. Look, it's late, and you're fucked up. You may as well crash till the morning. That's if you want to. I'm just trying to be nice. No pressure."

Portia shook her head and wondered what she meant about Fatima. "What time is it now?"

Charlene laughed. "Girl, it's four-thirty. You were out for a *minute*. Your car is parked in the city. I'll take you to get it in the morning. I'm tired."

"I'll call a cab."

"There's your purse. And don't mention this to anyone, Portia. Are we clear?"

"Yeah, whatever. We're clear. What's this address?" Portia dialed a cab, and three minutes later, she was on her way home. She decided she'd go get her car in the morning.

When Portia got home, Jay was mad as shit. "Yo, I called your phone mad times. Where the fuck you comin' from this time of night? And why you just got out of a cab? Where the fuck is your Benz?"

Portia was too exhausted to explain. She just went upstairs and lay across the bed. Jay followed her and kept on demanding answers. She could only mumble, "They put something in my drink. Please just let me sleep it off. I love you." Then she fell out in her clothes.

Portia dreamed of waterfalls. She was running down a beautiful beach, and suddenly, a strange force grabbed her and carried her toward the ocean. She couldn't see it, but it rushed into the water and lifted her in the air. Though she kicked and pleaded for it not to drown her, her protests were in vain. It tossed her in the water, and she held on to it, screaming and clawing.

"Portia! Portia, what the fuck did you take? I'm taking you to the hospital!"

Portia opened her eyes and saw panic in Jay's face. Then she saw blood on his neck from her scratches. She realized Jay had her in the shower, with cold water pouring in her face.

When Jay saw her come out of it, he turned off the water and grabbed her face. "Do you know who I am? You all right, Portia?" He shook her by the shoulders to accelerate her response.

She nodded. "I'm freezing. Are you trying to kill me?"

Jay grabbed two fluffy towels from the armoire and wrapped them around her head and shoulders. "You scared me, Ma. You came in babbling about 'they' spiked your drink, and then you fell out and wouldn't wake up. I didn't know what else to do, so I put you in the shower. I figured the cold water would help, but you started wildin', scratching me up and shit. I was about to rush your ass to the hospital 'cause I thought you was going crazy. Tell me what happened. Who's 'they'? Who spiked your drink, Ma?"

He helped her get up and put on some dry clothing while she told him everything she remembered about the night, except what Charlene had said about Fatima. Portia didn't know if that part was true. Even if it was, she didn't want Jay passing judgment on her friends.

Jay waited until she was finished to comment. "I'm glad you're okay, but why didn't you call me? You know I would've came and got you." He frowned. "So let me get this straight. Basically, your supervisor is a dyke, and you went with her to some industry party and wound up getting drugged. You told her you quit, right, Ma? I don't want you working for her, Portia. That bitch is bad luck, *and* she's sick."

"Baby, thanks for caring, but I'm not gonna quit. I have to be professional. I put Charlene in her place already, and if she doesn't mention it again, then neither will I. If she tries me at work, I'll slap that bitch with a sexual harassment suit so fast her damn head will spin. It wasn't her fault somebody slipped something in my drink. She was nowhere around. She got me out of the club safe and made sure I was okay before she pushed up on me. She didn't try me while I was passed out, and it didn't happen on company time. I didn't mean to make her sound like a rapist. I have to give her more credit than that. She just read me wrong, Jay, that's all. I don't think it will happen again."

"Well, that's your decision. But you need to stop dressing so sexy, Ma. Why everything gotta fit you so tight? You *make* niggas get curious. Look at them low-cut pants you came home in. I could damn near see the crack of your ass. You not leavin' the house in no more of that sexy shit. You sure you a'ight, man?" Jay looked real concerned.

Portia hugged him. "Yes, daddy. I'm home with you now, so I'm safe." She glimpsed at the clock. "Baby, it's six o'clock in the morning. Let's go to bed."

"Word. I'm tired too. Got me up all night waitin' for your ass. I know you calling in sick today. And that dyke bitch better not say shit. Matter of fact, I'm about to go get your car before you oversleep and wind up getting towed."

"Thanks, baby. Don't you need me to drive you? You can't drive the Benz and the truck home."

"Nah, sleepyhead. Call me a cab and go to bed. You want me to bring you some breakfast back?" Jay tied his Timbs and grabbed Portia's car keys.

"No, thank you. Just be careful. I parked on that little side street by the club. I forgot the name, but you can't miss it. It's a one-way, right off Sixth Avenue." Portia called Jay a cab, and then she fell in the bed. She was asleep before her head hit the pillow.

On the cab ride, Jay mused over Portia. He worried about her more than he cared to admit. He had bent his own bachelor rules and let her move in the house with him. She'd stored her bedroom set at her mother's house and given all of her other furniture to her cousin Melanie, and now they were shacking up. Their arrangement was working out good, because she wasn't suffocating him. Jay had a lot of space in the house, so he gave Portia her own walk-in closet to accommodate the millions of shoe boxes and clothes she had. He liked the woman's touch Portia brought to his crib. Her presence livened up the atmosphere.

She had changed her lifestyle for the better and was playing her position well, working and taking care of home. She was sophisticated, she cooked, and she was very clean. Portia hardly ever nagged him, and now she held down a good job, making her own money. Plus, she kept him satisfied. Jay thought of his name tattooed on her ass and smiled to himself. He couldn't complain about anything. He was stuck on Portia, so she was permanent. Unless she fucked up, and he really hoped she wouldn't.

Melancholy overcame Jay when he remembered that he had to leave her. He had to go away for a little while, a year at the most. He owed some time for a weapon-possession charge he got two years ago, when he was caught with an unregistered gun. He'd paid a lawyer to play tennis with it for a while in order to buy some time to organize, and he now knew the exact date his sentence would begin. On the eighth of November. That was three weeks away, and he hadn't told Portia a word about it yet. He would miss their first holidays together, Thanksgiving and Christmas. Jay decided to buy her an early gift and put it in a safe-deposit box until Christmas. If she stood up, he would call her and tell her where the key was.

Portia seemed like the stand-up type. Jay hoped she

wouldn't turn out to be one of those foul bitches who crossed a nigga when he went up north. Financially, he would leave her straight. She wouldn't need another nigga for nothing unless she couldn't keep her legs closed. If she fucked up, that was on her. That would be her only test: fidelity. He wasn't leaving Portia in charge of his finances yet. Jay took care of his own money business.

He and his partners had just sold their Virginia-based trucking company to a big corporation who'd been happy to pay them top dollar because the small company had cut into their business in that area substantially. Jay had put his share of the proceeds in a trust for Jayquan. And his real-estate business would be taken care of. That was where his moms came in. She would manage his property while he was away. He'd prepaid his property taxes for a year, so she didn't have to worry about that. And of course his mother would look after Jayquan financially. Mama-duke was the only woman Jay knew he could trust with his business. He loved Portia, but he wasn't ready to involve her that deeply yet. He was playing it safe.

His sisters didn't even think he should leave Portia in his house while he was gone. They didn't have anything against her, but they didn't trust any of Jay's girlfriends and never would. Jay loved Portia's chocolate ass and was really hoping that he could go do this mini-bid and come home without her becoming tarnished. Though he knew his mans would keep an eye on her without asking, he was counting on her doing the right thing.

Jay wasn't worried about doing the time. He had

done so much dirt without getting caught, he would do a year standing on his head. Shit wasn't always sweet. That's how the game went. You had to pay dues. Jay was fortunate enough to have been able to plan for his. He always followed a plan. And his next plan was to pursue that music shit full-time when he got out. Most important for right now, he would be comfortable while he was away, and his sisters would bring his son to visit him. He didn't want to see Stacy while he was locked up, because she was the type to piss you off, which could cause you to get in some unnecessary bullshit when you took your frustration from a bad visit back on the inside. Jay wanted to do this bid stress-free, and Stacy was already on his shit list about that child support mess.

Having taken care of Jayquan all these years, Jay didn't feel that the courts should force him to pay back support, as if he had been some deadbeat dad throughout his boy's life. Especially for Stacy or the welfare people to benefit from, because it wasn't like that money would go in Jayquan's pockets. Jay hadn't known that bitch was getting welfare for his son until Stacy stirred that shit up.

Jay spotted Portia's car and told the cabdriver to pull over. He paid the twenty-dollar fare and tipped the guy an extra five bucks. The Mercedes looked okay, so Jay got in and started her up. He yawned. Man, he was tired. After letting the car run for a second, he threw her in gear and headed back home to join his warm, soft lady in his warm, soft bed.

CAS WAS HEADING toward East Elmhurst on the Brooklyn-Queens Expressway when his cell phone rang. It was Jay's little sister, Kira, calling him again. Cas leaned back in his seat and regretted picking up.

Kira put on her best "1–900-SEX-ME-UP" voice and jumped right on him. "Hello, my hot, sexy soon-to-be lover. Are we on for the night?"

"Yo, don't come at me like that, Kira. What's wrong wit' you? Don't you have some homework or something to do?"

"Cas, why you be frontin'? I'm try'na see you. Seriously." Kira knew Jay was about to go bid for a few months, so this was her golden opportunity to get with Casino.

"Man, I'm busy. Bye, little girl. Go play somewhere." Cas hung up on her. He hadn't told Jay, but Kira had been pressing him on some real sex-her-type shit. He'd never looked at her that way, and he felt uncomfortable with her advances. Jay had been his man for the past eighteen years, so Cas remembered when she was like a year old. She was young and getting hot in the twat, but it wasn't his place to help her with that.

• • •

SIMONE HADN'T BEEN able to rest since she'd found that phone number. She looked in the Yellow Pages, and the Risqué Café was actually listed. Heaven was on her side so far. She dialed the number, and a guy picked up on the third ring. He said, "Risqué Café! Do you wish to play?"

Simone's heart sank. He was obviously gay. "Hello? Is this a nightclub?"

"Ye-es. May I help you, sweetie?"

"Umm, is Vanity there?"

"No, honey. She works nights, weekends, mostly." He sounded real bored with her.

Simone hesitated. "Is this a gay club?"

Sweet Pete laughed. "Darling. The Risqué Café is not a club. It's an experience!"

Simone was in denial. "Like a *gay* experience?"

"It's a boy fantasy world. *Hello?* What'sa matter, sweetie? Did you find a matchbook in your husband's pants pocket or something?" His voice dripped with gay sarcasm.

"Save your gay humor, RuPaul." Simone hung up. There was no point in debating, because she'd found out the naked truth. What normal heterosexual man walked around with a drag queen's telephone number in his pocket? A fog settled over Simone as she realized what she faced. Kyle had to be bisexual. She grabbed a seat and took a load off because her knees suddenly felt weak as hell.

What about AIDS? She knew she should've been concerned about it before, but Kyle's questionable sexuality had her extra-scared now. Her doctor had told her that they didn't automatically test pregnant women. Simone was too ashamed to tell her friends. Lord, had she picked a down-low faggot to knock her up? It was time to get tested.

FATIMA'S BREAST LUMP turned out to be nothing but a benign cyst. She was so relieved that she wanted to celebrate, so she summoned a brunch with her girl-friends that afternoon.

Fatima looked down at her watch for the millionth time. "Late as usual," she mumbled to no one in particular. She looked up and saw Portia heading her way, grinning. Fatima grinned back. "I see we movin' on black folks' time again."

Portia looked apologetic. "Hell yeah. I stopped at CVS to cop some Dr. Scholl's for these boots. My damn feet are killing me, girl."

"Them damn boots are smokin', though, so it's worth it," Fatima complimented. "That's the price of beauty, baby."

"Word. Look, I ain't the only one who's running late." Portia motioned toward the restaurant's entrance. "Here comes Belly."

She and Fatima laughed at Simone wobbling toward them. She was really starting to stick out there. "Hey, Miss Mommy," they shrieked in unison while Simone was still a good twenty feet away.

Simone rolled her eyes and grinned. "What's up, girls? Sorry I'm late. I'm moving a little slower these days 'cause I done put on a few pounds."

"We see," Portia said.

"Word, you better leave that cake alone," joked Fatima.

Simone grabbed a seat. "Thanks again for the baby shower, y'all. I have way more stuff than I'll probably even need. I love you bitches to death."

"That's what aunties are for," said Fatima.

"True," Portia cosigned.

"We may as well go on and order," Simone said. "Laila's not coming. She called me right before I got here. She said tell y'all she'll call you later, 'cause she got plans. I think she's with Khalil, because she told me they're try'na work some things out. I don't know about y'all, but I'm starving." She summoned a waitress, and they placed their orders.

Fatima informed them about her breast cancer scare, and together they thanked God that she was okay. The girlfriends enjoyed playing catch-up while they waited on their lunch.

When the food came, Simone picked at it while she tried to figure out how to approach the AIDS issue without alarming them. "I need some advice, y'all. I have a doctor's appointment this afternoon. A couple of weeks ago, I read this article on HIV testing. I've never been tested, and my doctor's urging me to. I was under the impression that pregnant women are automatically tested, but they're not. Last checkup I got, I was scared. But I want to do it today, just to make sure my baby's gon' be okay. I'm just a little worried." She looked at Fatima. "You ever been tested?"

Fatima shook her head. "To be honest, I'm scared to death. I don't even wanna know. I'd rather just drop dead from it." She and Simone looked at Portia. "What about you, P?"

"I have been tested. Several times. Believe it or not, Jay insisted when we first hooked up. I ain't gon' front, I was scared as shit, 'cause y'all know a bitch done been out there. It wasn't Jay's first time, but we went together and had it done. Thank God, the results came back negative all three times. My last test was almost a year ago, but I'm monogamous, and that mo'fucka better be too. Both of y'all should go get tested. Don't worry, Monie. You're fine. Just do it to ease your mind." As she spoke, Portia thought of her unprotected sex with Khalil, and a wave of insecurity swept over her. She played it off, but she would get tested again just to be on the safe side.

Simone faked a smile. "I feel fine, girl. I'ma still do it." She was lying. The truth was, since her suspicions about Kyle arose, she hadn't been feeling good at all. It was hard to keep food down; plus, she'd developed an irregular heartbeat and kept getting these weak spells. Dr. Garner said her blood sugar was fine, so it wasn't diabetes, thank God. It could be pregnancy side effects, or hypochondria, but Simone wanted to make sure. She didn't want to alarm her friends, so she kept her thoughts to herself.

"I hate to eat and run, but if I don't leave now, I'ma be late for my appointment."

Fatima grabbed Simone's hand. She knew her friend and could tell she was worrying. "You'll be all right, girl. I'll call you later."

"Me too. Be careful, Monie. Smooches," said Portia. Simone stood up and kissed two fingers and waved.

After they watched their friend depart, Fatima turned and asked Portia, "You up for a slice of that Dutch-apple pie?"

"À la mode? Hell yeah!"

Fatima shook her head. "No ice cream for me. I'm in the red zone, and you know cramps and dairy don't mix."

Portia understood. She'd had a bad experience with cramps and cereal and milk before. The ladies indulged and ordered. Portia decided to use this one-on-one time to grill Fatima about Charlene's insinuations that she was bisexual. "Tima, remember a couple of weeks ago, when I told you about that party I went to with Charlene?"

"When you got caught out there?"

"Yeah. Well, I didn't tell you, but Charlene made a pass at me."

"Girl, no! Get the fuck outta here!"

"Yeah. But I checked her, and she apologized. She said she assumed I fucked around because I was your friend. I didn't feed in to it, but I *have* been wondering what she meant by that. Now, I'm not here to judge you, but is that bitch lying or what?"

"First of all, she had no right telling you anything about me. Why is she worrying about what I do? That bitch don't know me that well. We only hung out a couple of times, so she damn sure shouldn't be promoting my business. Especially to my friends. Had she asked me, I would've told her you didn't get down like that. But she never asked."

"Well? You have my undivided attention," Portia told her.

"I see. Your ears just grew this big." Fatima spaced her hands three feet apart.

Portia feigned impatience. "You so silly. You can't even be serious for one conversation."

Fatima sipped her ice water and continued. "Now, don't think me and Charlene have anything going on. She just said that because we hung out at this gay club one night, and she knows I met this girl. She don't even know what happened after that." She sighed. "Fuck it, P, here's the truth. Straight up. I had my pussy ate by a bitch one or two times. That don't make me gay. Just curious. And hell no, bitch, I don't licky-licky, so don't give me that look. Come on, P, you used to dance. I know you done did some crazy shit too."

The waitress came with their dessert, and Portia waited until she was gone to comment. "Not with no bitch! I mean, don't get me wrong, I've *seen* it all. I done seen two bitches onstage fucking a duce-duce Heineken bottle, I seen a girl pour hot wax in her pussy and then pull out a candle, I've seen tricks with beer, ice cubes, *and* I seen a bitch spit handcuffs out her asshole. And you should see some of the shit those men do to the girls. Even *married* men. Girl, I'm open-minded, 'cause I done seen it all. Yo, this bitch named Lemon Joy even shoots lemons outta her pussy."

Fatima laughed. "You stupid."

"I'm dead serious. To each his own, but there's nothing no girl can do for me. No offense, Tima." Portia faked a Jamaican accent: "I like 'em hard and stiff. Lawd have mercy."

"So you mean to tell me that in your whole career as a stripper, you never once experimented?"

"I mean, I messed with a lot of niggas. I did a ménage à trois with some dudes twice, and I group-fucked five niggas. But I never messed with no chick. That's my word."

"Oh well, we all got skeletons in our closet. This is our little secret. Do *not* tell Laila. You know how old-fashioned she is. Simone don't need to know either. That's the past, I'm straight. And I must admit, P, I love dick way better. It's like a bonus. Luckily, my boo can do both, licky-licky *and* sticky-sticky, real good."

"Okay!" The homegirls hit high five.

"But damn, P, you done seen some shit, huh?"

"Girl, that ain't the half. I swear. I always practiced safe sex, but in the last three years, I led a fuckin' life you could write a book on."

"So write one, then. I'll buy a copy."

Portia laughed. "Yeah, a'ight. I'll title it 'Confessions of an Ex–Lap Dancer.'"

"Ooh, spicy. Yo, I'm dead-assed, P. You should write a fuckin' book. You could self-publish it, and we'll pump that bitch out the trunk Master P–style if we have to. And don't forget about the Internet. We can sell millions of copies. I'm with you, girl. Get them damn creative juices flowin', and make me a character in it." Fatima did some theatrical diva hand movements and put on a sexy voice. "Let me be a stripper!" They cracked up, and then Fatima got serious. "You got me an A on that paper you wrote for me in tenth grade, remember? And we all used to get you to write our love letters and shit. Couldn't nobody break it down like you could, P. You've always been great with words. You can write a book, girl. Sex sells, and the book will spark up controversy, which sells too. You can stir up some shit about both. Do it. Then we can turn it into a movie. Hell yeah."

"If you promise to go get tested for HIV, I'll write a book. Tima, you've been sexually active for over ten years, and it's time. This is the new millennium, girl. I'm sure you're fine, but regardless, there's a lot of advanced research and medicine today. And I'm pretty sure they have a cure, if you can afford it. Look at Magic. He looks better now than he did before he got it. Knowing is half the battle. Either way, you can live a long, healthy life. If you take care of yourself."

"You right. A bitch *do* wanna be here for a long time. I got a lotta plans, P. I'ma get tested. I should make Wise go too."

"Hell yeah, we need to make that a rule from now on. Let's get every new prospect tested *before* we do the do. No exclusions. Good dick shouldn't kill you. It ain't even worth it."

"Word. So bet. You write the book, and I'll get tested. It's a go."

"Let's pinky-swear," suggested Portia.

Tima laughed, but she intertwined pinkies with Portia.

On her way home later that evening, Portia toyed with the idea. Writing a book had been on her to-do list ever since she was eight and became fascinated with reading. As a child, Portia used to read under the covers with a flashlight after bedtime, and she still enjoyed a good book. She read everything from Alex Haley and Alice Walker to Zora Neale Hurston and Zane. Maybe it would work. She'd always aced English and writing courses, even in college, so she felt she had the makings of an author. Perhaps penning her memoirs would prove therapeutic. And maybe she'd get rid of those nightmares she still had every now and then.

But hell, she couldn't remember half of the guys she'd slept with, especially the times when nothing had gone wrong. The bad experiences stood out the most, though making money had outweighed them. That was part of the game. Usually, when you got caught out there, it was because you slipped. Bad shit happening now and then came along with the territory, and she had tried to forget it.

Portia knew from a psychology class that a person could repress bad memories and experiences, and those things could resurface in the subconscious, sometimes in the form of dreams, which were involuntary. Tackling those issues on paper could be purging for her soul.

The only factor that made her indecisive was Jay. She didn't want him to know some of the things she'd been involved in. But Jay wouldn't know what she was up to. That's it, she would do it. It was official. Portia grinned from ear to ear. She had just thought of her book title: "It's Official." Everything in it would be official too. Her book would be off the chain.

When Portia got home, the house was dimly lit. Jay had left a dozen red roses in a beautiful vase on the coffee table for her. There was a path of crushed rose petals leading to a candlelit lobster and shrimp dinner in the dining room. It was a lovely surprise, but Portia had the feeling something was up. Jay looked like he had something to tell her, and she had the feeling she wouldn't like it.

They ate in silence for a few minutes. Then Portia sipped her white wine, swallowed the shrimp scampi she was chewing, and asked, "What's wrong, baby?"

"I might as well be straight up with you. I gotta go away for a little while, Ma."

"So what's new? You always go outta town. What's so different about this time?"

"I'm not going out of town this time. Well, I am, but not like you think. I gotta do a little bit of time."

"What? How much time, Jay?"

"Just a few months. Nothing major."

"A few months! When do you go in?"

"Next week."

Portia looked like she was about to cry. "How long have you known, Jay?"

"A few months."

"I can't fuckin' believe this. How could you do this to me? Why are you just now telling me?"

Jay sighed. "Because I knew how you'd react. It's not the end of the world, Ma. Come on."

Portia just cried, so he went over and hugged her. "I need you to be strong, man. Talk to me, P. You stickin' by me or what?" Jay raised Portia's chin and forced her to look him in his eyes. "You wit' me?"

Portia put on her tough skin. "You my other half. Of course I'ma bid with you. I love you. No matter what."

"That's what I wanna hear. Listen, I set up a spending account for you. Just pay the phone bill and the light bill. I prepaid the satellite bill and all the insurance for a year, so you don't have to worry about that. There's fifteen thousand in the account. The bills won't take up half of that. The rest you can use to buy food and things you need for the house or whatever. Spend smart, Portia. I know you can throw that away in a day, how you love to shop. I'll be in regular contact, so if anything extra comes up, you can let me know and I'll make sure it's taken care of." He took a gold Visa debit card out of his wallet and handed it to her. "The pin number is your date of birth: 9676."

"Okay, be straight up with me. Just how long you gon' be gone? Honestly."

Jay tried to soften it up. "Well, it won't seem like so long, 'cause you can come visit me every week if you want to. I'll be on Rikers Island for a few weeks, and then I'll get transferred upstate to do a few months. I'm leaving you with two guns to hold the house down. For protection, just in case. I'ma take you to the range for a few days so you can practice your aim. You need to carry a ratchet anyway, Ma. Even in your car, because niggas get stupid sometimes."

"Answer my question. Exactly how long, Jay?"

Jay paused. "I'll be gone for about eight months, a year at the most."

Portia's heart sank, and she began to cry again. That news totally burst her bubble. How was she going to survive being away from Jay for a year?

"Ma, stop crying and listen to me. If you gon' be here by yourself, you gotta know how to defend yourself. What if somebody run up in here on you? What you gon' do?"

Portia shut off the waterworks and listened to her man. Seeing that he had her attention, Jay kept schooling her. "Outside of child safety, what's the number one rule about a burner, P?"

Portia blew her nose and said, "Shoot the motha-fucka before you get shot?"

Jay laughed. "Good guess. That's why I fuckin' love you, girl. You close, but that's rule number two. Rule number one is don't pull it if you scared to bust it. Unless you got a death wish. You got it, Ma?"

Portia nodded. "If you scared to bust it, don't even pull it out. I got it."

THE DAYS UNTIL Jay went in were sad for both of them, more for Portia. She stayed up under him as much as she could, cherishing their last precious moments together. She was taking it real hard. She cried during their lovemaking every night.

Finally, the day came, and though Jay played it cool, he was tight. He was so attached to Portia that it was like leaving a part of himself behind. He spent the entire morning inside of his honey pot. Her eyes were almost swollen shut from crying.

When it was time for him to go, Jay insisted that Portia stay home, even though she'd taken the day off work to go with him. Jay had Cas take him to turn himself in; he couldn't bear the thought of Portia breaking down in tears when they took him into custody.

WHILE JAY WAS incarcerated, Portia started marathon-writing her memoirs on her PC. It took her mind off of missing Jay. She felt she had some good stuff, though she didn't want anybody to see it yet, because it was so explicit. Portia wondered what her mother would think. She decided to publish her book under a pseudonym to protect her identity.

Writing had helped Portia survive the first six weeks of Jay's vacation. She'd visited him twice a week on Rikers Island, and now the holiday season had come. She wanted to do something creative, so she purchased a digital camera and a huge Christmas tree. After she decorated the tree, she had Laila do a photo shoot of her.

She started out modeling a long red sheer dress over a red sequined thong and thigh-high stiletto boots. Next, she took some sexy backside poses wearing only the thong and a Santa Claus hat. Portia ended her shoot horizontally in front of the tree, wearing nothing but sexy boots, a Santa hat, and a smile, with three stick-on Christmas bows strategically covering her breasts and crotch. All of the shots were provocative but tasteful.

Laila helped her select the best twelve photos, and

Portia arranged them in order from nicest to naughtiest and designed a glossy Christmas calendar on her PC. She mailed it to Jay the next day during her lunch break. There were about three weeks left before Christmas, so he was sure to get it in time.

WHEN SHE HEARD the doctor's news, Simone froze and turned white as death. She prayed she was having a nightmare. It was the wrong time for bad news. It was almost Christmas, and she was pregnant. The doctor's words had crushed her. She left his office in a fog.

Simone was in a state of shock, and the next thing she knew, she was on the elevator in her office building, riding up to the seventeenth floor, where she knew Kyle would be working late. Simone unzipped her Louis Vuitton bucket bag and removed her chrome .357. She stuck it in her jacket pocket just as the elevator doors opened.

The front desk was vacant; Raven, the receptionist, was gone for the day. The corridor was dark except for a ray of light that shone through a crack in Kyle's office door down the hall. As she neared the door, Simone heard voices. Damn, he wasn't alone. One of the voices was female, or so she thought. She crept up and peered through the door.

That bastard Kyle stood facing the window with his pants down around his ankles. He was apparently teaching the course "Deep-throating 101," because that disgusting disgrace was coaching gay white Clifton from human resources on how to suck a mean one. "That's it. Up and down slowly. Lick it like a lollipop. Suck this dick, bitch! Show me how many licks it takes." Kyle held the back of his head as Clifton followed his directions and moaned like he had a dick up his ass.

Simone pulled out and cocked her gun. Kyle had the nerve to be getting his dick sucked by a fucking faggot when she'd shown up to kill him for infecting her with AIDS. She wanted with a passion to put him out of his misery.

Kyle's moans grew louder. Simone knew him like a book. He couldn't stand up to some good head. His bitch ass was about to bust a nut. She was so disgusted, her stomach turned, and bile rose in her throat. Simone took a deep breath. It was time to make her move.

Kyle's eyes were rolled back in pleasure, so he never saw Simone push the door open. He gripped the back of Clifton's head and relieved his frustrations right down his throat. Clifton didn't even protest. Simone almost vomited again. He had no idea that a single drop of Kyle's venom could be the death of him, and he'd swallowed damn near half of a cup. Kyle was spreading his poison, and he needed to be stopped.

Simone's voice was as calm as still water when she spoke. "I see you gettin' you up in here, Kyle. You livin' a down-low double life, huh? Damn, I'm pregnant by a fuckin' faggot."

Kyle looked like he'd seen a ghost. His jaw dropped, and he let go of Clifton's head. Clifton scampered to the side and tried to look dignified while he straightened his clothes.

Simone shook her head in disbelief. "I can't believe this shit. You're really a faggot. What a waste of a six-foot, big-dick black man. You fuckin' bastard. I'ma kill you, Kyle."

Stunned, Kyle regained his voice. "Hold up, baby, this ain't what it look like. Simone, I wasn't expecting you. Come on, I'll make this right. Uh, let's go on a cruise. You want to go shopping? You want some new ice? Anything you say, baby. Just name it."

Simone started to cry. That was just how the mothafucka had allured her. With gifts and favors. And she'd fallen for the bait. She cursed the day she started having sex with Kyle. What the hell was wrong with her? He was married, and she'd never even really loved him. She'd been blinded by his extravagance, so she'd tried to make a dollar outta the fifteen cent his shit was worth. Something from nothing left nothing. Kyle had bought her with materialistic shit, and now she realized that he was the devil, and she had sold her soul.

Simone felt she had nothing to lose, so she pointed the gun at Kyle's head. "I'ma give you thirty seconds to pray, nigga. Go 'head and make peace with your maker, 'cause you goin' to hell, Kyle. You deserve to burn. Get on your knees, mothafucka! I'ma put you out your misery, you sick bitch!"

Kyle quickly pulled up his pants and started toward her. "Simone, put that damn gun down! Baby, you overreacting. My *wife* wouldn't even pull a gun on me. You know better than that! Give me that gun, girl!"

Simone couldn't stay calm any longer. "You infected me with AIDS, mothafucka! And my baby! Because of you, I'm gonna die! I'ma *die*, Kyle! And you are too, you fuckin' homo! 'Cause *I'm* the mothafuckin' judge and jury. And you got the death penalty today, Kyle. Get on your knees!"

Clifton stared wide-eyed. He was trembling and looked like he'd just shit on himself.

From the look on Kyle's face, he didn't know he had it. He vehemently denied Simone's accusations. "Bitch, is you *crazy*? I don't have no mothafuckin' AIDS! Unless *you* gave it to me. Simone, you got AIDS? If you gave me AIDS, I'll kill you, bitch! Fuck! Bitch, give me that fuckin' gun!" He stormed toward her.

Simone caught a flashback, and she saw her stepfather who'd molested her, Benny's face in place of Kyle's. Hell hath no fury like a woman scorned, and Simone felt her situation was a catch-22. The Monster was going to kill her anyway, so she didn't have shit to lose.

She snarled, "Take these bullets with you to hell, mothafucka!" She pulled the trigger and hit him in the chest.

Kyle staggered but didn't fall. Simone busted three more shots into his torso, and then she put one right between his eyes. That one put him flat on his back.

Simone immediately asked God for forgiveness. When she stood over Kyle's body and looked into his lifeless eyes, the harsh reality of her actions settled in. She doubled over and vomited right on Kyle's Armani-clad corpse.

Simone heard Clifton sobbing over in the corner. She wiped her mouth with the back of her hand. "Clifton, I guess you know by now, huh? He probably gave it to you too. Or did you give it to him? It don't even matter now. Don't nothin' matter no more." Clifton's sobs faded as she walked away.

On the elevator ride down, Simone called Portia on

her cell phone. When Portia picked up, she got straight to the point. "Raise my baby if she make it, P. I may be dead or in jail, 'cause I just put that bastard Kyle out of his misery."

"Stop playing, Simone. He must really be getting on your nerves." Portia's ears perked up. Wait a minute. Was Simone crying?

"I'm dead serious, P. I shot him!"

"Oh my God! Mone, where you at? Get in a cab and come over here! Right now!"

After they hung up, Portia was unsure what to do next. She called Fatima's cell phone and got her voice mail, so she left a message saying there was an emergency. She didn't get into details; she knew to use discretion over the phone. Next she called Laila.

EARLIER THAT DAY, Laila double-checked her rearview mirror on the Belt Parkway as she exited. She doubted she'd be spotted at the Marriott by the airport, where Cas had suggested they meet, but she wanted to make sure she wasn't being tailed. Laila was about to commit adultery, and she knew she was on her way down the road of sin. She was going to spend the afternoon with Casino. He'd phoned her a minute ago and given her the room number.

Aware that she was playing with fire, Laila parked and ducked into the lobby. She swore the middle-aged, three-piece-suit-clad innkeeper heard her heart pounding while she waited for the elevator and tried to stop fidgeting. On the ride up, her imagination ran wild, and she pictured Khalil standing there like Elmer Fudd with a shotgun when the doors opened, ready to blast his trifling wife for whoring around. She'd lied that morning and told him she was going to do some Christmas shopping after work. Laila held her breath until she got off and was positive Khalil wasn't around. When she got to the door of Suite 349, she lost her nerve and about-faced two times. Laila breathed deep and shook it off, and then she knocked.

Laila didn't know that Cas had been doing random peephole checks for the last ten minutes. He saw her when she first walked up. Her body language said she was contemplating leaving. Hopeful and amused, he watched until she knocked. Just so he wouldn't appear thirsty, Cas counted a few seconds before he opened the door. They greeted each other with a casual hug, and then Laila took off her cream-colored three-quarter-length sable coat.

"I need to use the bathroom, Cas." She needed to regain her composure: Cas was making her knees feel weak already. He smelled so good. Jesus! His caramel features were so perfect and defined, and his presence was so strong, that God must have fashioned him in His identical image. And when you heard that sexy voice, you knew he was worthy.

"So go 'head and use it." Casino sized Laila up as she moved across the room. He hadn't realized her hair was that long. He wondered if she had tracks in it. She looked stunning in a beige BCBG pantsuit and an expensive pair of cream and beige snakeskin stiletto boots. The footwear was very impressive, as usual. Cas was picky about a woman's feet. He preferred a girl who spent a little cash for her shoes. Casino was a dapper type of nigga, and he needed the right kind of woman by his side. Sexy high heels were an especial turn-on for him. And Laila wore them every time he saw her.

Cas couldn't front. Laila was an exotic enchantress and some kind of sexy, with her tantalizing slanted eyes and full lips. Her skin was smooth and flawless, like the finest dark chocolate. And her body was banging. The waist-to-ass ratio was crazy. The onion stood out even in conservative threads. Laila was like a hot-fudge sundae with an extra helping of bootie. It was one of the most perfect asses he'd ever laid eyes on. He'd yearned to touch it from day one, but he thought too highly of her to cop a feel. That was high school.

He was waiting until she was ready, like a gentleman. That was ironic, because Cas was the type to smack a bitch on the ass at a no-touching-allowed strip club. But Laila wasn't just some bitch. She had dazzled him with her poise and intelligence. So far, all they had done was talk during lunch dates since they met two months ago. Cas was feeling her, and he didn't want to pressure her, because sex wasn't everything. He could get pussy a dime a dozen. His name rang bells. Chicks dick-rode all day, but Cas was particular about the women he stuck his dick in. He wasn't about to let some nasty bitch be the death of him. He was real hard on females. He didn't respect chicken-heads and easy lays.

That's why he dug Laila so much. She was everything he'd ever wanted in a woman. But he knew her marriage situation, so he let her serve the ball. And now here she was, in the bathroom, taking too long, like women always do. Casino was satisfied simply by the fact that she'd shown up. He wasn't about to press her for pussy. In due time, it would come naturally. Her just being there said a hell of a lot. He appreciated her company. She was married, but it was obvious her husband wasn't taking care of home. So fuck that asshole.

Laila was in the bathroom wringing her hands and doing breathing exercises. She couldn't stifle her guilt. Casino wasn't a stranger, she reasoned. They'd been talking for over two months. Laila splashed cold water on her face and emerged from the bathroom feeling more confident. "What up, Cas?"

"I can't call it. How you feel today, Ma?"

Laila replied, "I'm good. What about you?"

"Better, if you stop actin' so uptight. I ain't gon' bite you. Why you standing over there like I got some type of plague? Relax, Laila. I didn't call you over here to try nothin'. I just enjoy your conversation. Sit down, man."

"I'm sorry. I'm all actin' like a little kid and shit."

Laila went over and sat beside Cas on the couch. He had the TV on CNN, so she flipped through the channels until she found BET. A rerun of *106 & Park* was just going off. Laila sparked her blunt and made small talk. She was a little nervous, but she was mad turned on from being so close to Casino. The chronic had her feeling mellow, and she desperately wanted to feel his touch. Frankly, she was getting wet from anticipation alone. She came to get wore out, and this cat was playing it too cool. She decided to flirt a little to draw his attention. Laila casually leaned over and laid her head on his shoulder.

She didn't know that Cas was already restraining himself. Now the scent of her hair and perfume teased his nostrils even more, further tempting him. He wanted to touch her bad as hell, but he refrained. "Yo, what do you wanna do, man?"

Laila only wanted to do him, but she just shrugged. "You hungry?"

She was hungry for him. "No, I just gotta go to the bathroom. I'll be right back."

In the bathroom, Laila got up the nerve to make her move. Fuck it, she was out there now. Furthermore, the sexual attraction was getting stronger than she could stand. It would be the first time she would be with another man since she'd been married, but the chronic and her curiosity combined convinced her that she was ready to take that step. It was now or never. She had never been around a man she wanted to give it to so bad. Laila reapplied her peach-flavored lip gloss and popped two mint Tic Tacs, and she went back out there.

She walked over and stood in front of Casino. "Cas, let's play this game. It goes like this. You have to voice your true thoughts, no matter what they are. No beating around the bush, and no holds barred."

"A'ight. You go first." Cas watched her, amused. Damn, that el she had puffed made her eyes look real low and sexy.

"Okay." Laila was frank. "I'm *extremely* attracted to you. I'm turned on, and I wanna make love to you . . . but I'm also terrified. Your turn."

"Take off your clothes."

"What? Don't cheat! You have to tell me your thoughts."

"I did. I want you to undress. Slowly."

"Can we turn out the lights first?"

"Nah, leave 'em on."

The way Casino stared at Laila made her dizzy with desire. They locked eyes, and she began slowly peeling off her clothing until she wore nothing but her apricot satin Vickie's Secret bra and panties. Khalil was the only man who'd ever seen Laila completely nude. She felt self-conscious because her stomach wasn't completely flat, and she had a few stretch marks from childbearing. Laila knew she had two beautiful babies to show for them, but she had a little complex. Cas didn't seem to have a problem with her tiger stripes, though, so Laila was relieved. Hell, he was looking at her like she was the *Mona Lisa*. Her confidence soared.

When Cas stood up, he realized how short Laila was without her heels. She was petite, but she was thick as hell. He bent down and ran his hands over her body. Her skin was like silk, and her ass seemed to melt in his hands like warm butter. It was even softer than he'd imagined. Cas thought out loud. "Your ass is softer than a pillow, shorty."

Laila blushed. She wanted to touch him also, so she lifted his shirt and helped him take it off. He had a real nice chest and broad shoulders. At six feet even, Cas looked like a tattooed bronze statue. Laila traced the art on his left arm and ran her fingers down his belly. He was hard, and she saw that he was packing, but she was too shy to touch it.

Cas wasn't the type to smooch, but he just had to feel her lips. He surprised himself when he laid Laila down and gently kissed her. To his pleasure, her lips tasted like sweet nectar. Cas kissed her on the neck while he unsnapped her bra. She smelled so good. Her breasts weren't huge, but they were very nice. He took the left one in his mouth, which caused Laila to squirm and breathe heavier. Casino slid off her panties and explored her with his fingers. Her pubic hair was like black silk, and the moisture in her valley told him she wanted him too. He removed his boxers and rolled on a condom.

When Laila guided Cas in with her hand, she noticed that he was larger than Khalil. His entrance was gentle, and he took his time. Their lovemaking was by no means distant and unattached. It was that of long-term lovers well familiar with each other's bodies. Before it was over, Casino made Laila purr like a kitten. She experienced two explosive orgasms—one before him and one along with him.

An hour after they'd used the last of a three-pack of Trojans, Cas and Laila lay intertwined in each other's arms. They were comfortable and were deep in conversation when Laila got a phone call on her cell. It was Portia. She told Laila to hurry to her house because there was an emergency with Simone. Laila's first thought was that something was wrong with the baby. She jumped up and started getting dressed.

"Baby, I gotta go. I'm sorry, but there's an emergency, and I have to go see about my friend. I had a wonderful time, Cas. I'll call you." She hugged him and rushed out of the room.

Laila exited the hotel lobby in a hurry, so she didn't see Khalil's cousin Vincent sitting in the blue van to her left. She jumped in her truck and pulled off fast.

Vincent owned a transportation company, and he was filling in for Jimmy, one of his drivers who had called in sick. Vince was making a pickup for his third run from the Marriott to La Guardia when he spotted an Escalade that looked just like his cousin Khalil's, twenty-two-inch Spreewells and all. A second later he saw Khalil's wife, Laila, duck into the truck and speed away like somebody was after her. He didn't have to guess what she was doing at the hotel. Not as guilty as she looked. He sat there for a second, hoping to catch a glimpse of the lame she was creeping with.

"Typical fuckin' bitch," Vince said aloud, and shook his head. Laila seemed like such a goody-goody, but she was just your average whore. That's why he stayed single. Because bitches couldn't be trusted. And now he had to tell his cousin. Hell, family had to stick together.

His fare came out of the lobby, so Vincent was forced to leave before seeing the mothafucka. It didn't matter who he was, though. That bitch was creeping with somebody.

After Laila left, Casino got dressed and mused about her. He was kind of glad she'd made a quick exit, because he had business to take care of. He really should've left over an hour ago, but he didn't want to hit and run. Not Laila. Damn, she put it on him. He could still see that heart-shaped ass up in the air when he hit it from the back. Boy, shorty had a snapper. And she rode him like a champion. Her having good pussy was the icing on the cake. Laila was wifey material. She was married already, with two kids. That shit was twisted, but Cas dug her.

He knew that chances were he'd wind up disappointed, but Casino was a gambling man. And he didn't wear his emotions on display. Laila would never know exactly how much he was feeling her. A man had to be icy. You could never let a woman know her power. And Laila was a refined sister with superpowers. Casino would deal with her just as he dealt with the dirt he did in the streets. He knew the consequences of all of his acts, and he stayed prepared to be held accountable for them on any given day. He was never afraid of repercussions.

WHEN JAY GOT the calendar Portia made for him, he was extremely pleased. His dick stood up from the first page. On June, July, and August's pages, he could see his name tattooed on her ass in sexy back shots. By the time he flipped to December, Portia was lying in front of a Christmas tree, smiling at him seductively, with just bows and boots on. After seeing that calendar, Jay had to go back to his cell to spend a little time with himself. Damn, his baby looked scrumptious.

On his way to his cell, he ran into his man Skee. Jay just had to brag a little bit. "Look, son. This my wife. Check this shit out." Jay flossed the first few pages on him.

Skee said, "*Damn!* That's wifey? She mad pretty. She look like a movie star, son. Shorty thick as *hell!*"

Jay turned a few more pages, and Skee's eyes got bigger and bigger. Jay snapped the calendar shut. "That's enough, nigga."

Skee looked real disappointed. "Yo, let me see the rest, son. It look like every month gets more interesting. I can just imagine what's goin' on around November and December. Damn, lemme see, son." Skee was dead serious. He grabbed Jay's arm.

Jay laughed. "Nah, duke. You won't be beatin' off to visions of *my* boo flicks. You can't see after July. Them for my eyes only."

Skee felt him on that. "No doubt. But you better hide that calendar. A nigga be more than happy to gank you for it. Better guard *that* wit' your life, son, 'cause I ain't gon' tell you no mo'fuckin' lie. I'm thinkin' 'bout stealing that bitch myself!"

Jay laughed. "I know, mothafucka. That's why you won't see it *no* more." He looked around. "Son, a nigga 'bout to retreat to his cell for a little while."

Skee nodded knowingly. "Don't fuck around and beat blood out yo' dick, nigga. I done did it before, son. Trust me."

Jay shook his head. Skee was a fool. "See you in the mess hall, son." He gave his man a pound and went to make love to his girl.

N A TEARY-EYED assembly, Portia and Laila comforted Simone after she'd murdered Kyle. They hadn't cried that much together since Tupac got killed. They knew for sure Kyle was dead because it was on the news that evening. The reporter said the police had no suspect at press time, but the crime scene was sealed off, and a thorough investigation was under way.

The friends spent the entire night debating. Laila thought it would be easier on Simone if she went forward and turned herself in to the police. Portia disagreed and said they should hide her out until they hired a good lawyer and then deal with it. Simone preferred to wait until the authorities came for her. Clifton was a witness, so she knew it was only a matter of time.

Simone said she'd use the time to draw up papers for Portia to have guardianship of the baby. Being supportive and true friends regardless, Laila and Portia backed off and let her go about it her way. It wasn't like they were fiending to see their best friend locked up for murder.

The next day, Laila had to go home to her kids. And she had to figure out a way to explain to her husband why she'd stayed out overnight, without telling him Simone's business. Portia begged Mone to stay with her; she had plenty of room. Jay was locked up, so there wouldn't be any intrusions. But Simone passed on the offer and went home about five that evening.

Portia didn't really trust Simone's mental state; it seemed like she was playing it too cool. She called Simone at least once every hour to check on her. The last few tries, she wasn't able to reach her. After a few hours, Portia began to really worry.

About eleven o'clock that night, Portia drove across town to Simone's apartment in Canarsie, hoping to find her there. On the way, she tried Simone's cell and house phones again; still no luck. She decided that when she got there, she would pack some things and make Simone come back to her house. It was a week before Christmas, and Portia really wanted to keep her friend's spirits as high as possible.

There was a couple coming out of Simone's lobby, so Portia gained access to the building without ringing the bell. The elevator took too long, so she went up the stairs, two at a time, to the fourth floor and banged on Simone's apartment door like she was the police. Nobody answered. Portia's guess was that she was depressed and holed up in the dark. Or maybe she'd packed a bag and hauled ass.

After knocking for about ten minutes, Portia knew she had to get inside the apartment. She wouldn't be able to sleep until she had a clue where girlfriend had disappeared. Her gut told her something was wrong. She tried to block the unthinkable from her mind. She hoped Simone hadn't been arrested.

Fortunately, the building's superintendent, Mr. Kales, lived on the same floor. He heard the ruckus and stuck his head into the hallway. "Miss, she's obviously not home. Keep it down out here. Some of these folks have to go to work in the morning, you know."

Portia leaped on the opportunity. "I'm sorry, but this is an emergency. I really need you to open this door. My sister is in there. She has a high-risk pregnancy, and something could really be wrong. Please? I know you have keys to every apartment in this building. Open the door, *please*. I have to see about my sister."

Though Kales had seen Portia with Simone on various occasions, he thought better of letting her into the apartment. But Portia convinced him that there might really be a medical emergency. He finally agreed, if he could accompany her inside to make sure she didn't do anything suspicious or steal anything.

When Kales ducked back into his apartment to retrieve the keys, he gargled with a capful of Scope and sprayed on some cologne. That was one little chocolate hottie in that hallway. Old or not, he was still a man and had to at least give it a shot. If she wasn't stuck-up, like that old light-skinned sister of hers, maybe he could give her ten or twenty dollars like the crack whores he sometimes paid to service him. No, she had class. He would offer her fifty or sixty. Getting excited at the thought, Kales hurried back into the hallway.

Once they were inside the apartment, Portia knew Simone was there, because the TV was on and there was loud music coming from the bedroom. Relieved, she hurried down the hall, yelling, "Mone! It's me, Portia. Simone!"

Simone still didn't answer. Portia peeked into the bedroom, where the TV was on, but she wasn't in there. Old man Kales was so close on her heels, Portia could feel his hot breath on her neck. She inched away from him and noticed a white sheet of paper on the nightstand. It looked like a letter. She hurried around the bed to see what it was.

Portia tripped over something on the way. When she saw what it was, she was overcome with disbelief. "No! No, no, no! God, please! No!" She gasped and staggered backward with her hand over her mouth.

Simone lay belly-up in a small pool of blood, with her gun and her Bible inches away. Portia knew she was dead because a small stream of blood trickled from her left temple onto the bone-colored carpet. Simone had shot herself in the head. The look of nothingness in her dear friend's once beautiful and bewitching gray eyes would forever be embedded in Portia's memory.

Portia's knees turned to jelly. She sank to the floor and grabbed Simone's hand and broke down and cried. "Why, baby? Oh my God, Simone. Why did you do this to yourself? God would've made a way. Why you do this? Why you do this?"

When she remembered the baby, Portia fought for control of herself. "Oh my God, call the ambulance! The baby!" Simone's body was still warm, so she couldn't have been dead long.

Kales used his cell phone to call 911. He couldn't believe his eyes. That poor child done went and killed herself. He had a daughter about her age. Kacy would be twenty-five come April. And the girl's poor sister was taking it real hard. He tried to comfort her and felt ashamed of his earlier intentions. "Come on, now. It'll be okay. She must've not been happy here. God will fix it, baby. Turn it over to the Lord," he told Portia. He pitied her, even though he was pretty sure her sister was already in hell, because he knew that anybody who took his or her own life was automatically barred from the kingdom of heaven.

Snotty-nosed, Portia just stared at him blankly. She was in a state of shock. This was one of those moments she wished she could rewind and delete. It couldn't be real life. Rocking back and forth, she prayed for the baby and Simone's soul until help came.

When the paramedics arrived, they found a faint heartbeat from the baby. It was holding on for dear life. To get the baby oxygen, they immediately removed it from Simone's womb by C-section. It was a girl. They rushed Simone and her tiny fetus to the hospital.

Fatima and Laila had shown up as soon as Portia called them. When the police finished their detective work and took Kales's and Portia's statements, the teary-eyed friends made sure Simone's apartment was locked, and then they hurried to the hospital to check on the baby.

At the hospital, they notified whatever members of Simone's family they could contact. Laila named the baby Imani, which translated to "faith." The name was symbolic of the faith in God that they had in her survival.

After a couple of hours, the doctor told them that Imani would live for the present time, but she had sustained massive brain damage from lack of oxygen. The doctor said her chances were even less great because she was also HIV-positive. The girlfriends said a prayer together. At three o'clock in the morning, they all went home because it was too unbearable to stay.

Laila had driven the Escalade so she rode solo. Portia gave Fatima a ride because she had taken a cab. On the way, R. Kelly's "I Wish" came on the radio, and they sang along with the hook. The song made each of them recollect their times with Simone. They could barely sing the words without crying. *I wish that I could talk to you and be with you somehow. I know you're in a better place, even though I can't see your face. I know you're smiling down on me, saying everything's okay.*

When the song was over, the homegirls continued their journey in peace.

In the days that followed, Portia spent her spare time at the hospital with Imani while trying to get over the passing of her sister from another mother. Damn, she would miss Simone. They'd been friends for thirteen years.

Portia thought about the day they'd met in seventh grade. They'd hit it off immediately, and by lunchtime they had a crowd surrounding them while they did that dance "Da Butt" from Spike Lee's movie *School Daze.* While they freaked it, they kept on repeating, "Portia got a big ole butt! Oh yeah! Simone got a big ole butt! Oh yeah!" The onlooking girls' expressions said they wanted to hang with them because they were crazy.

Together, she and Simone had come of age. Back when Laila and Fatima were still squares, they'd gone through all of their 'hood rites of passage together, from boosting clothes from Macy's at Kings Plaza to smoking weed. When they were in eighth grade, they sneaked to the Reggae Lounge on Marcy Avenue and learned how to wind, do the bogle, how to tick and grind on niggas. Then they taught Tima and Laila how to do the dances, and they formed a clique called NIB (New Improved Bitches). They made all of the other chicks jealous when they came through and freaked it at parties. They'd all make an entrance, yelling, "NIB up in this bitch!" while doing the vogue. Even back then, they all stayed jiggy as hell, so their rival cliques used to be sick.

In eleventh grade, Portia and Simone had tried hustling. They bagged up some weed and sold nicks and dimes at school and at parties. In '91, they got their cherries broke in adjoining hotel rooms by Hasaan, Portia's first, and his cousin Nashawn, who was with Simone. Afterward in the bathroom, they compared notes and giggled like the fifteen-year-old girls they were.

Simone used to remind everybody to carry their blades when they went to parties, because a lot of girls were jealous of their clique and acted like they wanted it. If they got caught out there unprepared, Simone was always the first one to break a bottle on the curb and holler, "Bring it, bitches!" to the girls they had beef with.

In the ninth grade, when those three bitches from Red Hook jumped Portia over Wayne-o, Simone had stolen her mother's boyfriend's gun, and their crew had gone up in Gowanus Projects to retaliate. Portia set it off on Michelle, who was fucking Wayne, and Simone backed her friends down with the gun so they could shoot a fair one. Portia represented for NIB and beat Michelle's ass, and Simone busted shots up in the air and ran them away. Then they all giggled and jumped in a cab and got the hell out of Dodge before their asses got in trouble.

After they'd gotten back around the way and split up, Wayne-o caught Portia walking home alone and blacked her eye, just because she'd caught him cheating. The next day, when Simone saw Portia's shiner, she was so mad that she ran up in Wayne-o's face to fight him. They never told Portia's parents who'd really hit her. They had blamed it on a lucky punch in a fight Portia had in school.

One weekend Simone stayed at Portia's, and they had a real heart-to-heart. Simone revealed the fact that she had been molested by her stepfather, Benny, when she was seven; she'd kept it a secret because she was afraid and ashamed of what he had done to her. He used to perform oral sex on her and then make her do him. She said the bastard had threatened to kill her little sister, Callie, if she told anyone. Simone hadn't told a soul until she told Portia that night.

Portia convinced her that it would be therapeutic to tell her mother what her ex-boyfriend had done. Instead of playing the God-appointed mother role, Ms. Benson had reacted by saying that Simone had made it up and that it was her half-white slut ass that had run her man away. Simone didn't despise her for it, but her mother's hatred of her light skin had caused her to grow up with some real self-esteem issues. Still, Simone handled it like a champ. She felt sorry for her mother and even blamed herself a little; she used the excuse that her mother was too drunk to know right from wrong. She did vow to kill the next mothafucka who violated her like Benny had. Portia had sworn to keep her secret and had done so until this day.

When they got older, Simone always carried a gun. She used to say, "I'd rather have it and not need it than need it and not have it." Girlfriend feared the thought of being caught out there powerless.

Portia's soul was wounded, and her heart ached. Tears rolled down her face for her dear friend whom fate had driven to such an untimely death. Simone was no doubt a "true blue, keep a weapon all the time, back-having, you could count on for a laugh every day, you get once in a lifetime" homegirl whom Portia would miss dearly.

THE DAY OF the funeral, it was raining cats and dogs. It was as if God too were weeping from their loss. The friends were sure the rain was a sign that Simone had made it on in and her soul could rest. It was four days before Christmas, and the turnout was huge, though none of them could make out any of the faces as they made their way to their seats. They were sitting in the front with the family because they were family too. They were seated right behind Simone's mother, sister, and aunts.

Laila tried hard to hold it together and comfort Fatima and Portia, who cried uncontrollably through-out the beginning of the service. She prayed for their strength because she needed their support to go up there and deliver the eulogy.

Laila went up to the podium and did her best, but she broke down two or three times before she was done. Although Portia and Tima stood on either side of her and held her up, they cried also. The three of them wound up having to be escorted back to their seats by relatives and ushers. Simone's cousin Tracy sang a tear-jerking rendition of "Precious Lord, Take My Hand" and another woman sang a soul-stirring version of "There's a God Who Knows It All."

Since they'd all shared a love for soul oldies, each of the friends chose one of Simone's favorite songs to pay homage. When it was time to view the body, Portia's tribute, Lenny Williams's "Because I Love You," began to play. It was followed by Laila's selection, "I Miss You," by Harold Melvin and the Blue Notes. Then Fatima's dedication, "Stairway to Heaven," by the O'Jays. The three friends sat together and wept. They purposely waited until everyone else was done; they knew they each needed time to say goodbye. It would be their last time seeing their friend in the flesh, and their hearts were heavy.

After a dreaded wait, it was their turn to go up. Simone's ivory and gold casket was beautiful. It was lined with baby-pink satin. Simone looked angelic and peaceful, like Sleeping Beauty. She had drop curls in her hair and was dressed in an ivory Anna Sui suit and ivory satin gloves. She looked like herself and had a smile on her face. Portia took that as a sign that Simone had made peace with God. She stood over her homegirl's casket and blinked in disbelief. *I can't believe my best friend is lying here dead,* she thought as she stroked Simone's face and hair. Girlfriend was as cold as ice. The undertaker had done a good job on her makeup, but you could still see the bullet's point of entry on her left temple.

Portia bent over and whispered her last words to

Simone. "I'll see you again one day, sis. I'ma treat Imani as if she were my own. I'll love her for both of us, I promise. Don't worry, I got your back. You know you always had mine. I still need you, Mone. God, I still need my friend. Why you had to go like this?" Portia broke into a fresh set of tears. "It wasn't supposed to end like this. We were supposed to grow into little old ladies together and become grandmas. I wish I could take it all back. I'd do anything to bring you back. I know you'll still be around in spirit. I'ma miss you, Monie. NIB forever, girl! Love you."

Portia tried hard to maintain control. She mustered as much strength as she could. Two of her tears fell on Simone's right cheek. Portia wiped them away and planted a kiss on her friend's forehead, then placed a solitary long-stemmed pink rose across her chest. She made way for Laila and Fatima to say their farewells. They each took their time. They knew saying goodbye to Simone was one of the hardest obstacles they would ever face together, but they had to let her go. The three friends walked on hand in hand.

The girlfriends rode in the limo to the cemetery with the immediate family. They heard the inappropriate bickering between Simone's mother and sister but were in no way prepared for what would come next. Those heifers had to go and make a scene. Simone wasn't even in the ground before they showed their behinds. Reverend Finley had blessed the casket, and it was being lowered into Simone's final resting place, and right at the saddest, most emotional part of the day, they had to be ghetto. People cope with their grief differently, but they played themselves.

Ms. Benson looked the part of a bereaved mother, complete with black dress, hat, and gloves; Callie was apparently pissed off. Unlike everyone else, Callie didn't seem moved by the sight of her mother hollering and asking God why he had taken her baby. It must've driven her mad, because she went off on Ms. Benson. "I can't believe you try'na fool all these people with them crocodile tears. You might can fool them, but you can't fool God! He knows your drunk ass wasn't no *real* mother!"

Ms. Benson shouted, "Lord, give me strength. I lost my child, and you disrespectin' me like this. You ain't nothin' but the devil, girl!"

"The devil? You want *respect*? What for? I will not give you the satisfaction of lookin' like some respectable, caring mother. Yeah, you lost a child. That's all you *did* do was birth us. You didn't even know my sister. You never gave a fuck about her. You was jealous of Simone, bitch! Just 'cause she was light-skinned with gray eyes. You made her feel bad about that. She used to hate who she was. She used to wish she was darker, like me, 'cause she thought you would love her more. Hell, I told her you didn't love me either! It wasn't her fault you had her by some damn-near-white man! You fuckin' hypocrite! You were jealous of your own child! You used to say she wanted your men. What kind of mother were you, competing with your own daughter? You ain't shit! I hate you, you drunk bitch! You never did *shit* for us. My grandmother raised us, and you didn't even have the decency to thank *her* before she died. You didn't even show up at her funeral. Your own mama, bitch! I hate you! Get the fuck away from me!"

Callie was trembling and had tears and snot all over her face. She was being disrespectful to her mother but Portia knew a lot of the things she said were true.

Ms. Benson was crying too. She got all up in Callie's face. "That should've been your hateful ass goin' down in that ground instead of Simone, you evil, ungrateful bitch!"

If looks could kill, Callie would've been a vigilante. "No, it should've been you! I can smell liquor on your breath right now. You pitiful. You had to get drunk to come to your own daughter's funeral? That's pathetic!" She pointed a finger in her mother's face and hissed, "God don't like ugly! You gon' pay."

"Oh, so now you gonna judge *me*? I'm your mother! You could've came at me like a woman if you needed to get something off your chest. I don't need this shit today, Callie, your no-class-havin' ass, with your public displays!"

That did it. Callie broke fool. "Class? You ain't *never* had no class! Who the fuck you try'na fool? You gon' bust hell wide open for disrespectin' my sister's memory like this!" Callie drew back and slapped the shit out of Ms. Benson.

Her mother looked surprised but not dazed. She grabbed Callie by her hair and punched her in the face. It was on then. They fought like hell. They were all over the ground, overturning chairs and the whole nine. A few men were still around to break it up, though most people had gone home by then.

When Simone's cousins Phil and Jerome managed to subdue them, Callie broke loose again and shoved Ms. Benson right into Simone's grave. She fell a good five feet down. *Boom!* The casket shook. The older women all hollered, and everybody just looked at each other, like *No, she didn't just push her mother in the grave!*

They probably made Simone turn over in her grave, literally. And she wasn't even properly buried yet. Everyone rushed to help Ms. Benson, figuring she might really be hurt. They pulled her out of the grave, and the fiancé of her sister Bea hauled hysterical Callie to the car. Ms. Benson was pissed off and probably real embarrassed, but she was okay. Portia wondered how Simone could rest in peace with her family carrying on like that.

INCE PORTIA HAD a little time to kill before going to visit Jay, she decided to work on her manuscript. She had written a lot of material, and now she had to fashion it into a story. She'd chosen to alter her main character to a Dominican girl named Dolce, to protect her identity. She began her intro:

> Dolce peeped out onto the floor from the dressing room. She could see that Jerome, one of her regulars, was waiting by the VIP room. It was a slow night, and she was about to make an exit, because she could leave and hump up more scratch in an hour than she could hustle up in the club that night. She gave Jerome the eye, and then she went to get changed.
>
> Ten minutes later, Dolce met Jerome outside, and they went to her place. When he left an hour later, she was five hundred dollars richer. She reshowered, and made phone calls to secure two more "privates" for the night. If all went well, she would be done with the last one by five a.m. . . .

The phone rang again and broke Portia's train of thought. Aggravated, she picked it up and slammed it down for the third time. That bitch Stacy just wouldn't give up.

It rang once more, so she answered curtly, "Yes?"

Stacy said, "Bitch, I'll come over there and fuckin' *kill* you. Don't you ever hang up on—"

Portia cut her off. "Look, little girl, what do you want? I'm about to go visit my man. I don't have time for this kiddie shit. Get a life and stop calling my house, bitch!"

"Trick, you only got Jay 'cause I passed him on to your black ass. You still ain't nothing but a fuckin' *stripper*. I'll come over there and bust a cap in your ass, hoe!"

Portia dared her. "Ugly-assed, freckle-faced bitch, come on!" She was tired of Stacy patronizing her. Hell, Jay knew she used to dance. "When you get here, I'ma leave you where the fuck you stand, and the jury will rule in *my* favor. Self-defense, bitch! That's justifiable homicide, so come on and give me a reason! Grow the fuck up!" Portia slammed the phone down.

True to his word, Jay had taken Portia to the shooting range and made sure she had a steady hand before he went in. She hoped that stupid bitch Stacy wouldn't have to be the first one she tested her aim on. Stacy didn't call back, so Portia saved her work, locked up the house, and started up her Benz for the biweekly drive to Rikers Island. For relaxation, she puffed an el along the way.

When Portia got to the island, she went through the long ritual again. Civilians weren't allowed to drive past the security checkpoint, so she locked her cell phone in the glove compartment, parked in the lot, and hopped on the bus to go over the bridge to the prison. When she got off, she followed the swarm of people rushing to line up and show their ID to the CO at the gate in order to register and visit their loved ones.

Inside the registration building, Portia took off her Gucci boots and belt and placed them in the bin along with her pocketbook and the bag of stuff she had for Jay so the CO could scan it, and then she went through the metal detector. Once she was given clearance, Portia went through the process to get her visitor's pass. Finally, she sat on an old blue, white, and orange corrections bus en route to C-95, where Jay was housed.

When she arrived at C-95, Portia was searched and scanned again, and she stood on the long line to leave Jay new white T-shirts and socks, newspapers and magazines, and money in his commissary. Portia put her belongings in a prison-issued locker and sat down to wait until they called for her visit. Even after all that time, she was forced to wait almost thirty more minutes before seeing her man. It was as if the system had designed all of the red tape and bullshit to discourage people from visiting their loved ones.

A short, broad-shouldered female CO with wire-framed glasses and red finger waves in her hair came out and called some names. "Thomas, Sidney, Mitchell . . ."

Hearing Jay's last name, Portia bounced up and hurried to line up at the final frontier, the last metal detector. This was by far the most thorough search, because it was the last one before the outsider came in contact with the inmate. Everyone knew how easy it was to smuggle contraband to an inmate on the island.

The officer in charge of that post was also a woman.

She looked Portia square in the eye and said nastily, "Look, stay behind the line until I call you!"

Portia rolled her eyes and backed up two steps because she didn't want to give that bitch a reason to hassle her further. Why did some female officers act like they were always on a menstrual trip? If they hated their job that much, they should consider a career change. Portia peeped how homegirl was purposely ignoring her and straightening the same papers on the table over and over again, but she didn't say anything.

At last the spiteful CO looked up and innocently called, "Next!"

When Portia stepped up, the CO gave her the business. "Take off your shoes and socks, and roll your pants up. Now pull your pockets out, lift up your shirt, and shake your bra. No, pull your bra away from your body and shake it. Run your fingers around your waistline. Now turn around and do it. Stick your hands in your back pockets. Turn back around. Wait, what's that?" She was clocking Portia so hard, she saw her navel ring. "You can't wear that in there. You gotta take it out or you can't visit." She looked Portia up and down. "Oh, and that necklace. You gotta take that off too."

Portia pulled the gold chain out of her blouse and showed the CO the diamond pendant. "This is a cross, so it's allowed."

"Religious items and wedding rings are allowed, but not that navel thing. If you wanna go in, you gon' hafta take it out. Now, you holdin' up my line. Step to the side, please. Next!"

Portia knew the woman was just being a bitch—she'd never been required to take out her navel ring before—but she played along because she had to. She wasn't about to walk around on that nasty floor barefoot, so she put her socks and boots back on and left the line to go back to her locker and put the belly ring in her pocketbook.

When Portia got back on the line, she held her tongue but thought about cussing that hoe out on her way out. That evil, jealous, out-of-shape, hating cunt wasn't going to stand between her and Jay. She had to see him. But it was a damn shame that a one-hour visit necessitated no fewer than four hours of bullshit every single time she came.

Jay was waiting the longest to be called for his visit before an officer came and called his name. It was that big Amazon chick, Officer Hines. She'd been flirting with him a lot lately. Jay wondered if it was Hines who'd sent him that love letter. It was one of the female officers on his cellblock. Whoever it was, he wasn't interested. Unlike some of the guys he was locked up with, Jay wasn't about to start fucking or getting head from a CO. He wouldn't be in jail that long, so jerking off to Portia's pictures and magazines served him just fine. Jay didn't want to catch something he couldn't get rid of. A lot of his peoples in there fucked with those loose officers, and he wasn't fond of sharing pussy no way.

When Jay and Officer Hines got out of the others' view on the walk to his visit, she turned around and grabbed Jay's crotch. "Right about now, you lookin' real tasty, Mitchell. I know you read my letter. I wanna fuck you. Later on today. I know you get transferred the day after tomorrow, and I'm try'na get up on that dick ASAP!" She massaged his manhood through the gray jail jumper he wore.

Jay hadn't had any in a while, but he wasn't about to hit that. He pushed her hand away. "Nah, I don't think so, shorty. Any- and everybody don't get this dick. I know how you get down, but I don't freak off like that. You got a bad reputation, Ma. Niggas talk, you know. Stop being so easy, and try to act more like a lady. This is your workplace. Where's the professionalism?"

Jay's rejection turned Hines on even more. Fuck what he said about niggas talking. Hell, the crazy hours she worked, she had to get her swerve on at the job. Some of them jailhouse niggas just looked so good, and temptation was a mothafucka. She would fuck with them as long as nobody with the authority to fire her found out. That was her only concern, so she was persistent with Jay.

"My number is on the letter. Call me when you get up north. You can call collect." Fine as that nigga was, she would let him move in with her when he came home. They always needed a place to crash when they came out. She knew he didn't have to serve much time because she had already checked his record. She pinched Jay on the ass.

Jay ignored Bigfoot's advances. Ironically, here was a woman, sexually harassing him. He wasn't thinking about Hines's big goofy ass. His mind was on Portia. Hines didn't have shit on his brown sugar.

Portia hadn't been holding up so well after the suicide of her friend last week. That poor little baby had her stressed out too. It was sad how Simone had caught the Monster and killed herself. Jay hoped his man Nate hadn't piped her. At least not raw.

With all of that going on in her life, Portia still came to visit him twice every week. And Jay called her three times every day to check on her. She hadn't looked well the first few visits, which had consisted of her crying through the whole hour. The next few she became harder, turning into the rock Jay needed her to be. She just looked so sad. He wished he was out there to comfort her, but he reasoned that her plight would make her strong in the long run. If she could get through these arduous times, she'd be seasoned for life. Portia put up a good front but was still green in a lot of ways. Today was visit number thirteen, and it was the last time they would see each other on the island. Jay was being shipped up north the day after tomorrow, and he wasn't about to force her to come all the way up by Canada to see him.

When Jay went out on the visit floor, Portia stood up and hugged him. He immediately became erect. "Damn, I miss you, Kit Kat," Jay said. She looked and smelled so delicious, his groin ached. Seeing her but not being able to make love to her was the hardest part.

He studied her. She looked better, like she'd gotten some rest before she came this time. "You look good, Ma."

"Look at *you*, baby. Lookin' all handsome. I know these CO bitches be pressin' you. I know what time it is." Portia smiled.

Jay wondered if she was psychic. "You a'ight, Ma?"

"I'm good. Except for your baby mama's death threats." She put Jay down on Stacy's harassing phone calls, and he promised to straighten her out. Portia then gave him the rundown on the past week, told him the house was fine. She assured him not to worry about her.

Then her face looked like a lightbulb had come on. "Oh yeah! You gon' kill me, Jay. Your mother came by the other day, and me and Laila had just finished smoking a blunt. I raced around frantically, spraying air freshener and shit before I opened the door, but I know she still smelled it. I wish she would've called first. I'm sorry, daddy. I just wanted to tell you first, in case she says something about it to you."

Jay laughed. "Damn, you scared me for a minute. I thought you was 'bout to tell me she caught you with a nigga up in there or something. And if she did smell it, so what? That won't be the first time she ever smelled weed."

Jay filled Portia in on the electrician's classes he'd been taking to kill time and the library books he was reading. He suddenly looked real serious. "You know I go up Thursday, Ma."

"I know. I left you a box with two new pairs of sneakers, some clothes, and some other stuff I got you for Christmas. Make sure your stuff goes up with you. Jay, I'm about to slide you this money in my hand. I know you got money in your account, but ain't nothing like having cash on hand."

Jay laughed. He didn't need it but would take it anyway. He was glad she thought on her toes. Like all of the other couples, he and Portia sat as close as possible while forced to sit on separate sides of a table. He stared at her and held her hands. He just wanted to look at her and capture her scent so he could take it back in with him and keep it as long as possible. They communicated silently, and the message was clear to both parties. They longed to be with each other somewhere other than on a jail visit on Rikers Island.

On the low, Jay took the money from Portia's hand and stashed it in his sock. He wouldn't have a hard time sneaking it back in; he did it every week when Cas sent Blair to visit him. That wasn't for Portia to know, but Blair was this shorty they used to smuggle stuff on the inside. She was just a homegirl, but any of them could pipe her if they wanted, because she was all about a dollar. Jay took care of the officers in exchange for leniency. He had all kinds of forbidden shit up in there. The greedy bastards looked the other way when Jay greased their palms. "When I go up, you ain't gotta come see me, Ma. Okay?"

"Is you crazy? Why, you got somebody else comin' up there?"

"Nah, it's just up there by Canada, and I don't wanna put that kind of burden on you. You got enough on your plate right now. I know you're tired of gettin' damn near strip-searched just to come see a nigga. Plus, it's wintertime now. It's mad cold up there. I'll call you, and we can write each other."

"What? I'm comin' up there to see you. I don't care how cold it is. You misunderstand, Jay. Comin' to see you ain't no inconvenience for me. It's like the only bright spot in my life right now, and I look *so* forward to it. Jay, I miss you so much it hurts. A part of me is caged away, and I need to come see you 'cause you're a part of me, and that makes me complete. Jay, look at me. I'm wit' you forever, no matter what the circumstances are. Whatever, whenever, and wherever."

"A'ight." Jay was moved. Deep down inside, he really wanted to hear that she wanted to come. He needed her too, more than he cared to admit.

"Boo, I'll run up to Canada butt-naked over hot coals to come see you." Jay laughed, and Portia got sad again. "Tomorrow is Christmas. I wish I could break you outta here. At least for a day. I miss you so much, baby."

"Don't worry, Ma. It'll get greater later. Just stick with me." Jay remembered the five-carat diamond bracelet he had stashed away for Portia's Christmas present. It was an original by Jacob the Jeweler, and it matched the earrings he'd bought her for her birthday. "When you get home, look in the bottom drawer in my left nightstand. Inside a little gray Bible, there's a key to a safe-deposit box. Look in my sneaker closet in the Jordan section, in the last row of shoe boxes on the left. Open the top box, and you'll find directions in there." Jay leaned back and smiled when he remembered the calendar she'd sent him. "Ma, thanks again for that calendar. Wit' your sexy chocolate ass."

"You better not be bustin' all over my pictures, 'cause I know you be jerking off on them."

"Hell yeah. It be landing all up in there." Jay traced her lips.

"Ooh, you so nasty." She leaned forward and kissed him. "I masturbate while I think about you too. I bought a toy, baby. But it's not a dildo. It's a little vibrating massager. Sometimes I just rub it on my clit until I cum. I don't want any form of penetration until you come home."

Pleasant visions of Portia getting herself off filled Jay's head, so he was candid. "Right about now, Ma, I'd pay a million dollars to see you play with that shit."

Then the visit was over, just that fast. Bigfoot was hating. She called Jay off the floor first. He held Portia and kissed her with the compassion of a newly-wed. Hines coerced Jay spitefully. "Come on, let's go, Mitchell! Visit's over, move it!" That mothafucka wasn't getting any special treatment. Not if he wasn't giving her none.

Portia rolled her eyes at that bitch and kept on talking to her man. "Try and have a good Christmas, daddy. I love you. My gift is in your package. And don't forget to pray, Jay. Call me later, boo. Love you." She placed her right hand on her heart, then lightly placed two fingers on her lips and blew Jay a kiss. Tears welled up in her eyes.

"Love you too, Ma. Be careful. I'll call you tonight." As with every time they parted, each of their hearts left with the other. Jay turned to get a good look at Portia's ass as she strutted back into the world. He imagined it bouncing up in the air with his name tattooed on it while he hit it from the back.

Bigfoot Hines noticed him looking at Portia and turned green with envy. What did that bitch have that she didn't? Jay was a damn fool to turn down her offer. She nudged him, and he headed on back to the dungeon.

When Portia got home, she followed Jay's instructions and went to the bank to see what was in the safe-deposit box. She pulled out a black velvet box with a gold bow. At the sight of the five-carat diamond baguette bracelet inside, she gasped. It was absolutely beautiful. The card read in fancy silver print:

SOME CARATS FOR MY CHOCOLATE BUNNY
MERRY CHRISTMAS, MA
KEEP IT TIGHT!

Portia laughed out loud. What a delightful pick-me-up! Even from prison, Jay was making her feel like a woman. She needed that right about now. She thanked God for him again. Portia felt a lot better, so she decided to spend Christmas Day at her mother's house. She headed to the hospital to check on Imani.

IT WAS CHRISTMAS Eve, and Laila felt better than she had since the funeral. She'd just dropped Pebbles and Macy off with their paternal grandmother, Mama Atkins, and was heading to Pathmark to do some grocery shopping for Christmas dinner. She hummed along with Donny Hathaway's "This Christmas" on WBLS.

Laila had just lost one of her best friends, but she still had a lot to be thankful for. She was done with her holiday shopping and had all of her gifts wrapped; she'd earned a salary boost at the hospital; and things were better between her and Khalil. She was looking forward to spending a nice quiet Christmas at home with her family. Christmas was for the kids.

Now, New Year's Eve? That was a different story.

She had plans. Khalil could go on out with his boys that night. Laila had it all premeditated. About an hour after she brought in the New Year with Portia and Fatima at Times Square, she was making an exit to go be with her side thing. She would call Khalil and tell him she was staying at Portia's until the morning because they'd been drinking heavy that night, and then she would meet Casino, and off they would go to spend the night together.

Laila smiled at the thought of feeling him inside her again. Cas was her best-kept secret. They had messed around only twice, but they did lunch every week and talked on the phone almost every day. Ironically, Laila's infidelity made her marriage more tolerable, and it kept her from feeling so sad about Simone. Plus, having an affair of her own, she didn't stress about what Khalil was doing. Hell, she kept a little smile on her face, and Khalil loved the new non-nagging Laila. Hubby had no idea.

Laila went in the supermarket and was done shopping in under thirty minutes, which was an unbelievable record for Pathmark that time of year. Earlier, Cas had a dozen red roses and a little black velvet box that contained a pair of three-carat diamond earrings delivered to her office. For him to have sexed her so little, that wasn't a bad choice of Christmas gifts at all. On her way home, Laila called her part-time lover to thank him for his generosity.

Casino picked up on the second ring when he saw Laila's cell number on his caller ID. "What up, Ma? How you feeling?"

"Hey, Cas! I'm good. Just calling to thank you for

the gift. I'm almost impressed. You got good taste. Miss me?"

"No doubt. I'm try'na see you later."

Laila halfheartedly protested, "No, we agreed to meet next week. New Year's Eve, remember?"

"Whatever. I'm taking care of some business right now, so when I call you later, be ready."

"Not tonight, Cas. I can't get away." Even though Laila verbally refused, she searched her mental database for an alibi so she could meet him later. That boy did have some good loving.

"So *make* a way." Casino reminded himself that Laila was another man's wife, and he had to respect that, so he toned it down a little. "Just call me if you comin' out later, a'ight?" He wasn't used to being put on a back burner, but he reasoned that some of Laila was better than none of her.

"I really do wanna see you, Cas. I'll see if I can get away for a little while. I'll call you regardless, okay? I'm pulling up in front of my house. I'll talk to you later, sweetie."

"A'ight. One."

Laila parked and saw Khalil's cousin Vincent coming down the outside stairs. "What's up, Vince?"

Vincent just nodded and kept it moving, barely glancing in her direction. He hopped in his black Yukon and pulled off without looking back.

Where was Vince's usual shucking and jiving? Laila wondered what his problem was. She knew he'd seen her with all those damn grocery bags. Rude bastard. He hadn't even bothered to ask if she needed a hand. She made a mental note to act shady toward his ass next time he came up in her face, trying to be a comedian and shit.

She called the house phone to tell Khalil to come out and help her with the bags, but he didn't answer. He probably had the music turned up too damn loud to hear the phone ringing. Laila copped an attitude and carried as many bags in the house as she could. She would make Khalil's deaf ass come get the rest.

She didn't know that Khalil hadn't answered the phone because he was emotionally fucked up over what his cousin had just told him. Part of him prayed it wasn't true, while the other part was fuming and on the verge of punching a hole in the wall. He was mad as hell. How could Laila do this? He never thought his wife would turn out to be a slut. The pain in his chest felt like somebody had stomped on his heart and cut off his air supply.

He decided he'd give her the benefit of a doubt; Vince might've made a mistake. Maybe it wasn't Laila he saw. Khalil had been able to trust her so far in their marriage, so he kept a lid on his anger for the time being.

When Laila saw that Khalil wasn't in the kitchen, she yelled down the hall to him. "Khalil! Go get the rest of the bags out the trunk!" She was putting the eggs and milk in the refrigerator, and her back was turned, so she didn't see Khalil burst into the kitchen with fire in his eyes. Had she seen his face, she would've known he was terribly upset about something.

"You called me?"

"Yeah, go get the other bags from outside," she said without turning around.

"A'ight." Khalil peeped Laila's cell phone on the counter, picked it up, and put it in his pocket. He brought her the rest of the grocery bags, then disappeared upstairs to do some investigating while she was putting the food away. He checked Laila's phone book for strange numbers. There was nothing he didn't recognize. Then Khalil pressed redial to see whom she'd called lately. There was their house number, and then there was a number he didn't recognize. Khalil pressed the send key and hoped for Laila's sake that one of her girlfriends answered.

Casino was in the midst of discussing some business in a three-way conversation with Wise and Jay when his other line beeped. Upon noticing Laila's number, he put his mans on hold and took the call. "What's crackin', Ma? Yo' ass better be callin' with some good news."

Steam shot out of Khalil's ears. "Yo, who the *fuck* is this? You know my wife, homie?"

Casino paused, not out of fear but out of disbelief. He knew shorty wasn't that careless. He couldn't believe this was her husband calling his phone like he was some hard-core G. Cas would never go out like a bitch, but he didn't want to get Laila hurt, so he played it off. "Who the fuck is *this*? Your wife who?"

"My wife, Laila. She just called you, man. What's your name? You fuckin' her?"

Cas was getting tight. He wanted to tell that lame the truth, but he didn't want to blow Laila up like that, so he lied. "Nah, duke. I don't know your wife."

Khalil was enraged. "I see I'm dealing with a bitch-assed nigga here. Man up, bro! If you fuckin' her, then be a man about your shit. Did she tell you she was married with two kids?"

What kind of chump did that nigga think Cas was? He didn't know who he was fucking with. Casino lowered his voice to a menacing tone. "Nigga, I said I don't know your mothafuckin' wife! You better learn how to take care of home, chump. Now don't call my mothafuckin' phone no more!" Cas hung up. He was heated. His phone rang again immediately. He'd forgotten Wise and Jay were on the other line.

His mans knew Cas well enough to gather that something was eating him suddenly. When he pulled their coat about the drama that just went down, they agreed he should let it go. They figured that beef over a skirt was out of the question, no matter how sexy she was. Casino gave them his word that he wouldn't react, and he told Jay he was sending him something up there before the New Year came in. Jay accepted the lookout, and the men wished one another a merry Christmas and parted ways after arranging to talk again the following day.

Knowing that he, Jay, and Wise were dealing with three friends, Cas wondered why he had to end up with the married one. *Because you wanted her,* he told himself. Now he was caught up in drama. He didn't want to have to kill that nigga. Especially not over no woman. He dug Laila, but it wasn't that serious. Still, his pride was hurt, and he felt like less than a man for not being honest with her clown-assed husband about their affair. A part of him wanted to out it so that Khalil would leave and give them freedom to be openly involved. This down-low shit was starting to make Cas feel like the other woman.

No, Laila had to come better than that. If she really wanted to be with him and was as unhappy in her marriage as she claimed to be, Laila knew what to do. Cas was a real nigga, and he would protect her from Khalil at all costs if she made a move. She was married to a lame. If Laila's punk-assed husband wanted it, Cas would give it to him. He would knock that chump out. Casino was known to knock a nigga out.

Back in the day, Cas boxed in the Golden Gloves tournament, plus when he bidded three years up north at Oneida. That was how he'd earned his moniker, "Killa Cas." It was known over boroughs that once Casino smiled and flashed his fronts, a nigga was going down in one way or another. Cas wasn't a bragging man, but his hand game was lethal and his aim was excellent. He would give it to that punk with the hands, or they could take it to the guns. Whatever way that nigga wanted to do it.

Cas imagined that chump was harassing Laila by now. He'd better not fucking touch her. Cas knew the street she lived on, though he knew he'd be out of line if he went over there. She was that man's wife. How would he feel if the shoe were on the other foot and it was his wife cheating? Cas couldn't help feeling alarmed for her, but he wasn't about to go running to her rescue. He couldn't. She was a married woman.

• • •

WHEN THAT DUDE hung up on Khalil, he was totally convinced that Laila was guilty, and he was furious. It hurt like hell that another man was sharing his wife, so he reacted out of frustration and pain in a man's way. He decided to fix her cheating, whorish ass.

Khalil ran back downstairs to the kitchen and demanded her attention. "Laila! What you know about the Marriott?"

Oh, shit! Laila's heart almost stopped, but she played dumb. "Why, boo? Are we going on vacation?"

Khalil read her eyes. She was good, but he wasn't stupid. Why would his cousin make up a story about her out of the blue? And that nigga who called her Ma and then wouldn't even say his own name. How could she explain that?

Khalil grabbed her by the arm. "You fucked somebody else! What's his name?"

"What the hell is you talkin' about, Khalil? Are you out of your mind? Get out of my face with this nonsense."

He grabbed Laila by the shoulders and shook her real hard. "What the fuck is Vince talking about? Don't fuckin' lie to me! Who the fuck was you at the Marriott with?"

"Nobody! Get off of me, Khalil!"

Since she wouldn't tell him the truth, Khalil got angrier and angrier. "I knew it was only a matter of time before you turned into a hoe. That's all the fuck you hang around. *All* of your friends are hoes. Every last one of you bitches."

"Khalil, you better watch your fuckin' mouth. Ain't

nobody no damn hoe!" Laila regretted telling him her girlfriends' business. A husband and wife were supposed to be best friends who shared everything, but Khalil was throwing it back in her face.

"Y'all *is* hoes! Portia's a fuckin' stripper, Simone was fuckin' a married man, and Fatima always been a hoe. And you a married woman who sneaks around, probably sucking dick all afternoon. Then you come back here, try'na play like you mothafuckin' Clair Huxtable. You conniving bitch, I should kill you!"

Khalil snapped. He choked Laila's neck and slapped her so hard, she flew across the kitchen and hit the refrigerator. "I just talked to your nigga on your cell phone, you *fuckin' hoe*! Can't you be a woman about your shit? Why you gotta lie in my face, Laila?"

Laila couldn't believe Khalil had smacked fire out of her like that. She was frightened but yelled, "You crazy bastard! Put your fuckin' hands on me again!"

Khalil undid the buckle of his thick leather belt and yanked it off. Laila didn't recognize this vicious version of her husband. The look of disdain and disgust in his eyes was one that she had never seen in the entire seven years of their marriage. She sensed what he was about to do, so she ran around the counter.

Khalil stormed after her. "Don't run, mothafucka! I'm 'bout to put a straightening on yo' ass!"

Laila's goal was to make it upstairs to the safety of the bedroom so she could lock the door until Khalil calmed down, but he was dead on her heels.

Swoosh! With his first lash of the belt, the buckle caught her across the back. Laila winced in pain but kept running toward the stairs. "Stop, Khalil! Please!" she hollered.

Khalil was blind with fury and didn't hear her cries. He forgot that she was only five feet tall and 131 pounds. He didn't once consider that he was being a hypocrite by hitting Laila, because he'd cheated on her many times. Even once with her best friend Portia, whom he'd gotten pregnant.

If Khalil had looked in a mirror, he would've seen a crazed maniac sweating like a madman. He bombarded belt blows down on his petite wife with the speed and force of an angry master whipping a runaway slave.

When Laila slipped down three steps and hurt her leg, she gave up running. She tried to grab the belt, but the buckle struck her arms and hands. Instead, she balled up and covered her face, screaming and begging Khalil to stop. Laila prayed to God for him to tire of beating her or at least numb her body from the pain.

Khalil finally got tired. "Get the fuck up and go upstairs!" Though he was out of breath, he drew back the belt threateningly, like a chastising father. Laila scurried up the steps like a disobedient child trying to escape a thrashing.

When they got to the bedroom, Khalil picked up her cell phone and redialed that number and thrust the phone in Laila's face. "Call him, bitch! Tell that nigga he can have you!"

Laila prayed Casino wouldn't answer. "Call who? I don't even know what you talking about, Khalil." She pushed the phone away.

"You think I'm playin' with you?" Veins popped

out of Khalil's temples and neck. "I should knock your fuckin' teeth out!" He gritted his teeth and motioned like he was about to hit her again.

Laila threw her arms over her face in fear. At this point she believed he was capable of anything. She tasted blood from a busted lip and realized her nose was also bleeding. Laila began to fear for her life. Khalil was going to kill her.

Please watch over my kids, God, she prayed.

CASINO WAS IN his truck, driving, when he got the second call. He wondered if he should answer it. Was it duke again or Laila? Fuck it; he picked up. "Yo?"

Nobody said hello, but he could hear their conversation. Laila's husband was yelling at her. "Fuckin' whore! You wanna be a slut, Laila? I should fuckin' kill you!"

Cas could hear Laila sobbing and begging him to stop whatever he was doing to her. It was then that he realized the depth of his feelings for her. Cas busted a U-turn and headed across town. He wasn't planning to go kick their door in or anything. He never reacted to a situation without weighing the pros and cons. He just couldn't shake this bad feeling. Cas decided to ride through her block and scope the scene out. That chump was so angry, he didn't even realize that Casino had answered his phone. Cas could still hear him yelling.

KHALIL HAD LOST control again and commenced to old-fashioned ass-kicking. He knocked Laila down and kicked her in her stomach and ribs repeatedly. "Bitch, you thought you was gon' get away with this?

You fuckin' around on me? Huh, bitch? How long you been fuckin' him? You suckin' his dick too?"

Khalil suddenly stopped. He was breathing real heavy. "I'm taking my kids and I'm divorcing you, bitch! Watch!" He spat on Laila and gave her a look of contempt, and then he walked away. He left her lying there just like that.

Cas heard the whole thing. The phone must've fallen on the floor, because he could still hear Laila sobbing. He didn't hear her punk-assed husband's voice anymore. He wished that bitch nigga would try to pound on him like that.

When Cas turned the corner of Laila's block, he saw this dude getting into the white Escalade he had seen Laila driving. He didn't get a good look because duke pulled off so fast, the tires screeched. That had to be him.

Cas parked and reached under the seat to retrieve his heat, just in case. Then he did something he normally wouldn't have. He took a chance and went to Laila's house. He looked around to make sure the coast was clear, and he ducked around to the ground-floor entrance and rang the bell. No one answered, so he banged on the window. Still no answer. He tried the knob, and the door opened with no problem.

Casino stepped into the house, praying nobody else was there. He wasn't trying to get shot or catch a B&E charge. He patted his gun on his waist for reassurance and quietly tiptoed. Inside, he didn't hear anything. No radio, no TV, no nothing. He looked around the house. There was no sign of Laila in the kitchen, the den, the living room, or the dining room. Cas had to admit that they had a nice crib. It was clean too. He guessed the bedrooms were upstairs, so he crept up two steps at a time. There were four doors. Cas tried the one to his left. Barney wallpaper told him that was one of her kids' rooms. When he got to door number two, he saw Laila sprawled on the plush beige carpet, crying her heart out. She didn't even notice he was standing there. The sight of her all bloody and broken-down tore his heart out. Casino wanted to kill that nigga. He was glad that mothafucka was gone, because he would probably body him right now if he saw him. He ran over to her. "Laila! You a'ight?"

When Laila looked up, she thought she'd seen a ghost! How did he get there? She didn't want Cas to see her like this. She thought about Khalil. "Oh my God, Cas. What you doin' here? I'm sorry he called you. Cas, you have to leave. I am so sorry. I didn't mean to start no confusion." Laila was humiliated and feared Khalil would return. She attempted to get up off the floor. Pain struck her midsection. It was so sharp, it caused her to double over and gasp for air. Oh God, something was wrong. Khalil had really hurt her. This was far more serious than the little slaps and shoves they sometimes gave each other.

Casino helped Laila stand. "I'm takin' you to the hospital!" He didn't know what else to do.

"I'm not goin' to no hospital! Is you crazy? I'm a registered nurse. I can take care of myself. I'm fine, Cas."

As much as Laila tried to play tough, she was relieved to see him. She really needed someone in her corner right about then. The pain struck hard every time she moved. Laila realized that Khalil had broken her ribs. Damn, what now? If she went to the hospital, they would ask her all kinds of questions. Even though Khalil had beaten her down like somebody in the street, she didn't want to put her kids' father in jail. Especially not on Christmas Eve.

Casino shook his head. "Look, Laila. You need to go to the hospital. You can't even stand up. Come on, I'ma carry you."

"I can't have the police in my family business. What I'ma tell them when they start grilling me about what happened? I'm not puttin' my husband in jail. That's out of the question. My kids need to spend Christmas with their daddy."

That was Laila, always loving unselfishly. Casino could tell from prior conversations that she considered everybody's needs before hers. Her humility was part of his attraction to her. But at a time like this? "So what you gon' do, stay here and fall dead? Look at you! I heard on the phone how that nigga was pounding on you. Look at your face!"

Laila turned to her door mirror, and when she saw her reflection, she began to cry. Her right eye was more swollen than post-prison Sofia's in *The Color Purple*. She looked like a poster child for battered women. Casino soothingly rubbed her back. She appreciated the strength he gave her, and she knew he was right about her needing some medical attention. She definitely needed some X-rays. "I need to clean up my face first, Cas. I can't go like this."

Cas ran and wet a clean towel in the bathroom and helped her dab the blood from her bruises. They both knew Khalil could come in at any second, so Casino grabbed her coat and carried her to his truck. Luckily, they made it out of there before her husband came back. Cas sped to the emergency room.

Laila was diagnosed with two broken ribs, and she had plenty of bruises and a black eye. After they left the emergency room, Cas stopped at Rite Aid to get her prescriptions filled, and he picked up a toothbrush and some feminine things she requested. Then he took her to a remote hotel so she could rest and heal.

After Laila called to check on her kids, she fell asleep. Cas watched her affectionately. She looked so fragile. How could any man do that to her? Cas had some running around to do, so he nudged Laila and told her he'd be back.

CAS RETURNED THREE hours later with take-out food and chronic. Just as he thought, Laila needed a blunt. They stayed up late talking, and then she fell asleep in his arms.

The next morning Laila woke up feeling sore as hell. Nonetheless, she went home early to see her children open their Christmas gifts. When they asked what had happened to their mommy's face, Laila told them she'd fallen down the stairs but she was okay.

She and Khalil barely said two words to each other all day. Laila couldn't stand to look at him. She was just so hurt that he wouldn't apologize for doing her like he did. She had come home to work it out, but there was no way she could stay with a man who didn't regret almost killing her.

She called Portia and told her what had gone down, and her homegirl offered her a place of solace to cry and heal in private. Three days later, since Jay was locked up and Portia had the space, Laila took the girls and moved in with her until she figured out what to do.

ON HER WAY home from partying Friday night, Kira was forced to pull over in East New York because her engine died suddenly. She tried to restart it several times, but she wasn't getting any fire. The first person she thought to call for help was Casino. She fished his number out of her phone and hit him on his cell, dialing *67 to block her number from his caller ID.

Cas picked up. "Yo."

"Cas. Look, I need your help. My car cut off, and it won't start."

"So what you want me to do, Kira? Call your moms."

"Mommy went down south to see Granddaddy on Friday, and you know my brother's locked up. If Jay was home, I wouldn't have bothered you."

"So park and take a cab home."

"I don't got enough money. I only got like four dollars on me, and it's three o'clock in the morning. It might be my alternator, because the battery light came on a little while ago, but I ain't pay it no attention. I'm not too far from your house, and I really need a hand. Cas, I'm a damsel in distress."

She was more like a damn nuisance and a pest. "Call 911. They'll help you."

"I can't. I had a few drinks at the club. Cas, please. That's word on everything I love. I'm stranded, and it's mad cold out here. I'm dead serious." Kira sounded somber. "Look, just tell whatever her name is that you gotta come help your cousin. What the fuck, we family, right?"

Cas sighed. It wasn't Kira's business that he was alone, so he didn't bother to dispute that little slick shit she'd thrown in there. She'd better not be up to anything. "Jay didn't buy you that car for you to be drinking and driving. Yo, that's my word, Kira. If you lyin', I'm not fuckin' with you no more. Where you at, man?"

"I'm in the East. On Pennsylvania between Sutter and Blake."

"Stay in the car and lock your doors, man. I'm on my way."

Cas had just come in the house and was still fully dressed. He grabbed his snorkel from the coatrack by the door and hurried to assist Kira. If Cas had a little sister, Jay would've done the same thing.

When Casino pulled up, Kira's face lit up. Cas failed to get the car started too, so Kira steered while he pushed the Maxima out of the street until it was safely parked. Cas knew there was no point in messing with it tonight in the cold. It could be fixed in the morning.

After they were seated in his Range, Cas looked at Kira. "I'm takin' you home."

"I might as well stay at your house so I don't have to call you in the morning worrying you. I'll be good, Cas. I promise." Kira was freezing, so she turned the heat on full blast.

"I know you *are* cold with that little skirt on. Showin' all your ass."

Kira sucked her teeth and rolled her eyes. "Like I was saying, I might as well stay with you. I have to move the car by eight. Look, the sign says no parking from eight to ten."

"Then I'll come back and get you in the morning."

"That's only a couple of hours from now. That don't make no sense. You mad shaky! Cas, I know you're not scared of no little girl. Stop being such a punk. How could I possibly hurt you?"

Casino was tired and didn't feel like driving all over town, so he gave in and took Kira home with him, just until he could find her a mechanic in the morning.

When they got to his house, Cas dozed off on the recliner while Kira watched BET *Uncut* videos. Cas dreamed Laila was giving him a blow job, and he practically smiled in his sleep. He woke up and realized Kira had unzipped his pants and was massaging his penis. She had stripped down to her bra and her miniskirt.

Cas jumped up. "Yo, what the fuck you doin'?"

Kira acknowledged the big hard-on he was struggling to put away. "Look like you was lovin' it to me. Cas, look at what's behind door number one."

She sat down opposite him and spread her legs. She wasn't wearing any panties! Cas acted unimpressed and kept his expression icy. "Don't be so whorish, Kira. Why don't you act like a lady and stop being so hot in the ass. Show some respect for yourself, girl. You were raised better than that." Why was she doing this to him? Cas tried not to look, but his eyes had a mind of their own. He was still a man, and he couldn't help appreciating the sight of a pretty pussy. Kira had it spread open so he could get a good look at it.

She stood up, praying she'd enticed him enough to prove she'd become a woman. Standing five-nine, Kira was able to look Cas dead in the eyes. She stared him down and he looked away. To her, that was a sign that she had the upper hand. She continued her mission, rubbing his chest and arms.

Cas shoved her away. "Stop fuckin' playing, Kira!"

"Don't fight it, Cas. I know you want this too. I refuse to take no for an answer. Not this time." Kira took off her bra and massaged her breasts. "I'm tired of fantasizing about you and masturbating. I want the *real thing*, Cas," she boldly declared.

The thought of Kira playing with herself while thinking of him turned Cas on. It was getting real hard to think of her as "little Kira" when she looked so sexy. She was acting real grown up, standing in front of him topless, with no panties on.

Still, Cas fought his desire. "I can't fuck with you like that, Kira. You're too young, man. I watched you grow up. I knew you before you grew titties." His expression was hard, but his eyes were glued on her chest with the last sentence. She was about a size 34C, and they were real nice.

"I might be young, but I'm ready. And I'm pretty sure that *both* of us are mature enough to handle this. Relax, Cas. I just want you to touch me." Kira took his hands and placed them on her breasts, then ran them along her torso.

Kira was coming on strong, and she was too close to Cas for comfort. She was overpowering him. Her skin was soft and she smelled good. Damn. The testosterone was kicking in. It was that vulnerable horny time, just at the break of dawn, when nothing felt better for a man than to bust a nut. Cas's imagination got the best of him, and his hand slid under her skirt into the silky ebony curls of her female essence.

Kira passionately kissed Cas, as she had yearned to do for years. She stepped out of her skirt, and butt-naked, she sank to her knees and took him in her mouth.

Cas's protests were barely audible. "Don't do that, Kira. Stop." Good head was his Achilles' heel. She wasn't playing fair.

Kira ignored him and concentrated on her goal to fuck his head up and make him fiend for her. She suctioned her jaws around him until he jerked involuntarily.

Cas couldn't believe Kira was capable of giving such dream head. That couldn't have been her first time, because babygirl was a pro. Getting more and more curious about that pussy, he pulled her to her feet. Kira maintained control by pushing him down on the sofa, where she straddled him and rode until she pumped two orgasms out of him, back-to-back. When she finished, her legs were trembling.

Kira watched Cas's eyes roll back in his head, and she was extremely satisfied. She had that nigga moaning, so she knew her shit was good. She had been saving it for him for a while, so it was extra-tight. Mission finally accomplished. She had staked her claim on him since she was eleven, and now it was official. They'd had unprotected sex, and that meant they were a couple. Now she fucked with Casino. Kira was young and naive, so she really believed that having his semen inside her proved it.

That nut was a blast, but as his erection softened, Cas sat there, realizing he had fucked up. He shouldn't have been so weak. He didn't usually have such a tender dick. He turned down pussy all the time, so why hadn't he just rejected Kira again? Then he had the nerve to run up in her raw. That wasn't like him. Kira was bold and sexy as hell, and she was the first girl to ever make him bust back-to-back like that, but she was his main man's baby sister. Jay wouldn't appreciate that shit at all. As far as Cas was concerned, it never happened. He wouldn't tell a soul, and he hoped Kira wouldn't run her mouth either.

The next morning, after Cas had her car towed to a repair shop and made sure Kira was straight, he acted like the night before was a figment of her imagination. Kira was hurt and confused. She had sucked his dick a few hours ago, so why wasn't he acting like he was into her? What was with the nonchalant, distant shit?

When Cas was done talking to the mechanic, he came over and pulled out a brick and peeled off five hundred dollars and handed it to Kira. "Don't let this dude overcharge you. He already told me two hundred for everything, so don't pay him no more than that. Get home safe, man." Cas wouldn't meet Kira's gaze, and he left her at the repair shop without another word.

KHALIL LEFT THE club tipsy. He hurried to his ride before Zena, the Brazilian Amazon he'd invited home, came out. Not that she wasn't proper, but he'd changed his mind about the sex. All this unattached sex was getting old. He was going to sleep alone tonight. Khalil headed home solo.

When he got there, he looked around his empty house and felt a pang of loneliness. What a fool he was to have worked so hard to buy this house for his family and then run them off. He missed his woman, and he missed the joy of his children's laughter. What the fuck had he done?

He had lost it, and beaten the hell out of his beautiful wife of seven years, and she had taken his babies and run away. He hadn't meant to hurt her. Something in his mind had just snapped when he imagined her sexing some other dude. He had pictured her sexy faces, and he couldn't fathom the thought of another man being the cause of her making them. Khalil had been with Laila since high school. He was her first, and he considered that pussy officially his. His name was on it.

Khalil had to admit that he and Laila had been on their way to splitting up before that incident occurred, and he had been to blame. He hadn't respected her as his wife. He'd been going through some type of childish phase, so he could understand why she had run to the arms of another man for the things he was slacking on. He had been an asshole and neglected her. If he'd had her back, he wouldn't have hesitated to tell her how beautiful she was, and how much he loved and appreciated her for giving him two babies and so much more.

The months since his family had left felt like an eternity, and Khalil now had the wisdom of an old fool. He wished he'd done like that old Otis Redding record said and tried a little tenderness. Khalil didn't want a divorce. He couldn't do this anymore. He missed his family and needed them to come home. It was time for him to man up and apologize. He had to beg Laila to come back.

LAILA TRIED, BUT she couldn't let go of her marriage. She saw Khalil every day in her daughters. They both looked just like him. Macy and Pebbles missed their daddy something terrible, and they questioned her about Khalil's whereabouts every single day. They looked sad, and Laila knew she was wrong to keep them separated from him. She had grown up fatherless, and she knew how incomplete it could make a child feel. She didn't want her girls growing up with issues just because their parents were on a rocky road. Laila made up her mind. If she was going to make her family life right, she had to end it with Cas. She had invested too much love and time in her marriage to let it all go. She forgave Khalil before he came to apologize. She knew he'd flipped because he had indirectly caught her cheating. It would never happen again, because she would never cheat on him again. Ever.

That weekend, when Khalil stopped by to pick up the girls, he tearfully asked for Laila's forgiveness for hurting her, and he promised to do right by her from then on. He broke down and admitted his infidelity, and he forgave her for hers. Laila took the kids and went home, and they made love all night. She did love him. They had accomplished so much together, going from having nothing to having something, and it was hard to let that go. And she wouldn't, because they'd built something successful. She and Khalil had actually made a dollar outta fifteen cent.

She would be eternally grateful to Cas; during that period when she was down and feeling like nothing, he had lifted her up and restored her self-confidence and made her feel like a woman. Though Khalil had busted her, she didn't regret the affair. It was short but sweet, and she would cherish the fond memories. Laila knew how Cas felt about her, and she knew it would be selfish to string him along. He deserved way better than that. Maybe things would've gone differently if she didn't have the girls, but her children's happiness came first, and she wouldn't compromise it no matter what. Laila didn't have the makings of an adulteress. The family ethic was far too alive in her heart.

Not wanting to say goodbye over the phone, Laila called Cas and arranged a final meeting. He met her at their spot, and now they sat across from each other, equivocating direct eye contact. Though she'd told him how she felt, Cas hadn't displayed any type of emotion so far.

When they walked out of the restaurant, Cas was shocked to see Kira in the parking lot. She pulled in front of them diagonally and jumped out of her car. She must've been crazy.

Laila looked at him for an explanation.

"That's Jay's little sister. She got a crush on me."

Kira walked up with her hand on her hip. She had no intention of blowing her cool, but she had to know what was up. "What's up, Cas? Who's this?" She told Laila, "No disrespect, 'cause I don't know you, but I'm Kira. We have a relationship."

Cas couldn't believe her young ass. "Is you crazy, Kira? We don't have a relationship. There's nothing between us. Nothing, Kira, so stop it, okay? Take yo' ass home and find something to do."

Casino hurried up and got Laila to the car before Kira told his business. Since he'd piped her, she'd sworn they were a couple. Fucking young girls.

Kira fought back her tears and restrained herself. She wanted to jump on Cas for disrespecting her like that in front of that fucking midget-assed girl, but she didn't want to turn him off by acting immature. She knew he wasn't with that "rah-rah" shit. And that bitch was lucky, because if Kira had wilded out like she started to, her ass would've got slapped just for being with Cas.

Cas had made a fool of her again, but Kira wasn't giving up. She remembered his moans that night. The two of them definitely had a connection. She drove off feeling defeated, but her spirit wasn't broken. She was going to treat Cas just like her rap-career dream. She was going to pursue that nigga with vehemence.

While they sat in Cas's truck, Laila asked him, "Do you want your jewelry and stuff back?"

"Those were gifts, Laila. Don't play me like some slouch-assed nigga."

"I'm sorry. Cas, I'll always have mad love for you. You've given me more than you'll ever know. Thank you." She paused. "Well, I guess I'll see you next lifetime."

"Nah, you doin' the right thing. Go home to your family, shorty. Make sure that nigga take care of you. Have a nice life, Ma."

Laila leaned over and kissed Cas on the cheek and got out of his truck with watery eyes. Cas couldn't stop the lump rising in his throat. How ironic that he was being kicked to the curb by a married woman. He marveled at his situation. Right about then, he needed to be around somebody who knew what a prize he was, probably to heal his wounded ego. He started to dial Kira's cell phone number, then changed his mind. She came with too much drama.

FATIMA WAS AT work on Tuesday afternoon and suddenly thought of her Wise. A hunch told her to make sure he was behaving himself, so she called his cell phone. She trusted him but just felt like being assured of his loyalty. When Wise answered, she told him why she'd called and asked him flat out. "Baby, are you messin' with somebody else?"

"Nah, Ma. I'm faithful, and you better be too." Wise was lying through his teeth. When Fatima had called his celly talking about some premonition, Wise was piping Melanie doggy-style. Now she lay at the foot of the bed, waiting patiently for him to get off the phone and finish knocking her off. Not only was Melanie easy as hell, she was also slower than Kelly Bundy. Wise continued talking to Fatima while Melanie slipped off the condom and deep-throated him.

Wise nodded at Melanie to show her that he approved. "I'm waiting on Cas. We 'bout to go take care of somethin'. Here he comes now, Ma. I'll call you later. Love you too."

After Wise hung up, he grabbed the back of Melanie's head and mercilessly face-fucked her. Mel gagged so hard she almost vomited, but she didn't protest. Wise was certain he'd left skid marks in her throat that time. Damn, she was the type of freak you could do anything to during sex.

Wise made her lie down, and he titty-fucked her while she sucked on his tip. Unable to withstand two big, pretty titties, he shot hot cum all over her face. Melanie leaned up in an effort to catch every drop in her mouth, and then she giggled and licked her lips like a white girl. "Umm. Yummy!"

Wise looked at her and shook his head. He never would have disrespected Tima and busted in her face like that. And she never would have swallowed the shit. "Girl, you somethin' else." Melanie gloated because she thought he was giving her props, but Wise was really thinking, *Bitch, you nasty. Go clean up your face and gargle.* Wise laughed out loud because he realized that he had given Mel plenty to gargle on.

"What's so funny, boo?" Mel got up and wiped her mouth with the back of her hand.

Wise played it off, because he knew he would be back soon to let her service him again. "Nah, I was just thinkin' 'bout how good you make a nigga feel, shorty. That's all."

Melanie smiled. She knew Wise was telling the truth, because she made his toes curl every time she freaked him. He was neglecting Fatima for her, and she would keep freaking him in exchange. In her gullibility, she didn't realize that Wise was using her as the slut she behaved like, and he would never neglect Fatima for no cum-guzzling hoe.

Wise cleaned himself up and got ready to make his

exit. He asked Melanie if she was straight, and as usual, she told him she didn't need anything. Wise would've paid up front for the type of nag-free service she gave him, but she never cracked for no dough. He'd never had a problem tricking a little for some good head, but hell, she didn't want shit. Had he been a pimp, he would've put her dumb ass on the stroll, because a slow chick like her was a pimp's dream come true. Wise lied and told Mel he would be back later, then he left her apartment feeling chipper from his afternoon sexcapade.

He wondered if Fatima was some kind of psychic, because that made two times she had called him and asked him the same shit while he was piping another bitch. Wise loved the shit out of Tima. They had been together for months, and he considered her his wifey. She was the best girlfriend he'd ever had. She gave him everything a man needed and more. And he made sure home was taken care of, financially and sexually.

Wise couldn't explain why he couldn't keep his swipe out of those hoes. He just had a high sexual drive that one woman couldn't fulfill. He hated cheating on Tima, but what she didn't know wouldn't hurt her. She was a keeper, and he was holding that down. He just needed to curb his insatiable appetite for pussy before he fucked up a good thing.

PISSED OFF ABOUT Cas dissing her the other day, and ready to give him an ultimatum, Kira circled through his block. She spotted Cas and Wise in Cas's Hummer, just about to pull off. Kira double-parked and jumped out of her car.

Wise nudged Cas. "Son, look at Kira with them tight-assed jeans on. She got a nice gap."

Kira went over to Casino's window and barked on him. "Yo, what up, Cas? I called you like four times. You've been avoiding me. You think I'ma just let you do me like this? I don't fuckin' think so. You need to let me know something right now. That's what's up!"

Who was she trying to get gangsta on? Cas coldly laughed in her face. "Who you think you talkin' to like that, little girl? Go play with your dolls or somethin'. I ain't got time to play with you, Kira. I got shit to do. Grown-people shit."

Wise cosigned, "That's right, Kira. Take your young ass home." He was unaware of the depth of Kira's argument, but he noticed how fat her ass looked in them jeans. He hadn't known she was holding like that. Damn!

Kira shot him a screw face. "You ain't funny. Shut the fuck up, Wise. You only like three years older than me. Who you try'na clown? You don't know shit. Mind your business. This is between me and Cas. Cas, we have an understanding, right?"

"How you figure?" Cas wasn't smiling anymore. Why wouldn't she just lay off?

"Because." Kira looked at him like it was obvious. "We made love."

Wise inadvertently sat up in his seat. Kira looked like she was dead serious, and it was Jerry Springer out that mothafucka. Wise looked at Cas to see his reaction.

Cas looked at Kira like she was stupid and offhandedly told her, "Don't equate sex with love, Kira. That was just sex. Not emotional, just physical."

"Just sex? Is you crazy? You *splashed* up in me, nigga! That means a lot. I don't do that with just anybody!"

"Well, let this be your first adult lesson. Rule number one. Don't ever let a nigga run up in you raw on the first night. That ain't gon' make him love you no more or no less. Smarten up, shorty. Now, that's one to grow on." Cas pulled off before Kira could say another word.

Cas didn't even bother to look at Wise in the passenger seat. He just turned the music up. Kira had pushed his buttons, and he'd said too much. Fuck it, the shit was out there now. He knew what Wise was thinking, but he didn't want to hear it. Wise didn't have to tell him what he already knew.

Wise didn't question Cas for the rest of the ride. If Cas wanted to discuss Kira, he would do it on his terms. Wise knew Jay wouldn't like to hear about that shit. Kira was young, and Jay was mad overprotective of her. Personally, Wise could understand why Cas had done it. Kira was getting thick, and she dressed real sexy now, instead of all tomboyish, like she used to when she was into playing basketball. Wise wasn't about to judge his man. Whatever happened between Cas and Kira was obviously consensual, and Wise would be lying if he said he wouldn't have beat it too.

Freeway and Beanie's song came on next on the CD Cas was bumping. Wise sang the hook. *Even though what we do is wrong.*

AFTER CAS PULLED off, Kira immediately called his cell phone. He didn't answer the first few times, but she was persistent.

When Wise got out of the truck to go in the store on the corner of Putnam, Cas picked up. "What, man?"

She sounded like she was crying. "Cas, I'm tired of you hurtin' me like this. Why you keep playin' me? I'm in love with you. Can't you fuckin' understand that?"

He hadn't meant to make her cry. Cas softened his tone. "No, you're not, Kira. I'm not for you. You're a princess, and you deserve somebody that's gon' treat you like one. Not an old nigga like me. I'm not good enough for you. Trust and believe, lil' Ma."

"You're mad transparent, Cas. Don't run that reverse-psychology bullshit on me. You're only twenty-seven, and I'll be twenty next month. We ain't even eight years apart. That ain't shit! If I'm younger, that just means I have less mileage on me. That's to *your* benefit."

Casino laughed. No, Kira wasn't trying to fuck it up on him. "There *you* go with the reverse psychology. Now *I'm* supposed to fall for it?"

"I love you, Cas. What's keeping you from me? You scared of Jay? I'm grown, he can't tell me what to do."

"I don't fear Jay. That's my man fifty grand for over seventeen years. I respect your brother. We get money together and the whole nine. Why would I sour that over fuckin' with his baby sister? Now you done ran your mouth so much, the nigga Wise know. What the fuck you try'na do, start some shit?"

The attention Kira was giving him was flattering, but Cas didn't want Jay to come home and flip like Tony Montana did in *Scarface* when he found out about the affair between his man and his baby sister. Him and Jay didn't need that bullshit in the game, no matter how long and sexy Kira's legs were.

"Cas, I love you, and I don't give a fuck who know it. This ain't no puppy love. I'm not no fuckin' little kid. I'll tell anybody how I feel about you. That's my word, this is some of the realest shit I ever said. You better get up on this, Casino. I'm a good catch. I don't have no kids, and I'm going places in life. You need me on your team, boo. I'm your Bonnie. Trust me."

Wise came out of the store, so Cas cut the conversation short. "I'll call you back in a little while. A'ight?"

"Okay, Cas." At least he had given her that much. Kira hung up, cheesing from ear to ear.

Cas and Wise continued their trip downtown, and Cas pondered the Kira situation along the way. She was pressing him so much, he was starting to catch little feelings. Especially with Laila trying to resolve things with her husband. Casino realized that they'd never have what he thought they could. She was married, and he had to let her go. He'd gotten so into her, he'd become jealous of her husband. Cas decided he didn't care if he never saw Laila again. He needed a shorty he could deal with on his terms, not just on hers.

Against his will, his mind drifted back to crazy Kira and that night at his house. He couldn't front, she had put it on him.

Wise wanted to let Cas know he didn't think any kind of way about what he'd just witnessed, so he interrupted. "Yo, son. I understand, man. I mean, if you *did* pipe shorty, I can dig it. Well, it ain't none of my business, so don't think I'm no bitch who gon' run back and report some shit to Jay that I don't know nothin' about."

Cas was relieved Wise had said that, but he didn't respond for a minute. Then he simply said, "Shit happens, son. I ain't plan it." He thought too highly of Kira to tell Wise how she had seduced him. He didn't want Wise looking at her like some slut. He felt a sudden urge to protect her.

Two days later, Cas called her. Kira played it cool, but she was thrilled. Cas picked her up that evening, and that was when they officially started creeping.

Cas wouldn't sex her for a long time, but Kira was content just to be around him. Somehow the tables turned, and Cas really started to care about Kira. He didn't realize that it was because she built his ego back up after Laila unknowingly tore it down. He just knew that Kira's energy was contagious, and she really lit up his days. And she was sublime about that hip-hop shit she always talked about. Kira really loved to rap, and she was determined to get a foot in the industry door.

After he heard Kira spit, Cas acknowledged her unique flow. He tested her by putting her in a free-style battle against Wise and some other little dudes from the avenue who were nice too. Kira battled all of them, and she held her own and made them respect her. Cas kept it from her for the time being, but he was so impressed, he believed that he and Jay should put Kira out there. Her long-legged ass was crazy sexy, she was mad nice, and there wasn't a shy bone in her body. To Cas, that combination made her extremely marketable.

He wanted to get Jay's opinion first, because she was his little sister. Kira had already told him that Jay felt she should be in school and was wasting her time. But Jay didn't know how good she was. Cas knew hip-hop, and Kira was nicer than some of the best. She spit like a dude, and he was willing to put his money on her.

After weeks of sleeping in the same bed at night without being intimate, Cas hit that for the second time, and the sex was A1 again. He saw Kira in a new light, but Jay was coming home in a minute, so they had to keep it on the low. Come what may, Cas knew she had him. Unlike any woman he'd ever known, Kira's aggressive little hard-core ass had thugged her way into his heart. She had made him love her.

"**Y**OU FUCKIN' DIRTY bastard!" Wise was out of breath from pistol-whipping Clay for stealing from the spot. He'd hurt his hand hitting that mothafucka, so he picked up a bicycle chain and berated Clay while he whipped on him. "You gon' bite the hand that feed you? Is you *stupid*, mothafucka? I should cut them fuckin' sticky fingers off!"

Clay's pitiful ass just laid there crying, talking about how he deserved the beating because they had been so good to him, he never should have snaked them from jump.

Wise knew all of that crackhead con shit already, so Clay could save it. He wondered how that nigga was going to smoke some fucking crack with a broke jaw. That mothafucka would probably find a way.

"You gon' work off every penny, dusty mothafucka! Get the fuck outta here and go clean yourself up. Be back on the next shift, nigga, or I'ma put some lead in your ass." Wise hopped in his Navigator, and Clay nodded and ran off.

Since Jay went away, Wise had tried to stay on top of shit without running to Cas about every little thing. His hand hurt so bad, he wished he'd just clapped Clay. When he got home, he would tell Fatima he'd hurt it playing ball and get her to wrap it in an ice pack.

Wise didn't regret it. When a nigga stole from you, that forced you to step up and make an example out of his ass, or else another nigga might test you. Though Wise would really rather be loved than feared, in the streets, niggas took kindness for weakness, so you had no choice but to be icy. That was why niggas walked around with screw faces on like steel Batman masks. It was from force of habit.

Wise pulled up at Cas's house and went upstairs to drop off the scratch, which was a little light, thanks to Clay. To his surprise, Kira answered the door wearing a pair of short shorts. Seeing her long shapely legs was a treat. Wise was glad summertime was coming, because it gave chicks the green light to show some skin.

"What up, Wise?" Kira blew on her nails, which were obviously freshly painted and still wet.

"What it is, Kira? Where's Cas?"

Kira stepped aside, and Wise went inside. They had the music thumping in the crib, 50's "In da Club."

Cas came out of the kitchen and motioned for Wise to join him. "What's good, son?" He poured some kind of green liquid out of the blender into a glass. "Try this out, man. It's good for you."

Wise asked, "What the fuck is that? Fuck you drinkin', seaweed?"

Cas laughed. "Nah, nigga. It's a special energy formula I got from the health food store. My moms put me up on this shit. It really work, son. It combats all that stuff that can cause prostate cancer and a whole lotta other shit. It got all types of vitamins and minerals in it. It don't taste as bad as it looks, son. Don't knock it till you try it."

Cas was into all that healthy stuff and was constantly getting Wise and Jay to try something new and good for them. This stuff was by far the grossest-looking, so Wise shook his head. "Son, I'll pass."

Wise gave Cas the rundown on the day's happenings, and the financial short because of Clay, and then he handed over a brick of money secured by rubber bands.

"How short is it?" Cas asked, drinking that stuff with a straight face.

"Twenty-three hundred."

"Make him work it off."

"No doubt."

"Yo, this shit just kicked in." Cas hit his chest like he was Tarzan. "Let's arm-wrestle, son."

Wise laughed. "Hell no. My hand hurt, son. I'm about to go on in." He gave Cas a pound and headed out. On his way to the door, he saw Kira in the living room, on the couch with her leg up, painting her toes. Wise caught a glimpse of her inner thigh, and his curiosity rose. He knew it was too late to think about hitting that now, because Cas had undoubtedly taken possession of it. "Later, Kira."

Kira looked up and yelled over the music, "A'ight, be safe, Wise. Later, nigga."

Wise wondered if Jay knew about them yet. He was coming home next week.

AFTER DOING NINE and a half months, Jay came home in early June. He was eager to put his plans into effect immediately. But the first day, he just wanted to spend time with his son, enjoy his house, and enjoy his woman.

After Jay took Jayquan home at eleven o'clock and argued with Stacy over bringing him back so late, he went back home. His house was a royal palace compared to his cell up north, and Jay hadn't realized how much he'd missed it.

Later on, when he was relaxing in his black marble Jacuzzi, Portia came in looking delicious in a tiny bikini and joined him, and they engaged in aquatic sex. First Jay hit it from the back, and then Portia rode him right there in the Jacuzzi. Her pussy was even better than he remembered. Jay spent the whole night making love to his wiz.

He wanted to stay in shape and keep his "jail muscles," so he thought about joining a fitness center. Instead, he purchased all kinds of exercise equipment and converted one of his spare bedrooms to a gym so he could work out any time he wanted to.

Determined to get up in the music industry, Jay pursued that goal with fervor. He booked studio time for his artists and paid a producer named Sway to make some tracks.

Soon Jay smartened up and got tired of kicking out all that dough for studio time. So that he wouldn't have to foot the entire cost of building a studio, he propositioned his main man Casino on a partnership. They combined from their hustling stashes and bank accounts a total of three hundred thousand dollars and used the money to buy state-of-the-art recording equipment. They soundproofed the walls of Jay's finished basement and set up shop down there.

Neither of them knew much about working the equipment, so Jay brought in his nephew Dave. When his sister Laurie had started earning too much money for Dave to qualify for financial aid, Jay had helped finance tuition so he could attend the Institute of Audio Research to study audio engineering. Now his investment would pay off. Dave was real nice on the beat tip. He could produce anything from hip-hop to pop.

The arrangement worked out well. Jay shut off the inside door and staircase to the basement, and they used the outside entrance. That way, nobody could get into his house from the studio, and there wasn't a lot of traffic in the house to disturb Portia. She could chill out in her underwear without worrying about some strange guy barging in on her. Another benefit was that Casino, Wise, and Dave would have access to the studio even if Jay was out of town. They all had keys.

The months to come would find a lot of traffic down there, from hopeful rappers and singers to a few groupies, not to mention the homies who came through to show love. Even other producers wanted to book time for sessions, but the partners agreed to use the studio exclusively for producing their own hits.

Night and day they worked, collaborating and swapping ideas. That was how their record company, Street Life Entertainment Inc., was born. Eventually, Portia and Fatima quit Black Reign Records to come on board. Fatima used her A&R experience, and Portia kept the books. They were more than willing to be assets to their men and help build the company from the ground up.

Jay's baby sister finally got a chance to show off her skills. She came to the studio and spit about a thousand bars off the top of her head. The fellas were all forced to give it up, because Kira ate it. Cas already knew about her awesome delivery, but he hadn't said a word; he'd wanted Jay to hear for himself. Jay was extremely impressed, so he and Cas signed Kira as the label's first female artist. Kira and Cas continued their secret affair.

Jay remained a man of his word, and as soon as Moe graduated, he had a legit salary working for the label. He'd majored in marketing, so they made him head of promotions in the South, and he oversaw operations from his Atlanta-based office.

The label released its first mainstream single, "Some Real Street Life Shit" by Wise, featuring Kira, over Dave's production. The track was the kind of beat that the East Coast, West Coast, and Dirty South could all groove to, and so far, hip-hop-heads were checking for it.

Before they knew it, the record was almost gold. The men enjoyed their success and continued to push and work hard. Their goal was to obtain a distribution deal through one of the majors so they could achieve international success.

THE PAST MONTHS, Portia had spent most of her spare time at the Children's Hospital with Imani. By God's grace, the baby lived to be sixteen months old before she died from pneumonia complications. Because Portia had felt that tiny, precious, cat-eyed Imani was the rebirth of Simone, she felt as if she'd lost her friend all over again. Portia arranged a beautiful home-going ceremony for the baby and fell into a deep depression for weeks after.

Portia had lost about fifteen pounds, and she looked exhausted. In an effort to revive her broken spirit, Jay decided to surprise her with a weeklong trip to Acapulco. He booked the flight and reserved a villa at an exclusive beachfront resort.

AS SOON AS they got off of the plane, Portia felt revitalized. It was barely dawn when they reached the resort, and the atmosphere was breathtaking. As soon as she and Jay got settled in the villa, they stood on the balcony overlooking the ocean. The tranquillity of the beach was undisturbed at that hour, except for a lone jogger running toward the sunrise. Portia gave Jay's hand a little squeeze to let him know how much she appreciated him bringing her there. "I really needed this, baby."

"I know, Ma. That's why we came."

Portia buried her face in his shoulder and cried tears of joy and relief. She wished she could freeze that moment. Jay held her and enjoyed the scent of the ocean's breeze, and they witnessed the sunrise.

Three days later, Jay had an epiphany. He was sitting on the beach when Portia emerged from the water in a yellow Dolce & Gabbana bikini. In the few days they had been in Mexico, the sun had kissed her skin and bronzed it to an even deeper shade of cocoa. She shook her hair, and the sunlight caused the beads of water that landed on her body to glisten as if she were draped in diamonds. From Portia's walk, you'd have sworn she had her own theme music. Jay noticed she had other admirers too, and with each step she took his way, he was more certain he had to spend his life with her.

Portia picked up her towel and dried off and noticed that Jay was in high spirits. She smiled back at him and wondered why he was grinning at her like that. Suddenly, his expression was serious again.

"Come here, Ma," he said.

Portia walked over and stood astride him on the beach chair he was lying on with his arms crossed behind his head. Jay had no shirt on, and he looked like a Hershey's Kiss. Portia stroked his chest and bent down and placed her lips to his ear. "Jay, you look so handsome. Let's go in for a little while so I can play with Rocky. I wanna fuck you, baby. Right now."

Jay laughed. "What I told you about actin' mannish?" He pushed her hair back out of her eyes. "What up, P? You try'na be my wife?"

"That's already official. I *am* your wife," Portia affirmed.

"I'm talking 'bout *officially* official."

Portia sat up and looked directly in his eyes. "Are you saying what I think you're saying?"

"Maybe. Give me some output. I need to know how you *really* feel about a nigga. You gon' ride or what?"

"Ride or die, boo. I'ma still love you fat, old, fucked up, and dead broke, the whole nine."

"So would you sign a prenuptial?" That was a trick question Jay threw out there.

"Of course. I don't need you for your money. I'm goin' places too, baby. I might have to make *you* sign one. What you hollerin' about?"

Jay laughed. "So how many carats the ring gotta be?"

"Jay, I don't care about that shit. I love you! You complete me. I'd marry you right this second, even if you had a fucked-up Afro with some tight-assed bell-bottoms and tied a piece of damn string around my finger."

Jay smiled and upped her diamond size a couple more carats for that answer. That's what he was talking about. "A'ight, Ma. It's a go. Let's get married."

Portia couldn't believe her ears. It wasn't the traditional proposal, with the man down on one knee, but Jay wasn't a traditional kind of guy. That was part of the reason she loved him so much. She looked into his eyes, and the tears beginning to form in hers confirmed her happiness. "Hell yeah, baby. I wanna be with you for eternity."

"Don't get mushy on me yet, crybaby. I ain't got the ring yet, 'cause this was some spontaneous shit. But I'll get you one later. You can pick it out yourself, okay?"

"Okay, whatever, daddy. I love you, Jay. This is *so* meant to be." Portia slipped her hands inside his, and she bent down and gently kissed him.

True to Jay's word, they went to an exquisite jewelry shop later that day. Portia tried to be considerate and select a modest, less expensive ring, but Jay picked out a six-carat solitaire marquise diamond. To avoid beefing with customs, he didn't travel with that kind of cash, so it set him back a handsome ransom on his platinum Visa. He didn't give a fuck. He would pay it off when they got back to the States. Portia was special, so she deserved a rock. Plus, he'd always regarded expensive jewelry as an investment. If worse came to worst, you could pawn it to get back on your feet if you fell.

Portia was careful with his money, which was one

of her good points. When he'd come home from doing his time, she still had most of the fifteen thousand. She had used her own money to pay bills, just in case he needed a boost when he got out. Jay was impressed then and again now. She kept on passing tests. Portia was a breath of fresh air compared to Stacy and her greed. Jay could never satisfy Stacy. If he had picked out six carats for her, she would've demanded eight.

As they dined outdoors under the sunset, Portia was awed by her engagement rock's brilliance. She counted her blessings and sent praises up to God so He'd continue sending them down. Portia was drunk with happiness, and she beamed at her soon-to-be husband. It had been a long time since she'd felt that good.

BACK IN BROOKLYN, Stacy heard that Jay had taken his bitch to Acapulco, but she was too busy celebrating the arrears from child support to dwell on it. Jay's success equaled her prosperity, so he could take Portia to Acapulco all he wanted. Stacy was the one with papers on his ass. The more he made, the more he had to give her. Stacy decided to pick up Maisha and drive to Club Envy to have a few drinks and talk a little shit, because she was feeling cocky about her newfound wealth.

After the club closed, Maisha never should've let Stacy drive. And Stacy should've known better than to drive home that drunk. She had way too much faith in her driving skills, because she and Maisha didn't make it home that night.

WHEN JAY AND Portia got back to the States, he was hit with the unfortunate news that his son's mother and her homegirl Maisha had been involved in a head-on collision on their way home from Club Envy the previous night. The impact had broken Stacy's neck, and Maisha was thrown through the windshield. They both died within minutes of the crash.

Jay was granted immediate custody of Jayquan. Stacy's mother protested at first, but she knew she had no wins. She offered to help out as much as Jay needed. Portia stood by his side through it all, the funeral and the whole nine. She vowed she'd do everything in her power to help with his parental obligations. Her heart went out to little Jay for losing his mother. Though Portia wasn't particularly fond of Stacy personally, her death was something she wouldn't have wished on her worst enemy. She felt sorry for Maisha's family too.

Jay went by to express sympathy to his man Wings for the lost of his PYT. When Jay gave him a pound and a hug, Wings's eyes were watery. He said he'd paid for Maisha's funeral service and made sure she had plenty of flowers there. But his wife had found out and was giving him hell about his dead mistress. He said he didn't give a fuck because he'd molded Maisha, and she was his heart. She had been his shorty since she was sixteen, and he would really miss her.

Over the next few months, the motherly instinct that most decent women possess kicked in for Portia. Jayquan was a huge part of her life with Jay, and she was determined to do her part. Poor Jayquan was having nightmares about his mommy. He'd wake up in the middle of the night, screaming for Stacy, and Jay would comfort him. Most nights he slept in the king-size bed with Jay and Portia.

ONE SATURDAY MORNING, Jay woke up to the sounds of Portia tossing pots and pans around in the kitchen like a school bully on a playground. Jay knew her by now. She was either on her period or PMS'ing. Jay was careful around her that time of the month because she always acted real weird. She yelled and snapped at him about everything, then she apologized and blamed her hormones and shit. Jay took a shower and got dressed before he went downstairs. If Portia spazzed out, he was ready to make an exit.

Portia looked pretty. She was seated at the table in a pink bathrobe, drinking from a pink coffee mug. Jay saw that she had made him breakfast. He bent down for a kiss, and she gave him her cheek. "Hey, Ma. You a'ight?"

"Yeah, I'm good. Kira came and got Jayquan a little while ago. She said your mother's bringing him back Tuesday morning." Portia's voice was deeper than usual, as if she'd just woken up.

Jay poured himself a glass of orange juice. "Yeah, she called last night and told me she was coming. What you drinking, coffee?"

"Hot water. You know I don't drink coffee, Jay."

"Hot water? Why?"

"Because, Jay."

"Because what?"

Portia rolled her eyes. "Just because! It soothes my cramps, okay?" She gave him the *duh* face.

Jay peeped her *leave me the fuck alone* tone of voice, but he kept on messing with her because Lord knows she didn't care when he didn't feel like talking. "Ma, you got a thousand boxes of green tea, peppermint tea, chamomile, jasmine, and all kind of herbal teas up in the cabinet. Won't you just drink tea?"

"Because I don't *want* tea. Tea hurts my stomach in the morning. Tea is for the afternoon. Why do you care anyway? Don't you have something to do?" Portia looked annoyed.

Jay was amused; Portia's worst attitude was harmless. He liked when she got sassy. "Nah, we can spend the whole day together, Ma. I'm free all day."

"Now all of a sudden you got the whole day free. Every other time *I'm* free and wanna do something, you got shit to do. Now *you* free for a change? Well, I don't *feel* good, and today I don't wanna do shit!" Portia glared at him.

"You got your period, Ma? Is that why you're actin' so mean to me?"

Portia softened up a tad. "Baby, I'm sorry. Look, my body is going through something right now, so please don't take it personal. It's not you, it's my—"

Jay cut her off. "I know. It's not me, it's your hormones, right?"

"Very cute," she told him sarcastically. "I'll try and be nice today. Now, if you'll excuse me, I'm going to dope myself up." She stood up from the table and stretched.

"Yeah, go 'head and smoke your blunt. You'll be all right." Jay laughed at his own humor.

"What? I was *talking* about taking a Motrin. What the fuck you think, Jay? If you think a blunt fixes every fucking thing for me, then you really don't know shit!" Portia rolled her eyes and stormed away.

She obviously didn't find him funny. "Thanks for the breakfast, Ma," Jay yelled after her. He didn't pay her any mind, because Portia was always "seven-thirty" that time of the month. He knew she was upstairs popping Motrin and plugging in her heating pad. That's what she called her cramps therapy. She was certainly a comical chick to have around.

The last few months, Portia had really held Jay down and helped take good care of his son. She treated Jayquan as if he were her own. Their schedules conflicted, because Portia preferred to work in the day, and Jay still kept late hours. Portia was a darling and usually let him sleep late while she got Jayquan up and gave him a bath, dressed him, and fixed him breakfast. Then she dropped him off at day care and picked him up some days too. She was home with little Jay in the evenings while Jay took care of his business, so it worked out well. Jay knew he had a champion on his team, and now that they were doing the family thing, she'd proved herself even more true blue.

Jay finished his breakfast and went upstairs to check on Portia the Grouch. She was asleep facedown on the bed, with a heating pad under her belly, just as Jay had predicted. He tiptoed to get his watch off of the night-stand so he wouldn't disturb her. It was almost eleven, and he was bored. He decided to go holler at Casino to see what he was up to this morning.

AFTER JAY RANG the bell about forty times, Cas answered his door in boxers. "What up, nigga?" Cas gave Jay a pound, and they went and sat on the sofa.

"If I call it, I might spoil it. What's good?" Jay noticed a new painting since he last came. "That's nice, man."

"Thanks." Cas yawned and stretched.

"You was still sleep? Man, get your mothafuckin' ass on the hot foot. Let's go to the park and play some ball, son. Come on, you been talkin' all that bullshit about dunking on niggas. Let's go!"

"Man, I'm tired. I pass. A nigga just laid down, son. I'm tired as a mothafucka. Fuck you get all this energy from so early? Take that battery out your ass, nigga. But since you out and feelin' all sunny, go pick up that money from Felly. The nigga called and said he was finished right before you came."

"A'ight, lazy-assed mo'fucka, I'll go get it. Get dressed and meet me at the park, son. Come out there so I can bust yo' ass." Jay playfully slap-boxed at Cas.

Cas blocked him and entertained him, slap-boxing with his friend for a few seconds. They called it a draw. "There you go with the Joe Frazier shit early in the morning. I'ma tell Portia to stop fixing you them mo-thafuckin' power breakfasts *and* shit. Fuck you had, Wheaties and a V8?"

Jay laughed. "Drink some of that green seaweed shit

you be making in the blender, and get you some energy too, nigga."

"Nah, son. I got a shorty up there." Cas nodded toward the stairs.

Now Jay understood why Cas was fronting on the hoops. He should've known that nigga was laid up with his new chick. "No wonder you was still sleep. I forgot you can't handle no puss. I'll give you a pass this time, son."

Jay knew Cas wasn't seeing Laila anymore, and he must've been getting serious about his new shorty, because he went home early quite a few nights. He'd stopped hanging out in strip clubs so much too. Jay was glad that he was digging somebody unattached this time. Cas shouldn't have messed with a married chick. That could lead to too much drama, and Jay didn't want his man to get caught up.

When Jay teased Casino about being whipped, Cas just shrugged and wouldn't comment. Jay didn't know Cas was hesitating to reveal information because his new PYT was his baby sister. When Jay rang the bell, Kira was asleep right next to him. She was probably eavesdropping as they spoke.

WHEN CAS OPENED the door for Kira the following Sunday night, she looked angry. Cas figured her attitude was with him, so he asked her, "What the fuck is wrong wit' you?"

"We got a big problem, that's what's wrong," Kira said with ethnic sistah neck movement. She folded her arms. "Look, I need to know where we at, Cas. Is you wit' me or what?"

Kira killed him with these demanding episodes. Cas put her back in her place quick. "Who you think you talkin' to? Watch your tone and stop talkin' in riddles. I don't read minds." He figured she must've heard a rumor about him with some chick or something.

Kira turned the attitude down. "I'm sorry. I hope this don't piss you off, but I stopped taking my pills, 'cause they were making me nauseous. Cas, I'm pregnant. Look." She showed him what must've been her pregnancy test results.

Oh shit! Cas experienced a loss of words for a minute. He didn't have any kids, so he should've been happy, but he hadn't meant to knock Kira up. Her family wasn't going to take this well. Damn, now shit was real complicated. Cas piped her raw sometimes, but only because she told him she was on birth control.

He said, "So what you wanna do, man?"

"What *you* wanna do, Cas? You ready to be a father? Or should I get rid of it?" Kira didn't really want to get an abortion.

"Hell no, you crazy? Just have it. Don't worry, lil' Ma. I'll take care of you. That's my word." Tears of relief flooded Kira's eyes from Cas's assurance, and he hugged her. "You ain't got nothin' to cry about. Don't worry, Kira."

Cas knew he had to be the one to break this to Jay.

FORCED TO OUT his affair with Kira, Casino told Jay face-to-face like a man and apologized for knocking his baby sister up. Cas admitted that he cared about her and said he would handle his responsibility.

Jay realized that the shorty Cas had been creeping

with had been Kira all along! That must've been how Kira was getting all that new jewelry. Jay was pretty upset, so he got in his truck and bounced. He couldn't believe his man had crossed him like that. If Cas were any other nigga, he probably would've spazzed out. But they'd been best friends for a long time.

That night, Jay filled Portia in, and she advised him to accept it because there was no point in becoming enemies with his best friend and his sister. Portia was right, and Jay had to admit that Cas had been a man about it and kept it real. He knew that was hard, so what more could he ask? Jay couldn't front, the nigga Cas had been different lately. Maybe he really did dig Kira.

Portia wasn't surprised when Jay told her Kira was pregnant, because Laila had told her about Kira popping up outside the restaurant the day she broke it off with Cas. Laila said she understood why Kira was attracted to Cas, but she wasn't sure if they were sexing, because Cas had treated Kira like a kid and told her to go home.

Though Portia had figured it out before, she knew Jay wasn't aware of anything between Cas and Kira, because he never spoke on it, so neither did she. She liked Cas, and she didn't want to stir up any ruckus. Portia and Cas had become real cool when he came and checked on her while Jay was locked up. Well, the shit was out there now, and there was nothing Jay could do, because his sister was grown.

Before Jay went to sleep that night, he said, "Fuck it." He wasn't about to go to war with his main man over something Cas and Kira both wanted. He'd known about Kira's crush on Cas ever since she was like ten and wanted to beat up all Cas's girlfriends. At least she wasn't fucking with some lame who couldn't do anything for her. Now Cas would be doing the family thing too.

Jay knew Cas was a good dude who would step to his business and make sure Kira was well taken care of. This would be his first seed. The kid would definitely be spoiled.

The next morning, Jay went over to Cas's crib to make amends and congratulate him. He told him there were no hard feelings whatsoever.

Being Street Life partners, Cas and Jay knew that, because of Kira and Wise's successful single, she needed to travel to do promos and shows. Jay wished she hadn't picked now to get pregnant, but Cas guaranteed him that the baby wouldn't hinder Kira's career. He said he would hire a nanny, and take care of the baby himself if he had to, so she could complete her solo album. Cas knew Kira was talented and marketable, and they would all profit from her continuing the rap thing. Plans were slightly altered, but overall, nothing would change.

ARLY SUNDAY AFTERNOON, Portia came home from attending church with her mother feeling high-spirited. The choir had torn it up and had the church rocking. Portia peeked at her fiancé sleeping upstairs in the bedroom. He was snoring lightly. She tiptoed over and pecked him on the lips. Jay opened his eyes and saw her smiling down at him.

Portia said, "Good morning, sunshine. You sleepin' like you got somebody pregnant."

Jay yawned and stretched. "Do I?"

"Ain't no bun in this oven. Better not be none nowhere else."

"Don't start. You know I didn't lay down till this morning. Ma, where you comin' from, church?"

Portia nodded. "I went with my mother. We had a good time." She began to change out of her church clothes.

"Did you pray for me?"

"Of course I did. I pray for you every day, baby. Not just when I go to church." Portia tossed her blouse on the bed and unzipped her skirt.

"That's good to know." Jay got up and headed for the bathroom. He looked back over his shoulder. Portia looked sweet. That skirt was fitting right.

"Ma, when you take that off, don't get dressed yet. Wait till I get back."

Portia smiled at him knowingly. He'd woken up feeling horny. It would be her pleasure to help him with that. It had been three days since they'd been intimate. Portia took off everything except her sexy Cesare-Paciotti open-toes and waited for Jay horizontally on the bed, propped up on one arm.

When Jay came back and saw Portia lying there nude, his boxers rose in the front. She looked so appetizing. He was about to tear that ass up.

Portia got up on all fours and crawled catlike to the edge of the bed with her ass cocked in the air. From where Jay was standing, he could see all up in it. It looked so inviting that he let his fingers do the walking.

After he played with her pussy and made it good and wet, Jay slid in doggy-style and proceeded to beat it. Portia threw it back, and ripples spread across her fat, juicy ass every time it smacked against him. Jay's name was on it, and it was so pretty that he bent down and kissed all over her back. Before he knew it, she suctioned a nut out of him. He stopped humping and slumped over Portia's back, still inside her.

Portia kept on throwing it before she noticed Jay wasn't moving anymore. She looked back at him. "Jay, no, you didn't! You came *already*?"

"Sorry, Ma," he whispered in her ear. "I couldn't help it."

"Get your two-minute ass off of me."

"Oh, shit." Jay laughed. "It's like that? You know I got you, Ma."

"Yeah yeah yeah. Let me go clean up this load you just dropped in me. Move, minute-man."

Jay rolled over and laughed. He deserved that one. He knew he'd barely lasted twenty humps that round. When Portia got up, he slapped her on the ass. Before he knew it, he'd dozed off again.

Portia freshened up and went downstairs to put on her Sunday dinner. She hummed gospel tunes while she decided what to do with the chicken. She had a taste for honey-barbecue chicken and baked macaroni and cheese. Portia wondered what Jay was in the mood for. She knew he wasn't a picky eater. He usually ate anything she cooked. She remembered that he had asked her to make broccoli the other night.

An hour and a half later, Portia was taking her chicken out of the oven when Jay came downstairs. "Ma, you got it smelling good up in here. The food ready?"

"In about thirty more minutes." Portia pointed to the macaroni pan on the counter. "I already prepared it. It just needs to bake for a little while. Do you want biscuits?"

"Hell yeah. I gotta run somewhere. I'll be back in about an hour. I hope you be finished cooking by then so I can eat."

"I will. What time you goin' to pick up Jayquan from your mother's?"

"She took him somewhere. She said she'd call when they get back. Later, Kit Kat."

"Be careful, boo," Portia said. Jay nodded and headed out.

When Portia was sure Jay was out of the house, she

placed the pan of macaroni in the oven and ran upstairs to try on her wedding dress again. She must've put on a few pounds, because her dress was tighter than it was last time. Portia frowned. It was two weeks before her wedding day. It was the wrong time to blow up. Lately, her appetite had grown. Portia knew she'd better quit munching so much when she smoked weed. Jay had commented on her getting thicker, and she'd disagreed, but now she saw it. She didn't want to burst out of her dress.

Three days later, Portia had an appointment for a routine GYN exam. She'd been so busy lately with working, taking care of home, and weekend wedding rehearsals, she'd had to work on her novel during what little spare time she had. Portia hauled her laptop to the doctor with her, and while she waited in the lobby, she wrote:

> Dolce dreamed she was in a sea of men, and the faces were all a blur. She awakened in a cold sweat and ran to get a drink of water. Dolce sat on the edge of her bed and thought about some of her experiences. She had slept with hundreds of men. Up and down the coast, from New York to Miami. She remembered select names and even cars. But the faces, she couldn't recall.
>
> She thought a little harder and was able to place a few of the numbers in her nightstand scribbled on match-books and crumpled napkins, with faces she could barely remember. There was Kenneth, whom she'd suspected was bisexual but still fucked her for five hundred dollars that he'd withdrawn at an ATM after he met her at a club.

Then that bastard Dallas, who'd paid her two hundred dollars to give him a blow job, and when she refused to let him take the condom off after he said he couldn't feel anything, he robbed her for his money back and her stash.

Then there was that crew from Norfolk. She'd done five of them at a slightly discounted group rate, but they were ballers, and she'd charged them per nut. When they left her hotel room, Dolce was four G's strong.

Oh yeah, there was that young guy Barry, who'd lied to his grandmother about his brother getting locked up for drunk driving and needing bail money, just so he could pay her four hundred dollars.

Then Neil, the dude who owned that restaurant in the mall down in Charlotte, who only wanted to eat her out, because he couldn't keep it up long enough to—

Portia heard her name being called, so she saved her work and went to the examination room.

Four days later, she found out she was over three months pregnant. She couldn't believe it, because she'd been having normal periods, but Dr. Jacobs said that was possible. She told Portia not to worry; she would monitor her closely throughout the pregnancy.

Portia decided to wait until after the wedding to tell Jay the good news. Now that she was pregnant, she needed to quit smoking marijuana. Portia decided to get tested for HIV again. Simone's situation had been a real wake-up call.

Portia was pleased with her results. She thanked God, because her lifestyle had been way more high-risk than Simone's. She was blessed, and she would never play with fire again. Monogamy was the only way.

Driving home from the doctor's office, Portia recollected her nights as a dancer and a call girl. She'd quit in part because she loathed the whore mentality she had developed, considering sex synonymous to wealth. If she hadn't been paper-chasing, then Khalil's money never would have been any good to her, and none of that foul bullshit would've occurred. Portia knew from the gate that it was wrong, but greed had caused her to ignore taboo barriers, and it had resulted in her having to abort a child. The ignominy of what she had done would haunt her forever.

That was the past. Things were different this time. She had Jay, and the odds were in her favor. Right? When Portia stopped at a red light, she rubbed her belly, and she couldn't shake the creepy feeling that she was going to pay for her transgression in some way or another. It was karma. Just when you squared up and did the right thing, old shit backfired on you, just like in the movies. It was inevitable.

Portia turned left off of Atlantic Avenue and pulled into an Exxon station to fill up. After she pumped the gas, she bumped into Tigress, an acquaintance from the club she used to work at. Tigress was like thirty-five and still stripping.

Portia greeted her. "Hey, girl! How you been?" She and way-too-much-makeup-wearing Tigress air-kissed diva-style, cheek to cheek.

Tigress said, "Hey, ma-ma. Where in the world you been? Mystique, it is good to see you. You remember Snow, that white girl? She's riding with me. She's over there in the car. We ain't seen you in such a long time. What you doin' for it these days? As a matter of fact, I got something for you to do!" Tigress grinned and pointed at Portia as if she were the Chosen One.

Portia knew Tigress was referring to a gig, so she shook her head and pointed to her belly. "Girl, I can't."

Tigress backed up and looked at Portia's stomach. "*What?* Get the fuck outta here, girl! You pregnant? Pigs must've done flew!"

Just then, Snow walked up. She was real excited. "What up, Mystique? Yo, I know *you* 'bout it. Come and go wit' us, yo! Tigress, put her down!"

Tigress happily informed Portia, "We on our way outta town, Mystique. We goin' to do a flick. That's where the money at now. Porno flicks. That's what's up." She nodded earnestly, as if pornography equated world peace. "I put Snow on, and now she's caking it too." Tigress looked at Snow. "Mystique can't do it, she pregnant."

Snow sucked her teeth real ethnic. "Word? Congratulations, boo! But so what? You ain't even showing yet. Plus, Brian, the director, he's real creative. He might like that. Pregnant women are really sexy. You know how men are. Is milk comin' out of your titties yet? 'Cause I knew this girl who made a bankroll just squirting milk on niggas. The fucking men would drink the milk. They don't give a fuck. You could get *paid*. Trust me." Snow stared at Portia as if expecting her to jump at the opportunity.

Snow was actually serious. This amused Portia, so she laughed out loud. "No, girl, I'm square now. I quit dancing and all that. I'm chillin' and doing the nine-to-five thing now. But y'all go do y'all. Cake it up."

"Word, you chillin'? That's good, mommy," Snow said. She and Tigress looked at each other, clearly thinking that Portia would have to come back to the life sooner or later.

Tigress said, "Well, don't get the wrong idea, Mystique. We don't mess with girls. We only do guys, and this shit is sweet. I got tired of that club shit. I'm getting too old to be shakin' my ass. My son is seventeen years old, and he's about to be a father next month. I'ma be a grandmama at thirty-five. Ain't that some bullshit?"

Portia said, "Hell yeah. Y'all just be careful. It was nice running into y'all. Take care of yourselves, ladies." She hugged each of them and went to her car.

Before she pulled off, they pulled up alongside her in Tigress's Mazda. Snow rolled down the passenger window. "That's you, Mystique?" She was referring to the Benz.

Portia let it be known. "Yeah, this me."

"*Okay!* You must've hit the jackpot with that nigga. You lucked up like a mothafucka, girl. Do that shit!" They pulled off, waving at her.

Portia felt light-years away from that lifestyle. She couldn't help feeling sorry for her former stage-mates. They were nice girls, but hustling and trick-ing were tantamount to survival for them, especially Tigress. She said she was getting tired of the life, but she didn't have a retirement plan, so her "out" was doing features in low-budget porno movies. Portia thanked God she'd gotten out when she did, because had she not, Tigress's fate could have been hers too. She easily could've been knocking on forty's door and still stuck.

ON THE CORNER, the spotlight was on Jay after several profitable bets in the Cee-lo game they'd just ended. It was customary to boast and break a nigga's balls a little when you beat 'em, so Jay rubbed Lite and Miz's noses in it.

"Don't worry, son. Lite, I'ma use this eight thousand I just dead-busted you for, and the six G's I got off you, Miz, for a good cause. You cocksuckas just financed my honeymoon. I'm taking wifey to the Caribbean courtesy of you two mo'fuckas. Good-lookin' dukes." Jay was feeling himself on a winner's high, so he was cocky. Plus, he had two ratchets on him, just in case one of those little niggas stepped up.

Lite and Miz were the only two men on the corner who didn't find Jay humorous. Jay could see that they were tight. He knew the little niggas were grinding for their cheddar, and they hated to part with it, but he had to teach them a lesson. They had been talking a lot of shit a little while ago, when he was losing. Now that the tables had turned, they were salty and looking all constipated. They really amused Jay.

Since they were such characters and Jay was feeling good, he was more than generous when he peeled off and threw them a couple of thousand apiece. "Here, sad lil' niggas. Take this walk and pick your little faces up off the ground. Now y'all got some re-up money. Don't go back to coppin' eight balls. You mini-niggas shouldn't try to play with the big dogs. Here's one to grow on. This New York City, not New York Pity. Now I'm out this bitch."

Jay gave his mans a pound and left the dice game with fat pockets. He hopped in his new G500 Mercedes truck with the Street Life logos on the sides. He, Cas, and Wise all had their trucks wrapped for company promotion. That was the latest shit mad niggas hated on them for.

Casino peeped how Miz was staring at Jay's back as if he had foul intentions, so he gave him a reality check. "Yo, son. Don't even think about it. It ain't worth it, Miz. Trust me." Cas smiled and shook his head and emphasized his words by patting the big .45 in his waist.

Seeing that Killa Cas had toast made Miz fall back on his plan. He'd been contemplating robbing that nigga Jay for his dough back, but he would see him again. He hated Jay for no other reason than that he was flamboyant and doing his damn thing. Miz hated their whole clique. Jay, Wise, and that bitch nigga Casino who'd just punked him. Them cats thought they were the shit because they were caking it on the streets and had their little record label. But Miz knew he would have the last laugh at niggas. They weren't the only ones with guns. He would see them again. Contrary to what everybody else seemed to think, those niggas weren't gods. And they damn sure weren't invincible.

EARLIER THAT EVENING, Jay, Casino, and Wise had gone to New Jersey to do some radio promotion for an upcoming show. On their way home, they stopped at a ta-ta bar in Jersey City, the Cat's Meow, to have some drinks.

It was almost closing time, and after they'd had four rounds of Hennessy and Hpnotiq, Cas and Jay were talking at the bar. Wise had gone to the VIP room for a private dance. He finally emerged with a drink in his hand. "Yo, let's take this hoe to a room. She mad stupid, son. We can *all* fuck for a buck. Matter of fact, I'll do y'all one better. The white-haired bitch over there named Destiny said thirty-five bones for head. I'm try'na get right. What y'all niggas gon' do? You see that bitch ass? Whoa!"

Cas schooled his little homie. "Destiny? Nigga, yo' destiny gon' fuck around and be catchin' AIDS if you hit that, you drunk mo'fucka. You better get tested, 'cause I done seen you fuck with some mutts. Have some discretion, man. Damn, you'd fuck a goat." He elbowed Jay. "Look at that high-risk, dusty-lookin' bitch, son. This nigga Wise will pipe anything. He done drunk that Incredible Hulk and went fool."

Jay nodded in agreement. Destiny did look cheap and broke with that nappy bleached-blond wig on. And she had on regular street shoes instead of the sexy stilettos they liked. Jay sided with Cas. He wasn't with it either.

Wise thought about it for a second and looked real serious. "Cas, you right. That's why a bitch I fuck shouldn't think too highly of herself. 'Cause I *will* fuck a goat. If she got a high ass."

Jay laughed. "Son, to hell with that easy pussy. We outta here. Go home to your girl, man." He slapped Wise on the back in a brotherly fashion. "We're probably saving your life, 'cause I think I seen a few pimples on Destiny booty. Move it, let's go."

The men loaded up in Cas's black Hummer. When they were settled, Wise took it there again. "Damn, son! I can still see that bitch's ass in my mind. I wish I would've drove my own shit tonight, man. Y'all old-ass, limp-dick niggas done got boring."

Cas turned around to face Wise in the backseat. "Nigga, you can say what you wanna say. I done got tested, and I got a clean bill of health. I ain't throwing my dick on the craps table no more. Any and every bitch can't even give me brains no more. I'm about to be a father, son. And Jay 'bout to get married! You need to stay outta the titty bars if you can't just look without trying to lay pipe to every bitch who looks desperate. You got a nice, respectable wifey. Won't you leave these fuckin' hoes alone?"

Wise said, "I can't help it if these bitches love it when I dig up in they ribs. That's what hoes are for. You fuck 'em."

Jay and Cas laughed, then Cas kept on. "One day you'll see. That's why you young mothafuckas gettin' AIDS at such an alarming rate. Because you fuckin' these hoes. Stupid mothafucka."

Jay said, "On the real, though, son, you never know. Shit is crazy. *Everybody* got it. From baby-faced little teenage girls to damn near the whole mothafuckin' continent of Africa is infected. Millions of people are dying over there, son. For something like that to happen in the motherland, that's a sign that the end of time is near. And don't think you safe 'cause we live in the United States either."

"Ahh, there you go with that socio-political-religious shit." Wise didn't want to hear that shit right now, because it hit home and scared him a little. He'd never been tested, though he usually used condoms. All the time lately, except with Fatima. He wondered if you could catch it from getting head. "I practice safe sex, nigga. I'm a grown-assed man, dog. I'm responsible. Fuck, I ain't piping these hoes raw. I just squirt in they throat sometimes."

Jay and Cas laughed again; they knew about his episodes with Melanie. The friends continued to debate the AIDS issue halfway home. Then they switched the topic to their favorite pastime, getting money.

AY COULDN'T BELIEVE what he'd just done. He stared at his new bride and wondered what it was she had over him to have made him want to tie the knot. No, he knew what it was: Portia loved him the way he needed to be loved. Everything with her was good. There was never any extra shit, and she'd better not change now that they were married.

They were riding home in a silver limo after their wedding reception, and Jay couldn't front. He was happy. He massaged Portia's feet while she sipped ginger ale from a champagne flute. He hoped the soda would help settle her stomach. "You feel better, Ma?"

Still unaware that Portia was pregnant, Jay assumed she had broken his embrace during the cutting of the cake and run to the bathroom to vomit because she'd drunk too much Cristal. Portia looked at her pink-diamond-and-platinum wedding rock and smiled at her knockout suit-wearing husband. "I feel wonderful. Today was beautiful, baby. I am so happy. I'ma be the best wife in the world. I promise."

"Yeah, you better. Yo, you sure you wanna get on the plane tonight? We could leave tomorrow if you still feel nauseous."

Portia straddled Jay and kissed him passionately,

and one of many hundred-dollar bills that their wedding guests had pinned to her ice-colored wedding gown fell to the limo floor. She lightly teased his earlobe with her tongue. He smelled so good. "We're sticking to our plans. Our bags are already packed, and our plane leaves in two and a half hours. We're going home to change, and this limo is takin' us to La Guardia, and we gettin' on that plane. And then as soon as we get in Jamaica, I'ma make the sweetest love to you that you ever experienced in your whole entire life." She kissed him again and felt his manhood harden against her inner thigh.

Jay pressed the intercom button and spoke to the driver. "Take a detour, man. Ride around the city for a little while." Portia looked so good in that dress, his mouth was starting to water. They could spare a few minutes and still make their flight. Jay began working Portia's silk stockings and panties down, so she got up and gave him a hand.

Jay was staring at her like he was really in love, and that made Portia feel even sexier, in her wedding gown with no underwear. She felt so close to him that she wanted him that second. Jay hiked up her expensive dress and sat her down and pleasured her orally until she cried out loud. When he was done, Portia had one more reason to stay with him. She sank to her knees and returned the favor by taking as much of him in her mouth as she could, simply because she wanted to please him.

Since the black partition was closed and music was playing in the limo, Jay didn't bother to stifle his moans. Portia had him right at climax, but he stopped her because he wanted to put that one inside her. He had high hopes of making a baby.

Jay slid into Portia's cocoon, and it was so hot and wet, he didn't last eleven humps. After the wave hit him, he thought out loud. "I'm ready for a daughter now, Ma. I'm try'na have you knocked up ASAP. We goin' half on a baby before this night is over."

Portia caressed her husband's back and held her tongue. If he only knew. She remembered their flight. "Jay, we'd better go change and get to the airport. Time is getting away from us."

Jay gave the driver the command to take them to the house. When they got home, he and Portia showered and changed, grabbed their luggage, and hurried to La Guardia. Shortly after, they boarded their plane at Gate 17. Jay snoozed during the flight, while Portia mentally replayed every second of their wedding ceremony.

Everything had gone fabulous. Jay had used a contact from the music industry to get Jagged Edge to perform; he knew they were Portia's favorite R&B group. They sang their hit "Let's Get Married" as she marched down the aisle. The wedding colors were baby pink and platinum; even Jagged Edge had on suits in those colors.

Since Portia's father was deceased, she'd elected to walk down the aisle alone. She didn't pick a substitute to give her away, because she knew her daddy was there walking with her in spirit. Laila was her maid of honor, and Fatima was her matron of honor. Her cousin Melanie; Simone's baby sister, Callie; and Jay's sisters, Kira and Laurie, were her bridesmaids. Each of them had sported different-styled lovely pink dresses.

How Portia wished Simone could've been there wearing one too.

Jay had chosen Cas as his best man, and he had five groomsmen: Wise, Moe, Wings, B.J., and his nephew, Dave. Each of them looked striking in their platinum tailored suits, which were not tuxedos, because Jay said he didn't do penguin suits and neither would his mans. Jayquan was the ring bearer, and Laila's daughters, Pebbles and Macy, were the flower girls. Portia's aunt Gracie confirmed their nuptials, and Patty-cake had cried through the entire ceremony.

Portia smiled. The reception had been off the chain. When the newlyweds left, their guests were still partying hardy. Portia couldn't wait to see the wedding pictures. Everyone looked so lovely. She looked over at her adorable, sleeping husband and thanked God again for sending her true love. Then she ran to the bathroom to vomit, because her baby obviously didn't like those peanuts she'd just eaten.

PORTIA PEELED POTATOES to go along with the roast she was baking for dinner that night, and she hummed along with the Dells's "Stay in My Corner," which played on an oldies radio station she had tuned in to. Two weeks had passed since she and Jay had returned from their Caribbean honeymoon, and she felt great. She'd succeeded in keeping the pregnancy a secret and was planning to announce it to Jay at dinner. She prayed that he and Jayquan would be thrilled about the addition to the family. Portia heard Jay's cell phone ringing. It was over on the kitchen table, and he was upstairs, so she answered it.

"Why is *you* answerin' Jay phone?"

It was some chick on the phone! Portia got on point. "Because I'm his wife, and what's his is mine. Who is this?"

"This is Tiffany. And Jay ain't your fuckin' man." Tiffany was overcome with sour grapes, and she jumped at the opportunity to put Jay's ass on Broadway with that bitch he thought so highly of. She got even more spiteful. "My pussy fits Jay dick better than yours ever will, bitch. That's why he can't stay away from me. You just fuckin' dumb."

"Well, Tiffany, you obviously ain't got what it takes to keep him, you low-budget skank. That's exactly why I'm wearing all these carats, and my husband comes home to me every night. Lose Jay number, you dirty, uncouth bitch!" Portia hung up feeling vexed, and she ran upstairs with her potato-peeling knife in her hand.

Portia ran up on Jay, slapped the shit out of him, and pointed the knife at his chest. Though she had caught him off guard, Jay subdued her and retrieved the knife. "You foul, Jay! We just got married, and your hoes disrespectin' me already. Do I need to know how your dick fits their pussy?" She threw the phone at him. "You fuckin' some bitch named *Tiffany*? I *never* cheated on you, mothafucka! Not once since we been together. Not even when you were in jail. This shit ain't fair. I've been good to you. I've been faithful. I stand by your side through everything, Jay." Angry tears flowed down Portia's cheeks.

"What the fuck is you talkin' about, Ma? I don't know no fuckin' Tiffany. Calm down, P." Jay was telling a bold-faced lie. He had messed with Tiffany again a few months ago, when he was out drinking and celebrating with his mans on that first weekend he came home. Promiscuity got the best of him, and he and Tiffany wound up in a hotel room in Queens. Jay had fucked her and dropped her off at home, all within an hour. Her pussy wasn't even all that, and she got salty when he voiced his critique.

Ever since then, Tiffany kept on calling his cell phone, harassing him. And now she'd disrespected Portia. That stupid bitch knew he had a wife. Jay was going to put a straightening on her for trying to mess up his happy home. He might pay some rowdy bitches to whip her ass. That was if he didn't leave that whore floating in a river.

"Listen to me, Ma." He turned Portia around to face him. "Listen! I said I don't know no bitch named Tiffany."

"Get the fuck off me, Jay! I don't need this shit right now! I'm four months pregnant, you asshole. So thank you for all this fuckin' stress." There, she'd told him.

Jay's eyes lit up. "Portia, you pregnant? Word?" He smiled and hugged her, but Portia broke down and cried as if somebody had died. She pushed Jay away and wouldn't say another word. She just looked at him and shook her head like, *How could you do this to me?* Portia walked away and gave Jay the silent treatment all day.

Later on, Jay was bumping slow jams on a mix CD in his truck while he drove from collecting some money from a new and thriving spot they had in Brownsville. Some of the song lyrics started getting to him. He felt real low for messing up Portia's mood like that. But he was in high spirits about his new baby. For both of these reasons, Jay decided to pick up something really nice for his wife.

When Jay got home, Portia was napping. He kissed her on the forehead and placed a slender box by her pillow with a dozen red roses and an apologetic greeting card, and then he went downstairs to eat.

When possum-playing Portia sat up and opened her gift, she couldn't help smiling. Jay had bought her a badass gold Rolex with a pink mother-of-pearl dial and diamond bezel. It was the watch she'd shown him in *Elle* magazine a week before. Portia added it to her collection of expensive jewels, and she forgave him that night when he came to bed.

LATE ONE THURSDAY evening, Jay rode around searching for an open fruit stand. His assignment from Portia that day was to bring home fresh fruit. And not easy-to-find fruit, like oranges and bananas. She was craving pomegranates, kiwis, and shit. When Jay spotted a fruit stand on Fulton Street, he double-parked and dashed inside. He hoped he wouldn't get a parking ticket. When he came out, he got into an argument with a fat lady cop who refused to give him a break. She kept saying that she was just trying to do her damn job.

Including the $105 ticket for double-parking, it turned out to be the most expensive fruit he'd ever bought. Portia better fucking enjoy it. Before Jay pulled off, he angrily balled the ticket up and stuck it in the glove compartment. He knew he had to pay the damn fine, but he was still tight.

When he got to a red light, somebody beeped the

horn on his left. Jay looked over and saw his man Nate, whom he hadn't seen in months. They pulled over and hopped out, and Jay greeted his peoples with a hearty pound. "A'ight, son! What's good, nigga? Niggas thought you done fell off the face of the earth. Fuck you been at, son? On Mars or some shit?"

Nate laughed. "What's crackin', man? I been OT. I got knocked in NC for some bullshit, son. A nigga had to lay down for 'bout six months. But it's gravy again. I got shit poppin' down in Greensboro. They lovin' that diesel out there. Son! You should see some of them bad-assed bitches hooked on heroin. Asses swole out to here! You would *never* guess they was dope-heads until you see one of them bitches noddin'."

Jay raised an eyebrow. "Son, you be fuckin' wit' them dope-heads? Let me find out."

Nate quickly disputed him. "Hell mothafuckin' no! A nigga ain't try'na fuck around and catch no AIDS. I ain't gon' let these bitches kill me! I got kids. I'm try'na see mines grow and make sure they become somethin'."

"No doubt, son. I know you heard about what happened to Simone, that chick you was talkin' to."

Nate shook his head. "What?"

"She caught the Monster from her baby father, so she rocked the nigga, then she shot herself in the head."

Nate looked shocked. "Word? That's fucked up, son. Damn, I was feelin' shorty. Yo, I'm glad I ain't pipe." He looked thoughtful for a second. "To be honest, that shit is actually a wake-up call, 'cause I ain't gon' front—pretty as she was, I probably would've hit that raw dog. She sure didn't look like she had AIDS. I see you can't never tell. That's fucked up she killed herself, though. She was mad cool, man."

Jay agreed. "That was fucked up. Things you *can't* tell just by looking at her. That should've been the name of that movie. I don't fuck around no more, son. I got me a wiz now. All that casual sex, that shit is over. Me and my shorty went and got tested three times together."

"Word? You married shorty from the party? Congratulations, man! That's real, son. I respect that. A clean bill of health is like peace of mind. That's what I need to do, find me a wife. Fuck it, son. I'ma start taking applications. These hoes need to be thoroughly screened. And tested. It's a lot of AIDS in the black community, man. This shit is *scary*."

"Word, son. I saw a documentary on TV. It don't make no sense. They said like one out of every five people in the city got it. And it's mostly these young kids. So don't be fuckin' with them young chicks."

"If pussy get any more dangerous, I'm just gon' beat my shit. Fuck it. A nigga try'na be here."

The men talked for a few more minutes, and Jay pulled Nate's coat about Street Life and the moves he and Cas were making. He guaranteed Nate a spot on their team whenever he was ready. He let him know that after they secured the distribution deal, they'd be making mega-moves. He and Cas knew that Nate was a stand-up dude, and they were recruiting all of their good men and storming into the industry with an army behind them. The industry was a lot like the streets, with its shady happenings, and they were going to be prepared.

Nate and Jay exchanged cell numbers and agreed to keep in touch. Nate believed every word Jay said. Jay and Cas had a history of making shit happen.

THE LAST FEW weeks of Kira's pregnancy were the longest ones. A week before her due date, Cas suggested that she stay at her mother's house, in case she went into labor when he wasn't at home. Kira pouted, but she knew how busy he was, so she agreed four days before her due date. Cas promised to drop everything he was doing and come to the hospital to witness the birth.

Cas was out taking care of some business in the city when he got a call from a number he didn't recognize. It was Ms. Mitchell, calling to tell him that Kira's water had broken. Cas hightailed through the city back to Brooklyn. On the way, he called his mother, who was away on vacation. She was thrilled and promised to be on a flight back to New York the following morning to see her first grandchild.

When Cas finally got across the heavily congested Brooklyn Bridge, he rushed to Brookdale Hospital to witness the birth of what he prayed was his son. His heart beat with the anticipation of what lay ahead. He was about to be a daddy. Cas would love Kira forever for this. She was giving him the honor of becoming a father for the first time, and no woman would ever be able to top that.

Ms. Mitchell greeted Cas in the hospital corridor. They hugged, and Cas kissed her on the cheek. She had a big Kool-Aid smile on her face. A few months ago, she had sent for Cas by Jay. Cas had been nervous and a little ashamed of the age difference between him and Kira, but Ms. Mitchell hadn't tried to make him feel like a pedophile. She'd spoken her peace about him getting her daughter pregnant, though her mother's intuition told her that Cas would do the right thing. Cas was glad there wasn't any bad blood between them. They'd known each other since he was in elementary school, and he'd always respected her like his own mother.

Ms. Mitchell looked like she was real proud. "Congratulations, Caseem! I have a *fine* grandson!"

"She had him already? Word?" Cas was more excited than he was after his first big gambling win.

"This one was fast, just like Kira was. He couldn't wait to come out and see what's going on." She handed Cas a disposable sanitary coverall. "Put this on over your clothes and go on in."

When Cas entered the room and saw Kira holding their tiny bundle of joy, he was overwhelmed. He stood at the door with his feet rooted, trying to photograph that moment in his mind so he could remember it forever. Kira had given birth to his prince. Suddenly, he loved her more than he ever thought he was capable of loving. He knew he would marry her.

Kira grinned at him. "Look, Cas. Come and meet your mini-me. He looks just like you with his big self. He was *eight pounds* and three ounces."

Cas got acquainted with his baby, examining every inch of him from his little head to his tiny toes. His son was perfect. He looked just like a doll baby, with a full head of curly hair. Kira had named him Jahseim, a derivative of Jay and Caseem.

Somebody knocked on the room door, and Cas and Kira looked up to see Jay coming in. He was grinning and filming them on a camcorder. "Congratulations!" Jay bent down and kissed his sister on the cheek and asked if she was okay. When Cas passed the baby to Kira, Jay gave his man a pound and a hearty hug. "Let me see that big-headed baby." Jay was impressed when he saw what Cas and his sister had produced. His little nephew was really adorable.

Kira was overjoyed. As she held Jahseim's tiny hand, she rapped to her newborn off the top of her head, like most women make up cute little baby songs. She cleverly put Cas and Jay in it too:

> Yo, I just had a son, so now I'm a mother
> There go your daddy, Cas, and that's my big brother
> I call him big head, but you'll call him Uncle Jay
> Against all odds, boo, Mommy will make a way
> Daddy bought you a little bed so we can accommodate you
> Jahseim's a little dream, too good to be true
> Day after tomorrow, you can come home wit' me
> And you, your daddy, and me, we'll be a family

She tickled her newborn's tiny thigh. "Just me, you, and daddy!"

Kira looked up and blushed when she caught Cas and Jay smiling at her. Cas looked like a proud father. She was so relieved.

Just then, Jay knew Kira would continue with her

music and be all right. She was freestyling right after giving birth. If that wasn't love for hip-hop, then what was? Jay was sincerely a happy uncle. This was his second nephew, and with Dave and Jayquan, that made three men in the next generation who could continue the family legacy.

Jay was glad for Cas, who'd gotten his boy. Every man needed a son to carry on his name. Kira looked like she was glowing. Jay knew she'd make a good mommy, with their mother's supervision, of course. Remembering his good fortune, he told Cas and Kira about Portia's condition. They were all thrilled that their babies would grow up together.

There was another knock at the door. Ms. Mitchell stuck her head in to tell Kira that Laurie and Portia were there. Jay and Cas stepped outside to talk so the girls could come in and see the baby. When the balloon-toting women went in, their high-pitched "oohs" and "aahs" could be heard all the way down the hall.

Jay reached into his inside jacket pocket to retrieve two of the expensive Cuban cigars he had purchased solely for the occasion. He handed one to Cas, who thanked his best friend, and the two men walked down the hall and discussed the power moves they would make to permanently secure their families' financial futures. Both of them had grown up without fathers. Unlike their fathers, they were concerned about their offspring and had intentions of being around to make sure they flourished.

FATIMA'S HEART WAS beating a mile a minute as she watched her doctor open the oak medical file cabinet that contained her fate. She was about to get her results from the confidential HIV testing she'd had done the previous week. Fatima wondered why she had let Portia talk her into doing it, because the anticipation alone had almost killed her. She crossed her fingers and said her trillionth prayer since signing the form to authorize the test.

"Dr. Phillips, I can't wait another second. I need to know right now, so I can get prepared." Fatima realized that she had a death grip on the doctor's arm and released it.

Dr. Phillips cleared her throat and looked Fatima in the eye. "I have your results right here, Ms. Sinclair. Please try and relax." The doctor flipped through the file until she found the paper she was searching for.

Fatima was more afraid than she'd ever been in her entire life. She just knew she had it. Larry probably had given it to her. And she'd probably given it to Wise. Or had Wise given it to her? Fatima wished she had never started having sex in the first place. Now she was done off. "How long do I have, Doc?"

Dr. Phillips smiled. "Calm down, Ms. Sinclair, you're fine. You tested negative."

Fatima could've sworn she heard heavenly bells and trumpets. The sheet of paper Dr. Phillips showed her was all a blur except for the words "No HIV antibodies detected." Fatima fell on her knees and threw up her hands in praise. "Thank you, Jesus! Oh, God is so good! Thank you, Lord. Thank you for sparing my life. Thank you, God, thank you, thank you!"

Dr. Phillips smiled at the sight of her patient celebrating her good health. She too was a woman of God, so she understood why Fatima was having church in her office. How she loved to be the bearer of good news. Unfortunately, that wasn't the case all the time. Sometimes she was forced to tell women they were positive, and they reacted in ways that tore her heart out. However, this scene was rewarding. She wished women would abstain from unhealthy, high-risk sexual behavior. They didn't understand how that virus could attack their bodies and shut them down.

Fatima got ahold of herself and stood up on two feet. "Pardon me, Dr. Phillips. I'm just so happy. I feel like this is my second chance in life. Finally knowing took such a burden off of my shoulders. God is just so good."

"God certainly is good, Ms. Sinclair. I'm refilling your birth control prescription, as per your request, but please be sure to practice safe sex from here on. Don't sacrifice your health for anybody. It's not worth it. I'll see you in six months for your next pap, and I'll instruct the nurse to give you a copy of these results. Have a good day."

Fatima thanked her and stopped at the front for her letter of clearance. She felt so good, she decided to take a walk. It was rather nice outside, to be November. Fatima remembered that Thanksgiving was only two weeks away. And boy, did she have a lot to be thankful for. She headed farther into Brooklyn Heights, toward the promenade and the water. Fatima stopped at a hot dog stand and bought a soft pretzel, and she broke off tiny pieces and fed the birds. She guessed it was due to her recent enlightening, but she sure felt appreciative of the simple things in life.

Fatima figured that Wise had to be safe too, since she'd been sexing him raw. She still wanted him to get tested. When she saw him later, she would show him her negative confirmation and insist that he get himself checked out as well. She wasn't taking no for an answer. If Fatima didn't have the Monster by now, she'd never get it, because if it didn't work out with Wise, she was locking up her stuff and putting the key in a vault. She couldn't go through that scare again. She'd almost had a heart attack. No more was she being anybody's cum dump.

About three weeks later, a relieved Wise tested negative too. He was so happy, he went home toting two bottles of Cristal, and he and Fatima celebrated by sipping champagne off of each other and making love all night long.

After Wise got his results, he started thinking like a new man. He figured it was time to put infidelity on a back burner, because life was more important than pussy.

The following day, Fatima was in such high spirits that she booked an all-expenses-paid-by-her weekend retreat for herself, pregnant Portia, and Laila at a spa in Valley Springs. She figured they could all use some pampering.

Friday evening, Laila drove them up to Valley Springs in Portia's Mercedes. When they arrived, the girlfriends dropped their luggage off in their suite. After that, the first stop was the bar. Tima ordered four apple-tinis, one for each of them, and the fourth for their homie who wasn't with them anymore. Then the ladies headed back to their suite to get right.

They stepped out onto the veranda, which over-looked acres of picturesque green landscaping. Por-tia, Fatima, and Laila reminisced about Simone, and Fatima held the fourth drink over the balcony. Before she poured it out, she said, "This for our sister who ain't here. I know you smilin' down on us right now, babygirl. We love you, ma-ma. Forever." She kissed two fingers to the sky.

"No doubt. You always with us in spirit, Mone," Portia added. "Tima, throw that shit up so she can catch it. Fuck that, don't pour it down."

"Hell yeah," said Laila. "Now we 'bout to put this el in the air for you too, Mone! Can't nobody roll one like you could, baby. Rest in peace, sis." Laila sparked up and blew the first smoke toward heaven, and Fatima threw Simone's apple-tini up in the air.

The friends smiled at one another, knowing that was what she would've wanted. Portia took a few pulls of the weed, even though she'd stopped smoking until she had her baby.

When the girlfriends were done with the bottle of Moët they'd had delivered to their suite, they went down to the spa to get facials and full-body massages. After the most invigorating rubdown they'd ever had, the ladies lounged in white terry-cloth robes, with avocado masks on their faces and cucumber slices on their eyes, relaxing before they got manicures and pedicures.

Later that night, they stayed up late, discussing their careers and relationships. Fatima sent Laila and Portia into a fit of giggles when she told them about her latest fetish, anal sex with Wise.

"See, y'all bitches laughing, but I'm for real. I was never into that before, but I love the shit outta Wise. He's always so gentle, and that makes the pain pleasure. That nigga freaks me out to where that shit feel good as hell."

Portia knew how freaky Wise was, from hearing about how he did Melanie, so she wasn't surprised. "Wise freaks you out? You mean he *turned* yo' ass out. Let me find out you into hot butt love now."

Fatima laughed and corrected her. "Only disease-free hot butt love. And it's wonderful with somebody you really love, P."

Portia asked, "Laila, you into HBL too?"

"I plead the fifth, yo. Nah, I ain't gon' front. Me and Khalil did it before, but I ain't like it. That shit hurt like a mo'fucka."

Fatima laughed. "You just have to relax, Lay. It's like making love on a whole new level. And y'all know a bitch get fucked up before we entertain that shit. We use lubrication, and we get so high, we be floating. So it feels natural, like I'm underwater. Yo, I'm telling you. Y'all gotta get up on that shit too."

Portia shook her head. "No, thank you, Madam Kama Sutra. Maybe after I drop this load. Lately, Jay's been getting straight-up missionary-style pussy. He's lucky if I give him some back shot on the weekend, shit. But it don't matter what position I give it to him in. That nigga be 'bout to lose his mind, regardless. He *loves* this pussy." They all laughed and hit high five. "Plus, I think I'm getting hemorrhoids, y'all. So ain't no way Jay sticking nothin' in my ass. At least not till I have this baby."

Laila and Tima cracked up. "I know that's right!" they said in unison.

Laila said, "Girl, you stupid. But love will make you do some crazy shit. Don't knock it till you try it, P. Tima, I done tried it, so I can knock that shit. Khalil don't smoke weed, so it didn't feel like we was floatin' under no damn water together. My booty was sore for a whole damn week!"

They cracked up again.

Late Sunday night, the girlfriends went back home to Brooklyn feeling like new women. They'd had a luxurious weekend, and though it set no-complaining Fatima back a few grand, she refused to take the money Portia and Laila offered. She had no regrets.

T WAS THE night after Christmas, and Portia was baking cookies. She took the Nestlé Tollhouses out of the oven and peeked in the living room at Jay and Jayquan. The Christmas-tree lights blinked on them as they did push-ups on the mink rug in front of the fireplace. They both looked so cute in their wifebeaters and jeans. Jay's son liked to dress just like him. Jayquan had the same sweat suits, the same Timbs, and the same sneakers Jay had, all in the same colors. Lil' Jay copied everything he saw his daddy do as well. That's why Jay was so careful about what he did around him.

When father and son were done exercising, they joined Portia in the kitchen. She sent Jayquan to wash his hands, and then they settled on the couch to eat cookies and watch *Jack Frost* on TV while Jay took a shower.

Portia had been having bouts of insecurity lately, due to her body changing from the pregnancy. She'd decided to go back to sleeping in sexy pajamas, instead of boxers, like she'd worn lately. But how sexy could she be, with that big belly? She decided to ask Jay how he felt about her figure. Jayquan laughed at the characters on TV, snapping Portia out of her daydream.

After Jayquan watched *Jack Frost*, Jay told him to

clean up his new toys. Portia made him a bubble bath, and after he got out of the tub, she and Jay tucked him in bed.

Afterward, Jay and Portia lounged around and listened to music and chatted about the record business and their baby-to-come. Portia was seven months, and the day before, she'd told Jay they were having a girl. He was elated, and he had no objections to Portia's decision to name the baby Jazmin Simone.

Jay stared out the window at the streetlight. It was snowing lightly, and the flurries fell peacefully on the concrete. The snowflakes were real big, and it looked nice outside. Jay was thinking how blessed he was. He had the good fortune of being with his family for Christmas that year. His son was with him, and Bighead was giving him a daughter in March.

A few minutes ago, he had laughed when Portia expressed her doubts about still turning him on. Jay was awed by the miracle he had planted inside her. She was carrying nice, and to him, she was getting sexier by the month. Jay turned around and teased Portia. "Ma, I hope my daughter don't inherit that big-assed dome head you got."

Portia laughed and gave Jay a jab to the ribs. "Or your big muscle neck. Why is your neck bigger than your head, Jay? What's up with that?"

That was a good one. Portia was silly, just like one of his homies. They played like that all the time. Just then Jay's cell phone rang. He forgot he'd left it on the sink in the bathroom. He went to go get it. Casino's number was on the caller ID, so Jay picked up.

Cas had called to let Jay know that one of their spots

had been set afire, probably by some competition. Jay told Cas to come get him so they could go check out the damage. They would have to relocate overnight, or they'd suffer a substantial revenue loss. That spot was pulling in over twelve G's a day, and after "Poppy" and all the bills were paid, they were left with a handsome profit. Jay and Cas had lots of other shit going on, but they weren't about to miss out on that money.

Lately, they kept close to home in getting money. The runs they had in Virginia and North Carolina were prosperous, but the feds were hot down south, so they'd relocated the soldiers back up top to work. Jay kept his soldiers close because there were so few niggas in New York who could be trusted.

He knew that he and Cas would regulate the spot situation, but they were both getting aggravated with that shit. There was always something. They had the record company, and shit was looking promising, but the brothers were still in the game because they were addicted to that cake. Maybe it was really time to give up the street life.

They were shopping their label for distribution with a major. Street Life was a flourishing independent company, so there was a little bidding war going on between Universal, Sony, and K Records. Jay and Cas were holding out for the best deal. After that, Jay was throwing down his hustling guns and putting all his dedicated niggas on the payroll legit. They wouldn't have time to hustle narcotics, because they'd be making international moves. Hell, they barely had time now; this hustling shit was a full-time gig, with crazy overtime.

Jay peeped in the bedroom at his sleeping son. He lingered for a second to make sure his little man was breathing okay. Since it was snowing outside, Jay went and got his black snorkel from his walk-in closet. It hung opposite the brown hooded mink Portia had given him for Christmas. Jay headed downstairs, then stopped short and did a 360 spin when he realized he'd forgotten his heat. He retrieved his favorite two ratchets from their hiding place and made sure they were both fully loaded and on safety, then he secured one in the front and one in the back of his waist and went downstairs.

Portia was sitting on the sofa and rubbing cocoa butter on her stomach. She had this thing about getting stretch marks. Jay walked over and knelt in front of her and kissed her belly. "Ma, I gotta make a run. Cas is 'bout to pick me up in a minute. Don't make that face, Kit Kat. I'll be back in a little while."

Jay didn't tell Portia what had happened to the spot or where he was going. There was no point in alarming her.

Portia had been looking forward to Jay staying in, but she didn't complain. "Okay, baby. Just be careful." She stood up and followed him to the door. That must've been Cas outside beeping his horn. Portia hugged Jay, and when she noticed he had guns on him, she ignored the urge to beg him to stay in the house. Instead, she stood on her tippy-toes and pecked him on the lips, and she whispered a prayer for him as she locked the door behind him.

After Jay left, she went upstairs and peeked in on her stepson, and then Portia went to get acquainted with the latest addition to her wardrobe, which she'd had to buy a size bigger because her feet swelled a little lately.

When Portia paraded in front of the full-length door mirror, she had no choice but to giggle at her reflection. She had on plaid boxers and a wifebeater and some bad-assed knee-high Manolo Blahnik boots. Portia turned sideways and admired her footwear. She didn't regret spending a penny of the seventeen hundred dollars she'd kicked for them. They went great with the floor-length chinchilla Jay had bought her for Christmas.

But Jay hadn't financed the Manolos. Portia had bought those bad boys with her own hard-earned money. Even though they were about two weeks' pay at her current salary, Portia didn't care; she loved a good shoe. Expensive shoes represented independence and freedom from the underworld, where she'd been held captive by fast money. Now she didn't have to risk her life just to have nice things.

It was funny to Portia how she measured her expenses differently—by paycheck instead of by the number of "privates" she did when she was in the life. Back then, she could've hustled up the boot money in a day, working nothing but her hips, lips, and fingertips. Portia felt she had good reason to rejoice because she'd shed her whore mentality. She'd never knock anyone's hustle, but she was proud of having worked a nine-to-five to get those babies.

Portia knew she had to count her blessings, because her transition from the nightlife to square society had gone pretty smooth. She'd quit two years ago, and things were going so great, she had no reason to go back. Portia recalled quite a few girls she knew from clubs who'd bragged about retiring. She'd seen some of those girls forced to come back just to make ends meet, or keep up with the latest fashions, or take care of their kids. It seemed like some of them were doomed.

Portia settled in front of her desktop and opened up the accounting books for Street Life. After she finished updating the books and filing some receipts, she thought about her novel. Over the last year, though she had written a lot, she didn't know what the climax was going to be. She just wanted to finish writing before she had the baby. She felt the intro was pretty solid, but she had no idea how to end it. Portia had disqualified quite a few possibilities because she wanted the last chapter to be real saucy.

BACK AROUND THE way, a plot was in effect to run up in a crib and stick something. Three black men, dressed in black hoodies and Timbs with big black guns, gathered their ammunition and loaded up a minivan with stocking caps, duct tape, and power tools intended for torture use. The men had intentions of coming off big, and they meant business.

Miz popped Lite in the back of the head. "Slow down, stupid! That's the house on the left. Park up the block, and make sure you call my cell phone if something don't look right out here. If you fuck this up, I'ma body you, son. That's my word. You better be here when I come out. Have this mothafucka running and ready to take off. If this bitch don't give it up, I'm shooting to kill, son. Fuck that nigga Jay!"

Wayne-o looked at his inexperienced little nineteen-year-old cousin. "Be cool, Miz." Wayne-o already knew Lite was shaky and had to go once they finished, because he was the type of nigga to crack. Wayne-o wasn't about to split the money three ways, so that was one more reason to put a bullet in Lite's skull. Miz was his flesh and blood, and he would be lucky to get a third. Half was out of the question.

"Miz, shut the fuck up, son," Lite said. "My heart don't pump no mothafuckin' Kool-Aid." Maybe it did, because Lite was having second thoughts. A little voice in the back of his head told him shit wasn't as sweet as Miz thought, with his itchy trigger-finger-having ass. And he knew Wayne-o's grimy ass was down to catch a body. Lite already had an open court case. He couldn't afford to get in any more trouble right now. This shit had to go smooth as a baby's ass.

PORTIA HEARD THE doorbell ring. She took off her Manolos and went downstairs. Through the peephole, she saw a young boy she recognized from the corner where Jay gambled. Since Jay wasn't home, she didn't answer.

But the guy kept on ringing the bell. Annoyed, Portia yelled through the door, "Jay is not here!"

Miz already knew Jay wasn't home. An hour ago, he'd paid crackhead Andy two hundred dollars to torch Jay and Cas's spot on Decatur, as a decoy to get Jay out of the house so they could rob his stash. Everybody knew he was sitting on a bundle. Politely, he said, "I'm sorry for knocking on your door this late, miss, but I just wanna drop this package off for Jay.

Here, just take it through the door. Keep the chain on. I don't need to come in."

Portia cracked the door and reached for the box, but it wouldn't fit through. Against her better judgment, she took the chain off and opened the door. Instead of a box, she got a gun in her face as Miz forced his way into the house, followed by another cat wearing a stocking cap over his face. Miz snarled, "Don't say a word, bitch. Where's Jay?"

Portia couldn't believe she'd fallen for the okie-doke. This shit couldn't be real. She was unarmed, and inconveniently dressed in boxers and a wifebeater, with no bra because her titties were sore, and now these niggas done ran up in the house. And she could see that they had silencers on their guns. Great, now they could kill her and nobody would even hear the shots. "Jay is gone for the night. So whatever you want, he's not here."

The stickup men backed Portia into the living room and scoped out the joint. When Miz went to look around and make sure no one else was in the house, Wayne-o took the opportunity to snatch the black stocking cap off his head. Portia's mouth hung open in disbelief. Wayne-o was satisfied by Portia's reaction. He smirked at her and couldn't help but stare at her breasts. They looked like huge overripe melons, with nipples as big as berries. That pregnancy had her looking real good. She was filled out, and her hair had grown past her shoulders. Wayne-o recalled that Portia did have some sweet pussy back in the day. He fondled her nipple and traced his gun barrel over her belly.

Portia recoiled in disgust, so he ripped her T-shirt

and painfully tweaked her left breast. From reflex, Portia slapped the shit out of him. Wayne-o grabbed her hair and shoved his gun under her chin. "Bitch, don't make me kill you! This always gon' be my pussy! I wonder how that nigga Jay will feel if I bust a nut on his baby head. Matter of fact, I want me some of this pregnant pussy right fuckin' now."

The thought gave Wayne-o a hard-on. He wrapped Portia's hair around his fist two more times and pulled it as hard as he could. Tears came to Portia's eyes. She knew from the past that Wayne-o was capable of just about anything. He used to beat her up and then force her legs open by painfully yanking her pubic hair until she let him have his way with her. Portia tried to stall him until she figured out how to make her move. She needed to get to the gun in the cabinet. "Please stop, Wayne-o. Let my hair go. It ain't even gotta be like this. Come on, we go back like recliners." She prayed those niggas wouldn't find Jayquan.

Wayne-o laughed in her face. He knew she didn't think he was that stupid. "I'm supposed to fall for that bullshit? Shut the fuck up! Don't talk unless I tell you to!" He shoved Portia on the couch and warned her, "Open your fuckin' mouth again. Matter of fact"—he unzipped his pants—"I got something to put in there."

Portia wanted to spit in that mothafucka's face for disrespecting her, but she wasn't crazy. She knew he had the upper hand with that gun in her face. She thought about the irony of her situation. She'd managed to avoid being raped and killed during her stint as a trick-turning stripper, and now that she was married and pregnant, it might be her fate. Portia knew the odds were against her. She'd grown up in the 'hood. She knew of people who'd been murdered in situations like hers.

She prayed they wouldn't kill her. *God, please don't let my life end like this. And watch over Jayquan, and my daughter too,* she thought.

When Miz came back and saw what was going on, he wondered what the fuck was wrong with Wayne-o. He knew his older cousin had to be more professional than that. Now wasn't the time to be horny. That nigga was trying to catch a rape charge. Then they'd definitely have to kill her. Miz wasn't with that. He talked tough, but he just wanted to take the money and run. He was no idiot. They weren't fucking with some lame. Jay was thorough and would have their heads for the heist itself, let alone raping his pregnant bitch. They had to come off big for sure, so they could blow town and lay low.

He tried to talk some sense into Wayne-o. "Son, let's get the money first. Fuck all that bullshit. Let's tie this bitch up."

"Hell yeah! Give it up, Portia! Where the fuck is the money?" Wayne-o placed his gun on her temple for emphasis.

"I swear to God, Jay keeps his money in the bank. I only got a few hundred dollars in the house, but I'll give you every penny I have."

Wayne-o lit a cigarette and pressed the gun against her lip. "Don't be a hero, shorty. Don't die for no nigga. Love ain't that mothafuckin' blind. You better smarten up and give it up! Don't die a hero, 'cause that nigga will have the next bitch knocked up, and you'll just be a fond memory."

"I can't give you what I don't have. I know you not playing no games, Wayne. I totally respect your gangsta, and there is no way I would lie to you. That's my word!"

Miz was tired of playing games with Portia. "Let's tie this bitch up. My power drill will make her talk! If I drill a few holes in her mothafuckin' ass, she'll be singing like a bird." He cemented his words with a look that told Portia he would kill her without hesitation. "You want a hole drilled in your fuckin' stomach?" Miz's ears perked up, and he raised an eyebrow in suspicion. "I heard something upstairs! Who the fuck is up there?" He raised his gun.

Portia's fear was confirmed. Jayquan had probably awakened to go to the bathroom and hadn't seen anyone around, so he was afraid and searching for her or Jay. He'd be coming downstairs hollering any second. She had to announce him before one of these assholes got trigger-happy. Oh, no, Jayquan was at the top of the stairs already. "That's my son! He's only four. Don't hurt him. Just let me get him. Please!"

"Daddy! Daddy!" Jayquan saw Portia with the strange men and rubbed his eyes. "I was scared! You left me by myself, Portia."

"I'm sorry, baby. Come here, Jay. It's okay." Jayquan ran into her arms, and Portia hugged him tight. She'd never felt so responsible for anyone in her whole life.

Miz could see Jay's resemblance in the boy. "Good, now I got somebody to use the power saw on." He snatched Jayquan from Portia's arms, and the boy started kicking and screaming. Miz tied Jayquan to a chair with his arms behind his back and gagged him, while Portia did her best to assure the boy that he would be okay. It took everything she had in her not to cry. The terrified look in his little eyes made Portia pray even harder. She wished she could make a move, but Wayne-o had his gun aimed at her.

Miz focused his attention back on Portia and warned her, "Bitch, if you don't tell us where the money at, you gon' watch lil' man get cut up in puzzle pieces. Then I'ma kill *you*!"

"Come on, he's just a baby! The money is in the bank. I swear! But we can get it out! I have an ATM card!" Portia was desperate to save their lives.

Miz was no fool. "You can't get but so much out of an ATM machine. Where's the fuckin' stash in the house?"

"It's all in the bank. I have ten thousand dollars in my account. You can have all of it."

"Ten thousand? That ain't shit! I know Jay got more than that. Bitch, you lyin', and I'm running out of patience with your ass. That's my mothafuckin' word!" Miz knew Jay was loaded, and he wanted that money.

"I don't have access to Jay's accounts. We don't rock like that. I don't know what he has. I swear!"

Wayne-o stepped in. "I'll bet that nigga will kick some ransom for his son and his wife. Let's kidnap 'em, son. Fuck it." The crazed lust returned to his eyes. "But first, take the lil' nigga in the other room. Go 'head, pick up the whole chair and just sit him in there. I'm 'bout to hit this pregnant pussy. You can go after me, son."

Wayne-o leered at Portia, and bile rose in her throat.

Miz didn't want to play that game. "Nah, son, I'm

good. The only thing I want is some mo'fuckin' cake. If we gonna kidnap these mothafuckas, we better get moving. Then we can get the ransom money, son. Besides, that shit ain't part of the plan. We ain't got time to be fuckin' this bitch."

Wayne-o scoffed, "I make my own mothafuckin' rules, nigga. Ain't no parameters. Now shut the fuck up and take that nigga in there."

"Whatever, man. Just don't fuck around and shoot her. Right now she's worth more alive. And hurry the fuck up! You got ten minutes." Miz carted Jayquan off so he wouldn't see Portia get raped.

Then Miz came back and uneasily watched Portia cry as Wayne-o choked her. He had ripped off her clothes and was shoving his gun barrel in and out of her pussy. Miz felt sorry for her. He didn't approve at all. His main girl was pregnant. But he and Wayne had to remain a united front, so there was nothing he could do. Personally, Miz didn't have to take pussy; he had too many girls dying to give him some. He was disappointed that his cousin, whom he'd always looked up to so much, had to stoop so low. Unable to watch, he left the room and strolled around, looking for something valuable to take while horny-assed Wayne got his jones off. There was no sense in leaving empty-handed.

Wayne-o withdrew the gun from Portia's vagina and rubbed it on her anus, then he rubbed it across her lips. "Suck it, bitch!" He laughed when Portia wouldn't open her mouth, and he lowered the pistol to her stomach. Just like back in the days, his hateful ass yanked her pubic hair hard as hell to gain access between her legs.

Portia yelped and was forced to unwillingly oblige. Wayne attempted to penetrate her, but it wouldn't go in. It hurt worse then the friction of carpet burn. Portia winced and dug her nails into his chest. She tried with all her might to push him off of her. Though her resistance turned Wayne-o's lunatic ass on, he gave her a backhand across the mouth for scraping his dick up with her dry pussy. He'd expected it to be nice and wet for him. That sick bastard had the nerve to believe he actually turned her on.

Portia's lip was busted, and it swelled up immediately. There wasn't much else she could do at that point, so she begged him, "At least use a condom! Please, Wayne-o."

Wayne-o laughed and smashed his cigarette out in Portia's navel. She screamed at the top of her lungs, and he disgustingly hawked spit on his hand and lubricated himself. He entered her roughly, and Portia choked back vomit from pain and disgust. She couldn't go out like this. She was a fighter. She clawed his throat with her nails.

"Bitch, if you scratch me again, I'll kill your mothafuckin' ass," Wayne-o snarled. He gave her pussy enough strokes to tease himself, and then without any type of warning or lubrication, he snatched out and rammed his dick up her ass.

Fire erupted in Portia's bowels, and she cried out in pain. From pure reflex, she tried to dig his eyes out of his head; her nails were the only weapon she had.

Wayne-o yelled, "Aah, you fuckin' bitch!" He and Portia struggled, and the gun went off.

Portia didn't hear the shot because of the silencer,

but when she realized she had a bullet in her collar-bone, only inches from her neck, she panicked and started screaming, "God, please help me! Somebody help me!"

Wayne-o hit Portia upside the head. "You stupid bitch, look what the fuck you made me do!" He pressed his ratchet into her rib cage. "Shut the fuck up 'fore I put a bullet in your baby skull!" He sped up his sexual rhythm to teach her a lesson.

During the excruciating pain, Portia was more worried about Jayquan's and her baby's safety than hers. She figured it out. This was the big payback for getting the abortion. That nightmare was back, but this time it was real. God was punishing her. She wanted to keep the baby this time, and she might not get the opportunity to do so.

At that point the only thing she was certain of was that if Wayne-o didn't kill her first, she was going to blow that fucking smirk right off of his face for violating, raping, and dehumanizing her. That mothafucka was so sick, not even the blood from her gunshot wound deterred him from trying to hump to the finish line.

When Portia was on the verge of praying for death's sweet escape, she realized she had found the saucy ending she needed for her novel, and she might not live to write it. God was merciful to her, and she blacked out during the unbearable affliction.

Portia regained consciousness shortly after. Wayne-o was still assaulting her, but vaginally now. He tore into her cervix mercilessly, and Portia realized she was bleeding down there. She remembered what she'd told God before she got that abortion. She had given Him her word that she would accept any punishment He saw fit for her sin. When Portia weighed the logic of the situation, her faith wavered. It must've been time to pay the piper, because she was certain Wayne-o was going to finish her off.

Before she accepted her fate and succumbed to her agony, Portia silently questioned Him. *So it's like that, God? You just left me to die like this, huh?*

LITE WAS DOUBLE-PARKED across the street from Jay's house when he saw Casino's black Range Rover pull up. Jay hopped out on the passenger side, and Wise got out of the back and jumped in the front seat.

Lite cursed. "Fuck!" Miz and Wayne-o done bullshitted around in the house so long, that nigga Jay came home already. As Jay stood at the driver's-side window talking to his mans, Lite made up his mind. He decided he wanted out. Seeing those dudes in person was a reminder. Them niggas were known for turning it up. They were some "for real, for real" cats and would annihilate them after this shit.

Lite didn't want to tango. Not with those dudes. He wasn't ready. Not for violating on this level, running up in niggas' cribs trying to take shit. The penalty for that was sure to be death, and he wasn't ready to die. Lite's ego deflated, and he lost every ounce of nerve he possessed.

Instead of calling Miz's cell to alert him and Wayne to Jay's arrival, Lite rolled down his passenger window. "Pssss. Yo, son!" When he got their attention, he was frank. "Jay, man, niggas ran up in your crib. They up in there right now. I'm supposed to be on lookout, but I had to pull your coat, man."

At the news, Cas immediately parked his truck a few doors down, and he and Wise hopped out. Wise went with Jay around to the back door of his house, where they crept inside with their heat cocked and drawn.

Casino didn't trust Lite, because if they hadn't shown up, he still would've been on lookout for them starving-assed niggas. He forced Lite out of the van at gunpoint, took his ratchet from him, and patted him down.

Lite didn't want any problems. He knew Cas wouldn't hesitate to bust his gun, so he sang like a bird. Casino assured him that he wouldn't kill him as long as he continued to cooperate.

JAY UNLOCKED THE back door, and he and Wise crept inside the house. They heard sobs coming from the living room, so they headed that way. Jay's knees weakened when he spotted Wayne-o on top of Portia on the couch, bucking like a bull. He staggered and clutched his heart for a brief second, and his eyes turned bloodred.

Wayne-o's back was facing Jay, and Jay saw that Portia had blood all over her. She was crying hysterically, and Jay could see that she had a gun shoved in her ribs. Jay couldn't believe he'd left her in harm's way like this. How the fuck did this shit happen? While he made his move, Jay said a quick prayer that his little son was okay, because he didn't see him in the living room.

Wise knew from Lite that Miz was also in the house, so he crept around looking for him while Jay took care of Wayne-o's foul ass. Wise had seen the look on Jay's face when he saw that nigga raping his woman. That'd be any man's Achilles' heel. He could fathom his man's pain and was ready to body them grimy niggas for crossing Jay like that.

ARE YOU JUST gon' let me die, God?

God's rebuttal to Portia's question was *Not today, my child,* because just then Portia spotted Jay creeping. She blinked twice to make sure she wasn't hallucinating. Praise God, it was really him. That was an act of God, and Portia was flooded with simultaneous relief and chagrin that Jay had found her helpless like that. They locked eyes for a second. In his, she read torment and vengeance, and in hers, he read agony and humiliation.

Gun drawn, Jay crept up on the side of Wayne-o to murder him. He had to be careful where he hit him so he wouldn't make a mistake and shoot Portia. He had to kill him quick before she got hurt any worse, but he wanted that mothafucka to see his face and feel his wrath.

Jay's eyes had water in them, and he bit his lip in rage as Wayne-o obviously climaxed, then slumped over Portia and shook a time or two. The pain of witnessing another man ejaculate inside of his pregnant wife tore at Jay's heart. Mortified, Portia stared up at him. A tear made its way down Jay's cheek as he placed the gun on Wayne-o's temple. His voice was an eerie whisper. "You got your fuckin' death wish, nigga."

Wayne-o was a little disoriented from his orgasmic high, so he didn't comprehend Jay's exact words. He could damn sure feel that cold steel pressed against the side of his face. Damn, that nigga Jay caught him slipping. Wayne-o had thought it was Miz creeping up behind him, wanting to get some skins. He tried to figure a quick way out. Though he had his gun on Portia, if he shot her, Jay could squeeze on him first. Wayne-o took a chance and aimed at Jay. Two shots were fired, and Portia screamed when the splatter of blood and skull fragments sprayed her face.

WISE SPOTTED MIZ in the den, unplugging the speakers and the big-screen. Wise couldn't believe that petty-ass nigga was blatantly preparing to steal Jay's electronics. He was relieved to see Lil' Jay unharmed in his Dragon Ball-Z pajamas, although he was tied to a chair with his mouth taped up. Jayquan's little eyes widened when he saw his uncle Wise, but he knew not to make a sound. Wise could see that Miz was slipping because his gun was on the floor at his feet. That clever move made it the ideal opportunity to kill him. Wise had the perfect shot, but he hated to kill Miz in front of little man. As soon as he raised his gun, there were shots fired in the living room, and a woman's scream could be heard all throughout the house.

Miz looked up and saw Wise creeping up on him. When he reached for his gun, Wise fired at his feet. Wise's goal was to run him out of the room, away from Lil' Jay, so he could put a bullet in his filthy vermin skull.

Miz took flight, and Wise chased him outside and emptied the clip after him. Somebody must've been praying for his ass, because he didn't fall. Wise stopped to reload. Even though he was certain he had hit Miz, he wanted to make sure he finished him off. He heard four more gunshots go off inside the house.

WHEN WAYNE-O'S BODY fell, Portia grabbed Jay's gun and stood over him and emptied the remaining slugs into him until she literally blew the fucking smirk off his face for violating her.

Jay called the paramedics and ran to untie Jayquan. Portia thanked God for sending her black knight to rescue her. She was in pain but glad she'd lived to tell. Her life and the children's lives had been spared, and now she could write her book's ending. Woozy from hemorrhaging, Portia passed out again.

MIZ FLED DOWN the stairs and managed to duck Wise's gunfire. He stumbled and realized he was hit in the leg. Lady Luck was his shorty upon notice of the minivan parked right across the street. Thank God, he would get away! Lite reached over and opened the door for him, and Miz jumped in.

"Drive, son! Hurry up, I'm hit!" Why the fuck wasn't Lite moving? "Drive, mothafucka!" Miz looked over, and his mouth dropped in shock. Casino sat in the driver's seat, smiling at him with his chrome .45 cocked and aimed at his heart.

"What up, Miz? You know you shouldn't have done this. Didn't I tell you it wasn't worth it?"

Miz had heard the rumors about Killa Cas's homicidal smile, but he wasn't going out like that. He reached, but not fast enough. His fate was already sealed. Casino pumped four shots in his chest. Miz's body slumped over the dashboard, and within seconds, the life drained from his being. Cas hopped out of the van and removed his gloves.

Lite lay on the floor in the back of the van, trembling and praying Cas would keep his word and not kill him. In all of his twenty years, he had never been so afraid. Lite realized he had pissed on himself. He looked up and saw Cas outside the window, laughing at him for looking like such a bitch, but he didn't care. He was thinking that if he made it home safely that night, he was going to take his aunt in North Carolina up on her offer and move down there to straighten up his life and go to school.

Casino gestured, and Lite's bitch ass got out on shaky legs with his hands up. Cas saw that he was petrified. "Yo, you seen anything?"

"Cas, man, I ain't see nothin'." Shit, he had amnesia.

"Good. Now, tell me why I shouldn't kill you. I should clap you in the ass on GP. Your bitch ass probably done shit on yourself by now. This shit ain't for you, lil' nigga. You ain't got enough heart. You need to go back to school or do *somethin'* with your life. Just don't let me see you no more. Yo, take this once-in-a-lifetime pass and disappear before I turn you into a ghost, mothafucka! Get the fuck up outta here, Lite."

That was the best advice Cas could give him. Lite nodded and took flight like a jet. As he turned the corner, he heard sirens in the distance.

AFTER THE PARAMEDICS got Portia to the emergency room, she was stabilized and admitted. Patricia, Laila, and Fatima waited and prayed until she came out of surgery. The bullet was removed, and her baby was born two months premature. Jazmin Simone weighed four pounds and two ounces. She stayed in the hospital until she was a healthy weight of five pounds, and then she was allowed to come home. Jayquan loved his little sister, Jazmin, and he was a big help to Portia with the baby.

Jay took the rap for Cas and said he'd chased Miz outside and killed him in the van. After a highly publicized trial, he was acquitted on two counts of second-degree murder, due to his high-paid team of lawyers' defense of temporary insanity, considering the brutal rape of his pregnant wife.

LATER, PATRICIA BABYSAT Jazmin evenings while Portia attended an intensive training program at New York Film Academy for a year. Jay upped the twenty-five grand for tuition and invested in her supplies and camera equipment. While Portia was in school, she and Fatima self-published *It's Official*, which went on to win accolades from the press, as well as making *Essence* magazine's top five best sellers of the month.

Street Life Entertainment Inc. signed a distribution deal with Universal for $100 million, and Cas and Jay purchased iced-out Street Life medallions for their whole team. Partial credit due to the marketing savvy of his wifey, Fatima, Wise's first album reached number seven on the *Billboard* charts. Kira's album release date was set for the next summer, and her first single, "Femme Phenomenal," reached number five with a bullet.

Portia directed Kira's video, and Melanie got a chance to strut her stuff in front of the camera, looking sexy but classy in a cameo. Street Life eventually branched off into straight-to-video movies, and Portia wrote and directed their first feature film, *Paper Chasing,* based on their real-life experiences. Fatima handled the casting and the sound track, which debuted singles from Street Life's new artists.

Their third project would be on the big screen, and they planned to take Hollywood by storm. Jay and Cas had two new acts in the studio, and along with their team of hustlers converted to levelheaded, legitimate businessmen, they were making those international moves Jay had predicted.

LAILA AND KHALIL stayed together and were renewing their wedding vows next year. Their business was successful, and they were happier than ever. They bought the building next to their sporting goods store and opened a video and record store, which also stocked the entire catalog of releases from Street Life.

Caught in an attempted robbery, Wise took a bullet to the chest in a shootout he had with the assailant and his accomplice. He made a full recovery, and he and Fatima set a wedding date. Wise had been totally faithful for a year, and Fatima traveled with him on tour. They were expecting a baby in six months.

Cas and Kira got married and lived together in a baby mansion on sprawling acreage in an upscale, posh section of New Jersey. Kira's career was going well, and Jahseim traveled everywhere with her and Cas.

Melanie slowed down a little but still got her swerve on. At an industry party, she bagged an A&R named Derek who worked for Sony. Apparently, she whipped it on homeboy, because he was infatuated with Mel and treated her like a queen. After finally learning how good it felt to be treated like a lady, Melanie grew to care for him exclusively. She was using her résumé of cameos from Portia's videos and films in order to pursue an acting career.

Jay, Cas, and Wise were still into real estate, and not counting a penny from their music business, each of them was worth millions. Jay, Portia, and the kids relocated to an estate among the urban elite, minutes from Cas and Kira's in New Jersey. With the help of God, Portia and Jay's union sufficed all tests. They successfully made a dollar outta fifteen cent, and it was a happy ending after all.

OR IS THERE really such a thing as a happy ending? Check out the second part of this riveting series, *A Dollar Outta Fifteen Cent II: Money Talks . . . Bullsh*t Walks.* Order it today and find out what it do in part two!

Sistas . . .

Lovely . . . Delicate . . . Flower . . . Had a bangin' body since she was twelve . . . Hood's version of America's Next Top Model

No plans . . . Just wanna be a balla's bottom bitch . . . Pipe dreams . . . Raw sex equal devotion—slow motion—oh shit!

Caught somethin' out there at places she never should've went—try'na make a dollar outta fifteen cent

Brothas . . .

Beautiful . . . Clever . . . Genius . . . Got his education in the dope game . . . Street-certified mathematician

Wishing . . . Kingpin aspirations . . . Dreaming . . . Scheming

The bait of the glitz and the glam was a scam—and now you got your third offense—try'na make a dollar outta fifteen cent

YOU ARE WORTH A LOT MORE THAN THAT!!!!

BLACK WOMEN ACCOUNT FOR 72% OF NEW HIV/AIDS CASES AMONG WOMEN IN THE US

WE AS AFRICAN AMERICAN WOMEN ARE TOO SMART AND TOO BEAUTIFUL TO BE IGNORANT ABOUT THE RISKS OF UNPROTECTED SEX—GET EDUCATED AND GET TESTED NOW! NOBODY'S GONNA PROTECT US BUT OURSELVES.

As a divine sisterhood, black women need to start speaking up and speaking out on HIV/AIDS. We have to use protection EVERY time we're sexually involved with a man. It's not about letting it slide this one time, nor is it about "the feeling" either, because every time we're intimate with someone, we put ourselves at risk for contracting HIV/AIDS. It's crucial that we hold one another accountable for getting tested.

FOR MORE INFORMATION CHECK OUT THE FOLLOWING RESOURCES:

HIV/AIDS AWARENESS INFORMATION RESOURCES

BlackAidsDay.org

BlackAids.org

BlackWomensHealth.com

SavingOurselves.org

LivingBeyondBelief.org

CDC.gov

AIDS.gov

TESTING RESOURCES

SafeCouples.com
1-800-456-9913

AdvancedTestingCenter.com
1-800-809-9252

Black AIDS Institute
1833 W. 8th Street, Ste. 200
Los Angeles, CA 90057
213-353-3610